**A MAJESTIC ISLAND WORLD CONSUMED
BY THE FLAMES OF REVOLUTION AND DESIRE . . .**

MELINDA SCOTT—From the moment her eyes first met Britt's she knew she would flee Philadelphia society and return to Java to claim her heritage and her heart's desire.

BRITT VANDEKKER—Caught between two worlds, his mixed blood made him a stranger to both. His passion for peace became a rage for justice. His love for Melinda made him willing to risk life itself.

ALDEN TOWNES—A suave diplomat, when he couldn't persuade, he instigated war, plotting to take Melinda back to America by force.

MAJOR WAKEFIELD—He led his brutal army against a proud, gentle people, determined to turn the islanders into His Majesty's subjects and their rich land into British revenue.

SAMARANG—His hired assassins cleared a path for his ruthless ambitions. His intrigues pitted brother against brother, setting the island afire with greed.

RAKATA MATARAMI—Heir to a Javanese ruler, he saw his half brother, Britt, as his most bitter enemy. Yet they were fated to fight together for the future of their golden land.

A LOVE MEANT TO RISE FROM THE ASHES OF WAR . . .

TO BURN AGAIN BRIGHTLY

TO BURN AGAIN BRIGHTLY

Joyce Verrette

A DELL TRADE PAPERBACK

A Dell Trade Paperback

Published by
Dell Publishing Co., Inc.
1 Dag Hammarskjold Plaza
New York, New York 10017

Printed in the United States of America
First printing—August 1985

Library of Congress Cataloging in Publication Data

Verrette, Joyce.
  To burn again brightly.

  I. Title.
PS3572.E764T58 1985   813'.54   85-4366
ISBN 0-440-58669-0

TO BURN
AGAIN BRIGHTLY

Chapter One

On a hillside's gentle slope the early sun sent a streak of pale fire that lit Britt's hair with gilt, making a spotlight of it among the lustrous black tresses of the Indonesian workers who had gathered at a respectful distance to await his decision.

The Java dawn spread dewy, golden light over the land, making columns of coral-tinted haze rise from the jungle valley like reflections of the smoke drifting from a volcano rising from one of the mountain ranges that formed the backbone of the island. Early morning gave Java an ethereal air. Most of the predators prowling the jungle's midnight floor had retired to their lairs and the fires always burning at Java's heart seemed quieted, but Britt knew otherwise. His father, Gerard Vandekker, and Gerard's friend, Charles Scott, had fought for every foot of their plantation, and during the several years since Gerard had been killed by a tigress, Britt had been Charles's partner, combating the endless succession of problems to be overcome.

This morning's trouble had been created during the night by a heavy rain in the mountains. Such storms were relatively common, but their results were so unpredictable that someone in the middle of fording a peaceful, shallow river could be suddenly washed away in a flash flood. Water from last night's rain had drained down the slopes to flood one of the tea fields.

Britt absently tapped the leg of his riding breeches with his crop, leaving faint smudges on the buff cloth as he contemplated the rows of plants that stood in water puddles. Chinese tea, Britt reminded himself, plants Gerard and Charles had brought to Java at great expense almost three decades ago, before he or Melinda had been born, before their fathers had even sought brides. The partners had borrowed money from the Netherlands government to invest in a plantation; in those days, they'd had to conserve their funds so closely that they'd lived in bamboo woven, thatched-roof houses like the natives.

The Indonesians, looking expectantly at Britt, understood that if the waist-high plants had to stand in water too long, their roots would be damaged. The shrubs might not produce tea for months while they were recovering, and they could even die. The workers saw Britt's frown, but didn't fear his anger as did the Javanese on so many other plantations, who were treated like slaves and cringed from their employers' displeasure. They knew Tuan Britt wouldn't punish them for not foreseeing that water would run down the slope from a rainstorm, which had touched only the high mountain tops. Tuan Britt even preferred they not perform *dodok,* the posture of lowering themselves to sit on their heels with palms pressed together as if in prayer to show homage to superiors, which these days meant all the foreigners who'd come from the western sea.

Britt turned slowly, hands on hips, still looking at the field, until he faced Arjuna, Phoenix House's overseer and his friend. The amber streaks in Britt's hazel eyes were an indication of his troubled inner thoughts as he spoke in the language of the Javanese court, his elegant accents a gift of his mother. "Can we spare enough workers from the factory or the other fields to get this drained before noon?"

Arjuna replied in the quietly modulated tone all Javanese used—and that Europeans had once mistakenly assumed indicated a placid people— "Many workers have already been taken off their regular jobs to help get the shipment ready for you to take to London. If more people are taken from the other fields, you'll lose some of the harvest."

"Then it will take all day to drain this field," Britt concluded.

Arjuna advised, "If you'll have the midday meal sent from the big house, these people will do it without grumbling."

"But not without suffering," Britt observed. The reason the workday began before dawn and ended at noon was that the afternoon sun made an oven of the fields. He glanced at the workers, knew they'd overheard and were willing. The women wore their long, traditional saronglike skirts, the men wide-legged pantaloons drawn snug at the ankles, but over the men's naked chests and the women's abbreviated blouses that bared their midriffs and arms, they wore the dark, long-sleeved jackets the missionaries insisted on. Though the jackets preserved modesty, they would be stifling in the growing heat.

Britt finally said, "Tell them to take off those damned jackets so they don't collapse later. I'll send Panji back to the house." He looked down at the round-cheeked little girl at Arjuna's side, lifted her chin so her great, dark eyes met his, and solemnly asked, "Do you think you'll be able to remember a long message, Panji?" She nodded hastily. "Tell Tuan Charles the field is flooded. Ask him to have someone bring plenty of drinking water as well as the tools we'll need. And when you tell Koki to pack lunch for us, remind her to give you some peppermints in reward."

Glowing with pride that she would be entrusted with the mission, Panji looked up at her father, who, like Britt, wore a shirt, riding boots, and breeches. Arjuna nodded approval, and her rosebud mouth bloomed into a dimpled smile.

Britt released her hand and faced Arjuna. "I'll stay and work with you," he said, loosening the bandana he wore knotted at his throat when he was in the fields.

The workers weren't surprised Tuan Britt would lend himself to the task. It wouldn't be the first time he'd worked at their side. One of them took Britt's horse while the others moved away to form a long line at the end of the rows of tea plants. Since there was nothing they could do until the tools arrived, they sat cross-legged on the ground to wait. Britt turned away, put one booted foot on a rock, and rested his forearms on his bent knee to watch Panji skipping and hopping down the slope toward the red-tiled roofs that were the plantation's heart.

Though Britt's Hollander father had given him height greater than that of the Javanese, who were the tallest of the many peoples that lived in the East Indies, his mother had given Britt their erect bearing and the supple grace of their carriage. When he attended tea auctions in London, Paris, Brussels, and Amsterdam, his loose-limbed, light-footed walk reminded Europeans of an animal they couldn't quite place, but their minds didn't readily turn to thoughts of tigers pacing jungle paths. His eyes, shadowed by thick, dark gold lashes, were long from corner to corner instead of round and wide-open like those of the Javanese. Though they were double-lidded and set straight on his face, European rather than having the Siamese-like slant of Java's people, they had an exotic cast women noticed. His mouth, not quite as full as his mother's, merely seemed enticing to western women, who privately speculated on how he'd kiss. The only thing about Britt that revealed his Javanese heritage was the willingness of his skin to turn deep honey in the sun, the same shade of the people of Siam, instead of burning like the Hollanders' did.

Britt had always been aware of the subtle difference between his nature and that of the Europeans he'd met when he was a boy traveling with his father. This hadn't troubled him until, when he was nineteen, something had happened to change his attitude. He'd proposed marriage to Elise Dampremy and she'd accepted. His fiancée had left Brussels for a visit to Java so she could acquaint herself with plantation life, but after she arrived, Britt quickly realized that all he'd said about Java while they were in Brussels had seemed like a fantasy to her. Faced with reality, Elise had been distressed.

Living on a mountainside almost a day's ride from Djakarta was less romantic, more lonely, than she'd dreamed. The social life had a different style than Elise had imagined, and she'd been unable to become at ease with it. The Indonesian servants made her uncomfortable, and it embarrassed her that Sukadana, Britt's mother, was Javanese. Britt had puzzled over why Elise felt that way; he'd told her about his background before their engagement. Elise had tried not to complain about the tropical climate, but Britt had known she didn't like it. She'd been terrified whenever she'd seen a harmless green lizard dozing in the sun, afraid of even a hummingbird, like a winged jewel that mistakenly flew through the house's open shutters. And when Britt's mother was killed by an Indonesian, nothing Britt said could convince Elise such murders weren't common in Java. She'd dropped all pretense of loving Britt and had fled back to Belgium. He had decided then, if he ever wished to marry, he'd best look for a girl nearer home—perhaps on Bali, Sumatra, or one of the Polynesian islands.

Grieved by Sukadana's death and secretly more wounded by Elise's rejection than pride allowed him to admit, Britt let his previous reserve become a wall that set him even farther apart from westerners. He never again mentioned his mother's being Javanese or spoke about anything personal to acquaintances in Europe. In Amsterdam he occasionally smiled, but never laughed, which made the good-natured Hollanders feel boisterous in his presence and comment on his moody temperament. He dressed as smartly as any Parisian, but with a careless kind of elegance that seemed to tweak the noses of Frenchmen.

His manners, impeccable as an English lord's, seemed bred into his bones, but his aloofness made him appear arrogant to Londoners. Even in Java, to almost everyone outside the plantation's boundaries, he seemed cool and humorless.

Britt lifted his gaze to the distance. The volcanoes in the area had spewed ashes on the plantation, and elephants had trampled the fields. Raden Matarami, wanting to drive Gerard and Charles away, had frequently sent his army sweeping down on them and had thrice burned the plantation. When the war in Europe had begun, Napoleon had sent soldiers and captured Java. Only a few years ago Britain had driven the French army out and had itself taken possession of the East Indies. Then a column of red-coated soldiers had filed through the rows of tea at Phoenix House, thinking to confiscate the plantation from two Hollanders. Instead, they'd discovered Charles Scott, an American, and Britt, whose mother had once been the *raden*'s daughter-in-law. The soldiers had turned away, though Hollanders on other plantations now worked them much like tenants with King George as their landlord. If these adversaries as well as the jungle, always ready to invade the fields and strangle the tea, had been kept at bay, Britt vowed that this old field would be saved now. He had lost his parents to the land and Elise had fled from it, but Britt loved Java. The house below was his inheritance.

As Britt wielded a pick to break up the earth between the shrubs, so the Javanese working in the row behind him could make a trench the standing water would seep into and then drain down the hillside, his thoughts again turned to the past.

Charles had gone back to America and had brought his bride from Philadelphia, one of the few cities in the fledgling country, the United States, large enough to have a formal social register. Jessica, like Elise, hadn't cared for life in Java, but because she was pregnant by the time she'd arrived, she'd stayed. Britt recalled the story of Charles and Jessica's daughter's birth in the kitchen—the only stone, therefore unburnable, building at the time—the night Matarami and his men had for the second time torched the cluster of buildings the Scotts and Vandekkers had lived in. When the Indonesian workers who'd remained faithful had seen the infant's auburn hair, they'd said the spirit of the fires had entered the girl-child. Britt, only three and unable to pronounce the name Jessica had chosen, Melinda, had called her Minda and had immediately become her protector. Their friendship had made them constant companions until Jessica had taken Minda away.

Britt had been eleven, and he still remembered the day clearly. Minda's eyes shimmering with tears as green as basket ferns, her fiery curls already awry from agitation as she'd handed Britt a keepsake, all she'd had to give—a child's gold locket he'd worn on his watch chain since. Through the years Charles had sent Jessica and Minda money and Minda had written to her father, but Britt had no idea if her letters were affectionate or duty letters thanking Charles and acknowledging the money's safe receipt. Charles seldom spoke of his daughter. Despite the passing years, he still was heartsick over losing her. Britt found himself wondering what sixteen years had done to Minda, then he decided that under Jessica's tutelage Minda had probably become as self-seeking as her mother. He wondered how a child born with the spirit of Java's fire in her could ever forget her island home. But as violent as the night had been when Minda was born, her birth had been less controversial than Britt's.

Britt's mother had been the young widow of Matarami's son. Her child of that marriage, Rakata, had been barely a toddler when she'd met and fallen in love with Gerard Vandekker. Sukadana's previous husband had been killed in an attack on a Hollander's plantation. Matarami's bitterness toward the foreigners settling on the island had increased tenfold at his son's death, and when Sukadana begged Matarami's permission to marry Gerard, the *raden* had aimed his anger at the Vandekker-Scott plantation. His previous affection for Sukadana had dissolved and he'd denounced her as a traitor to her people. The *raden* had taken little Rakata, his firstborn grandson, heir to the city of Talu and its province, and had banished Sukadana—a death sentence in Javanese eyes, and the reason Sukadana had been killed so many years later by an Indonesian who, trying to seek a favor from Matarami, thought of carrying out the much-delayed execution.

The Vandekker-Scott plantation had been burned a third time, which was what had decided Jessica, after nine years of incessant complaining about Java, to leave, despite Charles and Gerard's promise to rebuild. They'd just paid off their debt to the Netherlands government and could finally afford a proper house. But after Jessica had barely glanced at the plans Charles had shown her, she'd packed and left, never having seen the new house. They named it Phoenix House because the plantation had once again risen like the fabled bird from its ashes. This time the buildings were stone. The house had marble floors and high, airy ceilings. Because Jessica had constantly complained about the tropical heat—greatly lessened, in fact, by their living on a mountainside—Charles had designed the house as a square with an open center. All the rooms opened on the courtyard's garden and were filled with its fragrant breezes. One side of the house was the Vandekkers' suite, the opposite the Scotts', though only Charles had ever lived in it. The other sides of the square were common rooms and servants' quarters. The kitchen and the laundry were separate buildings, as was the bathhouse beside the walled bathing pool. Guest rooms were little pavilions, Javanese style, set away from the main house for privacy. The neatly clipped lawn and flower beds of the garden made an island of civilization in the heart of the jungle; visitors were welcomed into it by a driveway lined with stately royal palms.

Britt's thoughts were interrupted by the sound of hoofbeats, and he looked up from his work. Recognizing Charles on the horse trotting up the road, Britt leaned on his pick and waited. Charles drew his mount to a stop at the edge of the field and waved for Britt to come to him. Britt knew it wasn't a casual visit if they couldn't simply call to each other, so he laid aside the pick and hurried between the rows of tea plants to his partner's side.

Though the years hadn't dimmed Charles's spirit, the troubles and loneliness he'd suffered had helped the Indonesian sun line his face. His frown, as he looked down at Britt, deepened the wrinkles, making him appear older than he was as he said, "Major Wakefield has sent soldiers to the next village. They think one of the men is smuggling firearms to Rakata."

"They're always accusing Rakata of planning a revolt, but they never find firearms or anything else to prove their suspicions," Britt said in disgust. "I take it you're going to the village?"

"Lieutenant Blackburn's in charge of the search. I think someone besides Indonesians should see what will go on," Charles grimly replied.

Britt considered this information. Though Wakefield had often investigated one village or another, he tried to keep the uneasy peace. He'd sometimes even questioned the workers at Phoenix House, but Britt and Charles understood that was mostly to remind them of his authority. Charles was an American, not a Hollander, and Wakefield, nearing retirement, had had enough of fighting Americans during their revolution. He grudgingly respected their stand in the just-ended War of 1812. Britt's mother had been Javanese, and Wakefield preferred to stay on reasonably good terms with Britt, Rakata's half brother. Britt and Rakata's adult lives were as separate as their childhood had been and they virtually ignored each other, but the British commander seemed not to believe it.

Lieutenant Blackburn was another matter. Newly transferred to Java from the battlefields of Europe, hardened by the sight of the blood spilled in Napoleon's war, Blackburn was eager for promotion; at the same time he didn't understand the delicacy of the political situation in Java. The plantation owners from the Netherlands fiercely resented the British presence, and growing numbers of Indonesians wanted *all* foreigners to leave their island. Rakata was said to be a firebrand held in check only by Wakefield's cautious, even tolerant policies. Blackburn had already shown that he regarded the Javanese as less than human; if he were in command of soldiers entering a village so distant from Djakarta and Major Wakefield, he was likely to behave as he pleased. Knowing Charles's temper sometimes flared past discretion, Britt could see potential calamity.

He looked up at Charles. "I'm almost to the end of the field. Arjuna can take over for me. I'll go with you." Britt motioned to Arjuna, who nodded, then without another glance at Charles, who he knew would protest, walked with long, rapid strides to his horse.

Charles did begin to argue that Britt needn't accompany him, but Britt's attention seemed riveted on resaddling his mount. Not until he was finished checking his pistol to make sure it was properly loaded did Britt look up and brush aside Charles's protest with one terse comment: "I *am* going with you, Charles." Then he swung up into the saddle and gathered the reins in his hands.

Britt and Charles were almost a mile from the village when they saw smoke begin to boil over the treetops. The odor of it made them suspect Blackburn had torched the village's rice stores, which meant the Javanese would be hungry until the next harvest or would have to humiliate themselves by begging. Both men urged their trotting horses into a gallop.

As they approached the village, their fear was confirmed. The platforms, held above the ground by piles to protect the precious grain from animals and sheltered from rain by steeply angled roofs with sweeping eaves, were infernos. One beautifully carved and painted gable was already collapsing into itself.

The Javanese had been routed from their houses and were gathered in the center of the village, the children cowering against their mothers' skirts, the women huddling close to their men, whose eyes flashed with impotent anger under the soldiers' guns.

"You *will* tell me who Rakata's spy is and where he hides the firearms he smuggles or we'll burn everything in the village!" Blackburn shouted.

Thirty pairs of dark eyes stared at him, but no one spoke. Only the crackle of the flames and the sharp report of a timber snapping from heat were heard in the silence.

Charles flung himself from his saddle and started purposefully toward the lieutenant. "If you're all so certain Rakata is planning a revolt, why hasn't Major Wakefield given orders to arrest him and have it over with?" he demanded.

"This is military business, not your affair," Blackburn replied.

"You'd do better to explain what you want in Javanese, Lieutenant," Britt coldly advised from his horse. "I doubt they understand you."

Blackburn flushed. Like his men, he couldn't speak more than a few words in Javanese. Though Wakefield had told him to take an interpreter, he hadn't.

Knowing Charles's temper was high, Britt slid down from his saddle and approached. "Did Major Wakefield order you to do this?" he asked pointedly. At Blackburn's continued silence, Britt commented, "I'd thought not."

The lieutenant replied smartly, "I'm to do what's necessary."

"Bullying women and children is what you deem necessary for a quick promotion," Charles snapped. "Or is it simply that you enjoy frightening people?"

"That's quite enough, Scott. Your being an American doesn't impress *me*," Blackburn warned.

"That the Javanese are human beings is what *should* impress you. But I suppose, after serving in that bloodbath that's going on in Europe, a handful of villagers means nothing to you," Charles shot back. "If you harm anyone who's innocent, the major will hear about it from me."

Blackburn turned away, his face livid with anger. It was true Wakefield hadn't ordered him to go this far, but Wakefield was in Djakarta, some distance away. The lieutenant considered this assignment an opportunity to prove that Rakata was planning a revolt. The information he'd received *must* be valid, he reasoned; it came from Samarang, Rakata's cousin, who often secretly cooperated with the

British because he thought that would make it possible for him to inherit Matarami's title instead of Rakata if the British remained in Java. Why did Scott and Vandekker have to interfere? Blackburn thought angrily. What made them think they had any right to, when they lived in a country occupied by an army in which he was an officer? If they hadn't come, he might have done as he wished without any witnesses except his own men, who'd gone through too much with him in Europe to dream of peaching on him. Blackburn swore softly to himself as he wondered why he'd been transferred to the island anyway. Continuing in the fight against Napoleon would have distinguished his career more than searching little villages for a ragged gunrunner to prevent a revolt few in the civilized world cared about.

Finally, Blackburn again faced Britt and said derisively, "You, of course, speak the language more fluently than I."

Britt knew Blackburn meant to deride his mixed heritage and said with quiet control, "Yes."

The lieutenant waved to one of the soldiers, who, using the side of his rifle as a stave, pushed Charles back. Blackburn said brusquely, "Translate for me, Vandekker. Tell the headman to come forward."

That Blackburn had shown no hesitation in ordering his soldier to handle Charles roughly made Britt more uneasy. Though they'd come to safeguard the Javanese with their presence, Britt began to wonder if he and Charles might need protection themselves. Was Blackburn that brash? Britt decided that, perhaps as interpreter, he could keep the situation from worsening. In particularly courteous Javanese he asked the village leader to identify himself.

A wizened old man, his back bent from decades of laboring in the fields, separated himself from the tense gathering but warily came no closer. Impelled by ambition, despite Charles's warning that he would report what happened to Wakefield, and certain that his uniform was all the authority he needed at the moment, Blackburn gave orders to a pair of soldiers, who marched to the huddle of villagers. With lowered bayonets, they motioned the old man to approach the lieutenant.

The old mayor's eyes moved from the soldiers to Blackburn, then to Britt and Charles. He knew that Britt and Charles were just and, putting his faith in this, took a step forward. Two of his sons advanced with him, and though he paused to shrug off their grasp on his arms, they stolidly hung on. The mayor knew that if he declined his sons' support their pride would be stung, for they'd seem cowardly before the others. He let them remain with him.

Without looking at Britt, Blackburn said, "Tell the old man I want to know who's smuggling guns to Rakata."

Britt looked down at the three men squatting in the posture of homage and asked them to get up. To the lieutenant he said, "Even if someone in the village is smuggling guns, none of the elders are likely to know it. The smuggler would realize his operation could put the village under suspicion and he'd cache the guns somewhere else."

"Ask anyway. Do it loudly, so all the people will hear." Blackburn was adamant.

Britt realized then that Blackburn had been aware all along that the mayor wouldn't know about the gunrunner. Blackburn wanted to threaten the man before the others in the hope that anyone who knew about the possible smuggler would give information out of fear for the mayor. Britt asked the question Blackburn had demanded, but he also told the villagers that if they had any scrap of information they'd be wise to say so, because the lieutenant seemed not to be bluffing. He added that he and Charles might not be able to prevent Blackburn from doing what he wished.

"You said more than I asked," Blackburn surmised, "but from the expressions on their faces I can see it was effective. Nevertheless, kindly confine yourself to translating my words exactly."

After Britt repeated what he'd told the villagers, the lieutenant said, "You'd best accept the fact there's nothing you or Scott have to say about any of this or you'll have problems of your own."

One of the mayor's sons did understand some English, enough to follow Britt and the lieutenant's conversation. He hurriedly translated for his father, who considered the possibility that Britt and Charles were as helpless as he.

The mayor pressed his palms together before his face, bowed his head, and said quietly, "The officer-tuan must be made to understand, if there's a smuggler in our village, I don't know of it. This village is small, and everyone sees what the others do. It would be almost impossible for a smuggler to hide what he's doing."

Britt translated and Blackburn scoffed, "Does he think I came all the way from Djakarta without good reason? Do they suppose, at a word from this shifty native, I'll turn my men and go back? Even Wakefield would laugh at that. Me, foxed by an old snake who's too ignorant to sign his name."

Britt's narrowed eyes became a glaze of copper sparks as his own temper rose. He said stiffly, "Though the village is small, this man is its mayor. And he can write in his own language just as you do in yours. Java's royal court was as refined a thousand years ago as your King George's is today, so you shouldn't think these are ignorant people. They're only ignorant about *your* customs, a fact they're learning to rue."

Blackburn cast Britt a contemptuous glance, then moved to peer into the face of one of the mayor's sons. "What this one said to the mayor a moment ago makes me suspect he knows a little English. But you didn't tell me that, Vandekker. Is your mother's blood so compelling you're willing to take such risks with me?"

"He only told his father he was worried about the outcome of this," Britt lied.

"He has every reason to worry, something you might give thought to yourself," Blackburn observed. "So the mayor is his father. Perhaps I know a way to get them to say something useful." Addressing the soldiers who'd flushed the mayor from the other villagers, Blackburn ordered, "Take hold of this man and follow me."

Having no idea what the lieutenant intended, Britt watched apprehensively as the soldiers gripped the mayor's son's arms and tugged him toward a burning warehouse.

Blackburn stood aside and turned to regard Britt. "Now tell the mayor I'll have his son thrown into the fire if no one tells me the truth. Say it loudly, Vandekker, so all the villagers hear you."

"For the love of God, Blackburn!" Charles, still restrained by the rifle barring his way, exclaimed.

Britt stared at the lieutenant from eyes aflame with his own outrage, but forced himself to say quietly, "I assure you, Blackburn, if Rakata is considering leading a revolt, an ugly incident like this will only bring him closer to it. You could be touching off a powder keg."

"I can take that information as coming from one who knows Rakata's mind, seeing as how he's such a close relative," the lieutenant said venomously. "Tell them, Vandekker; make sure they understand I mean it."

Britt glanced at the villagers, who no longer were huddled together in fear. They were tense with fury, and only the soldiers' guns prevented them from rushing forward. "Look at them, Blackburn. If you throw that man into the fire, nothing will restrain them," Britt warned. "You'll have to kill them all—and me as well."

"You actually would fight for those beggars?" the lieutenant asked incredulously. "Your loyalty really is with the natives!"

"You're so fascinated with my mother's side of the family you've forgotten my father's. My name *is* Vandekker," Britt reminded. "I'll go to Major Wakefield, even the Colonial Office in London, if I must, and report this. The only way you'll be able to stop me now is to kill me, as I said."

"And me as well," Charles vowed.

Blackburn had counted on one of the villagers speaking up, though it wouldn't have plagued his conscience to toss a native or two into the warehouse. He hadn't dreamed Vandekker and Scott would raise such a row. But would it be possible that the jungle could hide what happened to them? The jungle concealed a great many secrets. He wondered. Vandekker had no family in Amsterdam that Blackburn knew of, and if he did, they were thousands of miles away. The only relatives Britt had on the island were Javanese, and no one would listen to their complaints. In fact, if Rakata began a revolt over this, it would only lend credence to Vandekker's implication in the smuggling. As far as Scott was concerned, his wife and daughter had lived in Philadelphia for years. They must not care about him if they hadn't even visited in all this time. Perhaps obliterating the village and Scott and Vandekker with it was the best way to bring the problem of Rakata to a head. Wakefield would have no choice then; he'd have to fight. Squashing any revolt that followed shouldn't take too long, Blackburn calculated. Then he'd go home a hero, having resolved the Javanese problem as well as firmly establishing in the minds of the government in Amsterdam that the East Indies no longer was their possession.

Certain the lieutenant would relent at their threats, Britt and Charles were stunned when Blackburn snapped off orders for his men to take them prisoner and the soldiers lowered guns on them.

"Are you insane, man?" Charles gasped.

"This situation has already gone too far. You'll complain to Wakefield about me no matter what I do now," Blackburn said.

"How do you expect to explain our deaths? What about the villagers? Your own men are witnesses!" Britt exclaimed as one of the soldiers took his revolver.

Blackburn glanced at the watching Javanese. "How many of them are there? Thirty? Forty at most? I've seen hundreds of corpses on battlefields," he said coolly. "These soldiers are *my* men. They fought with me in Europe and know from experience I always have reasons for what I do. They'll obey me now and won't say a word

against me later, especially after I explain how the outcome of this day
will send us home sooner, and heroes at that."

"You *are* mad," Charles concluded.

The leader of the Javanese, concealed with his men behind the wall
of foliage, understood English very well. He'd followed Blackburn's
conversation with Britt and Charles with great interest and growing
surprise that Britt and Charles were siding with the villagers.

Rakata's dark eyes intently watched Britt as he wondered about this
half brother who, as an adult, was a stranger to him. After Sukadana
had been banished, she'd somehow persuaded her old nursemaid to
bring Rakata for several meetings in a remote village, which had long
been abandoned because it was thought to be haunted by demons from
the nearby temple of Durga, goddess of death. Rakata had been seven
and Britt only four. Not knowing their people were enemies, the boys
had played together. But something had made Sukadana fear that
someone had become suspicious of the nurse's taking Matarami's heir
on outings, and the meetings had had to stop. Afterward, Sukadana
and her second son dared have no contact with Rakata or anyone in
Matarami's city, and Rakata had been reared as separately from Britt
as if they'd lived on opposite sides of the ocean. Each knew about the
other only what someone else had told him; they'd never spoken and
only occasionally had seen each other from a distance, though they'd
lived all their lives on the same island.

Rakata had assumed Britt's father had taught him to be as uncaring
toward the Javanese as the other foreigners seemed, but now he wasn't
sure.

His glance slid over the soldiers and chose one as he lifted his
blowpipe to his lips, but when Britt and Charles were taken prisoner,
Rakata's aim shifted to the soldier whose gun was pointed at Britt.
One breath sharply expelled sent the missile to its target.

Britt was the first to recognize that the soldier's silent death was
from a tiny dart in his throat. Even before the missiles from a dozen
blowpipes had reached other targets, Britt had caught up the fallen
soldier's rifle and whirled to fire at the man holding the mayor's son
by the burning warehouse. Though Britt saw the small force of
Javanese rush from the concealing foliage, he hadn't time to do more
than glance at them and hope they'd spare him and Charles. The rifle
had held only one shot, so when Britt turned, he bayoneted the soldier
holding Charles captive.

Charles immediately stooped to pick up the rifle the fallen man had dropped. "Don't worry about me! Help the mayor!" he cried, waving Britt away.

Britt turned his rifle around and, using its stock like a club, downed the soldier holding the village elder. "Get into one of the houses. Tell your people to stay out of the way," he urged.

"Do you think they'll listen?" the mayor asked, motioning toward the furious men who were struggling with the soldiers.

"Try to keep the women and children out of it," Britt snapped and turned away. Only then did he notice he'd splintered the rifle's stock, making it useless as any kind of weapon. "No matter," he muttered and threw it aside.

A Javanese boy flung himself against a soldier who was ready to fire at a villager. The soldier cursed at having his aim spoiled, lifted the boy by an arm, and swung him off the ground. He was ready to dash the boy against a tree when Britt's fist struck him. Being hit in the temple so hard normally would have killed a man, but the angle of Britt's blow blunted it. Staggering from the shock, the soldier released the boy's arm and dizzily turned to Britt, who caught him by both shoulders and rammed his head into the tree. Then Britt turned to attack another soldier, too intent on the fight to see that Charles had fallen.

Charles didn't immediately know how serious the bayonet wound in his chest was. There wasn't much blood he could see and not even much pain. He felt more as if he'd had the breath knocked out of him and might faint. He tried to rise, and because his legs didn't seem able to support him, he slowly crawled to one of the houses, intending to prop his back against the wall until he felt a little stronger. After a breathless struggle, he sat up and blood gushed from his mouth. He stared at the bright scarlet staining his shirt, dimly wondering about it a moment, until he finally realized his lung had been punctured. The bleeding was mostly internal. He'd seen a wound like that in one of his and Gerard's workers when Matarami's men had attacked the plantation the first time.

"The devil!" he whispered, knowing he was doomed.

Charles raised his eyes to search for Britt. He desperately needed to tell Britt something before he died. Charles picked Britt out from the melee when his hair caught golden lights from the sun as he leaped up to kick a soldier's chest. As Britt dived on the fallen man, Charles realized he couldn't catch Britt's eye and he wasn't able to call loudly enough for Britt to hear. He saw Rakata make a similar leap and mused at how alike their movements had been.

Charles wondered if he could survive until the battle was over. It was ironic, he thought, that his last moments should be comforted by the presence of another man's son, a friend and partner he knew better than his own child. He thought about Melinda and was surprised that his vision of her was as she'd been when she'd left Java. He now adjusted that mental image to match the miniature she'd sent for his last birthday. Though a lovely young woman looked at him from the painting, her eyes still had as direct a gaze as when she'd been a child. Brown hair piled in curls like a coronet on her head caught red tints from an unseen lamp. Charles liked to think the fire spirits of Java still lived in her and that she might consider returning. His daughter's coming home was the hope that had sustained him through all the lonely years. He wished he could see the bright, easy-smiling girl Britt had dubbed Minda, not Jessica's artificially polished Melinda. Charles remembered how annoyed Jessica had been when he, too, had fallen into the habit of calling their daughter Minda, and he smiled. A sharp pain stabbed his chest; he wondered if it was caused by his wound or his older torment, Jessica's leaving him and taking Minda away.

Charles renewed his determination to live just long enough to talk to Britt and beg a favor of him. If he concentrated on how much he loved Minda, he thought he might have the strength to survive until Britt noticed him. Charles closed his eyes to recall the letters Minda had written, remembered passages he'd memorized. Handwriting, dainty yet clear, devoid of the fancy flourishes Jessica had used. Perhaps Minda was, despite her mother's influence, still more like him than Jessica. Maybe she thought of Java from time to time. He hoped so.

The blow across Britt's shoulders sent him plunging to the ground. Momentarily stunned, he took an instant longer than he might have to roll over. When he did, he found himself looking up at Blackburn's pistol muzzle, the lieutenant's thumb on the hammer, pulling it back. But before Britt could move, Blackburn gasped and pitched forward to sprawl facedown beside Britt.

Britt glanced at Blackburn, then stared incredulously at the Javanese who bent to grasp the carved handle of the dagger in the lieutenant's back and pull it out. "Rakata!" Britt breathed.

Rakata extended his hand and tugged Britt to his feet. "Your partner needs you," he said, motioning toward Charles.

Britt glanced at where Rakata had pointed and, seeing Charles, felt fear flowing into him like an icy tide.

"Go to your friend," Rakata said. "The fight is almost ended."

Britt wordlessly hurried away to drop to his knees beside his partner, who was so pale and still that Britt was afraid he was already dead. "Charles," he said urgently. Charles's eyes opened, but Britt's relief was short-lived. Charles's life was so rapidly ebbing his eyes were losing their luster. Britt steeled himself and pulled open Charles's shirt. Horrified by the wound, he kept his face expressionless. He began to tear at his sleeves, thinking to use his shirt to try to stop the blood flow.

"Don't, Britt." Charles's words came with an ominous gurgling sound. "It will cause more pain, not change anything."

Reluctantly, Britt let his shirt fall back in place and caught Charles's hand in his. "You've been . . ." he began, then stopped, not knowing how to express his powerful emotions.

Charles whispered, "I know, Britt. From your eyes. They never could hide how you felt. It's a comfort to me, makes this easier to say. Just listen. I don't have long."

Britt nodded numbly and listened as Charles spoke in disjointed sentences, sometimes wheezing, sometimes gurgling, but always breathlessly. "You've been the best—partner a man could ask—since your father died. I'd once hoped—you and Minda. Never mind. Minda's what—I have to talk about. My will is—in my desk. Gives her, not Jessica, my share of Phoenix House." He paused to pant a moment, then said, "Will you go to Minda? Tell her yourself. Try to get her—to come back." He stared imploringly at Britt. "I know, it's a lot to ask."

"I'll do it," Britt said as firmly as his emotions allowed. "I'll leave the tea auction in London as quickly as possible and go on to Philadelphia."

"Promise?" Charles whispered.

"You have my word," was Britt's husky answer.

"I know you'll keep it." Despite his resolve, a moan escaped Charles's lips. He looked impatient that he'd used a precious moment on a moan, then resumed, "Got to get Minda—away from her mother. Jessica will ruin her life." Charles's voice was fading and he tried to say quickly, "Left nothing to Jessica. Fixed the will so Jessica won't—can't change . . ." Charles's breath escaped him, and he closed his eyes.

Britt waited a moment before he realized that Charles would say no more. He squeezed Charles's lifeless hand and whispered, "Yes, I'll keep my word." He turned his face aside and bowed his head in grief. Then he shut his eyes tightly, trying to dam his tears. Finally, Britt opened his eyes to see a pair of feet in jeweled sandals standing beside him, the wide legs of dark crimson pants gathered and held snug at the ankles by narrow gold bands. He looked up and saw Rakata.

The Javanese noted the moisture clinging to Britt's lashes and said quietly, "I'll have someone help you get him back to your house." When Britt glanced away, Rakata began to turn to go.

But Britt was suddenly angry that Charles had died for this village. As he got to one knee, he flashed, "Did your smuggler, at least, live through this?"

Surprised, Rakata quickly returned his attention to Britt. "This is not Durga, where you and I played spy-and-warrior games with sticks instead of swords. The villager who'd acted as my eyes and ears here has been killed. He never smuggled guns to me." Noting the fury in Britt's face, he asked, "If we had firearms, would we have come to meet the soldiers' guns with only blowpipes and knives? If you were in my place, wouldn't *you* have people in strategic villages gather information?"

Britt remained on one knee, now seeming to gaze down at Charles's body, though his eyes were again too blurred by tears to focus. Struggling to will them to recede, he didn't answer.

"It was my spy who warned me the soldiers were coming. If he hadn't, all these people would have been killed. You would have been killed too," Rakata pointed out.

"Didn't Raden Matarami tell you to kill us all anyway?" Britt asked bitterly.

"If you mean all foreigners, the weight of my grandfather's years has taught him to hope the animosity between the British and Hollanders will resolve our problem by causing them to kill each other for us," Rakata answered shortly.

Finally, Britt again looked up. "I've heard that *you* want a revolt."

"A man in prison must dream of freedom or he isn't a man."

"You aren't imprisoned," Britt said curtly.

"We all are. The island is a prison as long as we can't govern ourselves. But I see the wisdom of the *raden*'s thinking. I obey him." For the second time that day Rakata offered Britt his hand.

Britt ignored it and got to his feet. "If you want all the foreigners to get out, you might as well kill me now, while you have the chance, because I'm not leaving Java.''

"You're forgetting we had the same mother.''

Britt fastened his eyes on Rakata's, but couldn't read their midnight depths. "What does *that* mean?''

"Only what it seemed,'' Rakata answered. Then he said slowly, "One day I'll replace Matarami as a *raden* of this province, but I don't know what to think of you. You're part of both peoples. I want to learn more about you from you, not what others tell me of you.''

Britt looked at his half brother in a new light. Though he'd always been curious about Rakata, he'd never dreamed Rakata might feel that way about him. While Britt considered this new idea and wondered how far he dared trust Rakata, a Javanese approached and asked for instructions.

Rakata gave orders to bury the dead soldiers, to leave no evidence that Blackburn's men had ever come to the village. He instructed the Indonesian to have the soldiers' horses and guns collected, for two of his men to escort Britt with Charles's body back to the plantation. After he'd finished, the man left.

"You'll have your guns now,'' Britt commented.

Rakata turned to regard him a moment before he said, "I would be a fool to leave them. Farewell, Britt. We will talk more another time.''

Britt watched Rakata rejoin his men, recalling childhood memories of a brother who'd run beside him along the paths of a deserted village while their mother, knowing the visit would end too soon and there might not be another, had smiled sadly.

Rakata didn't glance back at Britt as he led his men into the foliage. Though curiosity plagued Britt to become better acquainted with his half brother, he knew he dared not trust Rakata too far. And he didn't like to be under so great an obligation as to owe Rakata his life.

Chapter Two

Melinda was aware of servants bustling past her room, but she ignored the sounds. Neither the downstairs door opening to laughing guests nor the musicians in the ballroom tuning their instruments caught her attention.

The party to celebrate her engagement was an event second in importance only to her wedding day, and Melinda had wanted solitude to prepare for the evening, time to assess the past that had led her to this moment. She didn't want servants distracting her. She didn't even look forward to chatting with the girls she knew about her fiancé and their plans, an odd attitude, she admitted to herself. Melinda wondered why she felt different from friends who'd gotten engaged. She was solemn and introspective; they'd been frivolous and gay, as if they'd been filled with rosy bubbles like pink champagne.

During the afternoon Melinda had turned away hairdresser, manicurist, messengers bringing flowers and notes, even June, her maid. She'd bathed, powdered, and perfumed herself without help. She'd arranged her hair, and grateful the high-waisted gowns of the day didn't need corsets, she'd been able to put on her lingerie alone. Melinda had sat on the window seat wrapped in her dressing gown watching the traffic dwindle on the street beyond the wrought-iron fence. The garden's shadows had lengthened, the patches of snow had become mauve, then purple, in the dust, and finally darkness had fallen as she'd reflected.

When Melinda had turned sixteen she'd wanted to be alone on the morning before her debut—the party to celebrate her entrance into adult society—but her mother hadn't allowed it. Today Melinda was older, more self-possessed, and would have demanded privacy. But demands hadn't been necessary. Jessica had been too engrossed in her own preparations. Melinda knew her mother hoped to catch Frederick Sinclair's eye, that Jessica had her love affairs. Affairs were all the relationships could be, because Jessica couldn't divorce Charles Scott. It was she who'd deserted him, though he'd supported his wife and daughter since, support that had grown in proportion to the success of Phoenix House Tea until Melinda realized her father was wealthy.

Money had high priority with Jessica, but position and social power stood at the same level. Melinda knew this about her mother and accepted it. She'd lived with this premise all her life except for the eight short years she'd spent in Java. Money hadn't mattered to a little girl who preferred sarongs to lace petticoats and loved the fragrance of exquisitely woven rush mats more than the fragile pastels of Aubusson carpets. She'd had her playmate, Britt, then, a more loyal friend than those she knew now. She'd had pets of extraordinary variety, anything that had wandered out of the jungle, though Jessica had sworn that keeping even a mouse deer in her room was unsanitary. Melinda smiled as she recalled how the tiny deer's hoof had fit on her child's thumb. He'd had huge, dark eyes and long lashes, and he had slept comfortably in her shoebox. She'd had her father then, whose attitudes toward sarongs, rush mats, and mouse deer were exactly opposite Jessica's.

When Melinda had become aware of her mother's love affairs, she'd sometimes wondered if Charles eased his solitary life with mistresses. She imagined sloe-eyed Javanese women, graceful and delicate of feature, gentle, soft-spoken women like Sukadana, Britt's mother. Melinda dared not ask such questions in her letters to Charles, but she'd wondered. There were many things she would have liked to ask her father, but years and distance had made her shy. Melinda's reticence had struck a similar chord in him, so their letters were newsy rather than personal and their hearts had to sense the unwritten emotions. Melinda had often puzzled over why her mother had left her father. She remembered that Jessica had disliked Java, had wept a great deal and complained about things Melinda hadn't understood, though they'd troubled her.

What would her father think of Alden Townes? Melinda had mentioned Alden in her letters; unlike Jessica, Charles had seemed less impressed that Alden's father was a knight in King George's court than that Alden had been an envoy to the United States since the War of 1812 had ended. Was it because Java had been occupied by British soldiers? Charles had assured her they weren't causing trouble at Phoenix House. Melinda's last letter had told Charles about her engagement to Alden, but that letter might not have reached him yet. It was odd, she thought, that she must describe the man she planned to marry in a letter to her own father. Perhaps this was why she felt so unsure. Melinda wished Charles could be with her tonight, that he could meet Alden and recommend or condemn him. She'd always trusted Charles's wisdom and unswerving honesty. He'd never tried to manipulate her in any way, had never lied as Jessica did. But Jessica's deceptions were fashionably acceptable lies, harmless enough, Melinda had decided, and she'd gotten used to them long ago.

Melinda knew Charles wouldn't have approved of her previous suitors, because though they'd desired her as a woman and often liked her as a person, they'd been drawn to her by Charles's fortune. Melinda had been disappointed each time she'd realized an admirer was more interested in her father's money than in her. Melinda had liked one or two of these suitors well enough, so she'd been wounded when she'd learned their motives. Instead of questioning their standards, she'd begun to doubt her own worth as a woman and a person and had become wary of the interest men showed in her, inwardly questioning if their compliments were merely flattery, because it seemed she got little more. But she hadn't had to worry about Alden's interest in her fortune. He had his own money.

Though Melinda and Alden never discussed it—that wasn't done in polite society—she understood that his family was wealthy. Everything about him spoke of refinement. His attitude of taking elegance for granted seemed to prove he was the product of a long line of aristocrats and wasn't impressed by money, simply because he'd always had it. Melinda was proud that Alden, who had the means to be a pleasure-loving but useless dandy, instead lent his hand to the intricacies of diplomacy. Working through peaceful means to bring order to his country's relationships with other lands was a noble cause.

Alden Townes was handsome and thoughtful; he seemed to adore her. He was the most eligible of bachelors. Why did something in Melinda's being always seem to prevent her from spontaneously showing affection? Melinda was almost twenty-four; Jessica had often reminded her that she was more than ripe for marriage—in fact, on her way to becoming a spinster—and that she must conquer her hesitation about men. Melinda realized Jessica was right at least in this. Even Alden had called her his little ice princess when she'd balked at affectionate kisses becoming amorous, but he'd seemed pleased at this sign that not any man could have her. He'd promised he would teach her how to melt after they were married. Melinda concluded she was probably the most fortunate of women to have won the heart of a man like Alden, who was so considerate and patient. She only hoped he was right and inwardly worried that she wasn't more excited about the prospect of making love.

"Melinda, what *have* you been doing?"

Melinda was startled from her thoughts by her mother's exclamation. She hastily got up and faced the woman standing in her open doorway. The light behind Jessica reflected the gentle sheen of her satin gown and glowed in her hair. Melinda, as usual, envied her mother's fragile coloring. Sky blue eyes and blond hair were much favored in this time of elegantly simple fashions and subtle colors, not dark green eyes and brown hair with flamboyant red tints like her own.

Jessica peered into the room's shadows and could see little more than that her daughter was standing by the window. "Melinda, don't you realize our guests are arriving? Haven't you even dressed yet?" Jessica walked quickly to the lamp on the dressing table and turned up its wick. Then she moved about the room turning up other lamps, talking irritably. "Why are you moping around in the dark on what should be one of the happiest evenings of your life? Other women would be excited and bubbling over with enthusiasm. June told me you wouldn't let her help you bathe, that you turned away even Madame Longet when she came to do your hair. What are you thinking of?" Jessica turned to face her daughter, who was slipping off her dressing gown. "Thank goodness you've dressed at least that far," she exclaimed as she noted Melinda's lingerie. "Come here so I can see what can be done with your hair."

"I've already arranged it myself." Melinda stepped out of the shadows cast by the cornice over the window seat and the curls piled on her head lit with auburn tints.

Jessica was momentarily silent as she stepped around her daughter to inspect the coif. Though she could find no fault in it, she commented, "I really can't understand why you'd insist on doing your own hair tonight. Madame Longet is the best, the very *best* hairdresser. She was insulted that you turned her away. June told me she left in a huff. Do you know how much she'll charge for her time?"

Unconcerned, Melinda turned to gaze in her mirror. "I don't know why you act as if you're worried about that. You never even look at the bills, just hand them to Mr. Henry when the accounts must be done."

"If you prefer to do your own hair, why can't you think of *me*? You *know* I can't manage mine. I'll be lucky if I can persuade Madame Longet to come again," Jessica said in a piteous tone as she moved away to get Melinda's ball gown. "I don't know why I deserve so selfish a daughter. I've done *everything* I could for you."

Melinda wasn't disturbed by her mother's bid for sympathy. She knew Jessica's sorrow was false. She tucked a diamond-studded ornament more securely into her curls and turned to let Jessica put on her gown. "I could have finished dressing alone, Mother. You needn't have left your guests to help me."

"My word, what a notion!" Jessica declared. "How could you know your hem would fall smoothly in back, that all your hooks would be correctly fastened? I really don't know where you get such ideas, Melinda. Independence isn't becoming to a woman. Sometimes I wonder how you ever managed to find a man like Alden."

"You made a great point of introducing us at the Foxworths' party," Melinda pertly reminded. "Alden rather likes a little spirit in a woman."

"Spirit, perhaps, but not sauciness," Jessica commented as she stooped to smooth Melinda's hem. She stood up to look appraisingly at her daughter. "I've done the best I can for you. Maybe, after you're married, Alden can smooth off your rough edges. Meantime, dear girl, if you have any sense at all in that pretty head, *don't* do anything to make him change his mind."

Suddenly acquiescent, Melinda nodded. "I won't, Mother. I do believe Alden may be the only man I've met who wants me for myself. That's what I like about him most of all."

Jessica studied her daughter's eyes a moment, as if trying to gauge whether Melinda was being sarcastic or serious. Deciding on the latter, she was relieved. "You'll certainly be the most beautiful girl at the party tonight, which is only right. It is *your* party." Jessica took

Melinda's hand. "Alden is already here and waiting for you. Come, dear, smile a bit, won't you?"

Melinda obeyed.

"Let's not waste any more time, dear. This will be a wonderful evening," Jessica promised as she hustled Melinda into the hall.

Having intended to carry out Charles's last request to the letter by trying to persuade Melinda to return to Java, Britt had spent his first week in Philadelphia trying to think of how to approach her. It would be awkward to tell Melinda and Jessica about Charles's death when he had no idea how either of them would react, and the situation was complicated by Charles's will.

Because Charles had never made an effort to divorce Jessica, his generosity in supporting her and Melinda would give Jessica every reason to expect she'd share in the inheritance. How would he explain that Charles's will was so carefully drawn Jessica would get nothing, even if she contested it, unless Melinda decided to give her a portion? Britt wanted to be gentle, if there was any grief in Jessica and Melinda, not to embarrass them or himself. How could he approach Melinda about Charles's wish that she return to Java when she hadn't shown a hint, as far as he knew, of even wanting to see her birthplace again? Then, while glancing through the newspaper one morning over breakfast, Britt's eyes had fallen on the announcement of Melinda's engagement and upcoming party.

Britt wasn't sure if he was relieved or saddened. This news might dash away any possibility of Melinda's returning to Java, but what if her fiancé decided he wanted to become Britt's partner in operating Phoenix House Tea? Britt didn't look forward to the possibility of having a stranger, who probably knew nothing about growing tea, interfere with the plantation's management. Britt had been able to think of only one thing to do: use the party as an opportunity to mingle anonymously with the crowd while he studied Jessica, Melinda, and Alden Townes; assess them before he made his identity known.

He'd gone to an exclusive wagering salon he'd assumed was frequented by some of the socialites who were invited to Melinda's party. After making a few discreet inquiries, much influenced by the money he passed into the hands of the salon's employees, he'd learned that one of the socialites present had been invited to Melinda's party, that the man was addicted to gambling and was always in debt; a little observation told Britt why. The dandy was a flamboyant but foolish cardplayer. A friendly word or two, a compliment, earned Britt a place at the gaming table, where he made sure the socialite lost so heavily the man was happy, incredulous that Britt wanted to attend the Scotts' party so badly he was willing to take the invitation in payment.

One of the Scotts' maids had been discreetly posted at the foot of the steps so word could be passed when Melinda was ready to make her entrance. The guests noticed Alden working his way to the stairway; Melinda's friends gathered near while more casual acquaintances merely turned from their conversations to watch.

As soon as the news flashed through the crowd that Melinda was finally ready to come downstairs, Britt stationed himself a little distance from the foot of the steps, near enough to see Melinda clearly, far enough so no one was likely to question his relationship to the Scotts. When he heard Jessica's voice on the landing above, he looked up, wondering what the years had done to Melinda.

The pale shimmer of a green hem, the tip of a dainty slipper, came into view. Then, as Melinda began down the stairs, step by step, the girl was revealed. She was wearing a gown that obviously had been imported from Paris at great cost despite Napoleon's war. He could see from the way the silk of the softly flowing skirt lifted then fell with each step Melinda took that she had long legs; he recalled the little girl who'd run like a gazelle whenever she was away from the house and out of her mother's sight. Though the dress was high-waisted, the fragile cloth skimming Melinda's hips gave glimpses of the uncorseted curves beneath. Folds of green silk gathered under her bosom by a wreath of silver beads and tiny diamonds accented the high, gentle roundness of her breasts, highlighted the cream of her skin. Shoulders as graceful as her throat were covered only by a narrow veil of delicate silver beads matching those under her bosom. Britt lifted his gaze to the slender oval of Melinda's face. Her eyes, as emerald as the shadows of the jungle, looked calmly at the waiting crowd. Her mouth wore a gracious smile, but it seemed practiced. Though Melinda's composure would have done justice to a queen, Britt wondered if a girl, newly engaged to be married, should be *that* unruffled, if her regal poise shouldn't be warmed by a sparkle in her eyes. The chestnut curls, gathered by diamonds, caught fiery lights from the chandelier. Though Melinda had grown into the most beautiful woman he'd ever seen, Britt decided that Jessica had had her way—Minda had been transformed into Melinda, an exquisite statue of frosted crystal.

Melinda's eyes traveled over the faces of the friends awaiting her, then moved to the guests beyond and met the gaze of a man standing to the side of the ballroom doorway. Unlike so many of the other guests, whose glances darted around, lingering on no one, as if they were embarrassed when they met another's face, his eyes touched then captured hers. Melinda felt as if his measuring gaze, now moving unhurriedly over her, somehow caressed her. Other men's glances had often held a deliberate message. This man seemed surprised at his desire, distracted from another purpose. He wasn't flirting; he was reacting to the sight of her as naturally and unthinkingly as he breathed. For one unguarded instant she was buffeted by a torrent of sensations that left her breathless, but fright at the unfamiliar feelings dammed them. Her eyes, momentarily lit by radiance, cooled, and her face was suddenly as poised as before. The man's lips, which had softened as if he might have smiled, again became a firm line.

Melinda turned her attention to Alden, whose eyes were predictably calm and aroused no disturbing emotions in her, but she was aware that the stranger had finally lowered his gaze to take a sip of champagne. When Melinda reached the base of the steps and Alden took her hand, she was again aware of the stranger's scrutiny on them both. A pulse in her temple throbbed; though she smiled warmly at Alden, she knew it wasn't her fiancé's nearness causing her reaction.

She was tempted to ask Alden if the man was an acquaintance of his she'd never met. Instead, Melinda said, "I'm sorry I kept you waiting. I'm more nervous than I'd anticipated."

Alden smiled indulgently. "You don't appear so, darling. You've never looked more beautiful."

"Will you stay close to me?" she whispered.

"As much as I can, my dear." One of the qualities Alden liked in Melinda was her seeming aloofness, which, in reality, was a foil to hide her shyness. He patted her hand. "You know I'll have to circulate a bit. Many people I do business with are here, and I mustn't ignore them."

"Yes, of course," Melinda agreed. She decided the stranger who'd looked so intently at her must be someone Alden knew. She wondered if, when they were introduced, he would still be fascinating; at the thought, her heart gave a little lurch. *No,* she silently argued with herself, he was just another man and probably not even likeable. That steady stare smacked of insolence.

*   *   *

Britt withdrew as the engaged couple passed, then waited to follow the crowd into the ballroom. Of course Melinda didn't recognize him, he was assuring himself. Sixteen summers lay between this evening and their last meeting, sixteen Philadelphia winters like the one just ending. He wouldn't have recognized Melinda except for knowing it was she about to descend those stairs. The look that had flashed through her eyes had been something other than recognition, he knew, just as the sensation that had rippled through him at the sight of her was something else. He recognized what *he'd* felt was desire, out of place, unwanted under the circumstances. But he didn't think it was desire that had flown through Melinda's eyes. He'd decided that the frosty-looking creature she'd become had no fire in her heart. It had been smothered; the flame that burnished her hair was false, reflecting nothing.

Britt looked appraisingly at Alden, wondering what kind of man would want to wed a lovely living statue. Townes appeared to be older than Melinda by ten years, perhaps more. An aristocrat, Britt guessed. But Britt sensed a vitality in Townes, a restlessness as he spoke politely though briefly with well-wishers, that gave Britt the impression Alden was always eager to move on and do other things. Had Townes chosen Melinda to grace his side as he would choose an exquisite porcelain piece to adorn his home? Maybe they'd be a good match then, she cold and beautiful, he polite and ambitious. In every gesture, each line of Townes's impeccably tailored evening clothes, his dark hair artfully brushed to show the streak of gray at his temples, Britt recognized a love of luxury. In Townes's brown eyes, Britt saw ambition, perhaps even a greed to match Jessica's.

Glancing past Melinda's shoulder at an associate as he skillfully guided her toward a group of chatting people, Alden said, "I must speak to Mr. Holliday for a moment. Will you excuse me, darling?"

Melinda nodded and moved on. She knew Alden would be longer than he promised and accepted an invitation to dance from one of her former suitors. Since she'd long ago forgiven the beau for his interest in her money and since he was charming, she enjoyed his company. Afterward, another man asked her to dance, then another before Alden returned.

As Melinda began to dance with Alden, she noticed the man she'd seen, when she'd come downstairs, watching them. Afraid to experience the same intimacy of his glance as before, Melinda lowered her eyes, then was disappointed by the awareness that he'd turned away to mingle with the crowd. After a moment she fastened her gaze on Alden's face and smiled at him.

"Are you enjoying your party, Melinda?" Alden asked.

"It's *our* party, Alden. Yes, I'm enjoying it," she replied, then wistfully added, "I just hope you won't have to discuss too much business and be away from me most of the evening."

"I'm sorry, darling. You know I'd rather be in your company than with all those other people, but there are a number of matters I have to resolve, and people tend to be more agreeable when they're drinking champagne and enjoying themselves." Alden drew her a little closer and dipped his head to brush his lips to her temple. "I must confess I've been trying to arrange something special for our wedding trip."

Melinda looked up at him, startled. Was it possible he'd thought of visiting her father? A little breathlessly she asked, "What are you planning?"

"A tour of Europe," he replied, smiling down on her. "It isn't easy with all the fighting going on. Of course I wouldn't take you near any of that, only some of the cities—whatever is possible and appealing."

Melinda murmured, "That sounds wonderful."

"You seem disappointed, darling. Did you have something else in mind?"

Melinda lowered her eyes as she admitted, "I'd wondered if we might visit Java so you could meet my father."

"I didn't know you thought fondly of Java; but I'll meet your father just as you'll meet my parents, at our wedding. Surely, he'll come," Alden said.

Melinda looked surprised, as if the idea hadn't occurred to her. "Mother will *have* to invite him, won't she?"

"Of course she'll invite him," Alden agreed. "Whatever made you think she wouldn't?"

"I guess, after all these years . . ." Melinda began, then smiled at herself. "Yes, I'm sure she'll invite him."

Melinda's mind was occupied with visions of finally seeing her father again, of his escorting her down the aisle at her wedding, until the dance was over. Then Alden, begging her indulgence, went to speak to another associate. Melinda looked after him, wishing they could talk longer about the honeymoon he was planning. She wanted to share just a bit more time with him, perhaps a dream or two, but Alden had never been a man to talk of dreaming. Melinda sighed in resignation; his work would always take much of his time. She resolved to get used to it.

"Melinda, how beautiful you look tonight!"

"Oh, do let us see your engagement ring!"

At the sound of the voices, Melinda turned, but she could see beyond her approaching friends that the man who'd watched her before was dancing with a girl named Eleanor Grimes. While Melinda acknowledged Priscilla Johnson's compliment, she observed that Eleanor was obviously enjoying the stranger's company. Melinda briefly wondered what he was saying; annoyed at herself, she turned her attention to her friends. Melinda showed Amanda Reed the diamond-blazing ring Alden had given her, but as she received admiring comments, she wondered if the stranger had escorted Eleanor to the ball or had just met her there. Melinda wondered if there was a discreet way to ask who he was if Alden didn't introduce them. She chatted with her friends, replied to the questions she'd expected them to ask with answers she'd previously decided upon. All the while she caught glimpses of the man on the dance floor and wondered about him.

He must have recently visited Europe, she decided, because his evening clothes were of a style only beginning to be seen in Philadelphia. Instead of the waist-length brocade jackets worn by most of the men at the ball, the stranger's frock coat was dark russet serge. Melinda couldn't help noticing how the unadorned material defined broad shoulders, suggested a trim waist, and fell smoothly over lean hips. Unlike so many other male guests, who wore knee-length pants and silk hose, the stranger's legs were covered by black trousers, gently tapered to hint of firm muscles beneath. Was he, like Alden, an envoy, perhaps from London? Maybe he was one of the men Alden was negotiating with about their honeymoon trip. But the stranger's sun-toasted face spoke of hours spent outdoors rather than in council chambers. The way he moved revealed he was used to long strides on open ground, not polite little steps in drawing rooms. He seemed more a man of action than negotiation, Melinda decided. Was he a plantation owner from the south or maybe one of the islands in the Caribbean? Perhaps he was enchanting his partner with descriptions of the Carolinas, Georgia, or even Trinidad. Melinda had heard that social customs in the Caribbean bore less reticence. Perhaps that was why he'd looked at her so boldly. Irritated at herself for indulging in speculations about a stranger, she returned her full attention to Priscilla and Amanda.

But they, having noticed Melinda's distraction, assumed she was searching the room for her fiancé, who appeared more interested in the guests than his intended. Promising to talk again later in the evening, Amanda discreetly withdrew. In a moment Priscilla followed, and Melinda was alone when the music ended.

She watched the intriguing stranger escort his partner to a chair, then move away, leaving the girl looking longingly after him. Melinda plucked a glass of champagne from the tray of a passing servant; when she looked up, she met the eyes of the stranger, who was standing at the opposite side of the room, again watching her. The space between them seemed to dissolve. As before, she felt as if he somehow were touching her. This time the sensation didn't surprise Melinda. Thinking she could keep her composure, she returned his gaze as steadily, defying him to affect her the same way again. It was as if, expecting to be burned by a fire, she had touched cool marble instead. Melinda's heart didn't leap crazily; her mind didn't blur. Instead, she saw him as if through a tunnel of heightening clarity. She realized he wasn't the sort of man to court a woman with flattery. Whatever he might say, it would be truth. Melinda knew honesty was what she'd wanted all along in her world of veneered rituals and deceptions veiled by courtesy. She needed the truth, though she wasn't sure, unused to it as she was, what she'd do with it or even if it would please her.

Melinda held her breath, wondering if he'd approach; when he began to walk across the room toward her, she suddenly wondered what she could say to him. She reminded herself that this stranger would ignore all the rules of coquetry that shielded women from facing the truth of their own passions. With him there would be no coy games a woman could seek refuge in. Suddenly she was terrified that she, so disarmed at the moment she'd first discovered what desire meant, must face such a man, and she hastily turned away to leave the ballroom.

Walking quickly down the corridor toward the back of the house, Melinda scolded herself for having given the stranger even one glance. She was engaged to Alden; how could she have completely forgotten him? Searching for excuses for her unusual behavior, Melinda was annoyed with Alden for spending so much time with their guests he had little left for her. Was business *that* important? Confused by her surge of conflicting emotions, Melinda knew only that she wanted a few minutes to think. Where could she find it in a houseful of people? To retire to her boudoir meant she'd have to reenter the ballroom, no doubt be stopped by friends, and have to make conversation when all she wanted was to escape. Where could she go at this side of the house? Suddenly the thought of the conservatory attached to the morning room appeared in Melinda's mind like a green refuge and she hurried toward it. No one would dream of visiting the ell of the building that sheltered the garden's more fragile plants through the winter.

The greenhouse was lit by moonlight falling through the glass panels that made its ceiling and three of its walls. Though snow patches still lay in the garden, Melinda was enveloped by warm, moist air, the perfume of foliage and flowers in bloom. Her heels made soft clicks on the flags as she wandered down aisles of greenery. Finally she stopped by a glass-paneled wall to gaze at the deserted garden and try to collect her disordered thoughts.

A guest looking admiringly at her was no reason to flee like a child. Melinda decided it was nerves; she was more agitated about her engagement than she'd dared admit. It was normal, Melinda argued with herself. She'd felt so rushed lately. Jessica making plans for an elaborate wedding that was less than a year away, Alden arranging a honeymoon without consulting her beforehand made her feel like a bystander. Everyone else was deciding her life for her; was she a pawn on someone's chessboard? But she wanted to marry Alden. He was a handsome, wealthy man. He adored her, Jessica had said. Melinda was almost twenty-four. She'd be passed over if she didn't marry soon, Jessica had said, perhaps too many times. Melinda sighed. Maybe her mother's enthusiasm was part of the problem. Jessica had too often manipulated Melinda into doing things she hadn't wanted to do. Maybe now she was automatically resisting everything Jessica said. If only Alden would spend more time with her. If only he . . .

"Hello, Minda."

The quiet voice behind Melinda stunned her, not only because she'd thought she was alone, but because she hadn't heard *that* name in almost sixteen years. No one had ever used it except her father. The possibility of Britt's having come didn't occur to Melinda; he was a childhood playmate from another world. All she could think of in that instant of confusion was that her father couldn't have come to her engagement party. He couldn't have yet gotten her letter telling him about her decision to marry Alden. She'd misunderstood, Melinda decided—not heard the nickname right.

"Minda?" the voice hesitantly inquired.

Melinda turned slowly and looked up at the face of the stranger. Her heart seemed to stop beating and she felt as if she were holding her breath. The moonlight flooding the greenhouse touched his golden hair, illuminated amber eyes that asked for nothing; no hint of desire was in them now.

"I'm sorry if I upset you," he said softly.

She finally whispered, "*What* did you call me?"

"You didn't recognize me, after all," he concluded. "No wonder you're frightened of a stranger staring at you, following you here."

"You walked so quietly I didn't know you'd followed," she replied, then again asked, "Did you call me *Minda*?"

He nodded, and a smile slowly crept over the solemn line of his mouth, transforming it into a more familiar shape. Suddenly Melinda saw the echoes of his boyhood, the face that had once been at her side through many happy hours.

"Can it be—am I dreaming—*Britt*?" she stammered.

"Yes. Britt." He took her gloved hands lightly in his. "I wasn't sure you'd remember anything from those days."

Melinda's eyes lost their puzzled look but didn't take on the cool composure of before. Her face lit with joy, and she threw away her poise as, with a little cry, she flung her arms around him. "How *could* I forget? Those were the happiest times of my life!"

Britt was amazed that the icy demeanor of the lady in the ballroom had shattered and fallen away, that she clung to him like the child he'd once known. But Minda wasn't a child now, Britt reminded himself. Her body, so surprisingly pressed to him, reawakened the desire he'd felt before. Gently, very carefully, he withdrew. Holding her hands so she stood a little away, still feeling her nearness like a magnet drawing him, he forced himself to say, "I wish you and your fiancé every happiness."

Melinda gazed up at Britt a moment. Then, at this reminder that they'd both grown up, that years lay between them, her smile faded. "Thank you," she replied quietly. Not wanting to talk about her wedding or Alden, she said, "Tell me how you've been. And my father! And how are your parents?"

Britt had expected a tumble of questions, but Melinda's haste in asking made him realize she didn't want to talk about herself. Something was wrong in her life, he concluded, then changed his mind. Melinda was overwrought by the excitement of her engagement, his sudden reappearance. He didn't want to tell her, especially this evening, about Charles's death or any of the other tragedies of the past. He *had* to say something, but what? Hating himself for lying, Britt said, "Everything is all right, but exchanging news, once begun, will take all night. Let's save it for tomorrow or whenever we can have more time."

Though Melinda wanted to hear all about her father and everything going on at Phoenix House, she realized it would take hours. Then, too, Britt was likely to ask about her life, and she wasn't in a mood to answer. She agreed before commenting, "I really didn't recognize you before. I thought you were flirting with me."

"I'm sorry I upset you," he said awkwardly.

Melinda wanted to ease the moment. Finally noticing the distant music in the ballroom slipping through the open doorway, she recalled how she and Britt had once watched adults dancing at a party in Java and tried to imitate them. As then, she made an elaborate curtsy and invited, "May I have this dance, sir?"

Remembrance flooded Britt's eyes, and he smiled. "I'm honored, miss."

As Britt took Melinda in his arms, she remarked, "I behaved like a fool in the ballroom, running away as if you were some footpad ready to pounce on me. Now you'll know I'm not afraid of you anymore."

"Not even of my stepping on your feet as I did the last time we danced?" he quipped.

"I could see, when you were dancing with Eleanor, how you've improved. You even know this new dance called the waltz," Melinda replied.

"So that was her name. I never asked it," Britt commented. "I was too distracted wondering how to approach you. You seemed so remote."

"I'm not remote now."

"No, you aren't at all," he agreed, and drew her closer. Minda's touch was a sweet fire running through him. The silk of her curls brushing his cheek, the perfume rising from her shoulders entranced him. But she was engaged to another man. Britt forced that knowledge from his mind; though he knew it wasn't wise, he let his senses focus on the rhythm of their bodies and the music.

"It seems appropriate to find you here in the greenhouse," he murmured. "The atmosphere is like Java's, balmy, fragrant."

"Winter is one thing I never liked about Philadelphia," she replied, pressing her cheek against his jacket lapel.

Britt realized there was more Melinda disliked, but he didn't ask. Instead, he said, "I've missed my little friend from Java."

"I've often thought about you, too, and wondered what you were doing, but I saw you as a boy, as I knew you then," she confessed. "How foolish of me that was. Probably you're married now with children of your own."

"I almost did get married once. I was nineteen then, too young and too naïve," he replied. Then he added, "But let's not discuss other people. Now that we're together and alone, I'd rather talk about you and me."

Melinda's heart leaped in surprise. She hesitantly asked, "What do you mean?"

Britt felt her tension, but he also noted she hadn't moved away. Again reminding himself he had no right to walk into her life and disrupt it, he answered, "We share so many happy memories. I suppose one of the reasons I've recalled them is that childhood was a simpler time, carefree, pleasant to think about in the midst of adult problems." Britt paused, the warmth of her closeness momentarily so distracting he forgot he was dancing and his steps faltered. He looked down the moment she tilted her head to gaze up at him. Melinda was silent, her eyes filled with moonlight. The curve of her waist under his hand made him want to enfold her in his arms.

Staring up at Britt, Melinda wondered if he was about to kiss her. She realized he was a relative stranger; she didn't really know how the years had changed him. Melinda knew she should withdraw, but couldn't. His lips looked so soft, inviting. She wondered how she would react if he kissed her.

But Britt suddenly released Melinda, stepped away, and turned to look out at the darkened garden. He began, "Minda, there's something I have to tell you . . ."

"What are you doing in the conservatory, Melinda?" Alden, entering the greenhouse, asked. Then, seeing Britt in the shadows, he demanded, *"And what, sir, are you doing here alone with my fiancée?"*

Britt had whirled at the sound of the accusing voice, but Melinda, having seen the flash of anger in his eyes, stepped between the men.

"Alden, I want you to meet Britt Vandekker," she said hurriedly. "His father, Gerard, is my father's partner in Java. Britt, my fiancé, Alden Townes."

Realizing how their being alone in such an unlikely place must have looked, Britt said quietly, "I surprised Minda with my visit tonight.

We were good friends once and we've been reminiscing.'' Britt extended his hand. "I must congratulate you, Mr. Townes, on your engagement. I wish you both much happiness.''

While Britt was speaking, Alden recalled that Melinda's sense of propriety was a wall he had yet to surmount, but his instincts warned that this childhood friend of hers could be a rival. He had no intention of allowing any man to interfere with his plans after he'd finally persuaded Melinda to accept his proposal. Deciding he *had* to accept Melinda's explanation of the couple's solitude or make an ugly scene that could turn her from him, he slipped his arm possessively around her waist. When Britt offered his hand, Alden had no choice.

"It's a propitious time for you to visit after all these years," Alden said. "What brings you to Philadelphia, Mr. Vandekker? Business?''

Britt briefly, but firmly, clasped Alden's hand, replying evasively, "Business of a sort.''

Still wary of Britt's motives, Alden said with casual sarcasm, "I do hope you haven't found it necessary to flee the British occupation of Java. If you're having any trouble, perhaps I could put in a word.''

The implication that Britt was part of a conquered people stung, but he said smoothly, "Your offer is generous, but unnecessary. There's nothing I need to run from.''

Disappointed, Alden smiled and replied, "You're more fortunate than others, or so I've heard. Of course, I'm also concerned about Melinda's father.''

Britt answered, "Charles has nothing to run from either.''

Unabashed, Alden said, "I'm happy to know that. Earlier this evening Melinda and I were discussing her father's invitation to our wedding. Now that I think of it, perhaps we should give it to you. Maybe you'll deliver it more quickly than a mail packet. Of course, that depends on how long you plan to remain in Philadelphia.''

Britt realized that Alden's request wasn't prompted by a need to know the best means of getting an invitation to Charles. He wasn't welcome, and Alden was hoping he'd leave Philadelphia soon. Britt said evenly, "I'm not sure how long I'll stay. Now that I've learned about the wedding, I'll consider remaining until after the ceremony.''

Alden was further discomfited, but he said, "You're welcome, certainly. Our invitation would include you. It is a long voyage to make twice in so short a time.''

Surmising that Alden wasn't likely to afford him another opportunity to talk with Melinda alone that evening, Britt said, "As I'd only intended to let Minda know I was in the city, I believe I'll leave now. It was a pleasure to meet you, Alden.'' Not waiting for Alden's reply, he turned to Melinda. "May I call on you and your mother? I have a message from your father for you both.''

Surprised at Britt's sudden decision to go, Melinda asked, "Can't I persuade you to rejoin the party?''

Britt glanced at Alden, then took her hand lightly in his and said softly, "I'm sorry, Minda. May I come tomorrow?'' His lips brushed her fingers and he released her hand.

"You're welcome anytime, Britt,'' Melinda assured. "Will you be free at tea?''

Britt nodded and said warmly, "It's been wonderful seeing you again.'' He turned as if to leave, but paused at Alden's call.

"Mr. Vandekker, if you decide not to stay for the wedding, do let us know before you leave.''

"I'm sure I'll be staying long enough that we'll meet again,'' Britt replied and began down the aisle of plants.

Alden watched until Britt disappeared through the doorway, then turned to kiss Melinda's cheek as he commented, "I daresay he has a way of walking so quietly it's a bit unnerving. I suppose it's a trait inherited from his native mother.''

Melinda didn't like the derision in Alden's voice, but explained, "Britt had to learn how to move silently in the jungle so as not to draw the attention of wild animals. I'm sure it's become a habit for him to walk that way all the time.''

Alden slid his arms around her waist as he remarked, "It reminds me more of the way footpads prowl the lanes at midnight.''

His arrogance made anger streak through Melinda. She gave him a sharp glance and said coolly, "That comment is unwarranted.''

Alden was instantly penitent. "I suppose I'm behaving this way because seeing you alone with him in the shadows made me jealous.'' His fingers under her chin tilted her face to his. "Forgive me, Melinda?''

Though her irritation still rankled, she replied, "Yes, Alden. I forgive you.''

His hands on her shoulders drew Melinda closer, and as Alden's lips met hers, his arms slid around her. His caressing mouth told her of his growing ardor, but she wasn't moved. As his kisses grew more avid, she stepped away. Alden's pulses beat a quick tattoo and his eyes were bright with desire, but he wordlessly tucked Melinda's hand around his arm and began to lead her to the door.

Though Alden was more attentive for the remainder of the party and Melinda's friends commented about his charm and gallantry, she was often distracted by memories of Britt and the exciting feelings his merely looking at her had inspired. Again she wondered how his kiss would have felt. Though Melinda had resigned herself to feeling little more than affectionate warmth when Alden kissed her, instinct told her Britt's caresses might be different.

Chapter Three

Jessica was stunned the next morning when, over a late breakfast, Melinda told her that Britt Vandekker had attended the engagement party. That he was coming to tea was anticlimactic, in Jessica's opinion, as her mind raced over the possible reasons Gerard's son had decided to come to Philadelphia after all these years. She was too surprised to answer Melinda immediately, then was glad for the interval silence had given her. Jessica noticed the light in Melinda's eyes when she'd spoken of Britt and was careful to seem enthusiastic about his visit. After breakfast, using a headache from too much champagne as an excuse, Jessica retired to her room to consider the situation.

Britt's coming all the way from Java to deliver a message portended momentous news. Jessica's first guess was that the plantation had suffered a setback owing to the British occupation and Britt was going to give her a message from Charles explaining that the income he was sending would be reduced. Then she wondered if Britt had some other purpose for coming to Philadelphia and Charles had merely sent them greetings. Maybe Britt was looking for additional markets for Phoenix House Tea. If he succeeded, Charles would become even more prosperous and she'd share in his good fortune. Jessica then wondered if Charles had seen the visit as a means to reintroduce Britt to Melinda. She remembered her husband had long ago hoped they'd make a match, after they'd grown up, and his recent letters had inquired about

Melinda's future. It seemed, in any event, that Britt had caught Melinda's interest.

Recalling the towheaded boy who'd been Melinda's playmate, Jessica wondered how he looked as an adult. She assumed he must seem an adventurous figure to Melinda, after traveling from the other side of the world to deliver a message, and she was afraid their past friendship could influence Melinda in his favor. Jessica had other plans for her daughter and would snuff out any spark of romance that might light between them. The last thing Jessica wanted was for Melinda to move back to Java after she'd so carefully maneuvered her daughter into accepting Alden's proposal.

Melinda's marriage to a Townes would give Jessica a key to British society. She intended to find a lover with enough money to effect her divorce from Charles, the money to provide her with a life of ease that didn't rely on Charles's largess. It was irksome to have to depend on her income from a man who lived too far away to influence, and she hated Java too much to consider returning. Love had so little to do with her plans it didn't even occur to her.

While Jessica speculated about Charles's message and how she would meet whatever challenge Britt might present, Melinda went through her day alternately wondering what she would have done if Britt had kissed her, reliving the sensation of being in his arms while they'd danced, and feeling guilty that she, an engaged woman, should have such thoughts about another man. As teatime approached, she went upstairs to change into a mauve gown she judged was too simple to be provocative and brushed her hair into a subdued chignon at her nape. But at the last moment, she pulled a few curls loose to fall prettily around her face and hoped Jessica would think they'd merely escaped their pins.

Melinda was partway down the stairs when the butler opened the door and Britt stepped into the entrance hall. He hadn't noticed her yet, and she paused to watch him shrug away his cloak; the lamp cast gilt lights in his hair as he peeled off his gloves. She told herself again he was merely a dear friend from long ago bringing a message from her father. Their dancing together had meant nothing. It had been only imagination making her think he'd been close to kissing her in the conservatory. She resumed going downstairs. When Britt looked up, his eyes were warm but held no desire, convincing her it had been tension that had caused her to misread their expression at the party.

Melinda couldn't know it was the message Britt had to deliver that sobered his expression.

"Mother will join us in a moment," Melinda said after greeting him, then confided, "She's been in her room all day with an aching head from staying up so late last night."

Britt expressed his regrets but privately thought Jessica's headache wouldn't be improved by the news he was bringing. As he looked into Melinda's eyes, he only hoped that time and distance would soften her grief. Though it had become apparent during their conversation last night that Charles had kept unpleasant news from his daughter, Britt didn't know how intimate their letters had been. Melinda led him into the parlor and offered him a sherry. He accepted, then sipped it wordlessly while they waited for Jessica, making Melinda wonder at his silence.

Jessica didn't delay long. When she appeared in the doorway, Britt immediately put down his glass and rose to greet her courteously.

One glance at Britt told Jessica he would be a formidable rival for Alden, if that was what Charles intended. Sukadana's features didn't war with Gerard's, but blended so subtly Britt's face was arresting, though not exotic. Snobbishly ever conscious of fashion, Jessica had hoped Britt, having spent his life in remote Java, would be dressed in outdated clothes. She noted in disappointment that his blue frock coat and matching trousers were the latest rage in London. The creamy jacquard waistcoat beneath was heavy silk, his shirt and neckcloth stitched from the finest linen. Jessica decided she must waste no time before trying to put him in a bad light with Melinda. But she would have to be careful, she warned herself, that Melinda, relatively naïve though she was, didn't catch on.

"It's ever so nice to see you again, Mr. Vandekker," Jessica greeted with a cordial smile, then signaled her maid to pour tea. As Britt seated Jessica, she commented, "It appears that you made a stop in London. Beau Brummell couldn't have turned himself out with better taste."

Feeling uneasily as if Jessica wanted to make it seem he'd had to pause in London to acquire a presentable wardrobe, Britt smoothly answered, "I'm pleased you like this suit, Mrs. Scott, but I bought it in Paris. I travel to the Continent quite often to attend tea auctions."

"An attractive rogue like you must leave a trail of broken hearts across Europe when you return to Java," Jessica lightly remarked.

"I'm afraid not. I have little time for that," Britt replied. Was she now trying to make it appear he was a rake?

Inwardly disappointed, Jessica smiled as she observed, "You must work very hard if you avoid the temptations I've heard every young man indulges in these days. Your devotion to duty is commendable. How do you like your tea?"

"Plain, Mrs. Scott," Britt answered, and accepted his cup from the maid.

"I've no doubt you'll find our tea inferior to what you're accustomed to. It isn't nearly as fresh after having been shipped such a distance. I'm sure your taste must be quite sensitive—or is it?" Jessica asked, hoping to maneuver Britt into an answer that would reveal him as a perfectionist impossible to please or, after all, an oaf who didn't care.

Britt glanced up at her remark, then took a sip. "Tea is my business, Mrs. Scott. I must be aware of the quality Phoenix House produces, but I don't conduct a critique on each cup, especially that of so gracious a hostess. If you're concerned about your hospitality and want a professional opinion, I can tell that this tea is from the first cutting of topmost leaves of a costly Chinese variety." He smiled engagingly as he added, "It's been so carefully packed it's lost little aroma despite its travels and has been excellently prepared."

"I'm very pleased you think so," Jessica returned as convincingly as if she meant it.

Britt again wondered why Jessica was trying to draw him into a trap. Had Alden confided in her about his suspicions concerning Melinda and him last night? Or did Jessica still hate everything Javanese so much? Not relishing the thought of sparring politely with her, he decided to come to the point of his journey.

"Mrs. Scott, Melinda, I see little purpose in delaying what I must tell you, and I know of no way to make the news prettier than it is." He put down the teacup and looked first at Jessica then at Melinda as he said, "I'm sorry to have to tell you, Mrs. Scott, that your husband, Melinda, your father, is dead." He kept his eyes fastened on Melinda, though he heard Jessica's gasp of surprise. Melinda looked frozen, as if she weren't capable of reacting just yet. He glanced at Jessica, saw merely surprise on her face, and asked, "Do you wish to know any details, Mrs. Scott?"

Jessica nodded hastily.

Britt told her briefly, all the while watching Melinda, who merely rested her forehead on her hand. After he'd finished, he gently asked, "Minda, are you all right?"

Melinda raised her head and regarded him from dry, but infinitely sad, eyes. "I didn't know Father very well, Britt, except in my memories. Though we corresponded, our letters were . . ." She paused, searched for a word, then said, "We were more like friends than father and daughter. I'd so looked forward to his coming to my wedding. I'd hoped we could learn more about each other then." She lowered her eyes to stare at her lap, but not quickly enough for Britt to miss her rising tears.

He gazed at the girl sitting with bowed head and wished fervently he could put his arms around her, give her comfort, but he dared not with Jessica watching. He said quietly, "I've brought his will. Are you sure you can bear hearing it?"

Melinda raised her head to address the maid. "June, please pour me a sherry. Yes, Britt, I'll manage."

"Mrs. Scott?" Britt asked out of courtesy, not that he thought Jessica was suffering. There was no grief shadowing her eyes.

"Yes, Mr. Vandekker, kindly continue," Jessica urged, thinking she and Melinda would share in the legacy.

Britt took a slim sheaf of folded paper from an inside pocket of his coat and offered it to Jessica. "This is a copy of your husband's will, which was drawn by his attorney in London. Although I'm sure you'll want to read it later, I can tell you briefly what it contains. Charles left his share of Phoenix House Tea as well as everything he owns to Minda."

Jessica's mouth fell open. "He left provision for *my* income, of course!" Britt shook his head and she gasped. "Nothing? *Nothing at all?* This is ludicrous, impossible! I'll contest it! You and your father have somehow persuaded him. Gerard knew I never liked Sukadana. He did this in revenge!"

Britt's face hardened. "My father was killed by a tigress four years ago and you'll notice this document is dated more recently. No one influenced Charles's decision. I never knew he'd made a will until he told me moments before his death. If you bring this document to the courts, you'll find that Charles had it drawn with exceeding care. I visited his attorney, who said Charles particularly instructed him to make it binding. I understand your disappointment, Mrs. Scott, but I see that as no reason to blame me or anyone in my family. I'll have to assume your shock at this news has made you say such things."

"Mother, you can't think I'd let you starve," Melinda said.

"Of course not," Jessica agreed, but was far from soothed. She was furious that, after all those years of wanting a generous divorce settlement from Charles, she finally found herself a widow with nothing.

Britt turned to Melinda and said gently, "Your father allowed you a handsome income from Phoenix House Tea, but it's a limited income. You'll have to decide what part of it you'll want to share with your mother, because that's all you'll be able to get unless you decide to live on the plantation or sell your share to me."

Jessica now began to weep in earnest. Melinda looked calm, but sad, as she realized that Charles had felt he had to protect her from Jessica. She asked, "What other provisions are in the will?"

Britt sighed in resignation. "The balance of your share's income, after your allowance is deducted, is to be held in trust. Only if you return to Java will you be able to take your full share of each year's profit."

"That's because Charles knew I'd never return to Java!" Jessica wailed. "I couldn't possibly—or I'd go mad!"

"I'm afraid that was exactly what Charles was relying on," Britt agreed, then fell silent.

"I have one of three choices—to sell my father's share of the plantation to you, to stay here and accept a limited income, or go to Java and take his place as your partner." Melinda looked at Britt as if begging his advice.

"I'm truly sorry, Minda. I can't tell you what to do," he said regretfully. "I'd thought the decision would be difficult, so I planned to stay in Philadelphia for a few months. If you decide to sell your half of Phoenix House to me, I can pay you immediately. If you decide to return to Java, I can accompany you."

Jessica cried, "You can't be considering *that,* Melinda! *What would I do?*"

"I have to think of Alden too," Melinda said slowly.

"Alden will tell you to sell it," Jessica sniffed. "What would a gentleman like him do in such a desolate place?"

Britt gave Jessica a hard look, but said nothing to her. Instead, he told Melinda, "I'll be staying at the Liberty Hotel." When he stood up, Melinda also rose.

"I'll walk with you to the door," she offered. Noticing Jessica's glare, Melinda said, an edge to her voice, "Mother, you must realize this hasn't been a pleasant task for Britt. The least I can do is be courteous.''

Jessica looked away without a word to either of them.

Melinda was silent as she accompanied Britt to the foyer, but when the butler brought Britt's cloak and gloves, she instructed him to lay them on a chair and leave. After the butler had obeyed, Melinda looked up at Britt. "I apologize for Mother's rudeness. This news has shocked her.''

"I know that," Britt replied. "My greatest concern now is for you, Minda. I know you loved your father and are grieving more than you show.''

Melinda began, "I can only remember Father as he was when I left Java. My grief is a little girl's, and . . .'' She stopped, tears shimmering in her eyes as they had in Djakarta the day Jessica had taken her away.

Britt put his arms around Melinda and she leaned on him, her face tightly pressed to his shoulder. After a moment he said, "If you can't bear to decide about all this, tell me. I'll return to Java and manage your share of the plantation as your agent.''

Melinda looked up at him, took a breath, and said more purposefully, "That would be taking advantage of you. I suppose the only decision fair to everyone would be if I sold my share of Phoenix House to you.''

Britt considered that a moment and decided it would be fair to everyone except Melinda. A chance to decide her own future was what Charles's strange will had been made to provide. Britt gently brushed away Melinda's tears as he said, "That isn't what Charles wanted. He asked me to come here and tell you all this personally so I could try to persuade you to return to Phoenix House and live there.''

"Father hadn't gotten my last letter and didn't know I was planning to marry Alden,'' Melinda surmised. "How could he have expected us, being single, to live in the same house without causing a scandal?''

"The house was built to accommodate two families without infringing on the privacy of either. You and I could live as separately as if we were merely neighbors,'' Britt explained.

"Even if I were to decide to sell my share to you, I'd like to see the plantation one last time,'' Melinda said.

"It would only be good business to do that. You must let your emotions settle a bit, then discuss it with your fiancé,'' Britt advised, privately hoping that if Melinda married Alden, they wouldn't immigrate to Java. As he put on his cloak, he was thinking that the way he felt about Melinda might make living in such close proximity awkward, whatever Alden's character was, but if his impression of Alden was right, Britt knew the man was more suited for drawing rooms and salons than running a tea plantation. He could foresee difficulties rising between them.

Watching Britt smooth on a glove, Melinda said, "I'm grateful you took the trouble to do all this. I know it hasn't been pleasant."

Britt glanced up, then returned his attention to his gloves. "I'm fulfilling my promise to your father. I didn't expect it to be easy, and neither did he."

"The least I can do is offer a little hospitality while you're waiting for me to decide. I could show you something of Philadelphia; we might go to a play or a symphony, if you'd enjoy it," she suggested.

Britt turned to regard her steadily. "I'd like that very much, Minda, but only if you want to do it, not if you think it's an obligation you owe me."

"I want to," Melinda assured as she gazed up at him. "Would you spend the day with me tomorrow?"

"I know of nothing I'd enjoy more," Britt returned, wishing he could put his arms around her again. Instead, he bent to kiss her cheek lightly, then turned to step outside and gesture for the carriage he'd rented to be brought up the driveway.

Aware that Melinda was still in the doorway watching, Britt got into the carriage and turned to look at her again, to wave before directing his driver to leave. Then Britt leaned back against the seat and closed his eyes, haunted by the vision of her standing in the doorway looking so lonely.

Alden arrived only an hour later and was escorted to the parlor, where Jessica sat over cold teacups looking more distressed than he'd ever seen her. Melinda stood by the window staring at the darkness outside, seeming too deep in her own thoughts to have noticed his entrance.

"Mrs. Scott, Melinda, what's wrong?"

Jessica started at his question, then tearfully began, "Oh, Alden, we've just received the most dreadful news."

Alden looked apprehensively at Melinda. She had turned and was watching her mother narrowly.

Though Jessica was weeping, Alden knew her tears weren't sincere.

She only briefly described Charles's death, then centered her attention on the terms of his will and how it affected her.

As Melinda listened to Jessica, her irritation at her mother's behavior toward Britt slowly dissolved to be replaced by a feeling of guilt that Jessica was suffering so much. She found herself feeling almost as if she'd somehow conspired with her father to make the bequest in her favor. It occurred to Melinda that Jessica had in the past made her feel this way about other matters she'd had no hand in, even situations Jessica had brought on herself by trying to manipulate others to her own advantage. Was it possible she was doing that even to her own daughter? Melinda was shocked at the idea.

Anger, like a briefly glowing spark, made Melinda suddenly say curtly, "I had nothing to do with Father's decision. Didn't I read my letters to you—that is, when you took the time to listen?"

Jessica looked at Melinda in surprise. "What do you mean, dear? I haven't accused you of anything."

But the spark had faded and Melinda answered less vehemently, "You make it sound as if I plotted with Father behind your back."

Jessica looked at Alden and said apologetically, "Melinda has been under so much strain lately." When Melinda glanced at her from eyes that seemed ready to flare again, Jessica's lips began to tremble as if she were on the brink of tears. "You misunderstood me, dear. If it seemed I was blaming you for anything, I'm sorry. I'm just so upset." Jessica looked imploringly at Alden and began to sniffle. "I've been under a strain, too, lately, trying to help Melinda with her wedding arrangements. It's difficult to manage a household and take care of a daughter alone, especially at a time like this. I want to make Melinda's wedding so nice. This news about Charles is terrible enough, but learning that he left me nothing is too much to endure." Her voice faded to a murmur as she concluded, "Now it seems my own daughter is turning on me, after all the sacrifices I've made for her. I don't know what to do. I feel like a beggar."

Melinda had finally turned away to take a sip of her almost forgotten sherry. She remembered other occasions when Jessica had described in almost the same words how difficult it was for her to bring up a child alone, listing the sacrifices she'd made for Melinda's benefit. And Melinda suspected that, when Jessica had wept before, there'd been more purpose than emotion in her tears. Was all this a display now? Melinda was aghast that Jessica could think she had to be tricked into taking care of her own mother. Melinda reminded herself that

Jessica had had a shock. She could understand how Jessica would be distressed, maybe beyond realizing how she sounded.

Even while Melinda argued with herself, the conscience Jessica had so carefully nurtured in her daughter all those years plagued Melinda with the inevitable question. Was Jessica *that* wrong? Except for Melinda, Jessica was alone in the world, not a comfortable feeling in a society where girls were taught from toddling age they would one day look to their husbands for everything. Melinda realized that now it was *she* who must do the deciding for them both. She didn't like being put in the position, for all practical purposes, of replacing her father. Wasn't she, after all, a woman too? If decision making was such a burden to a woman, couldn't Jessica learn to share *something* of that burden and lessen her daughter's load? As Melinda recognized that Jessica's tears and wheedling were slowly winning over her own reason, she was disgusted that she was subtly being forced to withdraw from this war of wills.

Melinda turned slowly to gaze at Jessica, who was bowed over her handkerchief, shoulders daintily trembling. She wearily apologized. "I'm sorry for what I said. I know it's been difficult for you, Mother. But it hasn't been easy for me either. We're both upset and not making much sense."

Alden stepped closer and took Melinda's hand. "This will turn out for the best. You'll see," he soothed as he patted Jessica's shoulder with his free hand.

"Nothing is so changed, Mother. You know I'll continue your allowance. Maybe it won't be too reduced, perhaps not at all. We haven't learned yet what I'll receive from the trust," Melinda reasoned. "And just think, now you can remarry if you wish."

Jessica dabbed her eyes. Whom could she marry? A woman had to display herself to advantage, which was expensive, especially when she was old enough to have a grown daughter. She saw her previous lovers only as dalliances, not suitors, because she wanted a husband of position, perhaps even a title. A bloodline was the only thing that lasted, no matter what else happened, she was convinced. A woman couldn't find a man like that in a newly established democracy. One found them in Europe, and to embark on a search like that took money, no doubt more money than Melinda could allow her. Jessica decided she must enlist Alden's help in persuading Melinda to sell Phoenix House and share the proceeds. She looked up at her daughter with a doleful expression.

"You're right, I suppose. We don't know what this allowance will amount to, and we shouldn't worry about it too much until we learn more." Jessica opened her arms to Melinda. "You must be patient with me until this difficult time is over."

Melinda went obediently to her mother.

As they embraced, Jessica reminded, "You have Alden to lean on, dear; an engaged woman must learn to rely on her future husband's guidance." She glanced at Alden over Melinda's shoulder as she slyly added, "After you're married, perhaps Alden will want to move to Java and become Mr. Vandekker's partner in managing Phoenix House Tea."

Alden was startled. "*Me, stranded in a jungle?* I think that unlikely. Can you imagine me overseeing a gang of natives while they pluck tea? They probably don't even speak English, and I doubt I'd enjoy learning their gibberish."

"Javanese isn't too difficult. I learned it as a child and spoke it as fluently as English," Melinda said as she drew away from Jessica. She added thoughtfully, "Of course, I'd have to relearn what I've forgotten since."

Appalled that Melinda seemed actually to be considering a move, Jessica tactfully said, "You and Alden will have to discuss this decision thoroughly. It concerns your future together, and you must agree on it."

Alden had a mental vision of learning the tea business from Britt and inwardly shuddered, but following Jessica's cautious example, he sighed and agreed. "We must talk later, darling, after your shock has subsided and we've learned more details about your inheritance."

Melinda looked at Alden and asked hesitantly, "Do you think we might travel to Phoenix House? It would be a sentimental visit for me; as Britt said, it would be wise to see it before I make a decision."

Though spending any time in Java was the last thing Alden wanted, he realized he could stall her off until after they were married. Preparations for the wedding would keep her busy; it was less than a year away. He said, "Britt is entirely right about that. We should examine it to make sure the selling price is fair, if for no other reason."

Alden had no illusions about what Jessica wanted—as much money from the sale as she could get. If he promised her a portion, she could be of great help in convincing Melinda to sell. After Melinda was his wife, he could legally sell the plantation whether or not she agreed.

Even after passing a share of the proceeds to Jessica, there would be enough money to keep them in elegant style until his father died and he inherited the family properties in England. Meanwhile, though his own funds were getting low, he couldn't allow his appearance to slip. Appearance was everything in society, though he'd heard gossip that many of the people he wanted to impress were deeply in debt from maintaining their own images. Alden's reflections were interrupted by the butler's entering with an armload of flowers and a parcel.

"Madame, a messenger just brought these with a note." The butler handed Jessica a mixed bouquet and an envelope. "Miss," he said as he gave Melinda the parcel and a second bouquet, this of pink roses and orange blossoms.

"Why, it's from Mr. Vandekker offering sympathy for Charles's death!" Jessica scanned the note, then looked at Melinda. "What does your letter say, dear?"

Melinda raised her eyes to answer. "It's just a note expressing sympathy and explaining the packet contains letters I sent Father. Britt found them in Father's desk." Melinda promptly tucked the note into her sleeve, because she didn't want either of them to read it. Though Britt's message was proper enough, it was affectionate. It reminded her that he would welcome her company to Java if she chose to go and offered to help in any way he could meanwhile. Melinda inhaled the scent of her bouquet a moment, then looked up at June. The maid had hovered in a corner of the room waiting for possible orders. "Please arrange my flowers in the vase my father sent last year and place it on my dressing table with the letters," she instructed.

Though Alden was miffed that Melinda would keep the bouquet in her bedroom, almost as if Britt were her beau, he put his arm around her waist and commented, "That was quite considerate of Vandekker. I wouldn't have thought so civilized a gesture would occur to him." Alden noted Melinda's vexation at his remark and quickly added, "I only meant that his being brought up in so remote and wild a place would seem to preclude such niceties."

"Java is abloom with flowers that people regularly give each other," Melinda coolly replied.

Not wanting to renew their previous tension, Jessica said, "Forgive me, Alden, but I've just realized you're dressed in evening clothes because I invited you to dinner. I'd forgotten all about it. Melinda and I are still in afternoon gowns. Dear me, my mind is a muddle tonight."

"Quite understandably, Mrs. Scott," he answered politely. "If you'd prefer I leave, I'll do so immediately."

"No, Alden, do stay," Jessica declared. She saw his presence as a buffer between her and Melinda, possibly even a means of influencing her daughter. "I only must beg your patience while Melinda and I change to proper gowns for dinner."

"Please don't trouble yourselves. You both look charming as you are," he gallantly returned.

After a dinner for which Melinda had little appetite, over dessert Jessica said slowly, as if she were musing, "Now that I've had a chance to mull this over a bit, I must say I shouldn't have been so surprised at Charles's will. He never was very considerate of my feelings." She looked at Melinda. "You, my dear, remember everything through a child's eyes; a little girl couldn't understand the problems adults have."

"I suppose not," Melinda conceded, though she felt like reminding her mother that she was an adult now. She prepared herself for another bout of Jessica's complaints. She was too weary of it all to openly resist and tried to fix her thoughts on something pleasant—Britt's flowers perfuming her room, the note in her sleeve gently scratching her wrist as if urging her to read it again. Was it wrong, she wondered, to be so happy about flowers and a note from a friend? Though she knew Jessica and Alden would disapprove the intimacy of Britt's addressing it to "my dear Minda" and his reminding her how happy he'd be to escort her to Java, she saw nothing untoward in it.

"A bamboo hut on a mountainside is hardly the place to bring a lady," Jessica was saying. "No conveniences of the most rudimentary sort . . ."

Melinda recalled the house they'd lived in during the days Charles and Gerard had been trying to repay their debt to the Netherlands government. It had had several airy rooms, and the Vandekkers had lived in another just as big. She affectionately remembered the smoothness of the teak floor under her bare feet when she'd been getting ready for bed, the fragrant, rush-woven walls she'd twined flowers in, the whispers of the roof's thatch in the tropical breezes. Nobility in Europe and the *nouveau riche* of America paid exorbitantly for teak parquet imported from Java to floor their mansions, grew flowers in conservatories to scent their dreary winters, and, during the summer, perspired in rigid houses whose maze of rooms allowed few breezes to penetrate. Melinda wondered how the house in Java could have been so inconvenient for her mother when bowing servants had hastened to fulfill Jessica's every whim.

"Charles was always meandering around the property and was of little comfort to me," Jessica complained.

Melinda recalled her father coming in from the fields after a day of teaching the Javanese workers how to tend the struggling tea plants. His shirt had been darkened by sweat and his face flushed with the heat, his hair bleached from the relentless sun. Charles's eyes had always lit at the sight of his small daughter hurrying to welcome him. Melinda would never forget the love in his smile.

"Howling natives always ready to pounce out of the jungle were frightening enough, but one didn't dare trust the servants, who were their relatives," Jessica said. "Even Sukadana, Gerard's wife, was one of them."

Melinda saw herself in her mind's eye, a little girl running to Sukadana because she was frightened by Jessica's raging at Charles. She vividly remembered Sukadana's arms gently enfolding her, Sukadana's pressing Melinda's face to her shoulder and humming to try to drown out the sounds of the argument.

Melinda's chin lifted in a warning Jessica should have recognized as she said, "Sukadana was gentle and kind. There was nothing dangerous about her."

"Javanese women are so subdued they hardly ever say a word," Jessica advised.

Melinda recalled Sukadana's sometimes spirited debates with Gerard about occasionally indulging too generously in gin, and she knew Jessica was wrong. Sukadana hadn't been downtrodden but had kept family discussions private—except when a little girl Sukadana hadn't noticed had eavesdropped.

"Though Mr. Vandekker's manners seem above reproach, I'm sure a colonial nobody like him must have to remind himself constantly to put his best foot forward in civilized company," Jessica was saying loftily. "There's one quality about him I cannot help but find distasteful. It's a sort of relentlessness that even frightens me, Alden. Now that I've recognized it in him as an adult, I must say I *know* I did the best thing for Melinda by leaving that island. Who can tell what might have happened if she'd grown up there? You realize, Alden, those people don't have the moral values we do—and his mother is one of them."

"Blood will tell," Alden readily agreed, glad for a chance to disparage Vandekker before Melinda. "There's no question that he's different from us. I noticed it last night."

"Then you met him?" Jessica inquired.

Melinda knew that when Alden described how he'd found her and Britt alone in the conservatory, Jessica would ferret out every detail of the scene and make much of it. At the thought, the spark of Melinda's temper flared again. Before Alden had a chance to begin, Melinda laid her napkin on the table and got up from her chair.

"Mother, Alden, please forgive me," she interrupted. "This afternoon was very trying and I think I must retire." At their surprised looks she added stiffly, "As a civilized gesture of my own, I offered to show Britt something of the city tomorrow. Seeing as you both have doubts that he's a reliable companion, I think I must go out early, so I may leave his company before dusk. Please continue enjoying your conversation. I wish you both a pleasant evening." Then she turned and left them staring after her.

Melinda was out of their line of vision when she approached the stairs; they couldn't know her courage had failed, that she fled up the steps with unladylike speed, her soft little slippers making less noise than the swishing of her skirts. Melinda's anger at these two people, who were supposed to be the most dear to her, surprised and grieved her. She wanted to escape them and, at the same time, the confused, unwanted emotions they'd aroused in her.

When she opened her door, the combined perfume of roses and orange blossoms reached out like a comforting hand. Melinda quickly closed the door behind her and turned the key. She needed to lock out a world that gave need and want, obligation and loyalty, love and guilt the same meanings, a world that shook her sense of right and wrong.

Melinda walked quickly to her dressing table and stood gazing down at the vase of flowers. Britt had, at no small cost in time and trouble, come from Java to fulfill his promise to Charles by delivering his message. Gerard and Sukadana had nothing at all to do with any of this, Melinda reflected. But Jessica and Alden had maligned them. Was Melinda supposed to side with them, wrong though they were, because one was her mother and the other her fiancé? It would be unjust to Britt and Sukadana as well as Gerard's memory. Her father had wished to protect her future; whatever his past conflicts with Jessica, he'd known Melinda wouldn't let her mother go wanting. Melinda looked at the packet of letters on her dressing table. It wasn't necessary to reread them to confirm she'd never written anything to her father hinting even obliquely at wanting his share of Phoenix House Tea for herself. Why was Jessica so angry simply because she wouldn't have complete control of the money? Melinda would have expected to consult with her mother about her needs. Charles had, evidently, thought Melinda would be too generous, that Jessica would take advantage of her, and he'd tried to protect his daughter through his will. Why was Jessica behaving as though Melinda were scheming otherwise? Why couldn't Jessica at least be a little more discreet until after the shock of Charles's death had a chance to fade?

Suddenly Melinda couldn't bear to think of any of it. As when she'd been a little girl trying not to hear angry, adult voices by playing pretend games with Britt, she sought refuge in fantasies of the past.

While Melinda prepared for bed, she recalled the sunsets, when Java had taken on a burnished light. Everything that was white had reflected a rosy tint and the grass had seemed to turn blue. She and Britt had caught fireflies and believed that if they made a wish before their glowing prisoners left their open palms, it would come true. Melinda wistfully reflected on how adulthood changed such dreams rather than granted them. One of hers had been the childish wish to marry Britt, for then he'd been the hero who rescued her from imaginary lurking tigers and fearsome-looking lizards.

When Melinda got into bed and found the remembrance of her troubles again invading her spirit, she reminded herself of the pleasant prospect of spending tomorrow away from the house. She knew that unless she introduced the subject, Britt wouldn't mention Charles's will or Jessica's attitude toward it.

Curling up under her blanket, Melinda closed her eyes contentedly. Tomorrow itself would be almost like a fantasy. She could pretend Britt was merely visiting, that he hadn't brought such disruptive news.

The fragrance of roses and orange blossoms became jasmine and frangipani in her slumber. The chiming of the hall clock took on the sound of gamelans, orchestras of bells, wafting through a sunny morning while a file of golden parasols wound down a green mountainside marking the return of a procession. Then she slipped deeper into a dream of walking with Britt through the incense-tinted haze of an ivory-lined Javanese temple, his arms full of flowers until he stopped and turned toward her. His eyes seemed like a glaze of amber flecks as he leaned closer to kiss her and let the flowers fall at her feet.

Chapter Four

Though the sky was a serenely unbroken azure dome wearing the sun like a gold bangle, the early March breezes were imps touching Melinda's cheeks with frosty fingers. She wore the fur-edged hood of her cloak close to her face and tucked her gloved hands into the plum velvet muff.

"The Declaration of Independence was signed in the state house so there's talk of renaming it Independence Hall," she was saying.

Britt took a last look at the building from the carriage window, tipped his head to follow the line of its tower, and observed, "As a man who lives in an occupied country, I can appreciate why the patriots fought so determinedly for freedom."

"Father wrote in his letters that the British soldiers weren't bothering Phoenix House," Melinda said slowly. She laid her hand on Britt's arm and asked, "Was he, perhaps, minimizing the danger?"

Britt turned to regard her from eyes shot with copper flecks in the sun. "Major Wakefield is more moderate in his policies than others, but as Rakata said, we're prisoners when we can't govern ourselves."

"Rakata! You mean your half brother?" Melinda asked. Britt nodded, and she inquired, "I gather the rift between your and Rakata's family has been mended?"

"Not really, though it was Rakata who came to rescue the village from Blackburn," Britt explained. "That was the first time we'd spoken, then only briefly."

"I find it hard to believe you have no curiosity about each other," she commented.

"We are curious," Britt replied. "Rakata admitted it and thought we should speak again."

Melinda noted Britt's expression and remarked, "You don't seem eager."

"I owe him my life, not an obligation I welcome, though I'm glad enough he saved it."

"But neither you nor he had anything to do with Matarami's condemning your mother," Melinda reminded. "You weren't even born and Rakata was a toddler."

"But my parents are dead because of it."

"Sukadana is dead?" Melinda gasped, then lowered her eyes. "I'm so sorry. I didn't know."

"A Javanese courting Matarami's favor killed her eight years ago. My father started drinking too much after that. It was because he was drunk that the tigress killed him," Britt said tightly.

"My father never mentioned all this in his letters. I guess he kept a lot of bad news from me."

"There was nothing you could have done, and the rest of the plantation's day-to-day problems didn't concern you, who were so far away," Britt said quickly.

Realizing he didn't want to dwell on the subject, Melinda decided to temporarily lay it aside and asked, "Would you like to drive past the College of Philadelphia now? The Pennsylvania Academy of Fine Arts, perhaps the Academy of Natural Sciences? All are the first schools of their kind in the United States."

Britt looked at Melinda. The rosiness the crisp March air had brought to her cheeks made her appear more like the vivacious little girl he'd known in Java, but her enthusiasm now, as all during their tour of the city, struck a false note. He wondered why shadows marred her eyes' clarity and made her smile look forced.

Melinda was surprised when Britt pulled off her muff and gloves and cast them on the carriage seat. He enclosed her hands between his and said, "Despite my coming from Java, I believe I'm better suited for Philadelphia's climate than you are. Let me warm these cold hands."

Britt lifted her palms to his lips and his warm breath cozily seeped through her chill, but Melinda was disconcerted by the easy familiarity of this man, who was yet a relative stranger. Jessica and Alden's comments that Britt's background made him different, his moral values looser, hung in her memory. She would have withdrawn, but it also occurred to her that it was Jessica's voice telling her to back away, that she hardly ever did anything without considering what Jessica would think of it. Melinda reminded herself she was old enough to let a man hold her hands even if he wasn't her fiancé. She'd planned to forget her problems with her mother on this outing, to enjoy the day, but Jessica's admonitions had crept into her thoughts to depress her. Melinda resolved again to forget Charles's will, Jessica's reaction to it, even Alden's derisive comments about Britt. She raised her eyes to meet Britt's as he pressed her palms to his cheeks, then covered her hands with his own. His touch was gentle yet strong, comforting to her.

Watching the changing expressions in Melinda's eyes, Britt was glad the shadows in them finally lifted. He said, "We've driven down Elfreth's Alley, which was charming, past Betsy Ross's former house and Christ Church. I've seen Benjamin Franklin's library company and think his idea of a library whose members' contributions are used to buy books they all can share is very clever." Britt lightly kissed the tip of Melinda's thumb. "We've visited Carpenter's Hall, and I was engrossed by your description of how the Continental Congress first met there to debate opposing King George's policies toward the Colonies. I felt as if the spirits of the men who signed your Declaration of Independence remain in 'Independence Hall.'" He smiled at Melinda with a boyishness she remembered well. "It all was informative and impressive, but having paid our respects even to the Liberty Bell, I think we might find some place less awe-inspiring to have luncheon."

Melinda suddenly realized it was past noon. Apologizing for her lapse as his hostess, she hastily ordered the driver to turn south.

The carriage soon entered the countryside beyond the city. The colorfully painted decorations at the peaks of houses and barns told Britt they were traveling through one of the areas where Dutch farmers had settled in Pennsylvania.

Melinda's thoughts had fallen again on Sukadana's death, and she looked at Britt's profile, wondering how many storms he'd weathered during their separation. While Melinda watched the glint of his hair in the sun, the golden fringe of his lashes as he gazed out the window at the farmland just beginning to take on a haze of green, she realized his mind, too, must bear scars, yet they seemed not to trouble him now. Maybe, like her, he was trying to forget his problems. Melinda resolved again not to cast shadows on their day and asked Britt about the people she'd known in Java before she'd left. She learned that Koki, whom she remembered as a young scullery maid, was now the cook and supervised a kitchenful of assistants and that Arjuna, a former playmate, had married Malili, another playmate.

Thoughts of Java recalled the variety of pets she'd kept, and Melinda admitted she'd had none in Philadelphia except a kitchen cat she'd befriended. She laughed at the memory of her first elephant ride, when she'd slipped off the animal's back and fallen in a stream. When Britt asked if she ever rode horses now, and Melinda said yes, but only sidesaddle as Jessica insisted a lady should; he silently resolved, if she returned to Java, he would give her a horse. It pleased him to think of Melinda again mounted astride, galloping with the wind blowing her hair like ribbons as she had so joyfully done as a child.

By the time the carriage stopped at a little inn, Melinda had been so distracted from her problems with Jessica that when Britt helped her out of the carriage she almost flew from his grasp to admire forsythia bushes blooming in front of the inn.

"They're the first I've seen this year, a sure sign of spring!" she happily exclaimed.

Britt duly admired the bright yellow flowers and was again reminded of Minda, the child, hunting for night-blooming tuberoses at the edge of the jungle. He knew, despite the changes time had caused in her appearance and Jessica had made in her demeanor, Melinda still had the soul of his little Minda. He took her arm and guided her through the doorway that welcomed them with a scalloped lintel of painted birds and hearts.

In a room of sturdy wooden tables and chairs decorated with flowers and patterned chintz curtains that let the sun stream through, they had a homey lunch of dumplings, duck, sweet-sour beets, apple butter, and popovers. Though Melinda reminisced about eating Javanese food— tiny shrimps in spicy sauce, stewed acacia blossoms, and dishes flavored with verbena—Britt noticed the shadows again gathering behind her eyes. He realized her chatter was an effort to distract herself from something.

Finally he quoted:

"the wan luster of thy features—caught
From contemplation—where serenely wrought,
Seems Sorrow's softness charmed from its despair—
Has thrown such speaking sadness in thine air,
That . . .
I should have deemed thee doomed to earthly care."

Melinda looked up at him in surprise. "You're quoting Lord Byron? I wouldn't have thought you'd be interested in poetry."

"Living on a plantation gives a man time in the evenings to read," he replied, then softly asked, "What's troubling you, Minda?"

"It's hard to believe a man as attractive as you has nothing else to do with his leisure," she hastily commented. "Is there no social life in Java these days?"

Noting she wanted to evade his question, he answered, "After a day's work, I'm usually content to spend evenings quietly." Because he didn't wish to explain that his lack of a social life was due less to weariness than a reluctance to again risk his heart, he changed the subject.

During the next several weeks, Melinda went on other outings with Britt, and though Jessica urged her to question Britt more closely about her possible allowance as well as what he was willing to pay Melinda for her share of Phoenix House, Melinda was reluctant. She was enjoying renewing their friendship too much to mention finances and turn their time together into a business discussion.

While Alden was eager to know what Melinda's legacy was worth, he was concerned that she spent so much time in Britt's company. Though Melinda claimed she was merely showing hospitality to a visitor, he suspected she was developing too great a liking for Vandekker. Finally, hoping to distract Britt from Melinda, Alden suggested he and Melinda take Britt to a symphony. Alden asked Eleanor, the girl Britt had danced with at the engagement ball, to make it a foursome. As Alden had foreseen, Eleanor was eager to accompany them.

Melinda discovered that, unlike previous evenings, when she'd easily lost herself in the spell music cast over her, even Beethoven's "Moonlight Sonata" couldn't distract her from noticing when Britt inclined his head toward Eleanor to hear a comment, when Eleanor put her hand on his arm as she gazed up into his eyes to listen to his reply. The girl's low laugh seemed unduly seductive, Melinda noted and flashed Eleanor a glance warning that others in the audience would be disturbed by the sound. In that moment Melinda saw that Britt's eyes weren't on Eleanor but on herself. She quickly looked away, thinking she must seem a stiff-necked prude in contrast with Eleanor's easy coquettishness. She wondered why she'd always felt she had to be so carefully circumspect, then realized that it was her mother's teaching, though Jessica was herself an incorrigible flirt. Melinda suddenly wished she was more outgoing—she liked to enjoy herself too—but all the while the knowledge clawed at the back of her mind that she really wanted to flirt with Britt, charm him as Eleanor was trying to do. She felt guilty at having such thoughts with her fiancé sitting beside her; but at the same time, Melinda felt an urge to compete with Eleanor. She grew morose.

When the evening finally ended, Melinda was glad Britt and Eleanor were waiting in the carriage so Alden could do no more than give her a circumspect kiss on the cheek when he escorted her to the door.

In Melinda's dreams that night Jessica admonished her to mind her manners and Alden pulled on her elbow while she tried to shake free of him and go to Britt, who silently watched.

During the morning Melinda argued with herself that her fantasies had no basis in reality. Alden was her intended and a far more suitable man than was a tea grower from another world, a Java that childhood's memories had probably made more attractive than it actually was. Melinda resolved, at her earliest opportunity, to ask Britt about the details of her inheritance, as Jessica had urged. The opportunity came sooner than she'd anticipated: Britt arrived to ask if she'd have lunch with him.

Despite her decision, while Melinda faced Britt across the table in the tearoom of the Liberty Hotel, she found herself hesitant to broach the subject. Britt again spoke about Java and reminisced about the things they had done together. She recalled the swing Gerard had made in the garden behind the house, how Britt had too gently pushed her while she'd begged to swing higher, ever higher. Melinda blushed and laughed at Britt's recollection of how he'd taught her to swim in a lagoon, surreptitiously, because they'd had to strip to their underdrawers and Jessica would have forbidden it. Melinda recalled floating in the flower-covered water, the music of the bells from a distant gamelan drifting on the scented air.

Britt saw Melinda's pleasure at her memories rising in golden-green flecks from the emerald of her eyes, like bubbles in the lagoon in Java. He didn't want to distract Melinda from the moment by asking why she'd behaved so coldly the previous evening, though the question had been his reason for the impromptu lunch. Britt sensed an undercurrent in Melinda's life that troubled her and knew happiness visited her too seldom and for too brief intervals.

Melinda's eyes shortly refocused on the present. "Those are only memories," she said quietly, as if they were something to fold up and pack in a trunk lined with tissue and sprinkle with dried lavender. With a sigh she added, "A child's impressions are different from an adult's."

Britt answered quietly. "Sometimes children have more accurate sight than adults because their perspective isn't distorted."

Melinda watched his hand, toasted by a tropical sun, creep across the snowy tablecloth until the tips of his tapering fingers just touched hers. Suddenly Melinda's sight was blurred by tears; she couldn't raise her eyes to look at Britt as she whispered, "Mother wants me to ask how much you'll pay for my share of Phoenix House. Alden wants me to spend less time with you."

Britt softly inquired, "What do *you* want?"

Every time Melinda had posed that question to herself, a pain had risen in her born of confusion and a vague feeling of disloyalty. And always the guilt. She tried to brush his question aside but found herself saying, "I don't know what I want and wonder if I ever did. It sometimes seems as if I've never made any choices, that I've only thought I did, for the outcome was of Mother's choosing." Melinda glanced up briefly, saw the concern on his face, then quickly looked down, blinking away the tears of her confusion. Britt's hand moved warmly over hers. After a moment, she whispered, "I'm so muddled lately I've even sometimes wondered if I chose Alden or Mother chose him for me."

"The man you marry should be your decision. If you're doubtful, you must delay the marriage till the uncertainty is resolved," he gently advised.

Melinda finally raised her eyes; Britt was startled to see resentment, not sorrow, in them as she blurted, "But don't you see? The longer I delay, the more Mother will press me. I'll end up feeling my opinion is hers and still not be sure! Sometimes she makes me feel like a rabbit in a snare. No matter how I try to free myself, even temporarily so I'll have time to rest and think, I get more entangled. She's done it before, you know—thwarted my plans in some way I couldn't resist unless I defied her.''

"What's so terrible about your taking a stand?''

"It wouldn't be just that. It would develop into an argument that would end with her crying and my feeling guilty. Or she would be very quietly, rigidly angry and make me seem ungrateful, foolish, as if I'd just vulgarly displayed my temper without having a valid reason.'' Melinda's tension revealed scars of the previous defeats she'd suffered.

"How many times have you hidden your own wishes from her or tried to ignore them to avoid such scenes?'' he prompted.

"Somehow she always gets her way,'' Melinda murmured.

"But surely you can't let someone else make such important choices as whom you'll marry and what you'll do with your father's legacy,'' Britt insisted. He waved away the serving girl, who was looking nervously in their direction, then took out a handkerchief to blot Melinda's eyes as he added, ''Charles must have anticipated all this. You should remember he wanted you to make up your own mind.''

Melinda looked as if a light had flashed behind her eyes as she said, "I'd thought Mother was bitter about her marriage's failure, but maybe when she spoke against Father, she was jealous, because I remembered him with affection. I wonder now if she suspected I wasn't showing her all his letters to me. Maybe she thought he was trying to turn me against her. But he never did!''

"Charles wasn't a man to scheme,'' Britt assured. "His will was the nearest he could approach to that sort of thing, and even then he gave you a choice.''

"You must think I'm hateful for saying such things about my own mother, but sometimes what she does disappoints me so,'' Melinda whispered. "I guess what they say is true—that you only hurt the ones you love.''

Britt commented coolly, "If that were true, it wouldn't make being loved very rewarding, would it?'' He stood up and helped Melinda from her chair as he said, ''I think everything that's happened so recently has presented you with decisions you've never had to make and now must. You're reappraising your life, trying to find some answer to guide you. It's upsetting and bewildering because there's no easy solution. If I can help you, call on me, Minda. I won't try to bend you in any direction of my own choosing.''

Melinda knew that was true. The first time she'd looked into his eyes at her engagement party she'd somehow known he'd tell her the truth whether she liked it or not. Suddenly Melinda felt as if Britt were a rock she could cling to in her storm and she felt safer. "I know and I'm grateful."

"To a stranger from Java?"

Melinda recognized the wry humor in his tone and, as she took his arm, replied, "I've discovered I trust you now exactly as I did when so long ago I was afraid I'd drown but let you teach me to swim."

Britt didn't speak again as he handed her into the carriage, and he let her think silently on the ride back. He was immersed in his own reflections. The restrictions society placed on behavior almost always made marriage a gamble. A man and a woman were initially caught up by physical attraction; while their minds were reeling with unrequited desire, they had to somehow decide if they were compatible—if their personal qualities would enable them to spend their lives together. He'd always wondered how it was possible for a man to see a woman clearly, get to know her well enough to make such a decision, when his thoughts were riveted on physical urges society wouldn't allow him to satisfy until after they were wed. He likened that perplexing situation to Minda's present state of mind. She was torn by loyalties to her past, fear of an uncertain future, while others tried to impose their decisions on her. Britt reflected on his engagement to Elise. They'd properly restrained themselves and had lived by society's rules, never truly getting to know each other while their yearnings had led them to misleading fantasies and ultimate disaster.

Britt gazed at Melinda, so delicate in profile, though the lift of her chin hinted an underlying courage she had yet to discover in herself. Her hair, sedately brown in shadow, seemed to burst into fire when the sun touched it. He likened it to her temperament—restrained and cool on the surface with passion beneath. If in confusion Melinda now made a mistake she couldn't later undo, her life would become a torment that would scorch her and everyone close to her.

Roused from her reflections when the carriage stopped, Melinda was embarrassed she hadn't said a word to Britt all through the ride. "I'm sorry I've been rude," she began.

He dismissed her apology. "You were absorbed in your thoughts."

Melinda smiled wanly. "How can I be comfortably silent with a man who has just come all the way from Java and will return there?"

"You own half of Phoenix House Tea and can go back with me if you wish," he reminded her.

"It's difficult to imagine."

"You should look the plantation over before you decide whether to sell it."

Although Melinda was still perplexed, her anger had calmed; Britt was glad of that. He leaned closer, intending to kiss her cheek lightly, then found himself lingering, inhaling the scent of her skin—roses and orange blossoms like his bouquet. He realized he'd inadvertently chosen flowers that matched her perfume. Britt smiled against Melinda's cheek and felt a light trembling run through her. It made him forget he was merely a friend and his lips remained to softly nibble at her cheek. She shivered again.

"You're doing what the Javanese call 'sniff-kiss,' " she murmured.

Britt withdrew. Melinda's eyes were closed, her face alight. He had been ready to apologize for his untoward gesture; instead he said softly, "You were only eight when you left Java. How did you learn about sniff-kissing?"

An impish smile tugged at the corners of Melinda's lips as she murmured, "You told me about it. I'd seen Koki and her beau do it, and I asked you." Melinda opened eyes glimmering with sun sparkles. "You said the Javanese thought a fragrant skin was very important as physical charms go."

"Did I demonstrate it for you?"

She nodded, her smile still softening her mouth. "I think you didn't know how to kiss a girl western style then anyway."

"I do now," he murmured and touched his lips to hers.

The chill of the March day receded and the sunlight of Java seemed to envelop Melinda as Britt's mouth caressed hers, lightly, tenderly, then more sensually. She felt his arms sliding around her; she leaned closer, her lips responding to his as if they had finally found the purpose they'd been shaped for. Her breasts against his chest, even through their clothes, seemed to have been formed only for the pleasure of pressing close to him. The sensations he was creating in her were like nothing she'd ever felt before. She caught her breath, turned her face, and put her fingers against his lips as if asking him to pause. He kissed them away. Then Britt's mouth moved to Melinda's cheek so he could nuzzle her, kiss Javanese fashion; she responded in kind, drawing more emotion from this delicate caressing than she had from Alden's most passionate kiss.

Britt's hands slipping into Melinda's cloak moved lightly, briefly, over her bodice, as if he couldn't resist the need to explore her but dared not linger. She felt like clasping his hands and moving them back, but she wasn't bold enough. His fingers slid to her waist, then around her back, drawing her to him as his mouth again reached for hers. His lips nibbled along the edges of hers, then his mouth covered hers, sending so sweet an ache through her she trembled. He felt it; a rush of desire flooded him. Suddenly remembering where they were and who she was—his partner and affianced to another man—Britt reluctantly withdrew.

"I promised not to influence you, but here I am, a moment later, kissing you. I'm sorry, Minda. I forgot myself," he said.

Melinda gazed at him while a shaft of sun falling through the carriage window turned his eyes to copper sparks. Finally what Britt had said sank into Melinda's consciousness and cooled her impulses. "It wasn't your fault. I forgot myself too," she awkwardly replied, though she wanted to kiss him again.

"Think of it only as you did in Java, a stolen kiss inspired by mischief," Britt said slowly.

Melinda recalled that he hadn't stolen the childish kiss in Java— she'd asked for it—but she nodded agreement. "I'd best go now. Thank you for listening to my troubles."

Britt nodded distractedly and got out of the carriage. As he swung Melinda to the ground, he thought his hands on her waist might, of their own accord, slide around Melinda's back and clasp her to him again. He quickly released her. "Don't let what just happened make you hesitate if you want to talk to me. I *will* help you any way I can and I'll have better manners in the future."

"I won't be hesitant," Melinda promised, then hurried into the house.

As the butler eased off her cloak, Melinda resolved to be less impetuous the next time she was alone with Britt and suddenly realized it was exactly the opposite of what she'd wished of herself the previous evening. She wondered why, though she was reticent with Alden and had always been so restrained with previous suitors that she'd earned the reputation of being a frosty lady, she'd become a flame in Britt's arms. This unexpected change in her made Melinda wonder uneasily what other surprising turns in her character she might learn about. Then she decided that her voyage of self-discovery, finally begun, must be seen through to its end—if it had an end. She must face whatever truth it gave her, because truth was the only sword or shield she'd ever have against the manipulations of others.

Melinda's steps made no sound on the thick carpeting as she headed toward the kitchen intending to get a cup of chocolate. The occupants of the library didn't hear her approaching.

"Really, Alden, this Javanese nobody is going to spirit her away yet if you aren't more attentive."

Melinda stopped at Jessica's remark and guiltily wondered if someone in the house had seen her kissing Britt in the carriage and had reported to her mother.

"You won't get a penny to save your dwindling fortunes if she goes off to Java—and I won't likely get more than some trifling allowance. I'd thought we'd made an agreement . . ."

Melinda caught her breath. An *agreement* between Alden and her mother? She was aghast at what this seemed to imply. Melinda urged herself not to jump to conclusions, to go into the library and get an explanation, but her feet remained solidly where they were as she listened.

"I would have been content to live on the income from the investments Charles made for her," Alden said.

"And meanwhile periodically beg your father to send money so you could pay one or another bill you'd run up, or be embarrassed?" Jessica laughed harshly. "I'd thought then I'd be grateful to have the allowance Charles was sending to support me and Melinda for my *sole* use. I foresaw going to New York in the hope of meeting an eligible man, possibly on a visit from England, Scotland, or even France," Jessica declared, unaware that every word she uttered shocked her listening daughter. "But if Melinda sells that miserable piece of Javanese jungle and you marry her, you and I can share its price. You'll have more than enough money to tide you over until you inherit your family's properties in England. I'd be able to travel to Europe like a queen and *choose* the man I'd marry rather than accept any bumpkin here who seemed reasonably suitable for my purposes."

The maelstrom of emotions building in Melinda suddenly compressed to a cold, hard knot in her heart. She stepped into the doorway. "And what would you have *me* do, Mother? Your plans don't seem to have any provision for my feelings."

Jessica and Alden, sitting across from each other, stiffened in shock. Jessica turned slowly, incredulously, to stare at her daughter, whose eyes were as expressionless as if they were a doll's made of glass. Having no idea what Melinda was thinking, Jessica didn't know what to say.

"Of course I'm *merely* your daughter. That never really meant anything to you—a daughter is nothing but a creature to be taught manners and obedience, to be groomed and polished until she can be sold on the market,'' Melinda said with a calm that shriveled Alden's heart.

Jessica gathered her courage and ventured, ''I can't imagine what you mean, dear. You've heard a fragment of our conversation, I must assume, and misunderstanding, you've come to a wrong conclusion.''

''Isn't that what I should have expected you'd answer? I'm always mistaken, have jumped to a wrong conclusion, or am under such strain I can't think clearly. If all else fails, you'll begin to weep, tell me how much you've sacrificed for me, feign illness to get my sympathy,'' Melinda observed. ''But today those tricks won't convince me, because *anyone* hearing a tenth of what I just did would recognize what you both were scheming.''

''Truly, Melinda, you've made a dreadful mistake,'' Jessica insisted, her lips quivering as if she were ready to weep just as Melinda had predicted.

''Darling, you surely can't think . . .'' Alden began.

''That's where both of you have always been wrong. Yes, I *can* think,'' Melinda corrected, then added contemptuously, ''Alden, you'll simply have to budget yourself more strictly while you wait like a vulture for your father's death. Seeing as you, Mother, won't be splitting my legacy with Alden because you won't be part of the Townes family by marriage, you'll *have* to make do with a colonial bumpkin like Frederick Sinclair unless you can lure some larger prey into your web.'' Melinda tugged Alden's ring from her finger, then dropped it on the floor and, daintily raising her skirt hem, smashed it under her heel. Diamonds bounced in sparkles around her. She let her skirt fall back into place and raised eyes no longer as blank as glass but flashing with anger.

''I've been agonizing over turning my heart from the decision it all along wanted me to make, trying to convince myself to do what both of you wanted instead, but I no longer need to do that. Now I'll go with that 'colonial nobody' to at least take a look at that 'miserable piece of Javanese jungle' you'd wanted to make you rich.''

Melinda turned and walked out of the room. Though the pain at what she'd learned about her mother and fiancé was a tempest battering at her anger like the ocean pounding a seawall, Melinda maintained her outward poise until after she'd gone upstairs. When she reached her bedroom door, Melinda's knees all but collapsed from

under her, and she hurried into her chamber to lock the door with a
violently shaking hand. Then, tears streaming, she threw herself across
the bed and buried her face in a pillow to muffle the sobs that tore
from her soul.

Melinda had no idea how long she lay helplessly weeping or how
many times Jessica and Alden might have knocked on the door alternately demanding and begging she come out. It wasn't that Jessica
didn't matter to Melinda, but that Melinda loved her, and betrayal by
someone you love hurts all the more. Melinda reasoned she'd been too
blinded by love to see what Jessica had been doing all along. Finally,
when it seemed there was not another tear left in her, Melinda turned
her head on the drenched pillow and saw through the window that
darkness had fallen. Slowly, wearily, she sat up and swung her legs
off the bed.

Her first impulse was to wonder how she could face her mother
now. Then, as she remembered the way Jessica had coldly plotted to
pluck her inheritance from her hands without a care for her, Melinda's
concern vanished. Unless Jessica could explain the conversation she'd
overheard—and Melinda could imagine nothing that would convince
her—there was no more to say.

Reflecting on all her previous suitors' interest in her father's money,
Melinda realized that grief at Jessica's scheme was part of her distress.
The old fear that she was undesirable without her father's fortune
seemed to be confirmed by Alden's perfidy, and she'd been crushed.
Melinda sat on the edge of the bed, feeling her aloneness as acutely as
if it were a vise tightening around her. Finally she remembered the
conversation she'd had with Britt and his assurance that he would help
in any way he could. She desperately needed to talk with him now.
Britt was the only person she could confide in, the one man she *had* to
tell about the decision she'd just made.

Melinda pulled a cloak from her wardrobe, heedless that it was old
and much worn, then hastily wrapped a woolen shawl around her
head.

She hoped she wouldn't have to confront Jessica or Alden a second
time so soon after the first and, hiding her fear under a mask of
determination, went downstairs and saw neither of them. Melinda
couldn't know that Jessica was so certain of the power she held over
her daughter, she'd assured Alden Melinda's courage would fail, that
they'd later convince her she was wrong. After their shock had

subsided they'd gone to a new play Jessica thought might be amusing—
Don Quixote, based on the famous novel by Cervantes.

Like a burglar breaking out rather than in, Melinda crept down the
servants' stairs at the back of the house, then began to let herself out
the kitchen door. Suddenly feeling foolish at her qualms, Melinda
realized just how strong an influence Jessica had always been if, even
now, she could be intimidated by her mother. She lifted her head,
stiffened her back, and turned to march through the house to the front
door, then imperiously told the butler to get a carriage. Melinda
waited in the foyer, bracing up her courage against Jessica or Alden's
coming, until the carriage was brought around.

The hotel clerk peered over his spectacles at the lovely young
woman in the run-down cloak and mismatched head shawl asking for
Mr. Vandekker's room number and tactfully said, "The hotel's policy
doesn't permit this sort of thing, miss." At the girl's perplexed look,
he added sternly, "This is a properly run establishment and young
women aren't allowed to visit male guests in their rooms."

When Melinda realized he thought her a prostitute, the blood drained
from her face. She said in the autocratic manner she'd learned to use
on pesky peddlers, "I am Melinda Scott, heiress to Charles Scott's
partnership with Mr. Vandekker in Phoenix House Tea. Mr. Vandekker
will be much put out to learn you turned me away when I have an
emergency to discuss with him. Neither will he be happy about what
you accused me of doing here tonight."

The clerk paled, involuntarily stepped back, as if the slightly down-
trodden-looking girl had somehow been transformed into a princess.
He swallowed, wondering if she were lying, but not daring to disbelieve.
In a newly respectful tone, he said, "I beg your pardon. I'll send
someone to Mr. Vandekker's suite to inform him of your presence."
The clerk came out from around the desk and, made more uneasy by a
glimpse of the hotel manager standing across the lobby watching, said,
"May I show you to a seat where you can wait?"

"Do you expect me to discuss a confidential matter with Mr.
Vandekker in the lobby?" Melinda inquired coldly. "You said he has
a suite? Why can't I speak with him in his sitting room?"

Glancing nervously at the manager, who hadn't moved, the clerk
began, "The hotel must protect its guests' reputations and . . ."

"Why should Mr. Vandekker pay for a suite he isn't allowed to use
to speak privately with a business associate?" Melinda pressed.

The clerk realized several passersby were listening and conceded, "Mr. Vandekker will have to decide what's best."

Melinda seated herself and waited until Britt came downstairs. Throwing the clerk a glare, he escorted Melinda into the now deserted tearoom.

After they'd sat in the same corner where they'd had lunch, he asked with concern, "What's wrong?" Before Melinda could answer, Britt snapped his fingers at a passing maid, who hurried to their table. "Miss Scott is chilled. Kindly get her a bit of brandy."

"The tearoom is closed and it doesn't serve spirits anyway, sir," the maid said.

"It will tonight, though it's after hours," Britt replied, looking pointedly at the manager, who was watching from the doorway. "Get me some brandy, too, and light one of these lamps."

The manager nodded approval and Britt threw him a grateful "Thank you, Ned." Then he turned to Melinda to ask worriedly, "What brought you here at this hour, Minda?"

Melinda managed to keep her composure as she related Jessica and Alden's conversation, but her eyes flashed with anger when she described smashing Alden's ring. She finished, "I'd sometimes wondered why, if Father was as inconsiderate as Mother always claimed, he'd been so generous in supporting us, though we were far away. Now I know, as never before, he was an angel best rid of so scheming a wife."

"But not best rid of you," Britt said softly.

"Why didn't he try to get me away from her? My life would have been so different if I'd grown up with him," Melinda said through lips she was valiantly trying to hold steady.

"He did try. What finally convinced him to leave you with her was Jessica's argument that you wouldn't get a decent education in Java and would have to be sent off to school anyway," Britt explained.

"Is that how you got your education?" Melinda asked.

"My father sent for a tutor—a series of them actually," Britt replied.

"And Mother calls you a 'colonial nobody,' " Melinda said disgustedly.

Britt looked faintly amused at the description. He sat back in his chair and remarked, "Forgive me for smiling, Melinda, but I met the DeWinters in Paris when they were touring Europe some years ago."

"My grandparents? I knew little of them, as they visited only a few times before they were killed in that accident," Melinda said slowly. "I do remember Grandfather always seemed a bit tipsy and Grandmother only talked about some new gown she was being fitted for, this or that piece of jewelry she wanted."

"Charles, as you can guess from all I've said, talked to me quite a lot; and he said he'd known the DeWinters wouldn't support you and Jessica while they lived, would leave you nothing when they died. Despite their prestigious family name, they weren't rich," Britt advised.

"It's true Mother inherited nothing. I'd wondered where Grandmother's beautiful jewelry went," Melinda mused. "What happened to the DeWinter money?"

Britt hesitated a moment, then finally said uncomfortably, "Charles told me everything went to pay off their debts."

"But why did they have such bills?" Melinda asked, already suspecting, then answered her own question. "For the same reason their carriage overturned, I'd warrant. Grandfather's drunkenness. He *was* a drunkard, wasn't he? And Grandmother was like Mother, a spendthrift concerned only with appearances. That's why Mother wants me to marry Alden, because he's a Townes. Being related to him will open doors for her. She wants an aristocratic husband, you know, a wealthy one."

Britt nodded solemnly, took a sip of brandy, and asked quietly, "Do you have any idea what you'll do now?"

"I'm going back to Java."

Afraid to assume anything, Britt inquired, "To look over your inheritance one last time before you sell it?"

Melinda took a breath, then answered purposefully, "I want to try to make my home there, learn to take my father's place as your partner."

Britt asked, "Are you certain you aren't merely looking for a way to escape Jessica? If so, you could be disappointed. I suspect such a flight would be more from yourself than from her. Jessica couldn't have put you in this position if your attitude hadn't allowed it."

"I know that, Britt," Melinda admitted. "But she had the advantage of being my mother. Even a rebellious child learns from its parents. Now I want to become acquainted with what I am. I could do that here in Philadelphia, but inheriting half a plantation opens a new avenue I think I should explore."

"I'm not trying to dissuade you. I just want you to see all sides of this," Britt advised. "Life on a plantation can be lonely, and running it is a difficult job."

"If I find that I dislike it or the task is beyond me, I'll sell my share to you," Melinda promised. "Then I'll think about whether I want to return here or establish myself somewhere else. I can't know where yet, because I've seen nothing of the world. If I hire a good solicitor, I could use the sale price of the plantation to make investments I could live on."

Surprised at the way Melinda had reasoned all this out so quickly, Britt commented, "Once started on the road to independence, you seem to do admirably."

Melinda smiled. "Father made investments in my name Mother has been supplementing our income with. She thought I didn't know about them, but I'd seen the papers when Mr. Henry was doing our accounting. I'll sign them over to Mother anyway before I leave for Java. She won't live quite as lavishly as she has unless she finds another husband, but she'll be well provided for."

"That's generous after what she tried to do to you," Britt said.

Melinda fell silent, as if reflecting in amazement on all the decisions she'd made. Finally she asked, "Do you think it's beyond me, a woman, to try to learn to be your partner?"

"After what you've told me this evening, I suspect no venture is beyond you," he replied. After a moment he added, "A few of the planters in Java are married to women they proudly say are their partners as well as wives."

Melinda's eyes lit with new encouragement as she raised her brandy glass and toasted their new partnership.

Britt smiled as he lifted his snifter, but he knew, despite Melinda's brave front, her decision made in anger could change as her temper cooled. He realized it was possible he was falling in love with her, and he was haunted by the fear that an adult Melinda wouldn't love Java as the child Minda had. Like Jessica and Elise, she might learn to hate life on a plantation. Britt reminded himself Melinda was Charles's heir. It was her right to try to carry on the partnership; it was what Charles had wanted. He resolved to control his own emotions until he learned what Melinda's reaction to Java would be.

Chapter Five

Having made the decision to go to Java, Melinda preferred to leave without delay; and at her urging, Britt arranged passage on the next ship bound for Djakarta, which was scheduled to sail in a month. The first fortnight passed as a weary procession of days with Alden repeatedly coming to the Scott house trying to change Melinda's mind and Jessica insisting she'd misjudged their motives because she'd heard only part of their conversation. Both of them talked their way around her pointed questions, neither offering a plausible explanation for the plans they'd been making to dispose of her inheritance.

Melinda didn't want Amanda Reed to give a farewell party because she knew everyone was speculating about her breaking her engagement with Alden to go to Java with Britt. Amanda insisted Melinda needed distraction and their circle of friends would think it even more odd if she left the country without a good-bye. Finally, Melinda reluctantly agreed, and Amanda arranged the event a week before the ship was scheduled to sail. Melinda asked Britt to be her escort.

Because Melinda wasn't looking forward to the party, especially since it involved spending a night in the Reed family's country house, she delayed packing the little she'd need for an overnight stay until the morning she was to leave. With only an hour left before Britt was to come for her, Melinda was interrupted by Jessica's coming to her room, supposedly to help her pack. Jessica kept up a steady stream of conversation, trying to persuade Melinda to consider reconciling with Alden and insisting that she was wrong about their intentions. Melinda answered as patiently as she could, though her annoyance was steadily growing.

Finally Jessica paused, thinking she'd made a point her daughter couldn't refute, but instead of answering, Melinda addressed her maid, who was offering several ball gowns for her choice.

"I won't want an elaborate gown for this evening, June, just something pretty for dinner. Give me a moment to choose." Melinda thumbed through the dresses in her wardrobe more slowly than necessary, using the time to decide how to answer Jessica without causing more animosity between them. She could think of nothing except the truth. "I'll take this gown," Melinda told the maid as she indicated her choice. Pulling a petticoat from the cabinet, she turned to Jessica to say wearily, "I just wish you could know how sad it makes me to have to tell you there seems no point in talking about any of this. You keep saying the same things over again and never give me one reasonable explanation for what I heard you tell Alden."

"You aren't sad," Jessica replied coolly. "You don't understand because you don't want to."

In her consternation Melinda dropped the petticoat she'd been folding. "That isn't so! Merely telling me your and Alden's plans were for my benefit is hardly convincing when it's obvious they were made for yours. A ten-year-old wouldn't believe that, and I'm not a child, though it seems you've tried to keep me as naïve as one."

"You *want* to run off to Java with that nobody!" Jessica accused.

Melinda forced herself to hold her temper and told the maid, "June, not the black slippers, but the green ones for that." Then she straightened to tell Jessica, "When I go to Java next month, it won't be to run off with Britt. It's a business arrangement. Our being friends certainly is preferable to having a partner I don't like."

"Everyone is gossiping about your decision to go to Java with him. Don't you care about what people think?" Jessica asked.

Melinda started to refold the petticoat. "Amanda told me anyone talking about Britt is doing so from jealousy—women who want to catch his eye, and beaus who resent him. I've already told you the plantation house was designed for two families."

"But taking Britt to the party seems to prove a romantic attachment and . . ." Jessica stopped, as if finally at a loss for words.

"My farewell party is a perfect time to formally introduce my new partner. If I didn't invite Britt, it would seem as if I had some reason to keep him away from my friends and acquaintances,'' Melinda said tightly.

"I wish everything were the way it used to be,'' Jessica said sadly.

Melinda wanted to tell her that if it hadn't been for Jessica and Alden's scheme there'd be no farewell party, but she felt worn down and didn't want to renew that line of discussion, which got her nowhere. She said disgustedly, "Alden will be at the party, which will make this event more chore than pleasure for me. I told Amanda not to invite him, that it would be awkward, but she insisted he's part of our social circle and it would be worse to leave him out. I sometimes suspect Amanda has an imp that goads her to do such things just to see what interesting mischief comes from it.''

"On that point we do agree, but for different reasons.'' Jessica sniffed. "It's perfectly scandalous for Amanda to give a party out of town.''

"She had little time to plan, much less prepare, this party and went through considerable trouble. It was her mother's idea to have it at their country house because their town house is being redecorated,'' Melinda patiently explained as she had during a dozen similar discussions.

"All those single men and women spending a night under the same roof isn't proper,'' Jessica insisted.

Melinda wondered if it was more proper for her mother to have had a string of lovers during these past years, but she said, "Amanda's parents will be there as well as a housekeeper and a staff of servants. That should be enough chaperons to satisfy anyone.''

"Ah, well, why should I think you'd listen to me? Since Britt came along, you don't hear a word I say.'' Jessica turned, shoulders drooping as if she'd suddenly been defeated. She walked slowly to the door.

Melinda felt a pang of remorse and took a step as if to stop her mother, but Jessica opened the door with so heavy a sigh Melinda suspected her sorrow was, as it had often been in the past, a ploy.

"It seems almost as if he's mesmerized you,'' Jessica added with a gesture Melinda was sure was rehearsed.

"All Britt did was tell us about Father's death and the will,'' Melinda answered quietly. "It was what you and Alden planned that decided me to return to Java.''

"You still don't understand what we meant. I don't know what you expect me to do after you're gone, but you aren't worrying about that.

I'm only your mother, and you have Britt," Jessica said as she stepped into the hall.

Melinda walked quickly to the door to tell Jessica's receding back, "You still can come to Java with me." As soon as the words were out, Melinda wondered why she'd said them. She could think of nothing more uncomfortable than trying to live in Java with Britt and Jessica.

Jessica only waved a limp hand as if utterly disheartened.

But Jessica was her *mother*, Melinda thought. She *couldn't* leave things this way. "I'm arranging to have the investments Father made in my name transferred to yours, as I'd promised," Melinda called as Jessica started down the steps. Though Jessica didn't answer, Melinda knew her mother had heard. Wondering if there was something else to do or say, other than surrender to Jessica's wishes, Melinda remained in the hall until Jessica disappeared around the curve in the staircase. Not knowing Jessica was smiling with satisfaction, Melinda returned to her room feeling depressed. Instead of resuming her packing, she went to the window to gaze sightlessly at the new leaves beginning to unfurl in the tree branches, the early spring flowers starting to dot the lawn. She wished she could think of a way to mend the situation with her mother before she left Philadelphia.

"Mr. Vandekker will be here soon, miss. You don't want to greet him lookin' so glum," the maid said sympathetically.

Melinda continued staring out the window. "I can't help imagining how I'd feel if my daughter were going to Java and I'd be left behind, especially when we're both so unhappy."

"You can't marry Mr. Townes if you don't care for him," the maid said gently. When she saw a tear fall from Melinda's lashes, she came to pat her shoulder. "There, there, now, miss." Several more tears spotted her mistress's bodice and she finally burst out, "I'll be oversteppin' my place, but I can't stand here watchin' you weep. Miss, I *have* to say the truth. If you sack me for it, I'll just have to go to my next job a couple of weeks sooner than I'd planned."

Melinda brushed away her tears with an impatient gesture but didn't look at the maid. "What is it?"

"Beggin' your pardon, miss, but you and Mrs. Scott are as different as acorns and strawberries. She don't feel like you think," the maid said quickly, as if she'd held back this opinion for so long it now came in a rush. "Mrs. Scott ain't cryin' behind no doors. It ain't right for me to let you break your heart over this."

Melinda finally looked up at the maid, whose blue eyes crackled with indignation. "What do you mean, June?"

"All this concern for your reputation ain't worth a snap. She's doin' more talkin' than anyone. Not a caller comes she don't tell—always makin' you look wrong, sayin' how ungrateful you are after all she done for you, you bein' just like your father and him so selfish. If anyone is makin' you look bad, it's her. Makes herself sound like a holy angel, she does," the maid said huffily.

Melinda flinched from this news but said, "Maybe it really seems that way to her."

"You think Mr. Townes been comin' all the time, sending you presents and posies on his own? No sirree. Mrs. Scott been tellin' him to do it. She's still tryin' to figure how to get you to marry him. Every time you and Mr. Vandekker been gone somewhere, Mr. Townes comes to talk to Mrs. Scott and see what new idea she got. Don't say much when I can hear, but they talk plainer in front of Kate. They think, after you're his wife, he'll have all the say-so 'bout your property and can sell it no matter what you want."

Melinda sighed. "It's just about what they were saying before."

"They ain't changed their minds," the maid declared. "Mrs. Scott still thinks, if she acts sad enough, you'll stay. She's sure, after Mr. Vandekker's gone, she can get you hooked up with Mr. Townes again. He's havin' that ring you busted fixed."

Melinda was startled. "Are you certain?"

"Sure as night follows day. You ask Mr. Conrad; he's the one doin' the work," the maid affirmed. "Kate heard Mrs. Scott say somethin' about Mr. Conrad's jewelry work. Heard Mrs. Scott tell Mr. Townes, 'Don't worry, Alden. Melinda's a tenderhearted girl and I know what moves her. I haven't groomed her all these years for nothing. I'll convince her yet.' That's the very words Mrs. Scott used, miss. I swear it."

Melinda stared at the maid, knowing neither June nor Kate would think of using those words quite that way. They *had* quoted Jessica. Before she could ask more, there was a tap on the door.

"Mr. Vandekker has arrived, Miss Scott," came the butler's voice.

Melinda noted June had finished packing and answered, "Tell the footman to come for my bag." She turned to the maid and prompted, "My cape, June?"

"You ain't sackin' me, miss?" the maid asked hesitantly.

"Even if I didn't need you till I sail for Java, I wouldn't dismiss you.

What you've said has reminded me not to be so gullible," Melinda assured. "Still, it's hard to turn my back on everything I've known and loved."

"I've seen the look in your eyes when you and Mr. Vandekker talk about Java. Seems to me you loved that place, too, and your daddy, God rest his soul."

Melinda nodded. "I should have realized before how selfish Mother is. There were questions in my mind I brushed aside, I guess, all along, I didn't want to know."

"Ain't easy to see the truth when it ain't so good 'bout someone you love," the maid agreed as she fastened Melinda's cape.

"I suppose I'm still wishing I'm wrong about her, that somehow everything will be all right," Melinda admitted.

"Don't much matter, miss. Right or wrong, she's your mother; you're just learning she's a human bein' too. Could be you two will make up yet," the maid said comfortingly, though she didn't believe it.

As the carriage rolled through Philadelphia's streets, Melinda chatted so tensely about the people Britt would meet at the party he knew she was trying to distract herself from something, but he didn't want to pry. When the carriage moved into the countryside, Melinda too eagerly pointed out each mark of spring's arrival. Britt inhaled the scent of the greening air and admired the budding of an orchard where the trees seemed like clusters of floating blossoms as enthusiastically as if he'd never stepped foot out of Java before and hadn't seen spring burst into carpets of daffodils in England, fill window boxes with tulips in Holland, or perfume the streets of Paris with lilacs. In the past this season of freshening life had exhilarated him, but today he wondered what Melinda was trying so hard to put out of her mind.

The carriage turned onto a road she said was the last leg of the journey; then, as the lane wound through a forest beginning to leaf, she finally fell silent. Watching her stare out the window, as if she'd forgotten his presence, Britt wondered if Melinda really wanted to go to the party. Finally he took her hands and turned her to face him.

"We can go back if you wish," he said quietly.

Melinda gazed up at Britt a moment, a series of thoughts he couldn't read leaving streaks in her eyes, like the cloud trails in the sky, before she answered, "The party is in my honor. How would it look if I didn't attend?"

"Does it matter what others think when in less than two weeks you'll sail for Java and need never see them again?

Melinda lowered her eyes before admitting, "I suppose they'd have a wonderful time without me at the party; a good part of their entertainment would be speculating about my absence—and yours."

"Is it gossip about me that's troubling you?" Britt inquired. Melinda shook her head. "Are you worried about Alden's being there?"

She finally looked up at Britt with eyes reflecting a swirl of conflicting emotions. "If I don't go to this party and face whatever Alden decides to do or say, I'll only have to return home and answer Mother's questions."

Britt found himself wishing they could spend the day alone, leisurely driving about as they had on their first outing in Philadelphia. But he also wished to pass the night with her in a feather bed by a cozy fire at the little Dutch inn where they'd had lunch. Made uneasy by the impulse, he shut it out of his mind and said, "It's all getting to be too much, isn't it? You're beginning to wonder if you should sell your share of the plantation."

Melinda turned again to stare out of the carriage window. Though her chin was lifted at the angle Britt had once thought defiant, he wondered now if it really meant she was trying to bolster her courage. "Whether it's Alden or Jessica that's bothering you, if you think you can't go to Java, you must tell me."

Melinda was quiet a long moment before she asked in a low, hesitant tone, "What do you think I should do?"

"Neither I, Jessica, Alden, nor any of your friends is wise enough to decide the kind of life that will make you happy," Britt said firmly.

Melinda nodded but said no more. Britt's devotion to reason annoyed her, but she knew he was right. Everyone had tugged her this way and that, sometimes subtly, often blatantly, except Britt. Yet without meaning to, he had influenced her more than anyone else. Britt's merely coming to Philadelphia had caused an irrevocable change in the way she perceived things; she'd never again be satisfied with her life as it had been. Even the kiss they'd shared the afternoon she'd heard Alden and Jessica discussing her legacy had changed her. Melinda was certain she'd never have had the courage to confront them if Britt hadn't awakened a spirit in her she'd forgotten existed. Melinda didn't hate Alden for scheming to gain control of her legacy. Other suitors had wanted her father's money and she'd forgiven them just as she had already, Melinda realized, forgiven Jessica. But going to Java was another matter.

Melinda realized her decision to become Britt's partner in Phoenix House Tea had been an impulse born of her turbulent emotions at the time. Since her anger had cooled, she'd begun to doubt that it would be wise to go to Java. She wondered if she'd been clinging to her decision out of pride or an inability to think of another solution to her problem. It was a possibility Britt had already pointed out. He was giving her time, the freedom to reverse her decision. Suddenly Britt's unswerving sense of integrity was no longer irritating but a blessing. As the carriage slowed to approach the Reeds' door, Melinda turned to look at him. His amber eyes gazed back at her as steadily and guilelessly as they had when he'd been a boy. A wheel seemed to move in Melinda's mind; something seemed to fall into place and make a connection.

A servant opened the carriage door. Britt rose to get out, then turned to help Melinda. She put her hands lightly on his shoulders and felt his hands at her waist as acutely as if she weren't wearing a woolen cape. After he'd lifted her from the carriage step, she wondered if he had held her a moment longer than necessary, a bit closer than proper. She saw his smile, almost imperceptible, a fleeting instant before he turned toward the house, where their host and hostess waited in the doorway.

The Reeds, as well as all of Philadelphia society, knew Melinda had broken her engagement with Alden and that her legacy was causing trouble between her and Jessica. Melinda had wondered what their reaction would be. They welcomed her as warmly as they had in the past, without showing a hint they were aware of any of the gossip. Mrs. Reed, always critical of the slightest lapse in manners, was charmed by Britt's inclining his head, as if he were being presented to nobility, before he brushed her hand with his lips. He thanked Amanda's father for his invitation with an air that was respectful yet not self-deprecating. Amanda, whose eyes had lit up at her first close look at Britt, was completely won as he bent over her hand and complimented her on her gown. Clinton, Amanda's brother, usually reserved, surprised Melinda by warmly greeting this visitor from Java. Relieved that none of the Reeds had seemed to let the gossip affect their opinions, Melinda reminded herself the other guests might be a different matter.

Everyone was wandering informally from room to room, pausing in little groups to chat, then moving on. The Reeds introduced Britt to several such groups. A few of the women, as Amanda had warned, discreetly flirted with Britt while their escorts restrained their pique. Britt behaved as if he weren't aware of either reaction, but Melinda knew he was.

Somewhere along the way to the drawing room Mr. and Mrs. Reed left them to greet other guests. After Clinton had made certain they each had a glass of claret, he also vanished; and Melinda and Britt were momentarily left with Amanda.

Glancing appreciatively at the wood lining the walls, Britt commented, "This paneling is beautiful."

"You must tell my father. It's his pride," Amanda said.

"I'm sure *you* are his pride, but the carving is . . ." Britt began.

"You don't have paneling like this in Java, I'll warrant," Alden, who had just approached, observed. "After all, it takes a certain refinement to fully appreciate its quality."

The copper flecks rising in Britt's eyes told Melinda that the derisive comment had struck home. She waited uneasily for his answer.

Britt said coolly, "The Javanese have very refined tastes, as anyone who has seen an example of their art or visited one of the palaces there can recognize, but it's true there's no paneling quite like this. The tropical climate would destroy walnut."

"I suppose you must be content with plain plaster," Alden said loftily.

Britt replied, "Phoenix House does have some plastered walls. Others are stone; but there is a lot of teak, which is plentiful in Java."

"Teak is precious in the West, but I suppose all you have to do is roll up your sleeves, take an ax, and chop some down," Alden said with a smile that revealed his disdain for physical labor.

"It's not easy to go into the jungle for anything," Britt answered tensely. "My father and Melinda's father had to take crews of Javanese on elephants so as not to be eaten by crocodiles in the swamp or tigers in the jungle."

"Yet your father, I understand, was killed by a tiger anyway," Alden observed, then cruelly added, "I'd heard he was drunk because some native woman he liked to bed died."

Melinda caught her breath at Alden's insult and was afraid of what Britt would do.

Not wanting to cause Melinda more distress, Britt leashed his temper and answered through lips stiff with anger, "Lady Sukadana, my mother, was the daughter of a nobleman in a kingdom far more ancient than yours. And she was my father's *wife*." Then Britt took Melinda's arm and guided her away from Alden.

It was the first of many conversations that afternoon and evening Melinda was to suffer through when Alden found some means to toss a jeer at Britt, always when others were present, in the hope Britt would lose his temper and make a fool of himself. Knowing Alden's purpose, Britt fended off the now more subtle taunts as if there was no end to his patience, replying always with a courtesy that mocked Alden's gibes. It became a contest. Everyone listened avidly, sometimes uneasily, for the next round, then turned away and smiled into their handkerchiefs or behind their fans. Though Britt had seemed to assume Alden was merely playing the dandy, whose cool contempt for everything was currently so fashionable, Melinda knew the steady glow of coppery flecks in his eyes meant Britt's anger was held on a tightening leash.

Melinda was grateful when the long evening ended and she could go to the room she shared with Amanda and Priscilla. Her friends chatted about the delicious gossip the situation had caused and speculated on what might have happened had Britt lost his temper, but Melinda said little to fuel their chatter and was glad when they turned down the lamps.

Afraid that Alden would resume baiting Britt the next morning, Melinda wished she and Britt were already on their way back to Philadelphia. Realizing she'd never fall asleep if she continued to think about Alden's insults, Melinda turned her mind to happier thoughts—and found they all concerned Britt.

After dinner there'd been dancing, and each time Britt had taken her in his arms, the tension Alden was causing had dissipated. Britt's nearness had set her heart fluttering as if it were a bird gingerly trying its wings, while his hands had guided her surely and smoothly through the steps. Melinda wondered at the expression in his eyes when he'd lowered them to meet hers. They'd still held copper sparks, but no longer seemed angry. A glimmer of another emotion had shot through their depths, then as quickly disappeared. Only now, after she was safely tucked in bed, did she realize that what she had seen was desire. It had surfaced as easily, as naturally, as the first time she'd seen him in Philadelphia; but tonight, while she'd been in his arms dancing, he'd banished it more quickly.

Such reflections kept Melinda awake until the first pale tints of dawn crept through the window. She watched the light grow, and as the sun's rim became a golden disk on the horizon, she gave up hope of sleeping. Too restless to lie in bed waiting for the household to awaken, she glanced at Amanda and Priscilla to confirm that hours would pass before they'd stir. She decided that a canter around the Reeds' property could fill her solitude.

When Melinda went to the stable, she wasn't surprised to find the stable attendant awake because horses always began calling for breakfast at first light. She didn't notice that one of the stalls was empty and a saddle and bridle were missing.

Melinda guided her mount along a path through the forest she knew ended at a meadow she expected to find blooming with lilies of the valley. She wasn't disappointed. The breeze swept their perfume over her before she even reached the clearing, and she slowed her mount to a walk. At the center of the meadow she stopped the horse.

The sky wore ruffles of lavender clouds dancing mischievously across the sun; and during a minute the golden light was free of them, Melinda tilted back her head to enjoy its warmth. She didn't notice Britt stop his horse at the far edge of the forest and gaze at her a moment before deciding to approach.

Not wanting to startle her, Britt said quietly, "Good morning, Minda."

Melinda enjoyed the sun a moment longer, then turned to look at him. Relieved that none of last night's anger remained in his eyes, they were as serene as if Alden had never taunted him, Melinda smiled and returned his greeting.

"It's early for you to be awake, isn't it?" Britt commented, then, realizing she'd been restless from worry, added, "You needn't have been *that* concerned about what Alden said."

"He wanted to hurt you, make you look like a fool. I was afraid . . ." She stopped, not knowing what else to say.

"He angered me, it's true," Britt admitted, "but no one can make another look like a fool unless he is one."

"Which you aren't," Melinda said vehemently.

"I hope not," Britt replied. Wanting to change the subject, he said as he dismounted, "I followed the perfume of these flowers all the way through the forest, but I was surprised to find you here as well. You made a charming picture a moment ago." He raised his hands, offering to help Melinda from the saddle. As she slid down, he added, "You make a lovely picture now." Britt didn't immediately release her. She became acutely aware of the warmth of his trim body so near hers before he stepped back.

She regathered her wits and asked, "Why are you out so early?"

"If you're thinking I lost sleep because of your former fiancé's remarks, I didn't," he replied. Melinda lowered her eyes in remembered embarrassment and Britt again came closer, this time to tilt her chin so she'd look up at him while he said gently, "I'm not used to having so many people around; and I'd thought, before they all woke up, I'd enjoy a little solitude. I always wake up early. One must on a tea plantation. You'll learn that for yourself, if you come to Java."

Melinda, looking steadily up at his eyes, began, "I think I'd like . . ."

"What a tender little vignette!"

Startled, Melinda turned quickly to see Alden on a horse, walking toward them. "How dare you spy on me?" she exclaimed.

"I wasn't spying, my dear, though I must say it does appear that Mr. Vandekker is more than merely a partner," Alden observed.

"You've said a thousand times you never get up before ten. You deliberately followed me—or Britt," Melinda accused.

"I never dreamed I'd disturb a tryst. Forgive me." Alden's apology was a lie that infuriated Melinda, but he went on, "Having decided I'd enjoy a ride this spring morning, I glimpsed Mr. Vandekker and feared he'd get lost in the forest. After all, this terrain is new to him."

Britt finally said, "Having hunted without mishap at Emperor Napoleon's Deer Park, I think I can manage to find my way around here."

"How interesting that your way happens also to be Melinda's," Alden commented acidly, "and how romantic a setting too."

"Alden, please don't say such things," Melinda implored. "It's embarrassing."

"But this will be a delightful picture to describe over breakfast," Alden persisted. "I'm sure everyone will be as enchanted as I—a field of flowers, a lovely young woman, her gallant suitor . . ."

"I'm Minda's partner, not her suitor," Britt interrupted, then warned, "I'm also her friend."

"Minda—how droll. I've wondered where you got that version of her name," Alden commented.

"It's a diminutive from her childhood," Britt answered tensely.

"Minda and Britt renewing a friendship begun while they were toddlers. It adds to the charm of the story," Alden said.

Melinda took a step closer and begged, "*Please,* Alden, don't say anything. You know how it will appear to the others."

"I know how it looked to *me.* Your business partner was about to kiss you," Alden replied with as pleasant a smile as if the gossip sure to result were a matter of no concern.

Still trying to hold his temper, Britt put a hand on Alden's reins as he began, "It was one thing last night when you tried to mock me, but it's another to make—"

"Get your hands off my horse, you half-breed," Alden snarled and rapped Britt's fingers with his riding crop.

Before Alden could raise his crop again, Britt's hand shot out, gripped his wrist, and gave it a quick turn and a sharp pull. Surprised and off balance, Alden instinctively reached out with his other hand to steady himself. Britt caught that wrist, too, and yanked Alden from his saddle.

Britt had reacted automatically out of contempt for Alden and he had no intention of doing more. But as Alden started to get up, he added another oath, a vulgar name more insulting than the first. Britt gave him a slap sideways across the face that sent him sprawling.

Looking down at Alden, who was momentarily too dazed to get up, Britt said derisively, "Now you have a different story, though just as false, to tell them over breakfast, that of how your face was purpled when your horse threw you." Britt hauled Alden to his feet and pushed the reins into his hand. Then, holding Alden by his jacket lapels, he vowed, "If you say one word to insult Minda, you'll get worse than bruises."

The moment Britt released him, Alden turned to his horse and hastily mounted. If Alden would have said more, Melinda never knew, because Britt slapped the horse's rump and the animal dashed into the forest.

Britt turned to Melinda. "I'm sorry this happened."

"It wasn't your fault," she said in a low tone, then hastily added, "Let's return to the house in case Alden does say something."

"I doubt he will, but if he did, our rushing back would make us look guiltier," Britt reasoned. "I think we should continue our walk or ride, whichever you prefer, and return in a calmer mood."

"It doesn't really matter how calm I appear to anyone at the Reeds'." Melinda looked plaintively up at Britt. "He'll report to Mother and she'll make a horror of my life until we sail."

Britt put his arms lightly around Melinda, gently drew her head to rest on his shoulder, and said soothingly, "I don't think Alden's likelier to tell Jessica than the others. He knows I'd learn about it. But if worse comes to worst and he does, you could stay at the hotel until we sail—unless, of course, you change your mind and remain in Philadelphia." Britt fell silent, wondering if Melinda was so upset because she really was reconsidering going to Java. Firmly setting aside his own opinion of that, he murmured, "Seeing you this way, torn in two by this decision, makes me wish I'd broken my promise to Charles and let his attorney write to you."

Melinda drew away to look up at him. "Then, out of ignorance, I'd have married a man I don't love and been cheated of my inheritance." She noted Britt's frown and was thoughtfully silent a moment before she said quietly, "I *am* going to Java."

"Because of this incident?"

"Despite how Alden may gossip or Mother scold, I *have* to make my own decisions, not go along with what they want because it seems easier," Melinda answered, again laying her head on his shoulder.

Britt suspected she was quietly weeping. He slipped his fingers under her chin and tipped her face toward his. Confirming that he was right—her eyes were brimming with tears—his frown deepened.

"It's just so painful," Melinda whispered.

"Life is often painful," Britt sighed and bent to kiss her eyelids. When he straightened, one of her tears clung to his lip. She reached up to brush it away. Her fingertip lingered on the curve of his mouth while she gazed up at him, and he said softly, "Alden wasn't completely wrong. I had been about to kiss you when he came." His lips caressed her fingertip as he spoke. She withdrew it slowly but continued to look steadily up at him. When he bent toward her, she didn't move away.

Britt touched the corner of her mouth with a soft kiss. Then, glancing up to see her eyes were closed, he let his lips slide along hers to the other side of her mouth to kiss her lightly, lingeringly. He wanted to kiss Melinda with all the passion in him, but instead let his lips wander over her face and finally pause by her cheek as he murmured against her skin, "I shouldn't do this and make Alden's gossip truth."

"Maybe you're right and he'll be too frightened of you to gossip," she whispered.

Britt said softly, "A circumspect lady like you should be frightened of the way you're making me feel."

She breathed, "But I'm not."

Britt caught the curls at each temple, and as if he would hold her to him with so fragile a bond, put his lips on hers, at first lightly caressing, then more firmly. He felt her mouth warming to his, beginning to cling, and trying to put off the desire insistently rising in him, moved away to brush his lips along her cheek. There was no use in it; his mouth again sought hers. The lips under his, softly moist as flower petals, parted slightly, and his need was a sweet pain flooding him. His arms locked around her, crushed her to him a moment before he controlled his impulse and loosened his embrace. Britt laid his cheek against Melinda's and waited to recover himself, but her lips teased his skin, the tip of her nose nuzzling him, Javanese fashion.

Britt took Melinda's temples between his palms, withdrew a little to look at her, but what he might have said was lost in his overwhelming need to hold her closer and closer yet.

Where Melinda had expected a renewal of the sweet madness she'd felt when Britt had crushed her to him, his embrace now was as light as if he held a bouquet of flowers. His lips, delicately kissing hers, seemed even more sensual. The tip of his tongue stirred her with a longing so piquant she wasn't aware of his hands slipping from her temples, along her throat, until they began to boldly caress the sides of her breasts. The unfamiliar sensation startled her, and Britt, feeling her tense, moved away. Melinda stared at him. She wished he'd continue but didn't have the courage to say it.

"I promised not to influence you, but I've broken that promise twice," he said quietly and released her.

"I already told you I've decided to go to Java," Melinda managed.

Knowing far better than she what a tempest his continuing would lead him to, Britt said quickly, "We haven't sailed yet. You can still change your mind." Then, not wanting to look at Minda, which would only make him long to gather her again in his arms, he glanced up at the sky. "It looks like it's going to shower. We should go back to the house."

Melinda had already felt a drop on her arm, but she didn't care if it stormed. "I'm not going to change my mind again. I *will* go to Java with you," she said firmly.

"Even if you do, it would be too difficult to concentrate on teaching you how to be my partner if we become lovers." Britt turned away to fetch their horses, which had wandered into the meadow.

"Lovers," Melinda breathed, and the word hung in her mind as if it were outlined with flames. She watched Britt move smoothly across the meadow to pick up the reins of one animal, then go for the other. The horse strolled away. Britt waited for it to become engrossed in a patch of dandelions before he followed and caught the reins. By the time he'd returned, a light rain was falling.

"It's as hard to predict how long these spring showers will last as when they'll begin," Melinda advised. "There's a cottage not far away. An employee of Mr. Reed's lives there. He'll give us shelter."

Britt glanced up at the sky. The clouds were thin but had completely covered the blue. The rain was fine, though steady. "Show me the way," he said.

Britt followed Melinda back into the forest and after a few minutes' walk saw a little stone building nestled among the trees. Noting that no smoke was coming from the chimney, he said, "I think the owner has gone away."

"There's no lock on the door. We can get inside," Melinda explained. "I've come here with Amanda before. Emmett, the man who lives here, is probably visiting his son for the day."

"Maybe I should take the horses to that little barn in the back," Britt said tensely and left her.

Once in the barn, Britt dawdled with unsaddling the horses and rubbing them dry. As he gave them hay, Britt realized he wanted to delay being alone with Melinda in the cottage. He returned to the cottage thinking time had fortified his resolve; but when he stepped inside, he noted it had only one room. The bed stood solidly before him. His eyes shifted to the far end of the cottage. It held a fireplace, cabinets, a table, and a couple of uninviting wooden chairs.

"Alden would enjoy describing *this* cozy little picture to your friends," he said dryly.

Melinda didn't answer. Having had a chance to give their solitude more thought, she uneasily went to stand in the open doorway and watch the rain.

Britt realized, now that Melinda's passions had had a chance to cool, she was as discomfited as he by the situation. Though his desire lay just under the surface like a trap, he reminded himself that she was a virgin and more naïve than most. At this moment in her life she was especially vulnerable, and he didn't want to seem to take advantage of her. He followed her to the doorway and leaned against the frame, as if to assure her by his distance he wouldn't touch her again.

The fragrance of the wet forest mingled with that of wool jackets moistened by the shower, a scent he grudgingly realized he'd associate with spring for the rest of his life. Britt became aware that Melinda was hugging herself, shivering in her damp riding habit. He wordlessly went to the bed, pulled off the quilt and draped it around her shoulders, then quickly stepped away.

Melinda gave him a grateful look and asked, "Aren't you chilled too? You're as wet as I."

Britt shrugged and answered, "I'll manage." But he found the chill gradually seeping into him. He wished he could close the door, but knew the feeling of privacy it would lend would be too tempting. He remembered the pile of kindling by the barn and realized it was too wet to start a fire.

Melinda noticed that Britt was trying to hide his shivering and glanced at the bed. There were no other blankets. A raindrop sliding down a strand of his hair fell on his forehead and he brushed it away with his sleeve. The boyish gesture eased Melinda's tension and she moved closer to drape one end of her quilt over his far shoulder. Britt glanced at her in surprise then quickly looked away.

All he could think of then was Melinda's nearness, her warmth reaching toward him over the circumspect little space between. He was acutely aware that she was still looking at him, couldn't think of a thing to say that wouldn't reveal how he wanted her, then decided he must silently endure his torment. Finally she turned away to stare out the door as rigidly as he, trying to resist the forces building between them. Again he searched for something to say that would lighten the tension.

An eternity seemed to pass.

Britt finally commented, "It rains for days in Java, but . . . ." As he spoke, he'd automatically turned to look at her. Melinda's eyes were great dark emeralds fixed on him. It was almost as if they exuded a power that drew him. He forgot what he'd been about to say.

Melinda didn't prompt him; she hadn't heard Britt's words, only his voice. They stared at each other a long moment until he surrendered, slid his hands under the quilt, and pulled her to him. The sensation of her body pressed to his made him ache with longing he couldn't disguise. His mouth moved restlessly over hers, kissing the corners of her lips, following the line of their parting. The edges of his teeth nibbled at her, his tonguetip lighting little fires that flashed along her nerves. When Britt felt Melinda's body molding itself to his, a tremor shot through him. His hands moved to her breasts and sensitively explored their curve. Then his fingertips found her nipples budding even through her clothes, and he caressed them with unhurried sensuality.

The exquisite sensations Britt was introducing in Melinda were like a current pulsing through her blood, spreading to every cell in her body until she thought she'd cry out with pleasure, but she only caught her breath in a soft gasp. Then Britt's arms again enclosed Melinda, one hand at the back of her head pressing her cheek against his shoulder as if, trying to restrain himself, he didn't want to be lured by the sight of her lips.

"I'm sorry, Minda. I shouldn't have kissed you at all," he murmured, rubbing his cheek against the silk of her hair. Finally realizing he couldn't prevent his senses from noticing the textures, the perfume of her, he released Melinda. "I'm not a man who can easily turn from love," he admitted, then bent to retrieve the quilt. He straightened and thrust it into her hands, urging, "Take it. The devil knows I'm warm enough now." He turned and walked quickly away to stand by the dark fireplace.

Melinda said, "When other men, even Alden, kissed me, I never felt this way."

Britt turned to look at her, his eyes flickering with surprise. "Why did you agree to marry him? Didn't you realize what a misery making love with a man you don't want would be?"

"I couldn't know because I'd never felt any other way until I kissed you. I accepted feeling nothing," she confessed. "It was probably part of the reason it was easy for Mother to persuade me to accept Alden's proposal."

"That's a hell of a reason to get married," Britt said gruffly.

"Now that you've taught me differently, I know I couldn't marry a man who doesn't make me feel the way you have," Melinda said thoughtfully. She walked closer, the quilt trailing on the floor behind her, and stopped an arm's length away. "I've made another decision, Britt."

He looked at her narrowly, wondering what surprise she had for him now.

Melinda lowered her eyes as she whispered, "I want you to be my first lover."

Britt was silent a moment before he said hastily, "That's because you're aroused now. The feeling will pass if we do nothing to stir it further."

Melinda didn't realize past affections had already become more complex emotions that were rapidly deepening. She was only aware of the intoxicating feelings coursing through her. Again she looked down, played nervously with the quilt edge as she admitted, "I feel as if a fire is incinerating me from the inside out, that if you don't quench it I'll die."

Britt listened in amazement to this confession; he'd never known a woman to be so candid. His suspicion, that he hesitated because he was falling in love with her, grew stronger, but he didn't want the words to bind her to him if she changed her mind about going to Java or, once there, wanted to return to Philadelphia. He came closer to take Melinda's hands in his and say, "This could begin something we won't be able to stop, yet it's also possible today is all we'll have or want."

"I know how uncertain our future can be. Whatever happens, I want you now," she breathed.

Britt's desire was like a coal glowing in his loins; her nearness was a wind fanning it to fresh life until he couldn't think for its heat. Britt turned to go to the door, closed it, and discovered a latch on the inside. He dropped it in place and returned. Halfway hoping if he didn't caress Melinda, she'd change her mind, he wordlessly knelt to pull off her boots, then rose to help her peel off the damp riding habit. Melinda never gave a hint that she'd reconsider. The sight of her body clad only in a lacy chemise blotted out Britt's restraint; and heart racing, he began to unbutton his shirt cuffs. He noticed her step backward and sensed she was shy about being naked. He gathered up her clothes and went to the far end of the cottage, taking a longer time than his eagerness demanded to arrange them over chairs. His eyes moved back to her as he pulled off his jacket. They kept flicking toward her while he continued undressing, as if he were anticipating she would change her mind.

Melinda, who had hastily scuttled under the quilt, watched Britt silently. She'd never seen a man in less than shirt-sleeves, and the sight of shoulders that hadn't been exaggerated by his tailor's skill, the narrow span of his waist, his flat hips, made her wonder how that lithe body, those sleekly moving muscles, would feel against her. Britt's skin was as toasted by the sun as his face, and she realized he still swam naked in Java, as he had when a boy. It never occurred to her to tell him to stop, not even when he walked toward her, as smoothly as an animal and as full of vibrant life.

Britt saw that Melinda's eyes had become a smoky green as she gazed up at him. He sat on the edge of the bed and offered, "You can still say no." She didn't answer, and he added quietly, "We should lie on the quilt, not under it."

Blushing furiously, Melinda crept from under the quilt and tensely lay on top, suddenly feeling shy under Britt's gaze, despite her desire.

He leaned over to cradle her shoulders in his arms and twine his hands through the back of her hair as he said softly, "You're beautiful, Minda, and need never hide your body." He kissed her eyelids as he spoke. "No one has told you much about love, and you're nervous, not knowing what to do this first time. It should be a special moment in your life, one you won't recall with regret or embarrassment." His lips traveled down her cheek to the side of her mouth, nibbled at her upper lip.

"But you?" she breathed.

"This isn't my first time," he murmured before his mouth covered hers.

His lips moved slowly on Melinda's, not hungrily as before, but as if he were allowing her to familiarize herself with him. When she lifted her head to reach for his kiss, he withdrew a little and, sliding his arms from under her shoulders, held her face steady with his hands. Britt's mouth sought Melinda's and claimed it, slowly grew harder, more compelling, his body moving seductively against her, making his entire length a caress. His hands slipped along her sides, tracing a fire over her hips' curving as his kisses trailed along her throat, then down to her breast. Melinda was surprised when his tongue teased her nipple. The warmth of his breath was as enticing as his lips, sending a shock of sensation through her nerves, a heat that flashed like a light at the base of her body then spread in ripples down her legs. His hands moved over her skin, coaxing her thighs then pausing between as his mouth reclaimed her lips.

The tip of his tongue matched the course of his caressing fingers as it circled the perimeter of her mouth, traced the line of its opening, and when her lips parted, caressed their inner curve. A glow suffused her, a brightening warmth that simmered through her blood to smolder in every pore. His searching mouth moved boldly against hers, making her tremble. His tonguetip delicately stroked her lips, relentlessly teased her, the lingering caress bringing her desire to a pitch too vivid to deny, advancing in a rush of piquant impulses, receding so she ached with a building urge until she felt as if she might burst from it. She held her breath, his caresses impelled her on, and finally her racing senses leaped their last barrier to ignite her like a torch that seared away her reason.

Afterward she reached up wonderingly to touch Britt's face as she breathed, "It's like knowing for the first time in your life that you're alive."

He nodded, then laid his cheek against hers. He still ached with desire and knew he should move away, but the silk of her hair was a snare, her perfume a spell holding him to her.

Melinda felt a tremor he couldn't disguise flow through him and she whispered, "You feel as I did, don't you?" When Britt didn't answer, she pulled a little away, turned his face so she could look at him, at eyes gleaming with copper flecks.

Britt leaned close to softly kiss her and gently say, "You've lost your innocence, but you're still a maid."

"I didn't want to remain a virgin; that's only a lie now," she protested, knowing his desire was a torment begging for release. "I don't know what our future holds or if we'll remain together, but even if we don't, I want to share this with you."

Britt was silent a moment, considering her situation. Melinda now knew about the ecstasy, but not the pain. Someone in her future could be clumsy . . . *No,* he didn't want to think of her with another man, not even a husband.

Britt moved over Melinda, seemed to hover a moment, barely touching, only enticing her; then, capturing her gaze with his shimmering eyes, he slowly descended. A pressure in Melinda grew until she caught her breath. He saw the flash of pain in her eyes, then cuddled her in his arms, tenderly kissed her face, murmured for her to lie still so he could wait until the last traces of her pang faded. He let his lips rest against her cheek, though he longed to kiss her; the arms that yearned to crush her merely enfolded, while his body, pulsing with desire, lay as quietly as if he were calm.

Melinda understood that Britt was giving her time like a gift and, in a rush of emotion, realized his concern must mean he loved her. For some reason he didn't want to say it; maybe he didn't know. Was it possible what she felt for him was love and she, too, was afraid to define it? She puzzled over this until he raised his head to gaze down at her. She reached up for his lips, caressed their curve, invited him to kiss her.

When he did, his mouth on hers was as provocatively supple as his body, moving slowly, shifting restlessly, as if he were searching for something in her being. A sharp delight suddenly shot through Melinda. Recognizing the reason for her tremor, Britt remained where he was, fighting to control the desire that threatened to erode his will so he could rebuild her passion. His mouth warmly covered Melinda's, caressed hers avidly to pique her beginning hunger. His hips, moving lithely, evoked a tingle that grew into a seething impulse. She reached for his kiss, wanting more of him; her body sought his, trying to cling, but he wouldn't allow it. When his insistent rhythm became too maddening, he changed it, and a new heat welled up in her to fuse body and thought into one driving force.

Melinda's hands joyously clung to Britt's back, her pulsing body eagerly reaching for the fulfillment he withheld a little longer as he paused to fondle her mouth with his. He felt her tremor growing in power and opened his eyes. Her face was tense with desire, but he kept his body still while he again captured her lips in a sultry kiss that whipped his ardor to a pace compelling his hips to fluently match its throb. She made a brief, soft noise, as if her beginning moan forgot itself in the growing fury of her passion. The knowledge scorched his dimming awareness. His senses rose like a wave of fire, poised to devour him. He felt her body shuddering at the edge of her ecstasy, and he could bear it no longer. Britt's racing impulses blended in a wild flood that overtook him, swept him into exploding forces that consumed them both.

He was too lost to know that, as passion shattered his mind, he whispered again and again, "I love you, Minda, love you, love you . . ."

Chapter Six

Melinda stood on tiptoe to watch as Britt moved away through the crowd on deck to talk with Captain Alkmaar, who was also from Java. Several passersby glanced curiously at her and she self-consciously slid down from her toes. It was easy enough for her eyes to follow the progress of a man who stood several inches taller than most others, whose hair was as yellow as the sun glancing brightly off the water. She was tempted to follow him, then hesitated again, wondering if her impulse to stay close to Britt was because she knew no one else on the ship and she'd never been alone among strangers before, never on a ship preparing to sail to Java. Melinda watched Britt a moment more; then, embarrassed that he'd noticed her staring, she turned away to walk to the rail and gaze at the wharf, listen to the cries of the circling gulls.

Harini, "Today," the ship was aptly named. It was for today she must live, Melinda bitterly reminded herself, not all the yesterdays the ship's sailing would leave behind, the past that held everything familiar to her, all the people she'd known. But how could she stop remembering, especially the memory that began in a cottage on a rainy morning a week ago? It was a memory of love she cherished and wanted to renew—a memory that had caused great trouble with Jessica.

After the rain had stopped that morning at the cottage, Britt had insisted they return to the Reed house together. If Alden had dared say he'd seen them and accuse them of anything, Britt didn't want Melinda to face the stares alone. It had appeared that Alden, as Britt had suggested, had told everyone the purple blotch on his swollen cheek was from a fall off his horse. But Alden had later told Jessica about his suspicions.

Melinda painfully recalled how Jessica's accusations had been added to her other complaints. And what could Melinda answer? Though a morning ride was hardly proof of a love affair, though it was plausible they'd been delayed from returning by the shower, Melinda's old obedience to Jessica had compelled her to say again and again that she and Britt were no more than friends and partners in Phoenix House Tea, a lie that rankled in Melinda's heart, making her feel guilty and disloyal.

Packing, transferring the investments Charles had made to Jessica's name, and closing other legal matters had made it impossible for Melinda to see Britt for anything other than a couple of luncheons and a dinner that ended the evening early. Melinda had no doubt that if she told Britt about the trouble Alden's gossiping to Jessica was causing he'd go after Alden to carry out his threat. Foreseeing more scandal, she'd told Britt that Alden seemed to have remained silent, another lie she'd hated herself for having to tell. Melinda and Britt had had little time to fully discuss the business of her inheritance; and feeling shy about bringing up their romantic situation, being so rushed and always in public, Melinda had avoided mentioning it at all. But the look in his eyes told her that his desire hadn't dimmed and that he wondered why she never spoke of their morning in the cottage. Finally the warmth in his eyes had receded, and as if he acquiesced to her wishes, he said nothing. She'd drawn what strength she could from merely being with Britt, but had spent her nights in fitful tossing, wanting him at the same time she'd wondered if it would be best to let desire fade.

Melinda's problems with Jessica had culminated the evening before the ship was to sail. Jessica had had the gall to invite Alden to dinner, and Melinda had known nothing about it until she'd come downstairs and seen him. The two had used every argument they could think of to persuade Melinda to cancel her plans and stay in Philadelphia. Melinda's dinner had gone untouched as she'd silently endured their voices, like stones raining on her head, until her temper finally burst past its limit and she'd answered angrily. The argument that resulted had sent her running upstairs in tears.

That morning, dreading to face her mother at the same time she'd yearned to become reconciled before sailing, Melinda had crept downstairs feeling as downcast as a beaten dog hoping for its master's forgiveness. But Jessica hadn't appeared. Melinda had wept so bitterly in the carriage that Britt's eyes had flashed with anger at Jessica even while he'd tried to soothe Melinda. By the time they'd reached the wharf, Melinda's tears had ceased. All her emotions seemed to have been exhausted save one—the need to cling to Britt.

As Melinda stood at the ship's rail, she reminded herself not to become a weight dragging after him. She resolved, despite what they'd been or might become to each other, she would learn to be his partner. She must behave that way, not like a little girl always ready to dissolve in tears.

When Melinda became aware of Britt's silent presence at her side, she longed to move closer, tuck her arm in his, but she forced herself to remain where she was, staring unseeingly at Philadelphia, hearing but not listening to the sailors' cries as they ran up sails and cast off lines. Her emotions were in such a turmoil she couldn't trust her judgment about anything. She was only determined not to weep.

"Are you so upset because you don't want to leave Philadelphia or because Jessica made it that difficult last night?" Britt asked quietly.

"Alden too. Mother had invited him to dinner." Britt's hand covered hers gripping the rail. Melinda swallowed the lump in her throat and, determined never to lie again, answered, "Now that we're ready to sail, I can tell you Alden did talk to Mother about finding us in the meadow and accused us of having a love affair. Among other things last night, they said you were trying to gain control of Phoenix House Tea by falsely courting me."

Britt imagined what Melinda had endured and wished she'd told him before. He could have challenged Alden to a duel and silenced Jessica at the same time he'd have eliminated Townes by honorably defending Melinda's reputation. Since it was too late for any of that, he only asked quietly, "You don't believe such accusations about me, do you?"

"Of course not, but I didn't even have the courage to tell them the truth," Melinda admitted, continuing to stare at, but not really see, the shore.

"We've had too little time together for you to know what to think of any of this. I'm sure you've even had doubts about my motives," Britt said. When Melinda began to deny that, he hushed her and continued, "It's understandable in so emotional a situation, especially when others are trying to persuade you.'' He stopped, taking a moment to choose his words with great care before he said, ''I'd thought you might wonder if I'd taken you lightly that morning when you were so vulnerable.''

Melinda glanced up at him, again ready to deny it, but Britt knew he was right and continued, ''There may be other times in the future, whatever it may hold for us, when you'll look back at that morning in the cottage and wonder about my intention. Then it may help for you to have something more tangible than memories, something your eyes can see and you can touch to reassure you.''

Melinda turned questioningly to Britt. He took her hand and pressed something into her palm. She looked down to see a gold locket, a child's locket. Recognition came rushing in to startle her. She'd given it to Britt when Jessica had taken her from Java.

Britt said softly, ''This was a boy's personal treasure, because it was all he had from you. That the man he became has worn it on his watch chain all these years should be proof I've never thought of you lightly. I suppose you didn't see it because when I'm with you, I don't think of passing time and never look at my watch.''

Melinda lifted her gaze to meet eyes that were as clear and open as those of the boy to whom she'd given the locket. Overcome with emotion, she couldn't speak.

Britt laid his hands gently on her shoulders and said, ''Such doubts are part of the reason becoming lovers could make our partnership difficult. Volatile emotions have no place in business.''

Melinda moved as if to draw away, but his hands held her more firmly. She forced herself to ask, ''You think, then, it would be wiser for us not to be lovers?''

''I want you, Minda. I've thought of little else since we left the cottage.'' He paused as visions flashed through his mind of starry nights on the ship, sunny mornings awakening at her side. He banished them and asked, ''Are you far enough along this road of self-discovery that you know for a certainty what you want of life? Are you so sure of your feelings, not those we shared for an hour in that cottage, but next month's or next year's, that you could say now you want to marry me and live in Java all your life?''

Melinda lowered her eyes and didn't answer.

''You want to say yes, but you know you can't.'' Britt released her and turned to gaze at the shore. ''The more often a man and woman make love, the stronger the bond between them grows. They learn intimate details about each other's bodies and responses. You said you want to be my partner and learn how to run Phoenix House Tea. What will you do when something I'm trying to teach you is hard and you want to avoid the lesson if you know that a certain caress will make me forget all else? What will happen if we disagree about a business decision and I can win my point by kissing you a particular way?''

Melinda kept her eyes on the water streaming along the ship's hull as she reminded, ''You said some of the planters have wives for partners.''

''They'd already learned to be partners in marriage before coming to Java. You and I have only just become lovers. We aren't sure enough of ourselves to even want to think of marriage yet,'' he answered.

''*You* aren't sure of yourself?'' she asked.

''I'm afraid to be—with you.''

Britt's quiet admission amazed Melinda. She hadn't thought he was afraid of anything, but taking a moment to reflect, she began to understand. Britt was, in his own way, as vulnerable as she. Perhaps it was wiser, after all, to let the one flame they'd lit fade than to add fuel to make a bonfire that could scorch their minds with emotion when they needed most to think clearly.

''The idea makes me feel more alone than ever,'' she murmured.

Britt motioned toward the open sea ahead. ''The ocean looks like your future feels to you now—lonely and frightening in its unfamiliarity. But there are millions of creatures in it you can't see, shores yet too far for you to imagine. And I *am* here.''

Melinda realized with a start that Philadelphia had already slipped from sight; she'd had no chance to mourn its last glimpse. She was alone with Britt on this ship called *Harini*—Today.

As the days at sea passed, Melinda grew familiar with the *Harini* and its routine, began to recognize the faces and learn the names of some of the passengers and crew and exchange greetings with them. She and Britt often had dinner with Captain Alkmaar, a friendly, affable man. But despite all this, she dreaded the day's end, when she closed her cabin door and was alone. Melinda scolded herself for being childish, afraid of shadows, but fell asleep each night only after hours of listening uneasily to every creak and groan the ship made, feeling its every shift in motion as a threat. She fervently wished Britt could be with her, if not as a lover, then as a reassuring presence to ease her solitude at night as he did during the day.

Britt spoke about Java and Phoenix House, described the trips he made to Europe for tea auctions she could also attend if she wished, and Melinda understood he was trying to distract her from brooding about the past. At first she wanted to be distracted. Then she realized what had already happened was the foundation of her future and decided she didn't want her future to be built on the sands of regret and bitterness. She must deal with the past and make peace with it.

Melinda candidly told Britt she feared that she'd come to hate Jessica, was horrified at the idea of hating her own mother. Britt reminded her that parents were human beings, not the paragons their offspring imagined, and that it was often disappointing for grown children to discover their parents' human faults. It had been as much a shock to him to realize Gerard was a drunk as it had been for Melinda to discover Jessica was a schemer. Manipulating someone to get your own way wasn't love, Melinda angrily flashed, but a self-perpetuating lie. Later she reflected on what she'd said and wondered if Britt's warning that being lovers could influence their business partnership was partly based on his wondering if she might follow Jessica's example to get her way. Chagrined by that idea, Melinda vowed to avoid saying or doing anything to even hint of it. She realized that keeping her resolution would also mean examining her own motives at every turn and decided it was what she needed to do anyway if she were to continue learning about herself.

No longer did Melinda wait for Britt to talk about Phoenix House, then merely listen. She questioned him about the plantation and asked if he'd help her relearn the Javanese language. Glad that Melinda wanted to try to prepare for her future, Britt became an enthusiastic teacher. Though Melinda's reasons for seeking Britt's company had changed, their instincts didn't acknowledge their agreement to avoid love; they were together almost constantly. While they strolled on deck, Melinda couldn't avoid feeling the warmth of the firm arm under the sleeve she tucked her hand around. She wasn't aware of drawing closer to Britt's side until, when she brushed him, she hastily stepped away—only to have to struggle with turning her thoughts from the smooth grace of his steps. When, after dinner, Melinda tried to practice Javanese by carrying on a conversation with Britt, her midsentence pauses weren't always due to her searching for a word. Too often they occurred because her gaze fell on the firm length of his crossed legs snugly enclosed in dark breeches, on the sun-toasted wrist revealed by the cuff of his shirt sliding back as he rested his chin on his hand, or on the shape of his hands and the taper of his fingers.

While they walked in the sun on deck, Britt sometimes imagined how it would feel to lie naked with Minda under Java's sun, and wondered if she'd like to make love with the sky as their ceiling. During the evenings Britt often rose to walk across the cabin and pour a glass of brandy because his eyes had rested overlong on Melinda's lips moving as she spoke, had followed the curve of her throat to the swell of her bosom and lingered. When Britt paced restlessly and paused behind Melinda, he was charged with an impulse to kiss the back of her neck, to run his fingers along a curl that fell to her shoulder, then slide them into her bodice. Sometimes Britt felt his yearnings so sharply he begged weariness and ended the evening early.

On one such night, as Britt escorted Melinda to her cabin, he was distracted from desire by a different sound in the sails' billowing. He looked up to note the wind had changed direction, had sharpened and taken on a suspicious tang. He scanned the sky appraisingly. Cloud banks had blotted out large sections of the stars.

Britt turned to Melinda and commented, "I think we may have a stormy night."

"Do you suppose it will be dangerous?" she asked uneasily.

Not sure if the shadows in her eyes were caused by alarm or by the clouds scurrying across the moon, he answered in a light, unworried tone, "A passage as long as this must meet at least one storm. During my voyage to Philadelphia we sailed through several. Just be sure to arrange some pillows along the open side of your bed so if the waves start rising, you won't roll out and fall while you're sleeping."

Still uneasy, but putting on an air of bravado, she smiled and said, "I'm sure the worst to come of this will be nightmares."

Britt glanced away at the sharp snap of a sail's billowing. His eyes moved back to meet hers. "If you're afraid, I can sit with you."

"Thank you, but I'm sure I'll be all right," she replied a little too quickly.

"If you change your mind, send a crewman for me," Britt said quietly. "More of them will be on deck tonight than usual."

Melinda promised she would, wished him fair dreams, and closed her door—with more reluctance than he would have guessed.

Britt returned to his cabin wondering if he should have insisted on staying with Melinda because he anticipated a violent storm. He argued with himself that he wasn't a sailor, but he knew that spending the night sitting with Melinda would only stir up the feelings he was trying so hard to ignore.

After he'd put away everything in his cabin that might fall or break, Britt took off his jacket and cravat. Then, still thinking about the storm's potential violence, he decided not to undress further. He aimlessly stalked around the room, knowing his uneasiness was caused by more than the weather. It was being in Melinda's company almost constantly, thinking of her when he wasn't, that unsettled him.

Britt regretted having surrendered to his desire even once. Maybe if he didn't know how Melinda felt moving pliantly against him, maybe if he couldn't remember how her hair had cascaded over the pillow, tasted in his mouth, he wouldn't be so stirred by her. Angry at his body's betrayal of his resolve, Britt finally turned his lamp down and, still clad in shirt and breeches, stretched out on his bunk. He closed his eyes and, like a moth already seared by a flame but lured back into it again and again, he succumbed to fantasies of caressing Melinda that later became dreams.

Snatched from slumber by raucous shouts, pounding noises, and crashes, Britt sat up dazed and confused, trying to sort out the sounds. When he realized the storm had struck but the shouts were coming from his own door, he got to his feet, momentarily staggered from the ship's lurching, and made his way across the cabin.

The wind almost tore the door from Britt's hand when he unlatched it. The sailor outside caught the door at the same time he thrust a hooded and cloaked figure into the cabin.

"Lady said she wanted to come here so I brung her," the sailor shouted against the wind. "Is it aright, sir?"

Britt nodded and thanked the seaman, who closed the door and held it firm while Britt secured it. This done, Britt turned to regard Melinda, who was still huddled in her cloak. "You're drenched," he observed and moved as if to unfasten the garment.

"No!" Melinda caught at his hands then breathlessly explained, "I was so frightened I forgot I was in my nightdress. I just put on this cape and ran out on deck after that sailor. Do you have a robe I could wear?"

Desire streaked through Britt like the lightning flashes regularly brightening the cabin, but he stepped back and turned away. "You'd have more trouble keeping my robe on than you'd get comfort from it.

Take off that sopping cloak and get into my bunk before you catch your death of cold.''

Melinda quickly obeyed. As he hung her sodden cloak on a peg in the corner, she said hastily, "I'm sorry for bothering you, Britt. It's just that the ship was rolling so far to its side I was afraid it would capsize. The lightning was so bright my cabin was lit like a ballroom. With the thunderclaps, the wind howling, sailors running past my door, I just didn't know what to think. I guess I panicked.''

"I told you to come if you were afraid," Britt said as he turned to face Melinda. Seeing that real terror of the storm was still reflected in her eyes, he made his way across the tilting room and sat on the edge of the bunk. Bracing himself with his hands to keep from being pitched to the floor, he said, "Alkmaar is a fine captain, and his ship is one of the sturdiest made. Violent storms are frightening, but they don't usually last very long.''

"I've never been in a storm at sea," she said, then quickly added, "I'm sorry about how this must appear to anyone who saw me on deck.''

"No one is on deck except sailors, and they have other things to think about," Britt replied. Then he gently asked, "Do you feel a little warmer now?''

Melinda nodded. Noticing he was still dressed, she surmised, "I guess you expected the storm to be pretty bad.''

"I didn't feel like sleeping," Britt replied in an offhand tone, but vividly remembered why he hadn't gone to bed. To distract himself he quickly added, "I've seen worse storms.''

"I'm not so frightened now that I'm with you," she murmured.

Wishing he could tear off the blankets and make her forget the storm by making love, Britt decided he'd better put a little more distance between them. He stood up and made his way to a chair across the room.

"I don't know how you can manage to walk so easily with the ship lurching around as it is," she commented drowsily. "It isn't fair for you to have to sit in a chair all night. Maybe I should just go back to my cabin now that I'm warm and know the ship isn't in danger.''

"You'd only get wet and chilled all over again. As long as you're here, you might as well stay. I've slept in chairs before," he said a little shortly as he pulled off his boots. "Close your eyes, Minda. Maybe you'll be able to sleep." Putting his feet on a table and slouching back, Britt tried unsuccessfully to keep his rebellious eyes from gazing at a long lock of chestnut hair that fell over Melinda's shoulder in the shimmering lamplight, at the curves her body made under the blanket. He couldn't help remembering the warm satin of her skin and how her lips softened under his.

Melinda fell into a fitful sleep the storm punctuated with nightmares. Britt's reverie was interrupted by little sounds she made that reminded him of a kitten's noises when it dreamed. He left his chair to look down at her. She was so restless he began to wonder if he should awaken her. She moaned plaintively, and he sat on the edge of the bunk, still hesitant to touch her. But when she cried out, his reluctance vanished. He gathered her in his arms.

"Minda, Minda, wake up!" he urgently whispered. Her eyes shot open and he said, "Everything's all right. Don't be afraid."

She clung to him, desperate with terror, still shivering with fright. "We aren't drowning? The ship isn't sinking?" she whispered.

"You've just had a nightmare," he assured.

Her eyes flashed over the cabin, then returned to his. "It was terrible, awful! Everyone was drowning."

Britt held Melinda too gently for her to guess that desire was like a serpent slowly uncoiling in him, but when her trembling finally stopped, he immediately released her.

"Please hold my hand, Britt," she pleaded.

He took a deep breath and drew away to gaze down at Melinda. She couldn't see his face because of the shadows cast by the lamp, but she finally recognized the desire in his voice as he said, "I don't think you realize how I feel. Minda . . ." He stopped when he saw from her expression that she knew. He waited for her to say something, but she was silent. He felt the tension crackling in the air around them and finally whispered, "You're safe from the storm here, but I won't be able to manage myself much longer if I have to sit beside you on the edge of this bunk."

"I've tried so hard not to think of . . ." she finally began in a low tone. He held his breath as she paused and then said quickly, "I guess this was a mistake. I should go back to my cabin." She propped herself up on her elbows as if she would sit up, but he didn't back away; her move had only brought her closer to him.

"The storm is . . ." Britt began to say, so close his breath warmed her face. Then he leaned forward to rub his cheek softly against Melinda's. When he felt her pressing closer, his fingers slowly threaded into her hair. "I don't care about our agreement or any of the problems this may cause later," he murmured, felt her shiver from his breath, then, with his face, brushed aside a lock of her hair.

When the tip of his tongue began to warmly explore her ear, Melinda felt as if a light had begun to glow in her. As his lips slid down her neck, then paused to press at its base, she felt herself moving closer and stopped. "I think you were right before, when you said we shouldn't be lovers," she breathed. "I should leave here while I still have the strength."

Britt withdrew to look at Melinda, saw that her eyes were glowing like smoky emeralds, and commented, "I don't think you can. It's already too late." Running his finger lightly along her jaw, he asked quietly, "Do you *really* want to leave?" When she didn't answer, he bent to nuzzle her breast. Even through the blanket he could hear her heartbeat quicken and he murmured, "Do you, Minda?" He turned his head to caress her lips with a restrained sensuality that maddened him, though she seemed momentarily not to respond. Was she *that* determined to avoid him? Beginning to feel as if he'd lost, he moved away.

She gazed at him a long moment before she finally breathed, "I don't want to go. I'll never want you to stop."

Britt's mouth reached more surely for Melinda's, moved insistently against her lips. His fingers knotted in her hair, holding her face to his. She laid her hands on his waist and slid her arms around his back, felt her breasts brushing his chest, and pressed closer.

The ship gave a lurch that flung Britt against Melinda, his weight pushing her back so he lay partially over her.

"Maybe the storm will prevent us," she gasped.

Britt straightened and began to unbutton his shirt. "Nothing will stop us," he said quietly. When his clothes were a heap on the floor, he slid into the narrow bed and, hooking his ankle over the foot of the bunk, pulled her down from the pillows.

While Britt's hands at Melinda's waist kept her from being moved by the ship's rolling, his lips made delicate circles around her breasts, spiraling in until his tongue sharpened her aching to a bright burst of flame. Melinda's hands at his temples mutely asked for more until she gasped with delight.

With a quick movement he planted a line of soft bites over her shoulder before lifting his head to delicately outline her mouth with his tonguetip and to capture her lower lip between his. He gently tugged at it, then at the upper lip, finally nipping them one by one, quickly back and forth, again and again before his mouth settled on Melinda's, drawing her into so eloquent a kiss she moaned in delight. His mouth continued to move so sensually on hers she didn't notice the thin silk of her nightdress sliding up her body until his naked length was against her. At his touch, his lissome movements, her senses rose in anticipation, but the ship made a sudden roll that slid her against the wall.

Knowing the storm was worsening, Britt caught the wooden spokes at the head of the bunk with one hand and, seeming not at all put off, whispered, "I'll only be able to keep one arm around you."

She glanced up at him in surprise, wondering how anything would be possible with the ship tossing and rolling.

A sultry glimmer went through Britt's eyes as his leg nudged then guided hers to fold over his hip and he said softly, "I told you the storm wouldn't stop me."

Britt's mouth again claimed Melinda's; she responded to his kiss as eagerly as to his body's possessing her. Though her hands on his back moved to hold him close, it wasn't necessary. The rolling of the ship locked them together. Britt let the sea's tossing dictate their lovemaking while his lips fluttered over Melinda's as surely as if they were in a bed on land. His tongue was a flame licking at her lips until the waves of pleasure running through her matched her quick little breaths. Britt's mouth caught hers, moved insistently, hungrily, while the rolling sea swept them into a new rush of sensations.

The hot sweetness of his lips, the lithe body united with hers, flooded Melinda's being with growing delight. Neither could step back from or in any way temper their responses. The storm directed their bodies with every wave that washed over the ship, capturing them with a new sensation before the last one had a moment to fade. Melinda thought she was at her limit only to find a new torrent of greater pleasure racing through her. When Britt suddenly kissed her with a force that bordered on violence, she responded with a ferocity that stunned her, but the storm still commanded them.

Britt heard Melinda's moan like a flame that reached through his darkness to sear him and he began to wonder if he were at the edge of madness. He opened his eyes to see her through the blur of his own senses and would have withdrawn a little to regain some thread of control, but the sea didn't allow the sensations it was creating in them to lessen.

Melinda strained toward Britt, groping blindly, her whispers becom-

ing wordless pleading. The storm continued to pulse through them
until their passion crested in the tidal wave that dissolved them with
ecstasy.

Britt slowly became aware that he was lying at Melinda's side, his
arms enclosing her. He couldn't remember having moved away and,
utterly spent, wasn't inclined to try.

"The storm has quieted," she finally murmured.

He sighed and answered, "You would think we'd made an offering
to the sea and it was accepted." Her eyes turned to glance at him and
he added softly, "But maybe it frightened you."

She considered this, then replied slowly, "Though basking in a
quiet lagoon is enough for now, if another storm comes, I suspect I'd
change my mind." She looked up at him to find he was smiling
faintly.

"Java's fire spirits seem to have returned to my little Minda's eyes
as well as her hair," he commented. Then, tenderly kissing her
forehead, he said quietly, "But now I think no one will ever be able to
snuff out your flame again." He laid his head on her breast and closed
his eyes to drowsily whisper, "No one should ever have tried."

The old troubles seemed to become as remote as the shores on
which they'd sprung. Memories of Melinda's heartaches dimmed and
Britt's misgivings about where love would lead their volatile spirits
blurred and softened on the ship called "Today" that was wrapped in
a blue cocoon of sea and sky.

Days and nights were blended in a kaleidoscope of shifting shapes
and colors: squares of billowing white sails in an azure sky, golden
triangles of sun reflected on the tips of turquoise waves, crescents of
smiles on oval faces, the silver sphere of the moon in a midnight sky
adorned with diamond sprays of stars.

Always the love in the warmth of bodies whose goals were the
same, to be close even while unblended. Eyes of smoky emerald
meeting those holding amber glow over hands always reaching to
clasp, lips eager to taste the kisses waiting on the other's mouth.

The captain smiled benevolently on the couple, who unknowingly
spread their joy around them like an enchanted ring. The crew smiled
just to see them pass, and the other passengers were warmed merely to
stand within their circle, absorb some of the magic while exchanging
greetings.

A shore approached, a port made, merely meant a shift in the kaleidoscope of colors and shapes. The cacophony of sounds was music that beat with a new rhythm for the ears of lovers. A stroll under fragrant arches of trees, a pause in the midst of a garden filled with the soft blaze of roses. Then, again, the sea. Another port to take on supplies, exchange passengers, visit a teeming market with new sounds and smells, exotically clothed people who recognized the circle of love following a golden-haired man and the woman whose green eyes were always on him.

Love was a shield that banished yesterday's troubles and held back the problems of tomorrow. Its fragile circle preserved every caress, distilled each kiss into the elixir of forgetfulness; and as Britt had foreseen, Melinda learned his every response while he grew to know her body as intimately as his own. The spell cast by the sorcery of their senses gave respite to their hearts and banked the embers of their volatile spirits as the ship called "Today" glided toward tomorrow.

Chapter Seven

The *Harini* sailed past a wreath of small islands Melinda tried to ignore, for she knew they signaled that the voyage was nearing its end. Then the ship was in sight of Sumatra, the island that was almost like the handle of a sword, whose blade was Java, Bali, and the islands trailing behind. Melinda viewed their destination with mixed emotions. Though the old lure of Java had begun to reach out, like a force drawing her, and the idea of being half owner of a tea plantation awakened a sense of potential power that was intoxicating to contemplate, Melinda regretted the passing of the idyllic interlude on the *Harini*. Unlike the sea and its fluidity, asking nothing specific of her and allowing her to follow a timetable determined only by the rise and fall of the sun, the land would insist she anchor herself in the earth or wither like an uprooted tree. Britt would become her teacher, not in love but in the running of Phoenix House. The sweet fire they'd freely basked in would often have to be banked, would give way to routines and schedules.

As the *Harini* glided past Krakatau into the Sundra Strait, she gazed at the thread of smoke coming from the island's heart and thought it was like her life, peaceful now in the sun while below its surface layers of earth were poised to shift and expose a fiery core. Would her life's shift erupt into explosions of flame to sear away the joy of her future? Or would it rumble, rearrange her life's mountains and valleys, then be content to occasionally warm her terrain with light?

It was impossible to hold back time; the sky was still smeared with orange and scattered with ribbons of crimson left from the dawn when Britt stepped from his cabin with Melinda on his arm.

Home. He didn't have to say the word. It was shining in the copper points of light that rose from the depths of his eyes when they looked at the island. It was glowing from his pores as the island exhaled its perfume of spices, flowers, and dripping leaves, shining in his hair that seemed to absorb the gold of the Javanese sun. Melinda knew then that if Britt ever left Java it would be only for trips; he would never stay away. His soul was welded to it. When they reached the ship's rail, the unspoken words were like a signal his eyes flashed to her—your home, too, if you want it.

Limestone cliffs gave way to shimmering white beaches that slid like ribbons under the turquoise water. Foliage of every tint of green blended into one glorious shade. Mountains seemed to float above the land, their bases lost in mist like golden froth ladled into the valleys. Over some of the peaks gray smoke curled like kittens' tails. On one slope Phoenix House waited. Which slope? Melinda had been too young to know when Jessica had taken her from the land Charles and Gerard had fought for and Britt loved so dearly. She'd loved it then, but would she now? Melinda dared not voice her fear and give substance to the now shapeless ghost of her doubt. But Britt knew it, and the knowledge was a cold streak of pain in his soul, like a sliver of ice that he desperately wished would melt and vanish.

From a distance the land seemed to have a fold an outrigger canoe disappeared into, but as the *Harini* sailed nearer, Melinda remembered the past an instant before her eyes beheld the mouth of the Liwung River, gateway to Djakarta beyond. The *Harini* floated unconcernedly past the city's garrison, and Melinda felt an automatic, smoldering anger at the sight of a flag that so recently had been the banner of her country's enemy. Her country, the United States? Or her country, Java? How *could* she ever have thought of wedding an envoy of the land so recently and now again an enemy? "So very civilized an attitude," she could almost hear Jessica saying and acknowledged that it had been from the beginning Jessica's decision, not hers, for her to marry Alden.

Fishing praus tied next to stone landing piers, nets like webs spread on poles to dry. An outrigger skimming past, guided by paddles in deftly moving hands. A cluster of Javanese women scrubbing laundry on the stones, a knot of girls taking baths, modestly covered all the while they bathed by loose, smocklike garments whose hems could be adjusted above water level.

"My memory was mistaken. I thought Djakarta was enclosed by walls," Melinda mused.

"It was, but Daendels had them torn down," Britt advised.

"Daendels, the Hollander Napoleon sent to rule Java?" Melinda inquired.

"After Bonaparte took the Netherlands," Britt confirmed. "Daendels was in political disgrace at home, but as governor-general here he proved himself efficient, though harsh."

"What do you mean?" Melinda asked.

"He had the old walls torn down, supposedly because they shut in the evil humors that caused so much disease, but he moved his garrison to high ground and left the lowlands to the Javanese, where they continued to die—when they weren't dying building his road. One of Daendels's first official acts as governor-general was to seek an audience with the *sunan*, the Javanese king. He had to wait but he got tired, so he and his soldiers rushed past the *sunan*'s guards. Daendels caught the king by the hair and dragged him to the garrison for their talk."

Melinda flinched at the vision of the Javanese ruler's humiliation, then ventured, "Was that Matarami?"

"No. It was Sunan Hamengky Bwono, the ruler of all Java. Matarami is a prince of the Javanese court, or at least he was when there was a court. His title is *raden*, and he's the ruler of a city named Talu and its district. Phoenix House happens to lie in that district," Britt explained, then continued to relate Javanese history of recent years and the series of occupations Java had suffered. "After Lord Minto rescued Java from France by driving Napoleon's troops out of the East Indies, the British army remained to occupy Java as effectively as the French had done. Raffles was appointed lieutenant governor and Hamengky Bwono was deposed shortly afterward. He lives in exile now while his brother, Notokusumo, who defected to the British side and was rewarded, lives in grand style as a figurehead."

"Who is this Major Wakefield you mentioned?" Melinda inquired.

"A sort of military supervisor. Who can know exactly what each in his echelon controls?" Britt said disgustedly. "The British have an army of officials here to direct an even greater army of soldiers—all to keep command of a handful of Dutch planters and Javanese leaders like Rakata, whose weaponry consists of little more than swords, blow-pipes, and bows and arrows.''

"How can Rakata even consider rebelling if that's all he has to fight with?'' Melinda asked.

Britt, still watching the shore, set one foot on a coil of rope as he slid his arm around her waist. "Rakata said one must hope or one is not a man. But if he were to meet Raffles, Raffles would expect him to perform *dokok,* too, I think.''

"*Dodok.* You mean when a Javanese sits back on his heels with his hands like so?'' Melinda pressed her palms together in a gesture much like praying.

"An effective posture to render one helpless, isn't it?'' Britt inquired pointedly. "That's one reason Rakata never shows his face where he'd meet any European. He's too proud to *dokok.* Also too smart.''

"And you, Britt, where is your place in all this?'' she asked.

"I guess no one knows quite how to categorize me. I'm very grateful I look like my father. If I'd taken after my mother, I, too, would be expected to squat in *dokok* to every passing European or stay out of their sight like Rakata,'' he said sarcastically.

Melinda threw him a sideways glance. She couldn't imagine Britt in so humble a gesture—not before Raffles, King George, or the Netherlands' King William. "You'd said before that you spend most of your evenings at home. Is that part of the reason you don't socialize much?''

"No,'' Britt answered quietly.

His eyes were unreadable as he continued to gaze at the nearing wharf, and Melinda knew there was more he wasn't saying. She wondered about it but didn't ask.

The breezes caught at her hair and impudently ruffled her skirt hem as she walked down the ramp to the dock, and she suddenly remembered it was always windy near the shore in Java. The odor of the sea mixed with that of bananas being loaded on a cargo ship was like a hand opening the trunk of her memories. Little details she'd long ago forgotten came pouring back. Suddenly, Melinda no longer was in a strange land, a refugee from her past. Everything was becoming familiar again.

Watching her expression, Britt commented, "It's odd the way one sniff of the air can change everything, isn't it?"

"Scent seems to instantly bypass civilized barriers, dissolve so many questions and doubts," she agreed.

"That's why Javanese sniff-kiss, Minda."

Melinda glanced up at Britt, then wanted to kiss the smile that tipped the corners of his mouth.

"Mr. Vandekker, I'm afraid Major Wakefield has a few questions to put to you."

The voice distracted Melinda from her thoughts and she turned to face a soldier.

"Sergeant Moore, miss," the soldier said. "Mr. Vandekker, will you come this way?"

Britt's hand on Melinda's arm held her back as he asked patiently, "If it's you, Sergeant, who are to ask the questions, do so here please. Miss Scott and I are anxious to go to Phoenix House."

"Miss Scott? Charles Scott's daughter?" the sergeant inquired. When Melinda nodded, he said, "My condolences, Miss Scott." Then he addressed Britt. "Major Wakefield himself wants to ask about Mr. Scott's demise, especially since the accident occurred about the time Lieutenant Blackburn's patrol disappeared."

Though Britt had told Melinda how Charles had been killed, he'd forgotten to explain how he'd reported the death to the authorities, that Charles was crushed under a load of teak logs that had broken their chains. He also hadn't told Melinda that Charles had been cremated immediately so the bayonet wound couldn't be examined if there were questions. Hoping to buy time to tell Melinda so she wouldn't make a contradictory remark, Britt said, "That all happened quite a while ago, and I don't see what one incident has to do with the other. Miss Scott is weary from the long voyage. Can't I take her home then return?"

"The major said to fetch you as soon as you stepped off the ship," Moore insisted.

Britt sighed disgustedly, remarked about the military caring nothing for sensibilities, as he knew an innocent in his position would, and casting Melinda a sideways warning look, led her after the sergeant.

Melinda realized Britt had never told her exactly how he'd hidden the circumstances surrounding her father's death, but she couldn't ask. The sergeant, seated in the carriage across from them, had eyes sharp enough, it seemed, to read even her thoughts. She stared silently at the passing scenery all the way to the major's headquarters.

Wakefield's iron-gray hair had receded to circle his head like a laurel wreath. Though his face was furrowed and scarred by battle, his light blue eyes, absorbed with business, weren't unkind when they regarded Melinda. "Major Wakefield, Miss Scott. I'm very sorry about your father's death and apologize for having to welcome you back to Java with what must seem like a tribunal," he said as the sergeant seated her. "Would you like a cup of tea?"

"Thank you, no," Melinda answered, hoping that if she behaved coolly the major would attribute her lack of cooperation to annoyance rather than ignorance. When Britt accepted a glass of Madeira, she knew he wanted to appear friendly and willing so Wakefield would direct most of the questions at him.

But Wakefield, hoping that Melinda would be caught by surprise and say something useful to him, asked, "Miss Scott, I'm curious about something perhaps you can answer about your father. It seems unlikely for the owner of a plantation to go into the jungle to supervise a load of teak. Why do you suppose he didn't leave the task to one of his workers?"

Melinda surmised the major was hoping to confirm or disprove Britt's report by casually interrogating *her,* for he'd carefully given no hint about the details of how Britt's report said Charles had died. She frowned and inquired, "How can I know?"

"I'd thought, being his daughter, you might be a better judge of Mr. Scott's inclinations," Wakefield answered.

Melinda raised her eyes to meet the major's. "This is the first time I've set foot in Java for sixteen years, because my mother hated the island. She was so bitter my father never even visited us in Philadelphia. My mother was aghast when I said I wanted to return to Java, and the friction between us was considerable. Between this, packing for the journey, saying good-bye to my friends, and closing matters there, Mr. Vandekker and I have had little opportunity to discuss details about my father's personal inclinations. There's a great deal I don't know about my father, Major, but I do intend to learn about the plantation so I can take his place as Mr. Vandekker's partner."

Wakefield was silent a moment, considering Melinda's surprising answer. He found it difficult to believe a woman would have the ambition to take on such a chore. Finally he said, "Miss Scott, why did you leave what must have been a comfortable life, despite your mother's protests? What did you and Mr. Vandekker talk about on so long a voyage, if not your father?''

Melinda realized, now that she'd begun to paint herself as eager and ambitious, she must convince the major her aspirations were so important everything else was of secondary interest. She frowned as she answered, ''We talked about the problems of growing tea and renewed my memories of Java. Mr. Vandekker helped reacquaint me with the Javanese language; but, Major, I was also distressed over some other problems I prefer not to discuss with you.''

''I'm not insensitive to your reluctance to confide in a stranger, but I have a job to do, and unfortunately, I must pry,'' Wakefield pressed.

Melinda sighed in resignation and went on, ''I was engaged to a gentleman, whom I decided I preferred not to marry. My mother was trying to convince me I should go through with the wedding. The situation was growing unbearable, and coming to Java seemed to provide an answer. In short, I wanted to escape.'' She looked up pointedly at Wakefield and inquired, *''Must* I describe intimate details of my mother's and my fiancé's quarrels with me?''

''No, Miss Scott. Please don't,'' Wakefield answered hastily.

''Why are you bringing up this matter now?'' Britt inquired. ''There was no question about my report at the time.''

''I had barely learned Mr. Scott was dead when his body had already been cremated and you'd left Java.'' Wakefield didn't miss Melinda's flinching at this and he wondered if she hadn't known about this either or if it was the sign of her returning grief to be reminded. She was staring at her folded hands on her lap so he couldn't see her face.

''There was no reason to delay. The ship was ready to sail and I might not have gotten passage on another for weeks, maybe months,'' Britt returned. ''Why does it matter?''

''After you'd left, a question rose about a patrol's vanishing approximately at the same time. Lieutenant Blackburn and his men still haven't been found and they were on a routine mission near Phoenix House. I wanted to know if you'd seen any trace of them.''

Britt said, ''I hadn't.'' As he remembered how Blackburn had turned the routine mission into violence that had resulted in so many deaths, his eyes narrowed, but Wakefield took this as a sign of his annoyance at being delayed going to the plantation.

''Nor did any of your people, according to the sergeant who questioned them,'' Wakefield said slowly.

''But you're wondering if I, being Rakata's half brother, might be privy to information you aren't,'' Britt surmised. ''As I've said hundreds of times before, Rakata and I have little contact.''

''The question is, if you did, would you tell me?'' Wakefield inquired. ''You know, Vandekker, it would be wise.''

''The very reason I've kept control of Phoenix House has been that I've avoided taking anyone's side,'' Britt reminded him. Then he suggested, ''Blackburn was new on the island. Maybe he led his men into a bog.''

Melinda remained silently staring at her gloved hands, noticing throughout the continuing discussion about the lost patrol that there was always an implication behind Wakefield's inquiries that Britt and Rakata were more friendly than they appeared. She realized Britt deliberately, though very subtly, encouraged this idea to keep Wakefield from confiscating the plantation, as he'd been ordered to do with the property of other planters from the Netherlands. Wakefield feared that leaving Rakata's half brother as barely a tenant on his own plantation might stir Javanese tempers too far. Melinda sensed, too, that her coming from the United States to replace her father as Britt's partner, rather than selling Phoenix House, would also help keep Wakefield's superiors from confiscating the plantation. They wouldn't want an irate American reporting to President Madison that her inheritance had been lost to a government trying to mend its relations with its former colonies. It would make Great Britain appear to want to colonize the world at a time when it supposedly was fighting to prevent Napoleon's doing that very thing in Europe.

When Britt and Melinda were allowed to leave Wakefield's headquarters, they returned to the wharf to find that the major had left orders to have the dock workers transfer Melinda's belongings from the *Harini* to a cart that, along with a carriage, had been provided for her and Britt's trip to Phoenix House.

As the carriage moved through Djakarta, Melinda didn't take much note of the stone houses built tightly side by side, Hollander fashion, along canals dug to drain the low-lying land. Her mind was on the precarious methods Britt had to use to keep control of the plantation. Melinda was grateful to leave the diplomacy needed in answering Wakefield's inquiries to Britt and conceded her temper wasn't suitable for the cat-and-mouse games they were playing. When the carriage was passing through the center of the city, the smells of coconut oil and flowers, shrimp and nutmeg, lured Melinda from her worrisome thoughts and she turned her attention to the passing scene.

The marketplace, where the Javanese spread their wares on mats on the ground and sat waiting for customers while sipping pear juice and exchanging gossip, was quieter than those in the other ports she'd visited during the journey because the Javanese were a soft-spoken people. Large eyes, like liquid pools of moonlight, rose to gaze at the carriage. Serene expressions camouflaged whatever emotions lay behind those eyes as people held their hands prayer fashion while the vehicle passed.

Melinda watched a pair of men lift a crate full of chickens for a girl whose tassel of hair falling loose from the lustrous double knot coiled at her nape denoted her as unmarried. Melinda supposed the men were trying to gain the comely girl's favor. The supple movements of the tall, slim men, their straightness when they drew themselves erect, reminded Melinda of Britt; and she wondered if his grace was inherited from Sukadana.

Melinda's reflections were halted. She caught her breath at the sudden rise of a high-pitched, wavering sound, a joyful music without pattern or pause, that delighted her ears.

"It's someone's flock of pigeons taking off," Britt pointed out.

Melinda tilted her head to stare at the birds flying in circles against the blaze of the sky, their song dipping and soaring with them. Finally recalling that people often tied tiny bells to their birds' feet and bamboo whistles to their tail feathers, she breathed, "How could I have forgotten?"

"There are probably a lot of things you've forgotten," Britt said quietly. "The Javanese like music, birds, flowers—just about everything that's pleasant to the senses."

Melinda glanced at him from the corners of her eyes. "For that quality in you, I'm grateful."

Britt smiled faintly. "My father, too, appreciated beauty. His nature certainly wasn't cold. I remember—" he did not get a chance to finish.

The carriage, just turning onto the coral road leading out of Djakarta, was stopped by a group of soldiers. Britt's hand briefly squeezed Melinda's as he glanced at the watchhouse they'd paused beside and said, "These men only act as police to keep order."

One soldier, a sergeant, nudged his horse carriage-side. "I'm afraid I'll have to ask you and the lady to step down," he said.

"Why?" The word was like a chip of ice against Britt's teeth because the sergeant's request was highly irregular.

"There's a new rule that all Javanese must be searched before leaving the city," the sergeant advised.

"Do you mean the driver?" Britt asked slowly, suspecting what would follow.

The soldier gave the answer Britt had hoped he wouldn't. "You as well."

"Mr. Vandekker?" Melinda gasped.

Britt silently obeyed; and as another soldier quickly patted his coat and trouser legs, Melinda couldn't help commenting sarcastically, "Shall he also make *dodok* for you?"

"No, miss. I do understand Mr. Vandekker has some privileges the others don't," the sergeant said coolly. "Please step out of the carriage."

Melinda was aghast. "Do you intend to handle me that way too?"

"You aren't Javanese," the soldier replied, then handed her out of the carriage and inquired, "What's in that cart?"

Melinda watched with amazed eyes as her bag was slipped from her wrist, the drawstrings opened, and the contents inspected. Despite Britt's warning glance, she snapped, "The cart contains my belongings shipped from Philadelphia. I'm an American, I might remind you, and not under your jurisdiction."

The sergeant gestured to his men to begin inspecting the cart's contents. "This road and anyone on it is my jurisdiction. Your baggage could conceal arms going to the Javanese rebels."

"I know no rebels! I just arrived this morning," she flashed, angered that the soldiers were sorting through her clothes.

"Until the matter of a lost patrol is resolved, we must assume they were done away with by rebels."

"Sergeant, we've come directly from Major Wakefield's office," Britt advised. "If he suspected us of anything, he wouldn't have released us."

"*Released* us!" Melinda exclaimed. "Were we under arrest?"

"In a way," Britt replied. "I'm always more or less under suspicion."

"How disgusting!" she declared. "How can you bear this treatment?"

"Be quiet, Minda," he warned as he propelled her back into the carriage.

Melinda sat in sullen silence while the soldiers continued to open trunks and even hatboxes. Though they were careful to minimize disturbing the contents, simply feeling among the layers of her clothes for weapons, she grew more incensed every moment. After everything had been reclosed and the soldiers had climbed out of the cart, the sergeant told Britt they could continue on their way. Melinda felt like flinging yet another accusation at the soldiers, but Britt again hushed her, his tight grip on her arm an effective warning.

By the time the carriage drew away from the soldiers, Melinda was sizzling with anger. "How *can* you be so docile about all that? Why didn't you say or do something? It was insulting to be searched as if we were criminals."

"If you'd said all you were thinking to that sergeant, the results could have been more than insulting," Britt returned, his eyes flashing with anger at her as well as disgust that she'd witnessed his humiliation. "If I'd resisted, they could have dragged us both from the carriage, *really* searched you, and spread what's in your trunks all over the road."

"They wouldn't have dared!"

"They could have done all I said and worse," Britt said tensely. "Then, if we'd have complained later, the sergeant would have said he was only following orders."

"Wakefield didn't seem like a man to give *those* orders," she persisted.

"They came from higher up, which means he must obey them too," Britt said curtly, trying to hold his rising temper in check.

"Why didn't he warn us about that roadblock?"

"Don't be foolish, Minda," Britt snapped. "Warning us would have given me a chance to hide any firearms I was carrying if I were a rebel."

"Foolish?" she echoed. "You're talking to me as if I were a child."

"You're behaving like one," he shot back. "You'd better recognize that martial law is different from civilian government. Do you think I enjoyed that little scene? Hardly, but I had no choice. You could have caused a very dangerous situation back there. We *have* to bend a little when necessary or they'll snap us like a twig. If you want to learn how to get along in Java, I advise you to listen more and talk less."

"I'm not your employee; I'm your partner," Melinda, angry at his tone, reminded him.

"A partner who knows little more about tea than how to drink it gracefully and who seems too hot-tempered to listen to anything," he said disgustedly. "I wonder if you'll be more trouble than help."

"You could have told me this sort of thing happens, should have prepared me for it," Melinda said, her face flushing with embarrassment. She knew he was right.

"I did try to explain the political situation. Maybe I would have succeeded in getting it through your head if I'd spent every minute of the voyage describing each detail instead of making love," he replied sharply. "This was the sort of thing I meant when I said being lovers would distract us from business. It surely did."

"I didn't come to your cabin to *seduce* you! I was afraid of the storm," she declared.

"Yes, in a silk nightdress looking as forlorn as a wet puppy," he returned. "Don't behave now as if it were all my fault. It was both our faults."

"If being lovers is going to cause us so much trouble, maybe we'd better stop it now," she flashed. "I thought Java would be a good place to start over, and now that I'm here, I intend to try."

Britt stared at a passing procession of chanting women on their way to a temple carrying offerings on their heads, but he didn't see them. He felt as if something inside him were shriveling into a hard, painful knot. Finally he said, "I'll keep my side of our bargain and teach you as much about running a tea plantation as you can learn. We'll be business partners only, as we previously agreed."

After that, Britt was silent, except for occasionally pointing out some sight as briskly as if it were Charles's son, not daughter, he was reintroducing to Java. Between comments he thought glumly of how different this homecoming was from the one he'd planned. His worst fears seemed to be turning into reality, for Melinda was as headstrong as he'd originally thought. She would find adjusting to life in Java, as it was now, far more difficult than she'd dreamed. The island's problems would add to their personal tension, for she'd overnight turned from Jessica's obedient, suppressed daughter into a woman with more volatile emotions than she yet knew how to manage. He could only hope that Melinda would learn all the lessons she had ahead before her fiery nature caused her to sail away in a fury even as Jessica, her mother, had done.

Night fell long before the carriage reached Phoenix House, and for Melinda the jungle road became a frightening tunnel through the shadowy trees. She looked suspiciously from side to side at each sound made by the wildlife hidden in the darkness, imagining all sorts of prowling things hungrily watching them pass. Grateful for Britt's company as well as the Javanese driving the carriage and the following wagon, Melinda was acutely aware that none of the three silent men had weapons. She recalled the soldiers' conviction that rebels were hidden in these jungles and hoped Britt's unwanted relationship to Rakata would turn any attacks aside. She gazed at the back of the Javanese driving the carriage and wondered if possible rebels would have compassion on their brothers who tried to live with the foreigners that had invaded their island. Life in Philadelphia didn't hold these terrors. At this time of night she would likely have been enjoying a play or a symphony with a new beau. But would she rather have been safely at the side of some tepid suitor, Melinda questioned herself, than with Britt, who scorched her with passion, then became a circumspect business associate? She wished she'd tempered her anger at the soldiers, not turned it on him. In the space of an hour it seemed as if she'd destroyed everything between them.

When the carriage neared the dim form of a rambling house hidden among the tree shadows, Melinda didn't try to discern its appearance. Though half of it belonged to her, was her home now, she felt more like an alien than ever.

Britt helped Melinda down from the carriage and, without a word, guided her to the door. Moments after he'd slammed it shut, Melinda heard the sound of bare feet hurrying from somewhere in the house and saw the glimmer of an approaching lamp.

It was Koki, the cook, who'd known Melinda as a child, but stood warily back gazing at the lovely young woman she'd grown into. Then Melinda offered her hands and Koki's face brightened. Enang, Koki's husband, now butler, welcomed the couple warmly. Suhadi, Britt's personal servant, then Dessa, a sloe-eyed maid, came.

Not even the coconut oil lamps they'd brought threw enough light to reveal the spacious entrance hall's corners, but Melinda was too weary from the long drive and her storm of emotions to be curious. She looked questioningly up at Britt, wishing she knew how to mend their situation, but she didn't know what to say.

Seeing Melinda's eyes, dark as emerald velvet, gazing up at him, all Britt wanted to do was scoop her up in his arms, carry her off to his room, and proclaim before them all that he and she were lovers. But they were lovers no more.

"Dessa, please show Miss Scott to her suite," Britt said. Then, without even wishing Melinda fair dreams, he stalked off. He knew what his dreams would be about.

Chapter Eight

A rush of air laden with the scent of camellias and limes fluttered Melinda's lashes till she opened her eyes. To her wondering mind it seemed as if she were wrapped in a shimmering orchid web until she realized the fine netting that surrounded the bed had been carried against her face by the breeze and its glisten was from sunshine. She brushed the silky gauze farther back and reclosed her eyes, not yet wanting to look at the room and face the reality of this strange place, this new life.

Yesterday's painful memories made her eyelids squeeze tighter. How could Britt have expected her to be mute while those soldiers had humiliated her with their search? No, not her, Melinda suddenly realized. It was Britt's submission that had shamed her. But how was she supposed to feel about it? The incident had been too mortifying. There was too much on her mind as it was, too much expected of her. How would she be able to learn to take her father's place on a huge plantation when there was so much else to worry about? She wanted to be a working partner, not merely a name on a sheaf of legal documents, but the task awed her. She'd never before had to earn a penny, hadn't made a decision more earthshaking than accepting Alden's proposal— and that had been mostly her mother's doing—until Britt had come back into her life.

Britt, with his sinuous walk and soft-spoken manner, his amber eyes measuring, caressing, making her forget Alden on the night of their engagement ball. It had seemed as if she'd been destined for Britt, almost as if he were part of her legacy. But no sooner had she set foot in Java to claim her inheritance than every beautiful feeling growing between them seemed to have been burned away by the quarrel, leaving among their ashes embers of pain her pride must somehow conceal.

Melinda was seized with the realization that she was beginning this morning with the same attitude she'd had yesterday—uncertainty, resentment that everything wasn't already as she wanted it to be. What had it brought her yesterday? From uncertainty had come foolish impulses; from resentment had come anger aimed at Britt instead of a situation in Java he could do nothing about. Melinda took a deep breath while she resolved that *this* day would be different. If she had to face unfamiliar situations, she would learn from them. It was why she'd come to Java—to learn. If she was afraid, she'd go carefully, think before she acted. Then, buoyed up by new determination, she propped herself on her elbows to look around.

The chamber had been black as pitch when Dessa had brought her there last night, and the lamp the maid carried had revealed little of the room. Melinda had been so exhausted she'd been in a stupor while she'd bathed. Then she'd put on the nightdress Dessa had handed her and fallen into bed already half asleep. Now Melinda decided that Dessa must have pulled the netting around the bed and opened the windows. Not windows, she noticed as she sat up, but French doors that lined one wall of the room. Running her fingers through her tousled hair, Melinda brushed aside the netting and swung her feet off the bed.

A table beside the bed held a carafe, and she bent close to learn that its steam carried the rich fragrance of hot chocolate; the camellia perfume came from bunchy pink blossoms floating in a porcelain bowl beside the carafe. Melinda pulled on a dressing gown and, sipping chocolate, slowly turned to look at the room: a dressing table and bench flounced by lavender satin, a divan made of teak with coral and violet cushions, a standing mirror framed with gold leaf, a row of cabinets.

Drawn by the scent of lime, Melinda stepped through the French doors to find herself in a corridor whose opposite wall was another line of doors, also open. Beyond them was the courtyard Britt had described as forming the house's center. Outside, whispering palm

fronds shaded brilliant red bougainvillaea, and flagged walks sprinkled
with fallen limes were bordered by ginger blossoms. Orchid sprays
crept among deep orange rhododendrons below bamboo cages set on
high poles at intervals around the courtyard. Melinda tilted her head to
gaze up at the brightly feathered throats that trembled with mixtures of
trills and warbles. One satin sleeve of the dressing gown slipped off
Melinda's shoulder, reminding her not to go outside, but she recalled
Britt had said all rooms could be entered from the corridor paralleling
the courtyard. She decided to explore her side of the house.

In the hush broken only by birdsong, Melinda soon discovered she
felt like an intruder creeping through a stranger's home, peeking into
doors: several bedchambers—apricot, rose, and pale green—a teak-
lined library, a sitting room of silver-gray damask, expanses of cool
marble floors unbroken by carpets. Charles seemed to have chosen the
decor with an eye toward a woman's taste, and Melinda wondered if
her father had always hoped Jessica would relent. Maybe that was why
he'd never divorced her or maybe he'd thought his daughter would
return. Now she'd come back too late to ask him the questions she
might have, too late to know him. Melinda wondered how her life
might have been if she'd returned to Java as soon as she'd gotten out
of school. What would Britt have been like? Not as harried, with less
on his mind, if her father were alive to help with the plantation.

But Melinda let her mind linger too long on Britt. She found herself
wishing she could have awakened in that lavender bed with him at her
side. During the voyage her skin had become so accustomed to his
morning's warmth it craved his touch; her hair hungered for his fingers
threading through it; her ears needed the deep rhythm of his heartbeat.
Lost in such thoughts, Melinda unknowingly rounded a turn in the
corridor. She opened a door and startled Britt, foot on a stool while he
adjusted his boot.

He quickly raised his head. Eyes lit at the sight of her slowly
deepened with amber shadows as he recalled their new agreement.

Melinda quickly said, "I didn't know I'd gone beyond my half of
the house."

Coppery pinpoints relit in Britt's eyes as they took in the dressing
gown and the lace that barely covered Melinda's breast, for the satin,
unnoticed by her, had again slid from her shoulder.

He said slowly, "I didn't have a chance last night to tell you there's
no wall between our sections." He took his foot from the stool and
straightened.

Britt's shirtfront was open, and Melinda's hands, as if they made decisions on their own, almost reached out with their impulse to grasp that lean waist, wrap around his back, draw that golden chest to her bosom.

Britt saw the smoke beginning to darken the green of Melinda's eyes, and desire was a silent messenger winging through his spirit, but he quickly began buttoning his shirt as he said, "Though locks were never put on any of these doors, I can have them installed if you wish."

Melinda's heart felt like a bird beating its wings against her ribs, yet she summoned her old poise to ask quietly, "How did my father and your family maintain their privacy?"

"Each respected the other's closed doors," Britt answered as he walked through the azure light of the room. He stopped to look down at Melinda, wondering how she could, as it seemed, snuff out her feelings like a candle no longer needed. He yearned to run his lips slowly along the swell of her bosom, but instead, fastened his sleeves. "I was getting ready to go for breakfast. Would you like to join me? Maybe afterward you can come with me on my rounds."

"Yes, of course," she quickly answered. "I want to see the plantation and should begin to learn about it too."

He raised his eyes to meet hers and said softly, "Then please, Minda, go to your room and put on something less revealing. If we're to keep our agreement, you must make it bearable for me."

Melinda hastily backed to step into the hall stammering, "I'm sorry, *truly* sorry, Britt. I didn't know this was your room."

"Now you do," he replied, then closed the door between them. Britt turned and stood leaning back against the wood. One touch, one word from Melinda, and he would gladly have thrown away all the reasons he knew it was wiser not to resume their love affair. After a moment he straightened and said with quiet vehemence, *"Damn."*

Britt was toying with the pomelo slices on his plate when Dessa brought Melinda into the dining room. Though she was now clad in a modestly high-necked dove-gray riding dress and he had leashed his desire, Britt missed her morning habit of stepping behind his chair and hugging him, laying her cheek against his. They exchanged greetings as if it were the first time today they'd met, but he fixed his eyes on the emerald-skinned fruit on his plate while Enang seated her.

"I think I'll just have tea and a muffin, if there are any," she told Dessa in a small, strained voice.

"You should have more of a breakfast than that if you're still planning to come with me," Britt advised. "We won't return to the house until after one o'clock, when the workers leave the fields."

"That's a short work day, isn't it?" she inquired.

"It's too hot to work in the sun after that, but they're in the fields at five in the morning. Ordinarily I'm out with them," Britt explained.

"No wonder you always awakened on the ship at what seemed like the middle of the night," she commented, then wished she hadn't reminded either of them about the languid mornings filled with love. She quickly added, "Now that you mention it, I do recall, when I was a child, creeping out of bed before dawn to be with my father awhile before he left the house." Her eyes focused on another time as memories came poignantly back. "Mother never got up that early, and he seemed so alone I kept him company." Melinda looked up at Britt. "Even then, I must have sensed he was lonely, but I'd forgotten since. I suppose being in Java will stir up a lot of memories." She sighed, adding, "Perhaps recalling them will help me learn more quickly about my new life here."

"I hope so," he said softly as his hand crept over the tablecloth to cover hers. Though Britt had meant to reassure Melinda, he felt the old thrill race through his arm to his shoulder. It seemed to settle like an ache in his heart.

"Must it always be this way?" she whispered.

Britt raised his eyes to meet hers looking intently at him. "You realize why we quarreled yesterday, don't you?"

Melinda lowered her gaze. She didn't want to admit she knew.

"How can you be expected to deal with all the things you just mentioned and at the same time manage the emotions involved in a love affair?" he asked softly. "Your loyalty to me as your lover wanted me to lash out at those soldiers, but I couldn't. You didn't want the romantic image of me in your mind to be tarnished by my submitting to their search. But Minda, I'm not an image. I'm a man. I have to deal with real problems. My position doesn't allow me to defy the soldiers. Until the occupation ends, there will be other times you'll see me have to swallow my pride and conceal my anger."

"But what if it never ends?" she asked.

"It will. It *must*," he answered firmly, not wanting to think otherwise. "Won't it be easier for you, for us both, if you see these things happen through the eyes of a friend and partner, not with the emotions of a lover?''

"How can I?" she murmured. "I can't pretend there was nothing between us."

Britt was silent, wondering how he would manage it himself. Yesterday, as he'd gotten out of the carriage to be searched, he'd felt as humiliated under her eyes as if he'd been stripped for a flogging in the town square. Finally he said, "What we have is still too fragile to withstand the strain of the conditions we must live with now. I don't want to end but suspend it for a while." He paused and sighed. "It won't be easy, but I think the emotional demand will be less. I don't want us to explode in an argument that could destroy what we've been to each other and send you from Java forever, Minda."

Melinda suddenly realized all the while she'd feared Britt might decide he didn't want her, he'd been afraid she would leave him. Wondering at this, wanting to ask about it, Melinda knew she couldn't. She tried to remember what they'd been talking about before. After a moment she said, "If I'm going to learn about growing tea, I guess I'll have to tell Dessa to awaken me earlier."

Britt understood Melinda wanted to talk about something safer than their emotions. Concluding that she really did intend to take Charles's place as his partner, Britt admired her resolution. He felt like gathering Melinda in his arms, but took his hand from hers and said in a falsely casual tone, "You'll be able to nap after lunch. If you remember, everyone rests in the afternoon; the house is very quiet then."

Acutely aware of Britt's withdrawing his touch, she forced herself to ask with seeming nonchalance, "Do you sleep?"

"I usually go through my account books, write letters, make lists, and the like," he answered.

"I should learn about that too," Melinda reminded and finally looked up at Britt. His eyes, which had been hard and bright with tension, slowly softened to an amber haze she'd never seen in them before.

Enang entered the room and approached them. "Arjuna has come."

The words were hardly out of his mouth when, like a golden bird, a little girl came flitting into the room, the lengths of her long, brown hair fluttering at each skip she took. She flashed Melinda an apprehensive glance as her own momentum carried her past, then stopped to face Britt. Pressing her hands together, she ducked her head in a quick gesture of respect, then looked solemnly up at him.

"A peppermint as reward, Tuan Britt?" she chirped.

"A reward for what?" he asked, already smiling agreement.

"Something I saw . . ." she began.

"Oh, that *child*!" A small, graceful woman wearing a floor-length sarong topped by a little jacket came into the room. Obviously trying to keep a stern look on her face as she gestured to the child to step away from Britt, she scolded in Javanese, "Daughter, where is your respect?"

Melinda had risen from her chair, and the woman, ready to hurry by, finally noticed her. She stopped before passing Melinda, pressed her hands together as if preparing to *dodok*.

"Please don't do that," Melinda said in Javanese as she put her hand under the woman's elbow. The woman raised her eyes, dark gray as the clouds during Java's rainy season. Melinda stared at her for a moment then whispered, "Malili?"

The woman smiled hesitantly. "Yes, it is I." She looked down again, nonplussed, not knowing how Melinda would treat her now that she was grown. But Melinda caught her hand.

Seeing Malili's expression and guessing what it meant, Melinda sobered and asked, "Did you think I'd forgotten we were friends? We used to steal sweets from the kitchen. I kept watch and you climbed up the cabinet doors."

"Things change when one grows up," Malili said reluctantly.

"Some things don't change." Melinda squeezed Malili's hand, then turned to the Javanese man who was watching silently. Taller than most Indonesians, as all Javanese, Arjuna was slender and fit. In the days of the Javanese court he would have been the kind of man who would have been chosen as a palace guard. Today he was dressed like Britt in a shirt and riding breeches. Though both Arjuna and Malili spoke English, Melinda decided to continue in their language to put them more at ease. "Arjuna, you were a friend, too, though more Britt's than mine. Do you remember me?"

"Yes, Mem Scott. I'd know those eyes a hundred years from now."

"You used to call me Minda," she said.

"Only when your mother couldn't hear. But we no longer are children." Arjuna's dark eyes were solemn. "My people don't call your people by first names."

"*I'll* call you Minda!" The childish offer was like a bell sweetly chiming in their adult silence.

"I wish you would call me Minda again, so I would know I'm really home." Melinda looked down into the little girl's face. "What, please, shall I call you?"

The child, remembering her mother's previous rebuke, demurred a moment before whispering with sudden shyness, "Panji."

Britt had observed Melinda's reaction to the family with interest. Noting that Panji as well as her parents were waiting to see what he thought of the little girl's addressing Melinda so informally, he said, "As you wish, Minda." He turned to his overseer. "I have a feeling you didn't come just to get reacquainted. What is it, Arjuna?"

"Malili wanted to help Minda with unpacking and I didn't want her and Panji to come down the path alone," Arjuna said. A worry crease appeared in his forehead. "Panji saw something near our village I thought you'd want to know about—tiger tracks."

Britt frowned. "I gather, from the look on your face, it may be our old enemy."

"One paw is twisted, as if it was born so," Arjuna confirmed.

A chill went through Melinda. "It's crippled?"

"Yes, an eater of human flesh," Arjuna said. "This tigress cannot catch normal prey, at least not enough to satisfy her appetite. A tiger cannot live on mice and birds like a housecat."

"She hasn't been around this district for some time. I'd hoped one of the soldiers had shot her," Britt said in a worried tone. Then he turned to Melinda and explained, "There were stories about a large tigress slinking around the battlefields when the Javanese were resisting the British, like a vulture waiting for a chance to snatch a body of one of the fallen. That crippled paw would have made it as difficult for her to escape the soldiers as it must be to catch her normal prey. I'm surprised she survived."

"She must be very clever to have lived even through her first year," Arjuna commented.

Britt calculated and said, "She must be seven or eight now and in her prime."

"My village will have a guard watching from dusk to dawn to prevent her carrying anyone off," Arjuna advised. "The other villages should do this too."

"But tigers don't usually approach villages, do they? Even maneaters will only take unburied dead or, if they're really desperate, children who stray from the village too far," Melinda said hopefully.

"This tigress is bolder. She's the one who killed my father." Britt's eyes reflected visions of remembered horror as he added, "He was half eaten when we found him."

Melinda shuddered.

"Before I do anything else, I'll have to take a look at those tracks to make sure this is the same tigress," Britt advised.

"I'm going too." Melinda saw that he was ready to protest and quickly asked, "I was supposed to go with you on your rounds, wasn't I? Isn't something like this part of what I should learn about? Wouldn't my father have gone with you?" As if the matter were settled, she turned to Malili. "I'm grateful for your offer to help me unpack, but if you're still willing, we'll have to do that tomorrow. Dessa can take out what I'll need until then."

"Dessa and I could still do it while you're gone, if you wish," Malili suggested. "It would keep Panji busy, too, and she wouldn't think so much about tigers. She's too brave sometimes and wanders too far."

"God forbid the child's curiosity should cause her to stray if that tigress is nearby," Britt said.

"Please, do stay," Melinda quickly agreed. "Panji's being here for the morning, at least until the heat rises, will keep her safe. Hopefully, her curiosity about the tigress will fade."

"So you remember tigers don't like the heat," Britt observed.

Melinda said ruefully, "Some of my returning memories may be more practical than others."

The tigress's tracks were impressively large, and Melinda was horrified when Britt estimated the animal to be over four hundred pounds—larger than other tigresses, though smaller than a male. As Melinda stared at the paw prints, her mind's eye saw four-inch fangs, imagined claws longer than her fingers. She was thankful Malili and Panji were safely at Phoenix House, not making their way through the jungle back to their village.

After Britt had chosen some workers from the nearest tea field to go to each village in the area and warn the people, he and Melinda rode on to the factory, where Arjuna said a mechanism appeared likely to break down soon. Melinda dutifully got off her horse to study the machine, which was powered by a donkey. It was a series of long, rectangular fan blades suspended above the racks of tea leaves. A system of cables moved the blades one way then the other to speed the tea's drying. It was these cables that had frayed in several places, seemingly overnight, because insects had attacked them. Britt judged they could last out the week, long enough for this load of tea to have dried, and decided to replace the cables then. Melinda carefully listened to Britt's explanation of how the mechanism worked and discovered its secrets weren't beyond her understanding. Afterward they continued strolling through the factory, a one-story building of bamboo woven walls, while Britt continued explaining how the tea was processed.

When they entered a section that extended for acres, Melinda noted that the stone floors were covered with tea leaves exuding a cloud of fragrance into the air. Britt explained that the leaves had been scattered on the floor so they'd wilt and not crack when they were gathered. The wilted leaves were spread on large cloths and curled by workers who gently shook the cloths so the leaves would roll. Great care was taken not to break the leaves, as they would bring a much lower price at the auctions in Europe.

It was well past noon when Britt suggested they return to the house. He promised to show Melinda on another day the fields, the nurseries for seedlings, and the places where the tea was finally graded and packed in boxes made on the plantation.

As Britt and Melinda passed a tree so full of birds it reminded her of a beehive, she heard singing in the distance. When they came closer to the sound, she recalled the song and its purpose. Women preparing a field for planting were singing as they worked. They had long rods of nibong wood they raised and thrust into the soil like spears until the holes they were making were big enough. Then, together, they pressed down on the rods, turned the earth, and moved on, using their song to keep their work in rhythm as well as make it more pleasant.

Melinda remembered such songs because they were monotonous, the kind a child would love and easily recall. As she and Britt passed the field, she sang along with the women, making Britt smile. Melinda was glad she could distract him from his worries, and she sang another Javanese melody to amuse him. She was humming a lighthearted tune when crashing noises in the forest ahead silenced her. It sounded like a large animal smashing the foliage and splintering branches. Alarmed, Melinda looked at Britt, who was sliding a rifle from the case attached to his saddle.

"It wouldn't be the tigress at this time of day, would it?" Melinda whispered fearfully.

"I think the horses would do more than prick their ears if it was something dangerous, unless the wind is carrying the scent away from us,'' Britt murmured, his eyes intently scanning the foliage ahead. "Tigers don't ordinarily make noise, but that man-eater isn't normal.'' He quietly cocked the gun, then kept it ready as the horses willingly continued down the lane. When he saw what was making the sounds, he let out a breath in relief and whispered, "Look there, Minda, through the trees, in that little clearing.''

Melinda peered in the direction he indicated. Her tension faded and was replaced by curiosity. Two rusta deer were in the clearing. One, a doe, was watching the other, which was causing the noises rummaging around in the foliage. Melinda couldn't see the second deer and wondered at its odd movements. Was it injured and suffering or defending itself from something near the ground? When the deer finally raised its head and emerged from the forest, Melinda saw it was a male, but rather than looking distressed, it seemed proud, almost swaggering in front of the doe. It had been thrusting its head through the greenery, and its antlers were festooned by leafy vines and flowers.

"It almost seems as if he wanted to decorate himself for her,'' Melinda breathed.

"He did,'' Britt's whisper confirmed.

As softly as they'd spoken, the deer heard them. The rusta whirled around, stared at them a moment, then ran leaping into the forest.

Britt slid his rifle back into its scabbard, commenting, "Even a deer wants to impress his ladylove.''

Melinda said wonderingly, "Despite the threats in his forest, he still courts his mate. How beautiful they are.''

"A deer hasn't the capacity to worry about danger until he perceives its possibility,'' Britt said, and nudged his horse to continue on the path.

"They're lucky they can't fret as we do,'' Melinda commented. "Though they thought they had to flee from us, maybe it was enough for her to appreciate his gesture.''

Still smarting from yesterday's incident with the soldiers, Britt hadn't forgotten its results and said curtly, "I'm not a rusta buck and you aren't a doe. Affectionate gestures would only remind me of how much more I want of you. Don't tease me, Minda.''

Melinda flashed him a startled glance. "I wasn't comparing them to us,'' she denied, then wistfully realized she had been. Recalling her morning's decision to think before acting, she realized wisdom didn't immediately follow resolution. She would have to remind herself about it often, to learn how it was possible to seal off the place in her heart Britt had so recently filled with love, safely dam up the emotions that threatened, if not to spill out in a rush, then leak in treacherous little trickles that tormented them more subtly.

Britt, too, was thinking regretfully that it was his own emotions driving him to see hidden meanings in casual remarks. He reflected on the vast difference between Minda's life in Philadelphia and the one she was being introduced to in Java, separated only by a voyage that had presented her with another situation that was new to her—days and nights of love. Recalling how Melinda had blanched at the sight of the tigress's tracks but had insisted on continuing with the morning's tour, how carefully she'd listened to his explanations and had surprised him with all the information she'd absorbed, Britt acknowledged, if she continued this way, if he gave her a fair chance, she would become an excellent partner.

Over lunch Britt complimented Melinda's efforts and found in her eager questions a desire to learn more. When she offered to spend the afternoon with him and the account books, Britt suggested instead that she rejoin Malili and Dessa. He knew a woman liked to decide the arrangement of her own bureaus and cabinets, inspect her wardrobe as each dress was shaken out, sprinkle her drawers with the potpourri of her choosing.

Melinda welcomed this chance but suspected Britt was putting her off—until she looked at his eyes. They were soft and hazy amber, like autumn in Philadelphia, a look she'd seen in them only once before, this morning. Although Melinda didn't know quite what it meant, she knew it had nothing to do with worry or pique. She was silently speculating on this when Arjuna again arrived with bad news.

The cables in the fanning machine had been in worse condition than they'd appeared and had snapped in several places. A couple of fan blades had fallen and scattered the drying tea. The machine had to be reassembled, new cables installed, and the undamaged tea sifted from the crumbled. Britt got up from his chair and stalked disgustedly from the room. Melinda anxiously followed him to the door.

"Can I help in some way?" she offered.

Looking down at her anxious eyes, Britt's vexation softened. "There's little you can learn from this, Minda. It's going to be a tedious, hot job. Arjuna and I will repair the machine, and a few of the workers who are especially nimble will sort out the tea without crushing too much more.'' He unthinkingly bent and kissed her cheek, then realizing what he'd done, quickly straightened. "How can I blame you for occasionally saying or doing things that stir me, when I only too easily forget my own resolution?'' he said quietly, then turned to walk swiftly through the garden toward the stable.

She watched until he disappeared. Finally, she went to her suite with his kiss burning her cheek like a spot of fire.

Melinda's bedchamber and sitting room were an obstacle course of opened trunks and stacked boxes. Dresses hung from anything that could hold them, and stacks of folded lingerie covered the bed. Dessa sat on the floor in a corner puzzling over a hodgepodge of shoes and slippers while Malili sorted an armful of petticoats. At Melinda's entrance both Javanese looked up in chagrin.

"It seems as if you need a little help,'' Melinda commented in Javanese.

Dessa rose, slippers tumbling from her lap. "I'm sorry, Mem Scott, the room is so disordered,'' she began.

Melinda shrugged. "It can be nothing else when you're unpacking. I can arrange those shoes, Dessa. You help Malili fold the petticoats.''

"Did you not plan to be with Tuan Britt this afternoon?'' Dessa inquired.

"Something broke at the factory and he had to see to it,'' Melinda said.

"The fan,'' Malili concluded, then looked curiously at Melinda. "You're troubled?''

Melinda delayed her answer by explaining to Panji how to fold the handkerchiefs she'd scattered over the dressing table.

"It isn't always easy to understand Tuan Britt,'' Dessa commented, assuming he and Melinda had quarreled.

Melinda glanced up in surprise.

"Secrets aren't kept very well in this household because the workers here are either related to each other or are friends,'' Dessa, embarrassed at her indiscretion, quickly said.

"I suppose gossip does fly, but I've been here less than a day,'' Melinda replied disgustedly.

Malili fixed her eyes on her work as she said, "It isn't so much your coming that's being talked about as the changes in Tuan Britt since that foreign woman's visit. Everyone is wondering what will happen if you stay.''

"What foreign woman?'' Melinda inquired.

"The one he had planned to marry. Elise she was called," Dessa promptly answered. Then she frowned. "She brought *lelembuts* with her and left them here when she departed."

Melinda searched her Javanese vocabulary; *lelembuts* were demons in the western view. "There are no *lelembuts* in Elise's land," Melinda denied. "How could she bring them here?"

"That foreign woman came to cause trouble," Dessa insisted. "She liked nothing about Java. I saw it in her eyes the moment she arrived, but she pretended so the *lelembuts* could do their mischief."

"Elise was new to Java. Some people can't get used to new places," Melinda explained.

"With her arrival came the death of Tuan Britt's mother. The foreign woman said she found Lady Sukadana dead in the garden, but we know she took her *lelembuts* to kill Lady Sukadana. She didn't like Tuan Britt's having a Javanese mother and wished to end Lady Sukadana's presence, which reminded her of it," Dessa said. When Melinda began to deny the story as fanciful, Dessa quickly continued, "Tuan Gerard went mad then, possessed by one of the spirits that foreign woman brought."

"Tuan Gerard was shocked and grieved," Melinda put in. "The man who killed Sukadana was caught."

"Tuan Gerard shot him," Dessa corrected, then explained her way of thinking. "Lady Sukadana's murderer was possessed by the foreign woman's demons too. Tuan Gerard wouldn't go to a *dukun* to be healed but drank brandy instead, which was as his *lelembut* wished. The spirit who lived in Lady Sukadana's murderer went to dwell in the tigress, which killed Tuan Gerard and now looks for Tuan Britt."

"Oh, please, Dessa, don't say such things!" Melinda implored. "I don't want to think of that beast stalking anyone, much less Britt."

"Tuan Britt loved the foreign woman and she wanted him, but when she learned she couldn't persuade him to go back to her land, she wanted revenge," Dessa said calmly. "It's proof that none of us, not even one of mixed blood, should look for love among those who come from across the water."

Malili put down the petticoat she'd been folding. Her dark eyes were grave as she said, "Tuan Britt was a lighthearted boy when we all were children together. His smile came easily to his lips before that foreign woman arrived. His sadness over Lady Sukadana's death and, later, Tuan Gerard's can be understood. But Tuan Britt hasn't returned to his old self yet. We believe it's because that woman's *lelembuts* remain in this house."

"Oh, really, both of you are telling such tales!" Melinda declared in exasperation. "Britt has had many worries on his mind, and even while my father was alive, this great house must have been a lonely place. *Lelembuts* can't be blamed for their being less than cheerful living alone in the middle of the jungle with such tragedies to contemplate. It has nothing to do with *lelembuts*. Lady Sukadana was killed because Matarami condemned her; Gerard died because his grief drove him to drink; a crippled tigress is a man-eater and nothing more."

"It's *lelembuts* who are already causing mischief between you and Tuan Britt. They know you love each other and wish to drive you away, for they also know your loving Tuan Britt will force them to leave," Dessa said placidly.

"But I only arrived last night!" Melinda declared. "Why should you think Britt and I are in love?"

"You loved each other as children. It's natural for you to love each other now as man and woman," Malili calmly answered. "You reveal it with every look that passes between you. Even your anger is proof."

"You said Britt shouldn't love someone from across the sea but that my love would drive away these *lelembuts*," Melinda reminded. "I'm from a land even farther away than Elise's. *I'm a foreign woman too*."

"No," Malili staunchly denied. "You were born here, and the fire spirits entered your being with your first breath. Your love will cleanse Tuan Britt of Elise's *lelembuts* as a volcano cleanses the earth of its impurities."

Seeing neither was likely to relent, Melinda dropped the subject, then bustled around the room to speed the unpacking. She didn't want to think of fire spirits or *lelembuts*, because to do so, even to deny the existence of the entire Javanese hierarchy of spirits, reminded her that Britt had loved Elise. Melinda had discovered a new quality in herself, one she didn't like—jealousy. The thought of Britt's loving any other woman brought visions so persistent they infuriated her. Elise was part of the past, she reminded herself; Elise had gone away. She herself didn't know what her and Britt's future would bring. But there was something deep in her being that couldn't prevent the images that rose in her mind of tender scenes between Britt and another woman.

Later, the unpacking finished, Dessa left with an armload of dresses to brush and air. Malili took Panji to the kitchen to chat with Koki while she waited for Arjuna's return. Wanting to get away from the house to sort out her thoughts, Melinda went for a stroll in the garden. Her jealousy was unreasonable, she reflected, and was shocked at herself for being so possessive. But Melinda couldn't deny that powerful feelings were the cause of her attitude, and there was only one answer for them she could think of. Love, so all-consuming it wouldn't tolerate reminders of Britt's even having had a past. The idea of being capable of such extreme emotions frightened Melinda because her parents' marriage had never given her even a glimpse of a love so passionate. Shaken by this discovery, trying desperately to somehow find another explanation, Melinda wandered farther from the house than she'd intended, to a place at the edge of the garden where she and Britt had played as children, where Panji was standing on the swing Charles had made for Melinda so long ago.

At the little girl's call, Melinda set her worries aside. As she approached, she said, "You shouldn't be so far from the house, Panji."

"There's nothing nearer the house to play with, Minda, and the kitchen cats have gone away somewhere," the child reasoned. Then she pleaded, "Do you know how to make this work? I can do nothing except climb on its chains or stand on this little step and jump off."

Melinda smiled. "My father made this for me when I was your age, but I think your legs are too short to make it work. You have to be able to touch the ground with your feet when you sit on it, unless there's someone to help you."

"Who helped you, Minda?" Panji inquired, not knowing her innocent question conjured up sunlit memories of Britt.

"Tuan Britt," Melinda answered.

"Please do it for me," Panji begged.

Melinda glanced apprehensively at the growing shadows of the nearby forest. "It's getting too near sunset. We shouldn't be so close to the trees."

"It's still light. Please, Minda, just a little, only once?" Panji pleaded.

Melinda surrendered to the dark liquid of the little girl's beseeching eyes. "Once only, just so you can know how it works."

After Melinda's repeated reminders for Panji to sit still—almost impossible for the excited little girl—and to hold the chains with both hands, Melinda drew the swing back and released it. As Panji glided forward, she let out a shriek of delight; then, when she returned to Melinda and found it wasn't the end of the ride, that Melinda gave her a little push, Panji screamed in surprise. Her continuing swings left arcs of laughter in her wake. Captivated by the little girl's happiness, Melinda, too, laughed aloud, got a strand of Panji's flying hair across her mouth and, lifting her head to shake it away, saw a pair of yellow eyes malevolently watching from the foliage. Melinda's heart gave a lurch. She caught the swing to stop it, hold it.

Panji turned to look questioningly up at Melinda.

"That's enough swinging for now, Panji," Melinda said, forcing her voice to remain low. "Go back to the house."

Panji's eyes clouded with suspicion as she noted Melinda's frozen expression. "What's wrong, Minda?" she asked. "Did I do something bad? Don't you like me anymore?"

"You did nothing wrong, Panji. I like you very much. But you must go to the house. *Now.* You must not look back, no matter what you hear. You must run," Melinda directed, all the while wondering how she kept her teeth from chattering.

Panji bowed her head and, still thinking Melinda was angry about something, turned to get off the swing seat. Then her sharp eyes glimpsed tawny stripes among the bushes. She gasped and ran behind Melinda.

The child didn't cry or even ask a question, but Melinda could feel Panji's small hands clutching at her skirts, the little girl leaning against her legs shivering in terror. Suddenly, all the day's pent-up emotions added to yesterday's gathered into an anger that exploded from Melinda like a volcanic eruption. She saw a heavy branch in the grass that had fallen from the tree and withered, caught it up, and screaming like a Fury, dashed straight toward the tigress.

"Get away, you devil! You got Gerard, but not Panji, not me!" Melinda shrieked and, with all the strength she could muster, hit the beast.

The tigress roared in pain as the dried twigs tore at her face, stabbed her nostrils, and seemed to claw at her sensitive ears. Melinda relentlessly thrust the branch again and again into the tigress's face, and the huge cat leaped back from the rustling weapon, from this human screaming, not in fear as she was accustomed to hearing, but in wordless rage. Melinda's reason had fled; she madly sprang after the tigress, lifted the branch and again swung it down on the beast's head in a resounding blow. Still insanely shrieking, she shoved the branch in the tigress's face, laughed in triumph at its screech of pain. The cat, astounded by the human's furious attack, hearing the sound of others coming, a gunshot, whirled away and bounded into the jungle.

Melinda stood transfixed, still gripping the branch as she watched the tigress vanish. Then, becoming aware of Panji's sobbing somewhere behind her as the little girl tried in disconnected words to tell someone what had happened, Melinda turned to collapse in Britt's arms.

Melinda opened dazed eyes. Seeing Britt's face near, aware of his arms enclosing her, she cried, "I'm all right! Shoot the tigress while you can, before she gets away!"

"She's long ago gone, Minda. You've been unconscious," he murmured, holding her even tighter.

"But Panji—where's Panji?" Melinda pulled away to glance wildly around. Expecting to see the edge of the jungle and its creeping shadows, her eyes leaped from orchid curtains to teak cabinets and a line of French doors, then returned to Britt.

"Panji's fine. Malili and Arjuna are soothing her," Britt was saying for the third time before he felt Melinda's arms reaching around him, clinging tightly, herself like a child trying to ward off the nightmarish memory. He continued repeating that she and Panji were safe, the tigress was gone, she was the bravest woman he'd ever met.

Melinda began to remember she'd awakened once dazedly as Britt had carried her into the house, then again several other times in her room, and realized she'd fainted repeatedly. Once Melinda accepted that she was in her own bedroom, her trembling lessened and finally stopped. She said against Britt's chest, "I shouldn't have let Panji coax me into giving her a swing. It was probably her laughter that drew the beast."

"I know how persuasive that child can be," he admitted, "but I never would have thought that tiger would come so close to the house. Maybe it was all for the best. No one was hurt, but now Panji understands very well why she should be more careful." Britt's hands on Melinda's shoulders moved her a little away so he could look at her face. "Do you know what a heroine you are? In half an hour the story has spread all over the plantation. By tomorrow morning even Djakarta will know how Mem Scott fought off the tigress."

"No, I didn't," Melinda denied. "She heard you coming, the gunshot. That was what drove her away."

"Not at all, Minda. A tiger is very quick and wastes no time killing something it attacks. From what Panji managed to describe, I'd judge that tigress was ready to spring on you. Even if you'd run, she could easily have caught and killed you both before we came," he said soberly. "When I saw you, the tigress seemed ready to run away. She never expected a human being to fight so ferociously. Like it or not, you're the heroine of the day."

Melinda laid her head on his shoulder.

"Try not to think about what might have happened," Britt said softly. "Instead, think about the celebration we're going to have."

"What celebration?" she murmured, not really interested. All she wanted was to stay close to him, be safe in his arms.

"I expected to have a party soon to introduce you to the other planters and their families, but the Javanese always celebrate a fortunate event, especially the saving of someone's life. The two can be combined into one party, though that will probably mean postponing it for a few weeks," Britt explained.

Minda sighed in resignation, then lifted her head to look at him and ask, "Did you ever get that fan thing repaired?"

Britt's expression of concern faded to amazement. "Yes, the fan is fixed and the tea was gathered up." He smiled and impulsively leaned closer to quickly kiss Melinda's nosetip, then laid his cheek against hers. "You're going to be a fine partner, if you can think about tea after you've driven away a man-eating tigress."

"I'll still be afraid to close my eyes tonight," Melinda admitted.

"No tiger or any other wild thing except birds can wander into this house; but if you wish, I can have a bed made in your sitting room and sleep there tonight," Britt offered. He waited for then felt her reluctant nod and remembered how he'd felt earlier. When he'd seen her in the distance confronting the tigress, he'd known in that brief moment exactly now precious she was to him. What he felt for Melinda transcended even physical love. Tonight he could have slept at her side without his body's demanding he do any more than protect her.

Chapter Nine

Though the Javanese on the plantation had treated Melinda with respectful courtesy from the moment she'd arrived, after she'd faced the tigress their attitude changed to joyous deference so lavish it embarrassed her. Where before she'd stopped them from making *dodok* with a word she'd not had to repeat, now when they began to sink into their graceful bow of respect and she tried to prevent it, they smilingly continued. They took to wearing head coverings in her presence, another complimentary gesture. Because in the Javanese court the heads of nobility always had to be higher than those of lesser rank, the Javanese paid Melinda this honor, often having to go through complicated maneuvers to keep their heads lower than hers. Dessa awakened Melinda in the morning by sitting on the floor, peering over the edge of the bed with one eye while reaching to touch her shoulder, and it was almost impossible for the maid to arrange her hair. Servants bent at the waist or knees struggled with heavy, covered tureens and hot, footed casserole dishes because Melinda was seated at the dining table. Out of compassion, Melinda found reasons to stand when she ordinarily would have sat, sit when she could have lain down, even step up on a footstool or stair when it was possible to tactfully do so.

Gifts of flowers, bells, colorful birds in ornately woven bamboo cages, bolts of cotton dyed with the preferred diagonal batik patterns called "soft rain," delicately painted fans, clusters of gorgeous feathers arrived till the house was filled with bouquets, twinkling bells, and birds.

Dessa said a little smugly that her people thought, if Melinda could drive away the feared tigress who was possessed by a *lelembut,* she'd send away all the demons that had been plaguing the plantation. Malili and Arjuna swore they'd do anything for her, and Panji was a golden shadow always skipping at her heels.

The honors paid Melinda made her self-conscious, but it also was impossible for her to be alone. She couldn't even step into the courtyard without someone producing a long-handled parasol—white, the color that shaded the *sunan*'s relatives—and followed until she went back indoors.

On the day of Melinda's party the women on the plantation began cooking before dawn, the men grating coconut, chopping spices, and digging pits to roast meat and fish. Even the children had been enlisted to decorate the grounds with strings of tiny bells, flower garlands, festoons of streamers, and fluttering fringes of tissue paper dyed every imaginable color. The workers were kept so busy by their tasks Melinda finally found a chance to slip away unnoticed in the afternoon.

She went to the farthest corner of the garden, where the old swing was and she'd confronted the tigress. There was no need to worry about the beast now because the noise and activity on the plantation would have frightened away even that man-eater.

Melinda's mind wasn't so much on the party as on what Dessa and Malili had told her about Britt; she reflected on how the events had affected him. While he'd already been shocked by Sukadana's death and must have been anxious about Gerard's state of mind, his first serious love affair had ended with his fiancée's desertion. Britt had had to take over the Vandekker share of the partnership almost immediately because of his father's dissipation, then had led the search party that had discovered Gerard's body. It all must have taken a heavy toll on his emotions, Melinda concluded. It was a wonder that he'd only become withdrawn, that his mind hadn't snapped after all these sorrows. Britt had never mentioned his reactions, talked as little as possible about any of it. Was this because the tragic events were still too painful or was it that he didn't want to seem to be seeking sympathy? Or was it both?

Though Melinda didn't believe in *lelembuts,* she wondered if everyone might have a kind of demon, a destructive part of themselves which, if allowed to dominate their decisions, eventually ruined their lives. Charles had been too stubborn to negotiate peace with her mother. Jessica had been too busy making her own life secure and comfortable to notice that Melinda's unhappiness was driving her away. Gerard had drowned his grief in brandy. Britt appeared to be too proud to confide in her and possibly find answers for his withdrawal. Melinda suddenly realized that Britt's readiness to suspend their love affair was not due to the problems it could cause their business partnership. *He didn't want to surrender to his emotions.* She wondered if he knew this. Did any of them understand the forces in their own beings, the fears that distorted their lives? With newfound wisdom, Melinda began to speculate about her own assortment of fears, but the sound of a gamelan beginning to rehearse for the party interrupted her chain of thought.

The sensuous but refined music so easily scattered the parts of Melinda's emotional puzzle she wondered if she wasn't ready yet to examine them that closely and finally stopped trying. The balmy afternoon seemed inappropriate for delving into hidden fears and motives. It had been made for more pleasant things, like listening to Javanese music. The music's intertwining elements were often incomprehensible to western ears, but not to Melinda's. She understood why the Javanese compared a song to a plant. The deeper drums and muffled gongs that kept the beat were the nourishing roots. The softer drums and vibrant bells carrying the melody—now accompanied by flutes and a bamboo zither—were the stem. The cymbals, bamboo, rattles, and delicate bells forming the ornamental accents were the leaves and blossoms. Melinda realized with a little jolt of surprise that she didn't know what the parts of western music meant and had never analyzed it.

Smiling at her ignorance of the world she'd spent most of her life in, Melinda stepped up on the swing's seat. She wondered about the long-lasting effects of her interrupted Java childhood, if her earliest years had more influence than later lessons. Melinda's musings were colored by the melody as she gazed at the thickly forested mountain slopes beyond the valley that surrounded the plantation, the fluted cone of a volcano, its smoke lazily drifting against the turquoise sky, and suddenly discovered that she felt as much a part of this land as Britt. She understood how Britt had felt on the *Harini* the day they'd seen Java in the distance. Finally, Melinda knew where she belonged. She'd go back to Philadelphia on visits, but not to stay. She'd enjoy Europe's charms while attending the tea auctions, yet she'd always return to Java. Melinda was no longer afraid she couldn't learn how to share the responsibilities of operating Phoenix House Tea; she knew it was possible to learn about anything one loved, even a puzzling man like Britt.

"I see that you finally found a way to escape the house without a parasol following."

Melinda smiled at Britt's approach. His presence was irrevocably merged with what she now knew she wanted. Britt's silent steps brought him to stop in front of the swing. Because Melinda was standing on the seat, she looked evenly into his eyes, clear amber regarding her. She felt as if he were drawing her closer, though he wasn't touching her. She knew he could see in her eyes how he was affecting her, but she didn't glance away. She no longer needed to ease the power of the magnetism between them.

Britt grasped the chains of the swing and wordlessly stepped up on the seat to face Melinda. His closeness stirred a welcome ache in her as she asked softly, "Do you remember how we played here as children, swung like this?"

He nodded, too absorbed in the nearness, the perfume of her, to speak. Then he moved so the swing began a gentle arc. "Just accommodate yourself to the rhythm. I'll do the rest," he murmured.

The swing's motion brought Britt's body to rest lightly against Melinda, then moved him away, his warmth reaching out, drawing her until, again, briefly, they touched, each arc lighting another copper spark in his eyes, one more fire in her. Melinda remembered the night of the storm on the *Harini;* the tempest luring her now was a more subtle one. She said nothing, though she recognized the same remembrance in his eyes. Wanting to wrap herself around him, she breathlessly endured the sweet pain of his nearness, stared at the message in his eyes that revealed he was as tempted as she. A kiss was trembling on her lips, ready for his taking, when Panji's voice broke in on them.

"Dessa said you should start getting ready for the party."

Britt hesitated, as if he wanted to prolong the moment, then reluctantly stepped off the swing. He steadied the chains, wordlessly took Melinda's hand to help her down, and kept her hand in his as they followed Panji back to the house. Though they occasionally answered the little girl's chatter with a comment, neither spoke to the other. They didn't need words to describe the emotion that flooded them. It radiated from their faces like a light neither could deny. There was nothing to do but let it exist.

* * *

While Dessa prepared Melinda for the party, Melinda didn't protest as she had during the last several days at the maid's elaborate ministrations. She was hardly aware of Dessa's presence. Her mind and heart were too full of Britt, her senses too absorbed in the memory of his touch. Time's passage meant little more than that she'd been bathed and perfumed and that her hair was suddenly a mass of curls falling from a flowered clasp at the crown of her head. Dessa, gathering up the gown Melinda had that morning chosen to wear for the party, laid it aside at a tap on the door.

It was Suhadi, Britt's servant, bringing an ebony box and an armful of apricot and gold silk with a note. The cloth became a shimmering, floor-length saronglike gown whose graceful folds softly clung to Melinda's body. The box revealed lustrous Javanese pearls set in Singapore gold sprinkled with diamond slivers—a necklace, bracelets, and an ornament to replace the clasp in her hair. The note explained that the jewels would have been Charles's surprise gift to Jessica had she stayed long enough for the pieces to be finished. The silk had caught Britt's eye in Rangoon on his way to Philadelphia, and on his return he'd had Malili sew the gown.

When Melinda, dazzled by both gifts, turned from her mirror, it was to face Dessa deep in the bow of *dodok*. "No, please," Melinda began, but the maid dipped forward to her knees and kissed the instep of her golden slippered foot. Melinda speechlessly watched Dessa rise.

"It's a gesture of respect deeper than *dodok*, one I know dismays you, Mem Scott, but one my heart wished to give," Dessa said warmly. As the maid led Melinda into the hall, she added, "Let the others show their gratitude without worrying that they debase themselves. They do not. It's an outpouring from their hearts also, and they won't be satisfied if you don't allow them to give you this gift."

Britt was waiting in the entrance hall near the door. His face lit at the sight of Melinda and he commented, "That gown fits you better than I'd dared hope. Malili was afraid she wouldn't get it right because she couldn't take apart the dress of yours she used as a pattern."

"The gown is beautiful; the silk's exquisite, Britt," Melinda sincerely replied, then commented, "I appreciate your thoughtfulness, but I have to wonder why you bought the cloth even before reaching Philadelphia."

"I'd intended to present you with some sort of gift and thought a bolt of silk wouldn't be considered too personal, but after I'd gotten a little acquainted with you and saw the problems you were having with Alden and your mother, I had doubts that any gift would be wise." Britt's eyes glowed with provocative warmth as he explained. "I'd remembered what you looked like as a child and could only hope the colors would suit you now, which I can see they do."

"Since you'd given me a sarong to wear to this party, I'd wondered if you'd be dressed Javanese style, if that was the kind of party it was going to be, but you're very handsome in a western suit." Melinda's eyes were unabashedly admiring the sun-toasted gold of his skin against his ivory jacket.

Britt smiled with pleasure at her compliment and tucked her arm under his. "Are you ready?"

"I wish this was just another party and everyone wasn't making such a fuss over what happened," she said doubtfully.

"It isn't every day that a child is rescued from a tiger, but everyone will be more dazzled by your beauty tonight than even the tale of your heroism, I think," Britt commented. He squeezed the hand holding his arm and smilingly led her through the doorway.

The house servants were gathered on the veranda, all sinking in *dodok* at Melinda's appearance, which embarrassed her. A crowd of plantation owners waited on the lawn. Melinda acknowledged their compliments and greeted them with smiles as Britt introduced them to her and was so taken by his pleasure at presenting her that she forgot her misgivings at meeting so many strangers. After they'd toasted Melinda's success as Britt's new partner and congratulated her on fending off the tigress, Britt led the company to a section of the grounds where chairs and a series of tables had been placed to form one long table on the lawn.

The fading day charged the air with an orange-gold tint that made the grass appear blue and everything white take on a deep rose reflection. A servant moving through the purple shadows became a boneless silhouette lighting torches, the glimmering flames he brought to life adding to the enchantment of the scene. Couples sipping wine from crystal goblets lit by the sinking sun strolled between scarlet torch ginger under trees lush with varicolored hibiscus. Jasmine climbing arbors exhaled a perfume that effectively competed with the gardenia bushes and the table bouquets of frangipani, which was called "charmers of the night" by the Javanese. The garden, a sensual delight, was taking on a strangely mystical atmosphere as the sun sank nearer the horizon, seeming like a dream to a dreamer who knew it to be an illusion, but whose senses were more vivid than during waking hours.

Several Javanese men, walking shoulder to shoulder to form a circle, held lengths of cloth above their heads as they carefully made their way to the middle of the open area. The cloths, which brushed the ground, made a round tent that screened what was at its center. The men stopped walking, then stood as motionlessly as if they were cast from bronze while the planters found their places at the tables and the Javanese workers settled themselves on mats in the grass. Britt led Melinda to the head of the table, where two chairs awaited them.

The makeshift tent was swept away; the men swiftly withdrew to the shadows. A pair of girls barely more than children were standing back to back, the folds of their skirts and the long, slim sleeves of their golden gowns lit to fire by the last rays of the sun. The tiny flowers nodding from wires in their headdresses danced in shimmering iridescence over their profiles, which were as serene as if they were carved from ivory. They seemed to take no notice of their captivated audience or the music softly rising from the gamelan. Of the same height, they were as much alike as twins. When one girl raised a hand, the other duplicated the motion, like a reflection in a mirror. They tilted their heads at the same angle, took a step forward, and still facing away from each other, began to dance.

They moved in stylized restraint. The fluid motions of their hands, the very arching of their fingers, were identical. It was like an optical illusion, Melinda thought, as if her eyes were out of focus and she was seeing double. The slowness of the dancers' gestures would have made it impossible to hide the smallest flaw in their performance, but there wasn't even a hint of tension on the girls' faces. They remained coolly expressionless, above human emotion. Another dancer appeared from the shadows, man or woman Melinda couldn't guess, wearing the mask of a demon and an elaborate robe that marked the demon as a tiger.

Melinda understood then that the dancers were portraying her encounter with the man-eater, and she tensely wondered if this performance would merely tell the story to honor her or be a celebration of the Javanese hopes that she could somehow destroy the beast.

At the appearance of the tiger-demon, the girls suddenly broke position, like an explosion of shattered glass, and darted in opposite directions. One dancer flitted about like a hummingbird, her fluttering hands and other fearful gestures accomplished with infinite elegance. The low, bell-like tones of the gamelan somehow took on the velvet padding of a stalking beast as the dancer portraying the tiger seemed to threaten the girls. But in one fluid movement the one who wasn't afraid shook out a fan and waved it gracefully in the tiger-demon's face, closed the fan and tapped the mask with its tip, then, with a little push away, caused the tiger-demon to sink to the grass, indicating its death. After a few slow circles the girls finally drew together, back to back, returning to a mirrored image so motionless that only the flower-tipped wires of their headdresses were left gently trembling.

Melinda was breathless at the beauty of the performance, but she recognized its full meaning only too well. The girl dancers weren't she and Panji but two sides of herself, one side mortal and afraid, the other given mystic power to kill the tiger. Because the animal was portrayed as a demon and Melinda had not, in reality, killed the beast, she knew the Javanese really were looking to her as somehow being able to deliver them from the jaws of the man-eater and the *lelembuts* causing the tragedies at Phoenix House.

Noting Melinda's expression, Britt commented, "You understand what the dancers were saying."

Melinda nodded but didn't speak.

He took her hand and brought it to his lips. When she glanced up in surprise at his kiss, he said softly, "For some, this dance was an expression of wishful thinking. The others, like Dessa, who really believe you have the power to destroy the tigress, don't expect you to personally kill the beast. They only think your presence at Phoenix House will set to rights the normal currents of the atmosphere that were displaced by Elise's coming."

Melinda stared at Britt. He'd never spoken about Elise other than to admit he'd been engaged to her. She said hesitantly, "Dessa told me they thought Elise brought *lelembuts* to Phoenix House, that she was evil and left them here."

Britt slowly shook his head. "Elise wasn't evil. My mother's death, my father's rage, frightened her. She used her fear as an excuse to leave, but she was only a girl from a faraway place who never felt comfortable in Java. The truth is, she didn't love me enough to stay."

"I don't know how any woman could love you in small portions if she loved you at all," Melinda mused.

Britt smiled as he turned Melinda's hand to kiss her palm. "I was naïve, as innocent when Elise left as I'd been when she arrived."

Melinda's eyes met his as he added, "I decided then that people couldn't very well judge each other's personal qualities, couldn't decide whether they'd be good partners in marriage, while their heads were spinning with unsatisfied desire. I resolved that the next time I thought I was in love I wouldn't restrain myself, but would even coax the lady into bed so I might afterward think more clearly."

Melinda stared at him as if mesmerized, afraid to ask a question or even breathe. Britt lifted one hand and lightly touched her cheek with his fingertips, lingering as if he really wanted to wind his hand into her hair, pull her to him.

"My theory didn't work," he said softly. "Making love with you didn't clear my mind but threw it into worse confusion." Then he withdrew and sat back in his chair to watch the line of servants coming to the table with dishes of food.

The couple seated nearest them, Mr. and Mrs. DeGroot, commented favorably on the party as the appetizers were set on the table: dishes of little red fish called *sambal*, which deliciously burned the mouth, shrimp and chunks of crab fried crisp and gold with saffron, skewers of *saté*, bites of turtlemeat basted with spiced oil and roasted on a charcoal fire. While tasting the appetizers, Mr. DeGroot began to discuss the possibilities of hunting the tigress with Britt. He drew Melinda into the conversation by asking questions about the man-eater's behavior during her encounter with it. While dishes of fluffy rice were carried in to be mixed with a variety of colorful sauces, some hot, others mild, Mr. DeGroot recalled previous hunts he'd taken part in for other animals that, in one way or another, had threatened the settlers from Holland. Melinda listened to his stories with great interest, because they gave insight on how Java had been when Charles and Gerard had first come.

Mrs. DeGroot, who not only had lived through these experiences but had heard them recounted many times, turned to another lady and in discreet whispers speculated about Britt and Melinda's living alone in the house except for servants. The subject flashed along the length of the table like a grass fire, leaving the women guessing where the possible affair would lead as they surveyed platters of artichokes, baskets of avocados, bowls of fried tomatoes, and *urab*, a finely chopped mixture of coconut and papaya. A roast pig came on a platter lined with banana leaves, its skin as brittle as thin glass, its meat richly perfumed from the spices and aromatic leaves it had been stuffed with, so tender as to finally still the tongues it melted on.

During the meal the gamelan continued to play and the music—a bright, clear sound broken into a mixture of patterns fluidly threading into each other—radiated a quiet joy.

As the company relaxed over cups of tea or coffee, dessert was served—grated coconut flavored with verbena and mixed with palm sugar, little balls of rice paste filled with sweet syrup, acacia blossoms, chunks of mangoes, and bananas sautéed with nutmeg.

Mrs. DeGroot, who had seen Britt kiss Melinda's hand and affectionately touch her face while they'd been talking in low tones, started a casual conversation with Melinda. Realizing that the woman's goal was to discover, if possible, whether the couple were lovers, Melinda put on an air of such cool formality that the woman was fooled, as all Philadelphia had once been, into believing Melinda to be as aloof as the moon, as passionless as a statue. Mrs. DeGroot couldn't guess how difficult it was becoming for Melinda to maintain her façade of composure when Mr. DeGroot's sprawling limbs allowed so little space under the table she had to keep one of her legs tightly pressed against Britt's. Melinda was finally rescued from the woman's questions by a troupe of actors coming into the clearing to begin a play.

At first it seemed the story was merely the traditional tale of a princess being carried from the arms of her intended, then being rescued by the prince. But as the play unfolded, Melinda and Britt exchanged glances as they recognized their own history being portrayed with only a few alterations. Under the table's sheltering flounce, they clasped hands, forcing themselves not to flinch as the prince's parents were one at a time devoured by a fantastic mystical animal. Britt and Melinda knew the creature symbolized the *lelembuts* the Javanese believed inhabited the plantation's grounds. The play's climax showed the prince bravely but unsuccessfully battling the animal, until the princess plucked one of the ornaments from her costume. She held the creature at bay with its magical power until, vanquished by the prince, the beast vanished.

Britt knew Melinda was troubled by this second referral to the mystical influence she was believed to have over the tigress. Hoping to lighten her mood, he turned to her and whispered, ''Wouldn't it be convenient if you really had a charm that would paralyze the tigress so I could kill it?''

Melinda sighed and answered, ''Everyone seems convinced *I'm* the charm.''

Britt was about to reassure Melinda that these tales were nothing to concern herself over, but he fell silent as the low murmur of other conversations at the table was abruptly hushed and a large group of Javanese men stepped out of the shadowy foliage.

The leader was dressed in white pantaloons gathered and held at the ankles by gold clasps that glimmered in the torchlight as he walked smoothly toward the table. His chest was bare except for an abbreviated gilt-embroidered jacket that had neither sleeves nor closings on the front. A rifle was slung from a tasseled strap over his shoulder, and a sword was fastened at his waist. Like the men accompanying him, his sword was worn with its handle toward the front of his hip within easy reach, not toward the back, as it would be worn by a man who thought himself among friends. The grim expression on his face made Melinda's heart hammer fearfully as Britt stood up and moved forward to meet the approaching men. She followed but stayed a few paces behind him.

Britt exchanged stiffly formal greetings with the leader, then said in quiet reproach, "There's no need to come to Phoenix House so heavily armed, unless you intend to restart the trouble between our families."

"Unlike my grandfather, I don't blame the Vandekkers for my father's death or my mother's wish to remarry," the Javanese answered quietly. Then he raised his voice and said in English so everyone could understand, "These weapons aren't meant to threaten you or your company but to kill the tigress that play just now portrayed."

Finally realizing this was Rakata, Melinda drew in a breath of surprise.

Rakata's dark eyes moved over her, then returned to Britt as he said, "Two days ago Raden Matarami was killed by the man-eater."

Although Britt was stunned by this news, he knew the Javanese thought that to express sorrow or even sympathy about a death did the departed's soul ill. He gave a traditionally courteous reply; "I'm sorry I wasn't able to see him before this happened."

Rakata nodded solemnly. Again lowering his voice so no one could hear except Britt and Melinda, he said in Javanese, "It is curious, is it not, that my grandfather and your father, bitter enemies as they were, should be killed by the same tigress? Perhaps the beast is, as many think, a demon of fate."

"The destinies of our houses seem to be interwoven, whether we wish it or not," Britt commented.

"So my grandfather's soul needn't fly into eternity with your rancor following, I must tell you that he never intended for Lady Sukadana to die, which was why he didn't have her executed immediately after her banishment. Matarami wished in his declining years that he could have seen her again, but he thought it was too late and he was too proud to admit he might have been wrong.''

"This is surprising news to me and difficult to accept," Britt admitted.

"Perhaps it will be easier for you to believe if I tell you my grandfather was aware that my nursemaid and her lover took me to Durga for visits with you and our mother when we were children. When the nursemaid became afraid that someone would betray her and stopped the visits, my grandfather could say nothing without revealing that he'd known about the trips, and he was too stubborn to admit he regretted banishing our mother,'' Rakata said in the same low tone, adding, "But perhaps you don't remember Durga.''

"I remember," Britt replied thoughtfully. He was silent a moment, absorbing this news. Then, realizing the other planters were curious about the hushed conversation, he finally said clearly, "How did Matarami's death come about? I would have thought he was too wise in the ways of the jungle to be trapped by any beast.''

Understanding that Britt meant to ease the planters' minds, Rakata replied in English, "He was wise, but sometimes willful. He told everyone he wished to nap and ordered them not to disturb him. He then slipped away so quietly no one knew he'd gone outside Talu's walls to a place where he liked to meditate. When his nap seemed overlong, I went to awaken him and discovered he was gone. We had to search for him well into the night because the tigress had hidden his body to finish later.''

Britt inwardly shuddered but said quietly, "It was as she'd done with my father.''

"Beast or demon, I will give her no peace until she's dead," Rakata vowed.

Britt asked softly, so the other planters couldn't hear, "What about *our* peace? Now that you're assuming Matarami's place, I must wonder if you'll rebel against the soldiers or the planters.''

"It would be fruitless for me to resist the foreigners now. I must continue to dream of freedom and hope the British and Hollanders will destroy each other," Rakata murmured.

Noting that Rakata's eyes were again flicking over Melinda, Britt said, "This is Charles Scott's daughter, Melinda, and my new partner in Phoenix House Tea."

"I know who she is as well as what she did," the Javanese advised. A glimmer Melinda couldn't read went through his dark eyes as he added, "If she is as favored by the gods as many of my people think, perhaps she'll rid the land not only of the tigress but of the British as well." Without another word he turned and vanished into the shadows with his men.

Though the Hollanders had heard Rakata's announcement about Matarami's death, few of them believed he would try to keep peace with the British. They had the same opinion as Major Wakefield, that the Javanese already had enough weapons to rebel and needed only some small excuse to begin a war. They speculated about this for a time; then, hoping to gain favor with the new *raden*, they began to discuss ways to kill the tigress and present its carcass to Rakata as a gift. The party broke up early because the plantation owners wanted to awaken before dawn so they could begin tracking the man-eater.

Watching the last of his guests depart down the driveway, Britt commented, "They'll never get that tigress merely by following her tracks. She'll lead them on a long trek through the jungle, and when she's had enough of her game, they'll suddenly lose her trail."

"Why do you say that?" Melinda asked. "They seem like men who know what they're about."

"So do I," Britt said softly. "But after she killed my father, Arjuna and I tracked that tigress for a long time—many times—always with the same result. I felt almost as if she were a demon taunting me."

Chapter Ten

Melinda looked apprehensively up at Britt. "Do you believe in *lelembuts, memedis,* and *tujuls*?"

"Demons, ghosts, and goblins? No, Minda. I was describing how intelligent that tigress is. It was an unfortunate choice of words," he answered, then tucked her hands between his as he noted, "Rakata's coming out of the jungle with his men that way was frightening after everything else that's happened, especially added to the stories Dessa's been telling you. I instructed the dancers and actors that this party was to welcome you to Java as well as celebrate your escape with Panji from the tigress. I never expected them to attach mystical significance to any of it; I'll never engage them again."

"The performances were wonderful. I'm sure the dancers and actors thought a little fantasy would add interest," Melinda said, excusing the artists. "It's just that the thought of Matarami's being killed by that beast is horrible." She shuddered, adding, "I keep remembering those awful fangs and how long its claws were. I think I'll see them for the rest of my life."

Britt made a mental note to tell Dessa not to upset Melinda with tales of *lelembuts* and *memedis*. He laid his hands gently on Melinda's shoulders and said sympathetically, "You must try not to think about things like that. The tigress is only one of nature's creatures, doing what she must, because of her crippled leg, to survive."

Melinda so badly needed Britt's strength she forgot the agreement they'd made and the temptation their closeness afforded. She leaned against him, her voice muffled by his chest as she asked, "Is that what you had to remind yourself of after your father was killed? Did it really help to ease the visions that must have been haunting you?"

Britt felt her breath like a flame searing him through his clothes, but he said softly, "Yes, eventually." He stepped back and looked down at her. "What happened to you was terrifying, my father and Matarami's deaths were tragic, but none of it has to do with demons or the supernatural. In fact, that brief look I got at the tigress, as she fled our garden, makes me suspect she's pregnant. If so, she's been hunting so persistently to nourish her unborn cubs."

Melinda glanced up at him in surprise. "Cubs?"

"*Lelembuts* don't have babies—or anyway, none I've heard of," Britt assured. Putting an arm around Melinda's waist, he suggested, "Let's go back to the garden and have a bit of sherry. It will help you relax."

Melinda wasn't able to hide the fear still clouding her eyes as she asked, "Do you think it's safe to sit in the garden at this hour with the tigress loose in the forest so close?"

"Talu, the city Rakata governs, is a day's ride away, and the tigress isn't likely to prowl here so soon again. I doubt she'll hunt tonight at all," he assured.

"Because she recently made a meal of Matarami?" Melinda shivered at the thought.

"Don't think about that, Minda." Britt firmly started guiding her back around the house. "Animals are wary of fire, and *any* creature will be frightened away by the torches. Don't you think it will be pleasant to sit quietly together without planters discussing how to track down marauding beasts while their wives are whispering about us?"

"I'd hoped you hadn't noticed the gossip," Melinda admitted as Britt seated her at the table.

He told Suhadi to get them sherry, then sat and regarded her silently a moment before he remarked, "They've been gossiping about me for a long time. I've gotten used to it."

"You mean because of Elise's leaving?" Melinda ventured.

"Yes, that, but also, because Rakata's my half brother, what happened to my father and Sukadana." Britt sighed and, noting Melinda's expression, asked, "Does it bother you too much to be linked with me in their gossip?"

Melinda smiled wanly. "We left all of Philadelphia society wagging their tongues about us, so I guess a few planters' wives won't concern me too much. I should have expected them to talk about our living in the same house this way, and the truth is, they're right. We were lovers, for a while." She noticed his brief frown and quickly added, "Romantic gossip is easier for me to contend with than a man-eating tigress and *lelembuts* anyway."

Their conversation was interrupted by Suhadi's bringing the sherry. After he stepped back into the shadows, Britt began to tell Melinda more about the people who had come to their party. Some, like Britt and Melinda, had tea plantations, others coffee and sugar. A few harvested spices or the milky liquid oozing from trees called rubber, which had recently found so many uses in the West. Mr. DeGroot's business, Melinda learned, was teak. As she grew more absorbed in the conversation, her mood began to lighten. Some of the anecdotes Britt told her were amusing and even made her smile.

The ominous feelings that had permeated the night gradually withdrew from the garden, and the darkness beyond the cheerful flickering of the torches lost its dread. Pockets of blackness once again were only shadows. The air, weighted by fear, became a balmy breeze floating with the perfume of jasmine and frangipani. No longer was the jungle populated by yellow glowing eyes malevolently watching Melinda. Instead, fireflies danced beneath the trees, their winking lights reminding her of long-ago dreams only beginning to be fulfilled before they'd been snatched away. She wished things could be different now for her and Britt, that this quiet moment could be the prelude to a night spent in his arms. The stars in the calm black dome of the sky were like dreams too distant to grasp, swirls of shimmering hopes she could only gaze at and long to someday touch again. But presently a thin film of clouds began to blur the diamond points of the stars into softly glowing specks; and Britt, feeling the change in the atmosphere, paused fom his conversation to glance up at the sky.

"*There's* something about Java I'm sure you'll remember—the rain. I think we'll have some tonight," he said.

Melinda, watching how the torchlight was reflected in his eyes as they scanned the heavens, wistfully remembered the spring shower at Amanda's party, the cottage where she and Britt had first made love. Captured by such memories, she murmured, "You're probably right. I suppose we should go inside."

Britt's eyes caught a glimmer from the torches as he looked uncertainly at her. She watched a series of thoughts flit through them, as if he briefly considered questions he might ask, but he said nothing. He finished his sherry without looking at her again, seeming lost in his thoughts, while Melinda longed to reach out to merely touch him, if nothing more could be allowed them.

The moon was a silver scimitar slicing at the gathering clouds, turning them into rags, when Britt lifted his eyes and said "Let's go in."

Melinda's pulses became a wild fluttering in her temples as she hoped Britt's words meant more than they said. She put down her glass and took his hand as she got to her feet. His touch sent a shock wave streaking along her nerves and she glanced up at him. He wasn't looking at her; she couldn't see if the same shimmering thrill had flashed through him.

Though Britt kept Melinda's hand in his as he led her into the house, he didn't pause at the doorway to his ell of the building. She wondered if he walked past it a bit too quickly, if that meant anything one way or another. Then they were in the courtyard standing before the French doors Dessa had left open. Across the corridor just a few steps away was Melinda's bedroom; the doors to that, too, were invitingly open.

Britt stood silently looking down at Melinda a long moment. The shadows obscured his features so she couldn't guess what he was thinking, though she was sure her face must reveal every desire pulsing through her. He lifted her hand, brushed it to his lips, lingered before he put a kiss in her palm and closed her fingers around it. Without a word, Britt turned and crossed the courtyard to his room. Melinda watched, her heart beating with the rhythm of his silent steps until he vanished in the shadows.

Melinda lay awake listening to the wind rustle the palm fronds, thinking that Britt had been right about a lot of things—he'd helped her learn much about herself she'd never have been able to accept in Philadelphia—but he wasn't right about their agreement to suspend making love. They'd *both* been wrong about that. The visions of the tigress that had been haunting her were replaced, as she fell into a fitful sleep, by memories of Britt's eyes on her, his passion mirrored in them like an amber flame waiting.

The sound of persistent thumping brought Melinda to vague awareness too unfocused for her to immediately understand what the noise was. A soft rush of cool air finally made her realize the wind was making the door bump against the wall. She was about to turn and sit up when a soft click told her the door had been snapped shut. Drowsily assuming it was Dessa, Melinda was about to reclose her eyes when a lightning flash revealed Britt's shadow on the wall.

Melinda's mind snapped to alertness; ready to sit up, to eagerly call to him, she hesitated. The brief glimpse hadn't told her whether Britt was inside the room or she'd seen him through the panes of glass. Had he heard the thumping and merely come to close the door? If so and she ran to him only to discover he'd already left and was on his way back across the courtyard, she'd be left standing alone in the doorway, looking after him. Melinda didn't want Britt to know she would go running after him even if he didn't want her to.

Then she heard a whisper of cloth, as if the folds of a robe were shifting while silent feet paced the room. She held her breath, wondering if she'd been mistaken. A soft, metallic sound revealed a hand on the door handle, considering. The handle turned slowly. Was Britt inside the room and, having found her adamantly asleep, ready to leave? Not caring about pride, forgetting that her newfound emotions could drown out wisdom, intending to run to Britt anyway, Melinda quickly turned and found herself in his arms.

Feeling as if he could crush Melinda to him, instead Britt held her lightly, steadied his voice enough to ask quietly, "Are you having trouble sleeping because of the storm?"

Against his cheek, the soft warmth of her breath said, "I haven't been afraid of storms since that night on the *Harini*."

The love they'd shared during the tempest on the ship was a flame wildly dancing through Britt's memory, and he couldn't prevent his head from turning, his mouth from seeking hers. Melinda's arms tightened around him as the warmth of his lips covered hers, moved restlessly, hungrily, for an instant before they abruptly withdrew.

Still clinging to him, she said breathlessly, "I can't sleep; I have no appetite. I can hardly think about anything except wanting you."

Gently but firmly, Britt broke Melinda's hold on him and moved a little away to look at her. The struggle he was having denying himself was shortening his patience, each day stirring up the coals of his temper, which might eventually explode with an impulsive flame that could cause more trouble between them than being lovers ever could.

"I can't bear the agreement we made," she whispered.

Another flash of lightning made a streak of amber in his eyes as he softly agreed, "Nor I."

His flattened hands moved to her temples. His fingers twining in her hair tilted her face again to his. Britt's mouth moved searchingly over Melinda's face, circling as the wind outside was swirling in the courtyard. He followed the line of her brows, caressed the fringe of her lashes, then slid to her ear, his tonguetip tracing its whorls until his breath made her shiver. Then his mouth captured her lips, stroked them sensually, so urgently she felt as if the lightning that lit the night flashed through her body and the passion seething in her erupted in an explosion of fire that incinerated her mind—anything left in her that might still have reminded her of caution.

Britt's hands left Melinda's temples, moved rapidly over her throat and shoulders, down her arms, hungrily renewing his knowledge of her skin. They ran along her hips, grew impatient with the gathers of the nightdress, then slid up her sides to her breasts. While Britt's mouth searched Melinda's, his fingers, heedless of the lace that shielded her flesh, sent new waves of desire through her. Stunned by the magnitude of the impulses bursting along her nerves, unable to contain them, she gasped aloud.

Britt's hands paused in their caresses and his lashes parted. Amber eyes, alive with copper sparks, intently watched Melinda as his fingertips continued to lightly, persistently, tease her nipples. Then, as if he couldn't endure even this brief moment of moderation, eyes still fixed on hers, Britt hooked his fingers in the gossamer of her gown, penetrated its lace, and tore it to the hem.

As the first sheet of rain lashed the windows, he swiftly untied his sash and tossed the robe aside, then, kicking away the last folds of net screening the bed, slid into the silken tent it formed around them.

Melinda closed her eyes and sighed as she felt Britt's hands grasping her shoulders, his chest hot against her breasts, firmly pushing her back. She welcomed the lips that took hers, caressed avidly, lingeringly, until she became a molten thing beginning to flow along his contours.

As Britt's legs began to curve around Melinda's, a flicker of lightning made an orchid flash around the bed and he stopped himself. Turning his face away, pressing his mouth to the side of her neck, he murmured, "It's too soon. I don't want this to go so quickly."

"I don't want to wait," Melinda said, her voice sharpened by desire.

Still intending to kiss her with more restraint, Britt was undone when her tongue became a flame licking at his lips, scorching him. His mouth grew harder, more demanding, and he claimed her kiss as if he were a conqueror ravishing a captured maiden.

As his mouth crushed hers, their legs groped eagerly, met like flames intertwining, fused them together. She whimpered against his lips, quickening his passion to heights that left him with only the last, rapidly disintegrating threads of his will. Trying to regain some shred of control, he paused.

Melinda's eyes flew open, their smoldering emerald depths silently imploring, while her body, trembling under his, swept away any thought of restraint. Britt's need became his master, an all-consuming force lashing his senses beyond their limits until his darkness, like the night, shimmered for an ecstatic moment in a lightning flash, then exploded with the thunder that bolted through them.

They lay unmoving, listening to the reverberations of the dimming storm, silent, but for their breathing, until the rain made a more gentle patter on the windows.

Finally Britt shifted, raised his head as if he would move to her side, but Melinda's arms tightened around his back.

"I want you never again to get any farther from me than this," she whispered.

No longer caring about the problems tomorrow could bring, wanting to remain forever lost in love, Britt lowered his head to rest on Melinda's breast and curled her arms around him.

Melinda awakened with sunshine warming her eyelids. She opened them and looked down to see Britt still sleeping with his head on her breast, his arms curled loosely around her, as if he hadn't moved one muscle the rest of the night. Reclosing her eyes, Melinda thought about the storm of love that had brought them together and wondered what she could do to prevent them from separating again. To manage that, Melinda realized she'd have to understand what had driven them apart.

Though Melinda's body was so relaxed she felt weightless, her mind was extraordinarily alert as she considered the factors that had brought them to this point. New insights, bright and clear, formed in her thoughts, then fell in line with the ease of crystal beads sliding into place on a waxed string. Finally she discovered she'd learned as much about Britt as she had about herself.

It was because their passion ran so high they lost themselves in it that all pretense was burned away to leave them as they were now, emotions as naked as their bodies. It was the intense emotion, the deep sensuality of their natures, that could destroy them or make everything they were building together possible. She doubted anything between those two extremes was likely. Normally not a gambler, Melinda knew she had no choice but to accept the challenge this situation offered—because she loved Britt.

Melinda recognized she'd have to learn how to sometimes leash or moderate her emotions, a feat many people well acquainted with passion never fully accomplished. She thought of how reserved Britt appeared, despite his volcanic nature, and knew even he wasn't always successful at controlling it. Comparing him with Alden, she understood that Alden only seemed controlled; in reality, he had no depths to struggle with. Finally, Melinda understood that this was why Alden had awakened no desire in her. His image faded in her mind, becoming as colorless as a picture left too long in the sun.

Her eyes moved down to gaze at the man sleeping on her bosom, this man whose future was merged with hers. Thinking about the enormity, the wonder, of their love as she gazed at Britt, she took in details about him she hadn't noticed before.

His hair, now so brightly gilded by the sun, was too thick to stay obediently in a part. Though his brows, set almost straight on his face, were finely drawn and unruffled by the turbulent night, his lashes were tangled. She could see now, as they lay lightly against his cheek catching the sun's gold at their tips, that they were longer than she'd guessed. There were a few freckles on his shoulders, like a sprinkle of cinnamon—the color of his eyes as they opened and looked up at her.

Britt's eyes were faintly surprised, as if he hadn't expected Melinda to be there, as if he'd thought the night had been a dream. He laid his fingertips softly against her cheek, confirming her reality. Then his eyes warmed, their cinnamon melting into amber, their corners forming little crinkles as they smiled and he observed, "All the time you've spent inspecting the plantation has lightened your hair, made it redder in the sun. Or maybe it's because you're back in Java that your fire spirits are getting stronger."

Her lips curved happily because she now was free enough to say, "It isn't Java or spirits, but you, tending my fires."

Britt moved away to lie on his side, head propped on his folded arm, though he didn't look at her as he concluded, "I suppose last night marks the end of our agreement."

Melinda stared at the ceiling as she said, "It seems that any storm coming along will be our undoing." She recalled what she'd been thinking about before he'd awakened. Though one of her resolutions had been to be frank with him because skirting the issues seemed to result in half-truths and needless confusion, she was shyer about talking than making love.

Britt's fingers on her chin turned her face to his. "It isn't going to be easy for us."

She made her beginning. "Before you woke up, I was thinking about why you'd said we shouldn't be lovers, and I finally understand, really understand, what you meant. We both have such tempestuous natures. They can be our salvation, but they can be our curse unless we can control them."

At this Britt wondered if Melinda intended to return to celibacy; but she saw the alarm that was gathering clouds in his eyes and quickly said, "The life I'd led in Philadelphia put a kind of buffer around me, and whenever my mother noticed even a hint of rebellion, any strong emotion rising in me, she quickly smothered it by making me think it was somehow wicked or, at least, not ladylike. Being with you, even before we made love that first time, introduced me to a new attitude, and coming to Java has stripped off the last of my veneer. My own feelings frighten me. I've had so little practice managing them I'm never sure if I'm too much of this, not enough of that. I've decided, while I'm still struggling with myself, the only answer that makes sense of any of it is to be absolutely honest so you can understand what I'm feeling and know that I'm really trying."

Britt was silent a moment, thinking how few people had the courage to look at themselves with such candor and speak so frankly. He finally said, "We *both* must try."

As if her confession had relieved her of part of a burden, Melinda sighed. "I feel the way a butterfly must when it first comes out of its cocoon and its wings are still too weak to be reliable."

"You aren't a butterfly, Minda," Britt said softly. "You're a woman." He began to lean closer, as if he would kiss her, then abruptly turned away and sat up. "If you took such a long, straight look at yourself, I suppose you did the same with me and have questions."

"I thought about what happened to you, tried to understand why you think the way you do." Melinda paused, then added thoughtfully, "Even if our partnership in Phoenix House proves viable despite our being lovers, I have a feeling you still might be wary of giving your heart to me, and I wonder why." At Britt's quick glance she said, "I don't really know very much about all this yet. Maybe I'm wrong about that."

"You didn't know much about growing tea a few weeks ago, but you learned quickly enough about that," Britt remarked, then without looking at Melinda, finished, "You're right about me too."

Amazed at her own bluntness, Melinda said faintly, "Probably having a Javanese mother affected you."

"Not as much as you might think." Britt decided he needed a few minutes to wake up before he plunged into this kind of conversation. Stalling for time, he turned to look at the table beside the bed and noted, "I was wondering if I should get up and leave because you might be uncomfortable if Dessa found me here, but it appears she's already come and gone. She brought my toilette articles and clothes. She knows I like coffee in the morning and left a carafe. Do you want some?"

Melinda moved closer to look at a tray and a bowl of flowers on the table. "Orchids," she murmured.

Britt turned to her and found their faces so close only a breath was between them. A thrill of desire ran poignantly through him. "The Javanese call them 'little doves,' " he said. Then, not wanting Melinda to think he'd use desire to distract her so he wouldn't have to answer, he added softly, "I would like to make love with you again, Minda, but I think we should talk a little first."

His eyes carried a warning Melinda understood. She moved away, but needing to divert herself from the warmth that had welled up in her at his nearness, she commented, "I like your calling me Minda. It's like having a new name for a new life."

"I've always thought Minda was what you really are as opposed to Melinda, what you'd been taught to be. I suppose Minda had become in my mind an affectionate name, as some would say 'darling,' " he explained.

"Then you've been calling me darling all along," she concluded, and took the cup Britt offered.

He considered this a moment before answering, "Yes, I suppose I have." Wanting to kiss her, but knowing where it would lead, Britt took a sip of coffee. "You were saying you thought I'm wary of love."

"I assumed Elise's leaving so soon after your mother was murdered and the change in your father must have added a great deal to your grief. Helping my father run the plantation as well as coping with Gerard's drinking couldn't have left much time for you to spend on women," Melinda said. "Then Gerard was killed, and I guess trying to track down the tigress must have occupied you."

"There's more to it than that," Britt said. "It's seemed as if everyone I've loved has been taken from me or didn't love me enough to accept what I am, wasn't willing to stay here at Phoenix House with me." He put down his coffee cup, then with sudden resolve took hers away too. Turning back to face Minda, Britt reached for her hands. "I haven't been quite the monk you seem to think. There were other women in Europe I was attracted to besides Elise. Of course, I didn't dash around collecting fiancées, falling in love at every turn, but each time I began to really like a woman and hinted something more might be possible with her, she started trying to persuade me to sell my share of Phoenix House and leave Java. I couldn't do that and got too discouraged to actively pursue any woman. I just threw myself into my work."

Melinda considered this silently a moment before commenting, "Then suddenly you had a new partner, someone you hadn't seen since childhood. And because my mother had hated Java, you thought she'd have taught me to dislike it."

"The very problem I'd been avoiding, falling in love with a woman who might not want to stay at Phoenix House, seemed to have been forced on me," he said quietly. When Minda flashed him a surprised glance, he admitted, "I loved you as a child and was afraid I'd love you as a man. It may seem foolish to have assumed that—children know little about adult love—yet I'd always felt there was something between us the years of separation couldn't change."

Melinda's eyes had been riveted on Britt as he spoke. Though she felt like joyfully throwing herself into his arms, she realized his confession of how he had felt didn't mean Britt was ready to propose anything more yet. Melinda lowered her eyes and said quietly, "Nevertheless, here we are in bed together. But I guess that isn't always necessarily love."

Britt released Minda's hands and tilted her face so she looked up at him. He said softly, "The reason I avoided women, when I knew love was doomed almost from the start, is that I can't play at love as many people do. Love means only one thing to me, Minda. I suspect it's the same with you.''

''Where can that lead us if we're afraid to follow and take a chance on our emotions?''

''I suppose I have to stop protecting myself, even stop protecting you,'' he said slowly.

''Do you think if I'd wanted to be safe I would have come to Java?'' she inquired.

Britt gazed at her a long moment. ''You're right, Minda.'' He smiled wryly. ''Who is teaching whom, after all?''

''I think we'll both learn about love from loving, which is as it should be and only proves you always were right, that men and women teach each other,'' she answered.

Britt swung his legs off the bed and sat thoughtfully gazing at the sunlight coming from the courtyard, contemplating Minda's reply. Running his hand through his hair, he finally recalled, ''Dessa will probably return before very long. I'd best get up and put on some clothes.'' Britt was surprised by Minda's cheek pressing his, her arms winding around his waist, the soft warmth of her against his back. He cast her a sideways glance and said, ''After breakfast, we'll have all day to share.''

''Aren't we going to supervise the running of our plantation?'' she asked.

''No,'' Britt murmured. He leaned back against Minda to enjoy the sensation of her a moment longer before he turned his head to briefly kiss the corner of her mouth. Then he got up.

She watched silently as Britt splashed water from the extra basin Dessa had provided and began to dress. His haste reminded her of the maid's imminent return. Minda got up and pulled on a dressing gown, but as she tied its ribbons, her eyes kept darting back to Britt, at the sleekly moving muscles across his shoulders, the motions of his arms and wrists as he lathered his face and prepared to shave. She wanted those arms around her again, those hands caressing her as before. Minda approached to lay her cheek against his back and slide her hands into his shirt, which he'd left open.

Between razor strokes Britt asked, ''Would you like to go to Djakarta tomorrow with me? I'm going to attend the ceremonies for Matarami.''

Minda stepped around to Britt's side to look up at him in surprise. "I didn't realize we'd be invited."

"Rakata's coming personally to tell us about Matarami's death implied an invitation to the funeral. It could be an opportunity for Rakata and me to improve our relationship. My not attending would be a snub. You needn't go if you don't want to, but the funeral of a *raden* is very colorful, something you don't see often." Britt picked up a towel and wiped the last traces of lather from his face. "We'd have to leave after breakfast tomorrow, travel most of the day, and stay overnight in Djakarta. The procession and ceremonies will last through the next morning. Afterward there will be a gathering rather like a party. We would return to Phoenix House the following day."

"Do the Javanese celebrate a death, as I've heard some peoples do?" Minda asked as Britt brushed his hair.

"They neither celebrate nor show any outward signs of grief. They think weeping distresses the spirit of the departed, so he'll hesitate to go to his reward." Britt laid down the brush and turned to put his hands at Melinda's waist. "One reason you might prefer not to attend is that Major Wakefield will probably be there with an escort for the procession."

Melinda realized the soldiers might inspect the Javanese for weapons and Britt, too, could be searched. "Do you think there will be any trouble?"

"Rakata won't want anything to interfere with Matarami's funeral and I doubt Wakefield wants to cause problems either, especially at a religious ceremony," Britt answered. "As I said, I don't want to seem to snub Rakata, but I also want to see if Wakefield has gotten any news about the war in Europe. You and I will have to leave for a tea auction in London in a few months and I hope the war won't prevent our attending." Britt leaned closer to kiss Melinda's cheek as he added, "If we continue to get along so well together and you agree, perhaps we can find some lovely old cathedral there to be married in."

Britt stepped back a little to gauge Minda's reaction. Green-gold flecks were rising from the emerald depths of her eyes, like bubbles from the ocean floor floating toward the sun. "It seems that possibility doesn't alarm you," he commented.

"As you said, it will depend on whether we continue to get along so well together," she answered easily, but her seeming nonchalance was betrayed by her joyously throwing her arms around him.

*   *   *

Though Dessa didn't bother to hide her pleasure at Britt and Minda's obvious happiness, she made no comments as she pulled a small table in front of the divan and laid out their breakfast on it. She hummed a Javanese love song as she efficiently went about her work, then left without delaying, as if she wanted to avoid intruding on the couple any longer than necessary.

Minda forgot the troubles that had plagued them and could almost imagine it was a morning on the *Harini,* because she and Britt fed each other bits of fruit and muffins and sipped from each other's cups as they had so often done on the ship.

Finally, Britt leaned toward Minda to kiss her eyelids and forehead with infinite tenderness, then, taking her hand, drew her to her feet.

"I don't need those months to know how I feel about you," she murmured as his lips brushed her cheeks, traced the outline of her face.

"I've always loved you as a companion, Minda," Britt said, the tone of his voice making a flurry of sparks whirl through her spirit. "I started loving you as a woman . . ." He paused to taste her skin, thoughtfully, as if he were sampling her for the first time, adding between caresses, "that afternoon in the carriage . . . when you teased me about Javanese kissing. I've been trying to fight it ever since."

Then his mouth found Minda's, caressed her lips with a delicacy that made her pulses flutter wildly. He moved to her ear, lingered until he felt her pressing closer; then, with unhurried deliberation, his lips slid softly down her throat. When Britt straightened to look at Minda, his eyes were a cloud of copper sparks in the sun; knowing they reflected the level of his arousal, she wondered at the quietness of his caresses.

To Minda's unasked question, Britt murmured, "We've always made such stormy love. I think this morning might be different. Didn't you say on the *Harini* that you'd like to bask in a lagoon?" When she nodded, looking surprised that he'd remembered, Britt said, "I remember everything you say when we make love."

He reached for the ribbons that held her dressing gown closed and leaned nearer to kiss the base of her neck by her shoulder. With little tugs he untied the ribbons and she felt the dressing gown loosen. Britt's lips nibbled languidly along Minda's shoulder; his hands slid under the gown, up her sides, bunched her breasts against his chest; and as he swayed slightly, his embrace became another caress. Without her deciding or even being aware of it, Minda's fingers began to unbutton his shirt. They fumbled with their unaccustomed task; and suddenly self-conscious, she glanced up at him.

Britt's lips paused from smoothing the fluttering pulses at her temples and softly invited, "Take as long as you need, Minda. I like your undressing me."

"I'm awkward," she murmured.

His hands replaced his lips at her temples and he kissed her brow as he whispered, "That you aren't used to doing such things has always added to your charm; but I can help, if you wish."

Minda nodded, though she noticed his assistance was slow in coming, then meagerly given.

After Britt was naked, his hands on her waist turned her and slid around Minda's midriff to draw her back against him. With a quick movement, his face brushed aside her hair, then dipped to burrow into the curve where her shoulder met her neck. Britt's lips nibbled and caressed, his tonguetip a flame searing into Minda's skin while his hands moved under the dressing gown to cup her breasts. The warmth of his kisses followed the base of her neck, ascended to pause where a pulse was throbbing at the side of her throat, and traced a fluttering path to her ear, where his breath brushed aside a rebellious curl. She shivered at his persistent tongue, at his fingertips coaxing the buds of her nipples into blossom.

When Britt felt Minda's back pressing tightly against him, his hands slid to her waist, along her hips to her thighs, then enticed Minda until her head turned so her cheek was against his chest, as if she hadn't the strength to stand alone.

The exquisite sensations flooding her blotted out even the awareness of being on her feet. All she knew was that Britt's caresses were lighting little fires that flickered and dimmed at his direction until the impulses running along her nerves ignited her being and she became a flame.

When Britt heard Minda sharply catch her breath, felt her body against him poise and tense, he smiled into her hair. After a moment his arms circled her, turned her to face him. Lips lightly caressing without really kissing, Britt slid his hands under the edge of the dressing gown at Minda's neck, slowly ran his fingers along her skin, and slipped the gown off her shoulders, down her arms. His fingertips guided the gown past her hips, then down her legs. It dropped in a slither of satin around Minda's ankles. Britt circled her hips with his arms and drew her to him.

"Do you think we might now make our way to the bed?" He breathed the question into her ear as he moved slowly, sensuously against her. The look in her eyes was his answer.

Expecting Britt to step back, Minda was surprised when his mouth sought hers. During their kiss, he picked her up and carried her to the bed, continuing to caress her lips until he laid her down. Britt noticed Minda's wondering look and, as he stretched out on his side, whispered, "I just didn't want to stop kissing you."

Britt's rounded lips nibbled Minda's, the tip of his tongue playing with her, teasing until it parted her lips and his mouth possessed her kiss. His hands moved along her arms, shifted so his fingertips tantalizingly caressed her breasts, arousing new and piquant fires until her nipples crowned with passion. Then his leg slid lazily up hers, folded over her hip, drew her to him.

Minda opened her eyes and saw that Britt's were like an autumn haze shifting with amber lights as his hand moved caressingly along her side, over the curve of her hip. Like a star outlined by fire, Britt's fingers spread against Minda's back and pressed her closer. He whispered about how he wanted her and Minda's heart quickened its beat as he moved with insistent persuasion. While his gaze held hers, his languidly pliant hips gave one quick little thrust that made a sharp fire streak through her eyes. Then he stopped.

The sweet, hot flame Britt aroused in Minda flared higher, her senses poised in expectation that, as always before, he would begin to move. But his hands grasping her hips held her still while he burrowed his face into her hair. The tip of Britt's tongue teased Minda's ear, commanded her attention, and between moist caresses he murmured that he was letting her be a quiet lagoon as she'd asked. His hips moved lazily with quiet sensuality, and instead of setting her ablaze, he enveloped her in a growing heat that coaxed rather than compelled.

He turned his head, his lips moving slowly across her cheek, until his mouth took hers. The teasing of Britt's tongue and the caressing of his lips matched his body's motions. She opened her eyes to discover his half-closed, the golden fringe of his lashes shadowing the smoldering embers beneath.

Britt's fingers pressing against Minda's back became her guide as he lissomely shifted, steadily building the quietly glowing flame he'd so carefully tempered. Tingles ran along Minda's nerves, little bursts of fire. When she closed her eyes, his lips moved to nibble at her lashes until she reopened them. The sunlight was a golden stream lighting the smoky shadows of his eyes with copper sparks that ignited her soul.

Minda's desire quickened; she clung when Britt would have moved away. She slid her hands around his back, holding him more firmly to her, refusing to allow the intensity to subside even a little.

"You want more than I'm giving," he whispered. Her answer was to press even closer and he murmured against her lips, "Then take me where you want to go."

Britt's words made Minda hesitate, but his hips moved confidently against hers, for he'd long ago measured the height and breadth of her passion and he wanted to entice her to continue. His fluently caressing body charged her with excitement she tried to contain. Britt watched Minda's face, gauging the brightness like a tide of fire growing in her eyes. When he paused, her hands tensed, flattened against his back, locked them together. She gave Britt a heated glance, then, abashed at herself, quickly lowered her lashes.

"Go on, Minda, please yourself with me," Britt coaxed, then caught his breath as her hips made a small, sensuous circle.

As he'd suggested, Britt gave himself over to Minda's command while she swayed against him, slowly at first, then, as her ardor reached a higher level, less hesitantly, until Britt's senses seethed with desire.

Minda felt Britt's body quiver as waves of increasing passion raced through him. She opened her eyes, saw the tension that hardened his features and the realization that she was controlling his arousal intoxicated her. Now Minda's mouth crushed Britt's; and as he responded eagerly, triumph flooded her. She moved even more avidly against him and shock after shock of delight streaked vividly along Minda's nerves, propelling her closer to her own surrender.

The power of the impulses raging in Britt's senses made him feel like a torch that flared and dimmed at her command. His body cried out for fulfillment, and in his struggle to withhold himself a little longer, he moaned softly.

The sound was a new flood of fire searing Minda's racing instincts, and all thought of prolonging her mastery of him was blasted from her mind. Minda's supple motions accelerated to an eagerness that maddened them both with approaching ecstasy. Britt's senses leaped to greater heights and the demands of his body overwhelmed him at the moment she was taken by the force of her own conquest of him. A fire seemed to explode in her with such fury she whimpered as she was carried into rapture.

Minda lay helplessly trembling, her arms now limply around Britt. As her mind slowly found its way back to awareness, she heard him whisper, "I love you Minda. I always will."

Still breathless, she couldn't answer, could only open her eyes and gaze mutely at him. Britt wasn't lost in passion now as he'd been at the cottage, and she realized that the first time they'd loved he'd known what he'd been saying. The amber haze in his closing eyes confirmed it. The amber haze meant love.

Chapter Eleven

Britt's eyes narrowed against the glare of the sun reflecting off the Java Sea as he gestured for Suhadi to stop the carriage. From this little rise in the land only a dozen paces from the beach, Minda, Dessa, and Suhadi would have a clear view of the colorful ritual about to begin for Matarami and at the same time he could keep an eye on the crowd. At the first sign of trouble, Britt intended to have the carriage retreat down the beach.

He looked over the Javanese who had followed Matarami's procession on foot as they gathered at the edge of the sand. It seemed almost as if they'd been given an order not to step on the beach while the priests were supervising the placement of the tower-like platform that held the coffin. The Indonesians seemed peaceful, Britt observed, but he didn't forget they were a people who'd become used to hiding their thoughts under a docile façade. They had turned out in great numbers. Britt wondered if every village in west Java had been emptied and the plantation owners had given most of their workers time off, as he had, so they could attend Matarami's funeral near Djakarta. Soldiers on horseback were warily threading their way through the throng, Britt noted, and knew Major Wakefield had brought every man he could spare to assure that order was maintained.

There had been no search for weapons except for the customary inspection at the city's limits, and the only Javanese who had undergone that were those who lived in Djakarta and had to leave to join the procession. Rakata and the mourners from outside the city had avoided entering it because, instead of having the preliminary ritual held in Djakarta's Temple of Souls, Rakata had had the ceremony conducted in a little-used smaller temple in the hills. Now, it was impossible for Wakefield and his soldiers to search such a crowd. Britt knew Wakefield and his men were at a disadvantage on this plain in the midst of so many Javanese, especially if there were any firearms hidden among them, and the soldiers were nervous.

Although Britt was sure Rakata had passed strict orders not to bring guns of any kind, the new *raden* couldn't forbid his people the other weapons they would have needed to protect themselves from animals during their trek through the jungle to the funeral. Britt noted that every man carried a sword or dagger, some had spears, others bows and arrows; and no one could see how many blowpipes and darts were tucked in sashes or sleeve linings. Even if Rakata and Wakefield had made it clear that they didn't want the funeral disrupted by violence, one wrong move from any of the resentful Javanese or nervous soldiers could put the match to this potential powder keg.

Minda had noticed the tension on each soldier's face they'd passed. When the carriage stopped and Britt, instead of getting out, sat silently studying the situation for a long moment, her apprehension grew. She realized the occasion was more potentially dangerous than Britt had anticipated and kept reminding herself, as she watched his amber eyes moving over the crowd, that he would take care of her. She drew courage from this, though she couldn't forget that, despite the Javanese being a pleasant, quiet people, they could be ferocious fighters when aroused. She wasn't aware that the box secreted under the carriage seat contained a pair of loaded pistols.

Having known Suhadi for years, Britt had learned to trust his ability to judge the Javanese mind. The servant also had friends close to Rakata who, since Sukadana's murder, had more sympathetic attitudes toward Britt and sometimes discreetly relayed bits of information through Suhadi. Though the servant had told Britt before they'd left Phoenix House that a violent incident was unlikely, no one had expected such numbers to come.

"Do you think, Suhadi, that so many people will remain calm?" Britt asked quietly in Javanese.

The servant was silent a moment before answering under his breath,

"They know the new *raden* desires peace today. If the major's soldiers listen as well to him, I believe there won't be trouble."

Britt considered this. That Wakefield's men were well disciplined was unquestionable, and the major had always tried to administer his command as peacefully as possible. Scattered incidents like the one in which Charles had been killed were unusual in this district and had always occurred when Wakefield wasn't present. The major's personally attending the funeral made it clear to his men that all orders would be issued by him, not lesser officers. Reassured by this, Britt turned to Minda with a more relaxed attitude.

"The Javanese would say you shouldn't have worn that dress so close to the sea," he commented lightly as he got out of the carriage.

Minda looked down at the pale green batiste gown as she closed her frilly parasol. She'd avoided wearing her white dimity because it was the color Javanese nobility would wear and she hadn't wanted to offend anyone. "I'd thought green would be coolest, but perhaps I'm breaking some custom, after all," she said as he turned to help her out of the carriage.

Britt grasped Minda's waist and lifted her to the ground saying, "They believe the goddess of the sea will sweep a person away who wears green so close to the water." He set Minda on her feet, held her a moment longer to add softly, "One glimpse of your eyes and the goddess would be jealous no matter what color dress you're wearing. I'll just have to keep you close to me in case she's too tempted."

Ready to tuck her hand under Britt's elbow, Minda was happily surprised when, instead, he put his arm lightly around her waist. She looked up at him and commented, "I like that legend better than the one about the tigress—or at least its results—though everyone is eyeing this public display of affection."

Britt gave a nearby soldier, who was staring at them, a sharp glance, then returned his attention to her. "That corporal is merely jealous of me, but the Indonesians think I'm shielding you from the goddess."

"Do they really believe she'd snatch me away?" Melinda asked.

"Most of them do," Britt answered. "Despite Java's size, it is an island surrounded by the ocean, and the sea is a powerful force in their lives."

"People everywhere who live along seacoasts tell all sorts of stories about the ocean. I'm sure there are legends in America too," she remarked, then added, "But not even tales about demon-tigresses frighten me while you're at my side."

Britt pressed her a little closer. "Tigresses, *lelembuts,* or goddesses would have to go *through* me before they could harm you."

The musicians who had ridden to the beach with the priests and the coffin resumed playing, and Britt, knowing the next part of the ceremony was beginning, turned Minda so she could watch. As he did, he saw in the distance that Major Wakefield and a pair of his officers had drawn their horses together. Wakefield noticed Britt watching and nodded, but instead of returning his full attention to his men, the major's eyes kept darting back to Britt, as if he had something on his mind. Britt fixed his attention on the ceremony, hoping the major wouldn't approach to ask more questions to embarrass Minda or make comments about the possible dangers of the crowd and frighten her.

Though Minda ordinarily loved Javanese music, the kind that had been played during the procession to the sea had left her cold and this song promised to do the same. It wasn't that the music was particularly mournful but that it was so colorless it was dull and monotonous. She pretended to listen dutifully and to watch the priests' graceful gestures as they prayed amid puffs of fragrant incense, but she was remembering how she and Britt had spent the day after the storm in her room, talking when it suited them, making love when they pleased, napping in each other's arms. The day and the following night had called up memories of their time on the *Harini.* Even traveling to Djakarta the next day and staying at the inn last night had reminded Minda of trips into ports when the *Harini* had docked, but for one difference. The time on the ship had held no real thoughts about their future, no plans to continue or end, for they'd seemed suspended in time. It had been like an enchantment cast over them, but now they were aware of all the tomorrows, the commitments to each other, not only to Phoenix House as partners. Rather than awing her, the unspoken promises were reassuring against future problems. They were stronger together than they'd been separately. There was no need to wonder if they'd want to be married in London. She knew Britt's decision as surely as she knew her own. The knowledge brought her a new confidence and, with it, a feeling that, with Britt at her side, she was freer than she could dream of being alone.

Britt's thoughts were not on romance, though they were concerned with love, because his mind had been alerted to a new danger and he questioned how he could keep Minda safe. Major Wakefield had finally sent his officers away and he and his aide had begun winding their way through the throng toward Britt and Minda. Britt noticed that several Javanese men seemed to be pacing the major. He wondered if it was merely the coincidental shifting of the crowd's movements that always left the same trio of men not more than twenty paces from Wakefield or if they were skillfully trailing him. If so, Britt knew their intentions weren't benevolent, that if they harmed the major, the soldiers would retaliate, which could spark off a riot.

Minda wasn't aware of Britt's suspicions. She'd decided that this ceremony was part of Java, and her and Britt's future was inextricably bound to the land. She wanted to understand the heart and soul of the island and its people, so she asked why Matarami's coffin was carved like a winged lion, why it was painted red, black, and orange and decorated with golden streamers. Dessa was happy to explain this as well as the meanings of other customs and rituals. Minda looked with new understanding at the tower that bore the pavilion of state, an elaborate structure with a series of pagodalike roofs, each smaller than the one below, with the topmost peak soaring as high above the crowd as the *Harini*'s mainmast had been over its deck. The steep ramp that led to the pavilion, where the musicians were playing and the priests performing their functions over the coffin amid brilliantly dyed paper garlands and flowers, held less mystery for Minda. By the time the music stopped and the priests and musicians began descending the ramp to set the pavilion afire, Minda was watching with the same attitude as the Javanese.

Britt, meanwhile, had become convinced that the men he was discreetly observing were stalking Wakefield, but they were being so cautious neither the major nor his aide had noticed. Britt stepped closer to the carriage and slid his hands into the box under its seat. Using his body to shield what he was doing from the sight of others so he wouldn't be accused of planning trouble himself, he cocked the hidden pistols. Although no one else had an inkling of what was happening, Britt was ready.

When Britt heard the beginning crackle of the flames for Matarami's pyre, he lifted his head and seemed to be watching, but his attention was focused on the trio of men, who had now moved closer to Wakefield. One man stood on each side of the major's horse near its withers; the third was in front of the horse with his back toward Britt. Though Britt dared not draw the guns into view until the last possible moment, he was sure he knew when the assassins planned to strike. They were waiting until the fire exploded into the pavilion and engulfed Matarami's coffin, becoming a spectacle no one's eyes could resist. Then the song the Javanese were singing in farewell to Matarami would rise in volume and help disguise any outcry from Wakefield. The assassins were hoping the distractions of the funeral's most dramatic moment would delay the onlookers' reactions just long enough for them to escape.

The assassins began to reach into the folds of their sashes; Britt knew they were locating blowpipes and darts. He realized he might not have a chance to shoot more than one of them so he chose the farthest from him. When Britt took out the pistols, he saw Wakefield's eyes on him widen with alarm, realized the major thought *he* was the assassin. But when the first of Britt's pistols fired, the Javanese at Wakefield's right seemed to leap backward before plunging to the grass, blowpipe and darts scattering from his outflung hands. People standing nearby, startled by the gunshot, turned quickly; and several stepped in the line of Britt's other targets. He tossed both pistols into the carriage, then launched himself at the nearest assassin.

Minda had whirled around and saw Britt's shoulders hit the Javanese at an angle that carried them both into the third assassin and sent all of them sprawling. One of the men was rising to his hands and knees when Britt leaped up and kicked him squarely in the face. The man crashed back down on his side. The second assassin struck out at Britt; Minda caught her breath to see a dagger flash in the sun. Before she could call out, Britt had moved away, easily eluding the blade. Then as quickly, Britt sprang back, caught the man's wrist, twisted it, and the man tumbled to the ground. Britt leaped on him, and Minda couldn't see, as they rolled, who had the dagger. All she knew was that it was between them. When the struggle suddenly stopped, so had her heartbeat.

Britt rose, his shirt spattered with the assassin's blood, turned to the major, and observed, "I gather none of them got a shot at you."

Wakefield lowered the pistol he'd drawn but had not had a chance to even aim during the fast-moving fight. He gestured for his aide to examine the assassins. The young soldier threw Britt a look of new respect and dismounted.

"None indeed," Wakefield said brusquely, then inquired, "*How* did you do that?"

Pinpoints of light gleamed in Britt's eyes as he raised them to regard the major. He said coolly, "There are some advantages to having a native mother. You can grow up with Javanese friends and learn their way of fighting." The fire in his eyes evened to a steady amber glow as he turned to Minda, who was standing beside the carriage staring at him as if he were a stranger. Britt extended his hand, inviting her to come to him. When she did, he put his arm around her waist and said quietly, "Everything is all right now. You needn't be afraid." Her eyes told him it was he she was in awe of and the corners of his mouth tipped in a wry smile as he pressed her a little closer.

A soldier who had arrived on horseback crowded his mount close and aimed his pistol at Britt. Not having seen the fight, he assumed Britt had shot all three Javanese, though he couldn't remember the sound of so many shots. "Hand over your weapon," he directed.

"He has none," Wakefield snapped. "Help Sergeant Moore with those bodies." He glanced around, distractedly muttering, "Where are the rest of my men?"

"Yes, sir. I'll flag some others down, sir," the soldier answered as he put away his gun. Realizing the struggle had been so quickly ended the soldiers circulating through the crowd farther away hadn't even noticed it, he turned his horse to hastily gesture to the nearest soldier.

Wakefield watched him until he was far enough away not to overhear, then said quietly, "I owe you my life, Mr. Vandekker, but I do not *ever* want to see you with a firearm in or near Djakarta again. I'll be forced by my orders to confiscate it."

"All three assassins are dead, sir," Sergeant Moore approached to advise.

"A pity," the major said. "I'd have liked to learn who put them up to this."

"I did not."

Everyone turned to the white-and-gold-clad figure who had made his way through the crowd.

"You aren't harmed?" Rakata's dark eyes briefly moved over Britt before he turned them on Wakefield and said, "I gave orders to my people not to make trouble at my grandfather's funeral."

"These seemed not to have heard that order," the major replied in a sarcastic tone as he cast a glance at the bodies now lying in a row near his horse.

"Perhaps not, but had they survived this, they would have died on a palm shoot," Rakata said coldly.

Despite his anger, Wakefield inwardly shuddered that the would-be assassins would have been impaled on a sprouting frond, which after two days' growth would have unfurled and torn them apart. Recovering himself, he demanded, "Who are they?"

Rakata glanced once, contemptuously, at the bodies. He recognized them as being some of his cousin Samarang's associates, but knew it would do no good to explain that Samarang wanted the title of *raden* and might have hoped an attempt on the major's life would end with Rakata's arrest. Neither would Rakata's pride allow him to admit he had an enemy among his own people. He said only, "The names of these criminals would mean nothing to you."

Britt saw the bitterness in Rakata's eyes, knew there was more to this than the new *raden* was admitting; and when Wakefield turned away to give an order to one of his men, Britt asked softly in Javanese, "Is there some other trouble, perhaps among your people, I should know about?"

"You have probably prevented a battle here. I'm grateful for that, but like the major I would have preferred you hadn't killed these men," Rakata said under his breath. "They could have been persuaded to give evidence I need to stop someone who wants to usurp my place." Rakata raised his eyes to fix them like spearpoints on a figure standing near Matarami's pyre on the beach.

Britt followed Rakata's stare to Samarang, but he was stunned to recognize another man on the beach standing near the Javanese. *Alden Townes.* A score of questions flew through Britt's mind. What was Townes doing in Java? Why was *he* with Samarang? Or was it merely coincidence that he was standing near Rakata's suspected enemy, an enemy who wanted Rakata's title?

Noticing the shock that registered in Britt's eyes, Rakata inquired, "You're so surprised at Samarang's plot?"

"It's something else, nothing to do with you, that surprised me," Britt said curtly and turned away.

Minda had understood part of Britt and Rakata's hurried conversation, but she wasn't tall enough to see beyond the surrounding crowd. "What is it?" she whispered.

"Just Javanese politics," Britt said impulsively, then, reconsidering, added, "I'll explain later."

"Mr. Vandekker?" Major Wakefield returned his attention to Britt.

"I'd like you to describe everything you noticed from the moment you first became suspicious of those assassins."

Britt complied, but midway through his description he noticed that Minda seemed to be growing pale and hurried through the rest of it. After he'd finished, he said, "I think I should take Miss Scott back to the inn. She looks a little faint."

Wakefield conceded, "I suppose the shock of all this has been a bit unnerving for a lady, and the noon heat hasn't helped. I'm sorry for keeping you so long, Miss Scott. Mr. Vandekker, I needn't remind you to keep yourself available in case I have more questions—you as well, Raden . . ." He stopped, perplexed that Rakata had vanished into the crowd.

"I'm sure Rakata has started back to Talu. You know where you'll be able to find me," Britt said, bid the major a good afternoon, then turned to guide Minda back to the carriage. They found Arjuna waiting with Dessa and Suhadi.

"The tigress has killed again," Arjuna said quietly.

Britt frowned as he helped Minda into the carriage. "Who was it this time?"

"The ancient one, Pemangku," Arjuna replied. "Maoke found him in the courtyard of the temple at the foot of Gunung Mrabu. Maoke came to me right away. He thought you might want to look at the tracks before someone else learns about it and disturbs anything."

Minda was freshly horrified by this news. Pemangku had been a priest, a benevolent old man she'd known before she'd left Java. She asked slowly, "Gunung Mrabu is a volcano, isn't it?"

"It's the one nearest Phoenix House, but it hasn't spat fire for many years," Arjuna answered.

Britt considered the situation a moment. "What was Pemangku doing there? I can't remember that temple having been used during my lifetime. I saw it last when I was fourteen. Even then the jungle had grown around it so I could hardly find the place."

"Pemangku thought it was a sacred place, that he could commune with the fire goddess. He recently claimed that the goddess was getting ready to stir in Gunung Mrabu," Arjuna explained. "Tigers like cool, shady places, and the temple is covered with moss. The inside of it must be as cool as a cave. Also, it's secluded and a stream runs nearby."

Britt looked speculative. "A tigress getting ready to bear young might think it was a comfortable den."

"If so, she will abandon it after anyone else learns about the attack on Pemangku and leaves human scent all over," Arjuna warned.

"The tigress might not stay there anyway, once she finds that Pemangku's body is gone," Britt said.

"That was why Maoke didn't take it. There was so little left he only recognized it as Pemangku's from the priest's insignia and prayer beads," Arjuna said. "Even that beast isn't hungry enough to eat bronze and wood."

"I see you've anticipated my decision and brought a spare horse," Britt noted. "I'll just go back to the inn to change my clothes before we leave."

"It won't take long for me to get ready," Minda promised.

Britt turned to look at her in surprise. "You aren't planning on going with us!" he exclaimed. When he saw that she was, he said, "You're pale and you look upset. You should rest overnight at the inn, then go home tomorrow with Dessa and Suhadi in the carriage."

"Anyone would be pale after watching three men fall dead at her feet, then hearing about a tigress eating Pemangku," Minda returned. "I don't want to rest. All I need to do is splash some cool water on my face and change my clothes. I can ride one of the carriage horses."

"Though I won't enter the temple before sunrise, when the tigress is most likely to be hunting, she might be nearby. Looking for a tiger's lair day or night, man-eater or not, is too dangerous," Britt warned.

"I've already seen how good your aim is with a gun; I'll trust to that if anything goes wrong," Minda reasoned, then, knowing Britt was going to argue, she quickly added, "Didn't you just say I could go home? *Home,* Britt, is what Phoenix House is to me too. Anything that affects it affects me just as it does you. Would my father have come with you or gone home? Am I your partner or not?"

"Of course you're my partner, but you're a lot more besides," Britt declared. "Wasn't it enough for you to face that beast once?"

"To be able to face what I'm afraid of is important to me," she insisted.

Britt took her hands and said more quietly, "You don't have to prove anything, Minda, to yourself or to me."

Minda looked up at him. "Maybe I just want to share everything with you, even the danger. How would you feel if you were in my place and had to stay home worrying about me while I went with Arjuna? Are you going to forbid me to go?''

Britt exchanged worried glances with Arjuna, but answered, "I can't do that. You know I wouldn't if I could.''

"If you did, I'd follow anyway. I *am* going to that temple," she said vehemently.

As a precaution against the tigress as well as any other nocturnal predators—such as the giant lizards, aptly nicknamed "dragons," that often weighed close to three hundred pounds and could outrun a man—Britt and Arjuna made a circle of fires around the campsite. They tethered the horses in the protective ring, then took turns on watch so the flames wouldn't die.

Standing guard for half the night, then rolling up in a blanket on the ground to sleep with his face smeared with grease to guard against insects wasn't how Britt had planned to spend the night. After finally having come to a loving understanding with Minda, he'd wanted to spend every night with her in his arms. But she was separated from him by space they couldn't even reach across to hold hands because some creature looking for warmth might crawl up their sleeves. Though Arjuna had the last watch, Britt thought he might as well have taken it, too, for he spent the few hours they'd allowed for sleeping alternately cursing the tigress, *lelembut* or not, and Alden Townes.

Britt felt as if Townes were an octopus trying to wrap yet another tentacle around Minda, that Jessica had attached invisible lines to her daughter and still was tugging on them trying to pull her back. Although Britt's apprehension about Minda's leaving Java had faded and he knew she loved him, he was weary of Jessica and Alden's interfering with their lives.

Britt wondered what might have brought Townes to Java, if not Minda. Though he tried to convince himself that the envoy might have merely been reassigned to Java, he couldn't make himself believe it. Britt recalled the servant who had stood a little behind Townes on the beach, and he thought, if Alden planned to stay in Java long enough to have engaged a servant, he must also have rented his own quarters. Britt couldn't understand why Townes hadn't already called on Minda if he intended to pursue her. Was it possible Jessica had relented, was worried about her daughter's well-being, and Townes had traveled on his embassy pass to discreetly check on Minda's situation? Britt found that, too, difficult to believe—Alden and Jessica had already shown themselves to be more concerned about money than about Minda. Might Townes have some other purpose he couldn't even begin to guess? Britt's conflicting theories collided with everything he knew about Townes until he was angry with himself out of frustration.

During the simple breakfast Arjuna had cooked over the campfire, Britt was quiet and sullen, but he decided not to mention Townes's having come to Java. If by chance Townes had come to the island on a matter having nothing to do with Minda, telling her he was there would only cause her needless worry. Britt concluded they'd eventually learn what Townes was up to if it concerned them, but he felt pessimistic.

When Britt noticed Minda uneasily glancing at the jungle's darkness beyond their fire circle, he said quietly, "We won't be able to speak again until after we've left the temple, so we'll have to make our plans now."

Arjuna came closer, but he already knew what Britt was going to say.

Britt took a last swallow of coffee, then sloshed the grounds in the grass before he regarded Minda. "You and Arjuna will wait together while I go into the temple."

"You're going inside alone?" She was aghast at the idea.

"You can't move as quietly as I will, Minda, and I don't want to be distracted by having to worry about your foot scraping a pebble loose or you brushing against a wall and making a sound to alert the tigress if she didn't go out hunting last night," he explained.

"Then take Arjuna inside with you. I can hold the horses. Give me one of your pistols," Minda said, terrified at the thought of Britt's being alone with the tigress in the dark.

"Arjuna would have stayed with the horses anyway. He'll have the pistol." Britt's tone was firm.

"You planned from the first to go inside alone," Minda suddenly realized.

"If you'd gone home as I suggested, you just wouldn't have known about it until it was over," Britt returned, becoming annoyed.

Minda looked helplessly at Arjuna, wishing he'd add his plea to hers, but he shrugged, then turned away to start kicking dirt over the fires.

"You *are* staying with Arjuna outside the temple, Minda," Britt said.

She knew from his tone that if she argued with him until dawn it wouldn't matter. She sighed and hung her head in hopelessness. Then Britt's hands were at her temples, lifting her face so she had to look up at him. The last flickers of the campfire revealed an amber haze in his eyes having nothing to do with annoyance.

"I love you, Minda. I'll come back," he said softly before he drew her close.

In the first gray light of the hour before sunrise, Minda held to Britt's promise as tightly as if it were a talisman in her clenched hands as she watched him creep across the ruined temple's broken paving stones, himself as stealthy as a jungle cat. He paused behind the fragment of a wall, scanned the open area, then ran, making no more sound than a drifting cobweb, to crouch in the shelter of another rubble heap. Again he was moving swiftly, his feet somehow missing every loose stone that was scattered over the courtyard. A statue, fallen so long ago that grass was growing in the spaces between its crumbling contours, lay across Britt's path. He leaped over it, dislodging not a pebble, landed soundlessly on its far side, then stopped to flatten his back against the wall to the side of the temple entrance.

The earth's shifting had caused the building's sections to sink haphazardly. The doorway had lost almost half its height, and Minda thought it looked more like a cave opening than the entrance to a once mighty temple. Britt drew his gun, cocked it so carefully it made only a soft click, but Minda felt Arjuna flinch beside her. She hoped the tigress hadn't heard, prayed that the man-eater was prowling far away and hadn't yet even thought of returning to her lair.

As Britt moved away from the wall, Minda prayed even more fervently that he would be safe. He bent to step quickly through the entrance, then vanished into the blackness beyond.

Minda stared at the doorway wondering how Britt would be able to see by the light of the one small candle he'd brought, if the tiny flame would only make it easier for the tigress to find him. She thought of the many treacherous passageways where rotting floors must have vanished into pits, or ceilings had collapsed, how many walls were teetering with age. Would one of them choose today, the moment Britt passed, to give up its long struggle to remain erect? Did the tigress—a fearful enough animal ordinarily, but this one the Javanese believed was possessed by a demon—lie in wait, like a machine of death, around some dark corner slavering to make a meal of Britt? Minda felt as if the entire weight of the temple bore down on her head and she couldn't bear to look at the doorway Britt had vanished through.

While her ears listened for a gunshot or the awful rumbling growl that marked a tiger's attack, her eyes moved along the length of the pockmarked walls, paused at a shattered column lying on its side, a crazily leaning doorframe open to nothing, a cracked staircase climbing nowhere. Minda's heart was pounding so hard it felt like a drum beating against the inside of her ribs as though it might crack them, when Britt finally reappeared in the doorway.

She was so relieved she would have leaped to her feet; but Arjuna's arms suddenly wrapping around her like an iron band, his hand sealing her mouth, prevented her from moving or crying out in joy. Minda realized his purpose—the tigress could be nearby—and remained where she was, but Arjuna felt the tremors running through her and didn't loosen his grip as Britt ran straight across the rubble-strewn courtyard to rejoin them. He gestured to Minda to say nothing, then, still holding the pistol in one hand and catching her wrist with the other, hastily guided her away. Arjuna managed to lead the horses, which, already nervous, were showing increasing signs of fear.

Not until after they'd walked some distance and turned onto a path did Britt pause and Arjuna remove the cloths he'd tied around the horses' noses to keep them quiet.

"Now we can talk," Britt said.

Then Minda didn't know what to say. All her anxious questions were pointless because Britt was there—he was safe. She'd forgotten his purpose had been to search for evidence that the tigress was living in the temple. Her mind had turned it all into the beast's hunt for him.

"It's where that man-eater's staying, all right," Britt said as he put his arm around Minda's waist and turned to Arjuna. "I could smell her as soon as I stepped into the place."

"Did you see her?" Melinda gasped in horror.

"No, but she was on her way back. That's why the horses were so afraid. They scented her in the area. Horses have a sense of smell to rival a bloodhound's, but they don't make such a show of it. If you ever go out riding alone, keep in mind that your mount will scent danger before you'll be aware of it," Britt said. Pulling Minda a little closer to his side, he went on, "It's a good thing tigers don't have such an acute sense of smell. That man-eater won't guess I visited her lair today. I went all the way to her nest. She does have a couple of cubs; I heard them mewing."

"If you kill her, I suppose they'll die," Minda said slowly.

Britt looked down at her. "I'm afraid so, but we don't know if the deformity in her leg was from an accident or inherited. If it's the latter, she might have passed it on to her babies, and we'd likely have another generation of man-eaters to contend with. I couldn't see the cubs well enough in the shadows to tell if they're normal. I dared not step into the room where the nest is, much less touch the cubs and leave my scent in a place the tigress couldn't fail to notice."

"How do you think we should trap her?" Arjuna asked.

"We can't use beaters on foot in the jungle making noise to drive her into a trap because noise doesn't frighten her. While I was in that temple, I heard quite a few sounds coming from the volcano in the mountain, and the noises would have been enough to scare any other tiger out," Britt said.

"She isn't afraid of people and might stalk the beaters the way a normal tiger would track a deer and separate it from its herd," Arjuna concluded. "If she escaped us, she probably would just come back to the temple to hide."

"That's why I think we'd better trap her in her lair and have it over with," Britt said.

Minda looked up at him and begged, "Oh no, Britt! Please don't go back into that cavernous place with her!"

"This entire mountain is honeycombed with caves. If the temple was made like them, I'd never consider it. But temples are built by human hands, mostly on the same pattern, and have a limited number of doors. If I take enough men from the plantation, divide them into groups that enter each door, then follow the corridors, they'll drive the tigress back to her nest, where I'll shoot her."

"But what about those men? Won't she attack them?" Minda asked anxiously.

"Since the occupation forbids all Javanese to use firearms, none of the workers except Arjuna and Maoke have had enough practice with guns, so I can be sure they won't hurt themselves or each other," Britt answered regretfully.

"They'll carry torches. No animal will keep coming if a flaming torch is being held in its way," Arjuna advised. "Though the workers can't shoot guns, they still have spears and bows, all we ever had before guns were brought to Java."

Resigned to the hunt because she knew the man-eater had to be stopped, Minda finally asked, "When will you do it?"

"As soon as everyone is ready," Britt answered. "From the sounds that mountain is making, I'm afraid Gunung Mrabu might erupt one of these days. I wouldn't want to be in the temple if the eruption is the kind that explodes in fire."

"Is there any other kind?" Minda inquired.

"Volcanos do many things. Sometimes they only shoot up sparks or hot mud runs out. Gunung Mrabu hasn't spilled lava in many years, but we can't be sure it won't," Arjuna said. "We must make certain that the tigress doesn't escape us. If we catch her tomorrow or the next day, she may not have a chance to kill another human."

"Which reminds me," Britt commented as he undid a couple of his buttons. Reaching into his shirt, he pulled out a bronze medallion and a few wooden beads knotted on a piece of twine. "These must have fallen off Pemangku's body when the tigress dragged it into the temple."

Minda got only a brief glimpse of the bloodstained medallion before Britt pushed it into his saddlebag, but she quickly turned away. "Pemangku sometimes paused to tell me stories when I was a child," she whispered. "I remember him as a gentle, kind man."

"Tigers kill their prey swiftly. He wouldn't have suffered long," Arjuna said, hoping to give Minda a little comfort.

Britt turned from his horse to put his arms lightly around her. After a moment he said gently, "Pemangku died in the place he loved most, the sacred mountain of his special goddess."

"Maybe we should go up the slope and drop his medallion and beads into the crater so Pemangku's spirit can take them," Arjuna suggested. "After the tigress is dead, we'll be able to find his bones. The other priests can pray over them."

"I think Pemangku would have wanted his priestly insignia to be given to the volcano," Britt agreed, wondering if, while they were at the crater, he might be able to guess whether Gunung Mrabu was likely to erupt.

The sun was an incandescent ball floating on the ocean and the eastern slopes of the mountains were washed with orange-gold light. But at the foot of Gunung Mrabu on its opposite side, the path was a pale thread woven among the purple shadows of the trees.

Despite Britt's keeping them at an unworried, leisurely pace on the ascending lane, Minda cast wary glances at the forest's darkness and wondered if the tigress was now peacefully tending her cubs or still patrolling the jungle. Vivid memories of long white fangs, claws like curving knives, conjured up visions of the creature, like a sleekly flowing shadow pacing them in the foliage. Each time her horse's ears pricked up and swiveled at a sound he alone could hear, Minda held her breath for the instant till he lost interest in it. Britt's having said her mount would scent danger and warn well in advance of its approach was reassuring, but she was uneasy till the forest gave way to a grassy slope.

Then the crest of Gunung Mrabu was a dark, gray-blue fluted cone taking on a greener tint in the shortening distance. Below the peak a layer of haze was like a wide ring that had been slipped down over its summit, because though the mountain wasn't so lofty its top reached into the clouds, the smoke and steam it exhaled settled around its slope each dawn and dusk. As the riders approached the cloud bank, Britt told Minda not to let her horse dawdle, to keep his back always in sight until after they'd passed through the smoke. Then he chirped to his mount and moved ahead while Arjuna protectively dropped behind her.

It was like stepping through a diaphanous wall and having it close around them. At first as innocently white as clouds, the vapor quickly became an ominous gray, then changed to black smoke that completely obscured their surroundings. Realizing how easily she could lose her way, even ride off the lip of a ravine, Minda kept her mount close behind Britt's and still could only see him as a shadowy figure.

A splinter of sunlight suddenly pierced the smoke like a needle drawing a golden cord through the blackness the riders clung to until the dark ahead was no longer a solid mass but a sooty veiling crushed by an invisible hand. The line of light became a beckoning finger that widened into a tunnel they followed, always ascending toward its source through the graying mist. Then, abruptly, they moved out of the clouds into turquoise sky.

Eyes dazzled by the sudden blaze of sunshine, Minda turned in her saddle to look at the path they'd followed. Beyond the smoke, lavender clouds were tinted with gold. At Gunung Mrabu's foot was a placid expanse of green no one would guess, if they didn't know, hid tigers' claws, deadly serpents' coils, and fanged dragons.

Britt guided his horse through a break in the wall of the crater. Minda, apprehensively following, discovered that its inside lip didn't immediately drop into a flaming cauldron but was a wide, level area. The volcano's inner wall wasn't a cliff but a steep hill that sloped to the molten fluid in the bottomless funnel at its center far below. Britt rode along the rim, choosing the gentlest angle, then dismounted.

They left the horses unconcernedly munching grass and picked their way down the slope. For a short distance the crater's inner wall was no harder to walk down than any stony hillside, but soon it became pitted from ancient boulders that had exploded out of the volcano and dug holes like meteors streaking from the heavens. Ridges were mighty humps of hardened lava flows scored by razor-edged gutters the molten rock had ploughed. Britt cautioned Minda to remain at the level where she was, so she wouldn't trip and tumble into the fires shimmering below, while he and Arjuna made their way farther down the slope. She eyed the steepening pitch and quickly agreed. She watched with hammering heart as Britt walked down the treacherous decline and quickly realized her fear for his safety was unfounded. His balance was as sure as if he were strolling along a tea field's furrows while he made his way on lightly moving feet halfway down the slope.

Minda watched Britt hand something to Arjuna and realized it was Pemangku's medallion. The Javanese held it high, as if offering it to the heavens, and Minda said a silent prayer for the old priest in the moment before Arjuna tossed the medallion into the lazily bubbling fluid at Mrabu's core. Then, while Britt and Arjuna studied the rocky walls discussing where the lava's previous risings and ebbings had marked the rocks, Minda stared at the flowing liquid far below, finally thinking not of its deadliness but its beauty.

She felt as if she were looking into the heart of a gentler sun than the brilliant sphere that hung in the sky. The surface, yellow as sulfur, moving slowly, restlessly among shifting orange waves and rippling gold fires, fascinated Minda. A line of blue flames occasionally sheeted higher than the others when the wind came in little gusts that whirled around the crater's inner curve and touched the molten surface. It blew the skin off one of the bubbles; escaping steam made a distant hiss, rose past Britt and Arjuna, then soared beyond Minda's head to float against the sky. She suddenly realized the puffs of vapor made the clouds she'd watched from the garden and had compared with kitten's tails. She knew she'd never again liken them to anything so harmless.

Not to be outdone by caves, where minerals dissolved by water formed the shimmering rock icicles called stalactites, Gunung Mrabu melted the elements, then splashed them on its wall. Ancient spatters, cooled and hardened, became crystals clinging to the wall like flower clusters. A streak of vermilion flashed amid a bouquet of the mineral blossoms, and curious about what it was, Minda picked her way along the rocky path to find that the glimmer had come from an orange-red crystal beyond a cleft in the path. If she could stretch far enough, she thought, she might be able to reach it. Bracing her hand against a stone outcropping, she leaned past the empty space at her feet to pluck a tangerine-colored crystal from the others.

Something tickled the hand Minda was using to hold herself steady; fearing a venomous insect, she quickly looked to see that only a large golden butterfly had lighted on her fingers. She remained at an awkward angle, leaning over the cleft, afraid to breathe and frighten the butterfly away.

"The wind has blown it to you and it's resting." Britt's voice came softly from behind her.

"It's a thing of life in this deadly place and that it came to you is supposed to be a sign of good fortune," Arjuna commented.

Minda gazed at the butterfly in wonder, thinking how incongruous it was that so sublimely beautiful, so fragile a creature should fly into the crater of Gunung Mrabu and choose to light on her until it had regained its strength. The butterfly again took flight. She watched it flutter, like a sprinkle of sunlight against the sky, till it finally vanished over the top of the crater. Then she turned to show Britt the crystal she'd found.

"It's a kind seldom seen," Arjuna breathed as he peered around Britt at the crystal, which scintillated orange-red lights. "This was born of Gunung Mrabu's flames. We call it a blossom of fire. Pemangku would have said the volcano's goddess came in the form of the butterfly to test if you're worthy of her gift. You gave the butterfly a moment of shelter and won the goddess's favor. She'll protect you as you did the butterfly."

Minda was ready to deny this as another of the myriad superstitions she'd heard in Java when Britt assured, "This crystal is truly a rare find, Minda. I've seen only one other this color. Pemangku had it. Now that he's dead, who can say where his crystal is?"

"It *is* beautiful," Minda agreed, then remembering what Arjuna had said, inquired in a tone that hinted skepticism, "What do you think would have happened if the goddess had decided I didn't deserve this?''

"If you so mistrusted nature that you were frightened of the butterfly or if you weren't kind enough to let it rest on you, you would have dropped the fire blossom. It would have fallen down the slope back into the volcano, the goddess's home,'' Arjuna answered. Noting the expression on Minda's face, he shrugged and finished, ''Pemangku once said, when you were born the spirit of the fires that destroyed your father's house entered you. If he were here now, I think he would say the crystal is a gift from the goddess, a sign that the spirit in you will burn again brightly.''

Chapter Twelve

The print Britt was reading blurred, and he finally realized, though he'd turned several pages, he had no idea what they held. Britt put the book down with a thump on the table beside his chair and impatiently shoved away the footstool. About to get up, he noticed the glass of sherry he'd forgotten and again leaned back to take a sip while he gazed at the light coming from Minda's room across the courtyard. Britt had told her he wanted to read awhile, then get some sleep before he left for the hunt in the morning, but he'd discovered he was too restless for either.

His unease wasn't because he was particularly afraid of hunting the tigress. Though anyone would be apprehensive about walking into a man-eater's den, Britt never allowed himself to think too much about dangerous situations until he had to face them. He'd learned that such thoughts could magnify fear so it might paralyze a man when he most needed his wits and he'd taught himself to expect nothing specific until it happened. It was an easier rule to follow when physical action was called for than when problems hinged on the motives of others.

Was his mood due to Alden Townes's being in Java? He dismissed the idea. Even if Townes had come to pursue Minda, Britt knew she'd never go back to Philadelphia with him. The man could present an annoyance, but not any threat Britt could think of. He just couldn't understand, if Townes had traveled to Java to try to win Minda back, why he was delaying visiting her.

Taking another sip of sherry, Britt considered the political situation on the island, which had been worsened by the attempt on Wakefield's life. If Samarang had planned the assassination intending Rakata to be convicted, Britt was sure he must have arranged for someone to step forward and swear to having witnessed the *raden*'s paying the assassins or giving them orders. That meant Samarang had agents in Talu's court or among Rakata's guards or servants who would be privy to the *raden*'s movements. If so, Rakata now dared not trust anyone near him, a situation likely to shorten his temper, which was especially dangerous in these uneasy times.

Pressure was sure to be growing among the British as well. Wakefield must have tightened his security and his alerted troops would be more suspicious. The assassination attempt had worked against everyone because the increasing tension on both sides could easily cause a relatively minor incident to explode into a battle. Britt's mixed background had made him a puzzle to the Indonesians and British alike, and they'd left him alone as long as he'd done nothing to provoke them. If a rebellion broke out, each camp might decide he was with the other side, because neither faction would trust an enigma like him in the heat of the moment. The danger to Minda in such an event chilled Britt.

He raised his eyes to stare at the light coming from her room. At the thought of Minda's being harmed because men fought over something she'd had nothing to do with, a red flood of anger overtook him; and the hand that held his sherry glass clenched. The sound of the snapping stem startled Britt back to reality, reminded him this all was speculation. None of it might happen. He dropped the glass on the table. It was empty. The sherry had done nothing to ease his tension anyway.

Britt heard Minda's door being closed against the night, and a sense of profound loneliness swept through him. Just the soft click of the door handle's turning made him feel as if he'd been locked out. He tried to reason that it was his thinking about Minda's being harmed that inspired the strange feeling, but the sense of loneliness didn't pass. He stood up, silently stalked around the room, then ended again staring across the courtyard at her light.

*   *   *

When after dinner Britt had told Minda he wanted to read, then go to bed early, she'd dismissed Dessa and spent her evening doing the personal tasks of a woman alone, but her thoughts were on Britt's returning to the crumbling temple to kill the dread tigress. Finally, Minda had gone, still brushing her hair, to the window that overlooked the garden and, gazing at the darkness of the jungle beyond, wondered if the tigress was peacefully tending her cubs or looking for prey on this, hopefully, last night of her life.

"Why must a courtyard stand between us?"

Startled by Britt's question, Minda turned in a whirl of lace, her hair, darkly burnished gossamer, spun around her shoulders. She stared silently at him standing in the doorway for the moment it took to collect her thoughts before she answered, "I thought you preferred separate rooms. You never said otherwise."

Despite the tension he radiated, which seemed to make the air almost crackle as Britt walked slowly toward her, his loose-limbed steps were deceptively calm. He stopped to look down at her. "I'm saying it now. If you want your own bedroom, Minda, let it be the one adjoining mine."

She gazed up at him, wondering what had caused his mood, then answered quietly, "I've always thought there should be only one master suite in a home."

Minda saw his agitation fading. The change was in Britt's eyes, the softening of their surface, the brightening of their lights. She knew what he was feeling, that he wanted to make love with her. The knowledge of the desire growing in him was a sweet ache running through Minda, and she was aware that her eyes were taking on the same look as his.

"This house has been in two sections long enough," he said softly. "It's time the walls between came down."

Minda reached up to lay her hands at his temples. The thrill that ran through her was reflected on his features, as if they shared a vibrant power that completed its circuit wherever they touched. She wanted her body, not just her arms and shoulders, to feel it, but as if Britt wished to introduce the smoldering shimmer more gradually to his skin, he bent closer to brush his cheeks to hers. Minda turned her face, searching for his lips, not questioning, not asking more of him. It was enough that he was there, his mouth touching hers softly, as if he would hold back the power of the need she sensed in him.

Minda felt the desire making invisible arcs flicker between their bodies, saw it mirrored in his eyes like amber lightning. His lips caressed rather than kissed her. It was a cherishing of the sensation growing in the breathless waiting of their hearts. She was aware of the soft tug on the ribbons circling her waist, of his fingers deftly loosening the dressing gown's bows, and she knew the unhurried delicacy of his touch was a deliberate denial of the urgency keening through his senses. It served only to tease them both, to heighten and intensify their need. When the dressing gown fell open and Britt's hands slipped inside to rest warmly on her waist, Minda felt their slight quiver as an echo of her own eagerness.

Her hands slid from his temples to lightly clasp the back of his neck, and she wove her fingers into his hair. He brought his mouth again to Minda's, softly, tentatively, as if awaiting her response. The touch of his quietly moving lips changed Minda's wavering currents to steady warmth, as embers in a flirtatious draft were lit to a constant glow by an unchanging breeze. Her mouth responded avidly, igniting a piquant flame in him.

As she swayed closer, Britt put his hands on hers. Eyes gleaming in warning, he took her hands out of his hair and held them to his lips. His teeth brushed the curve of her fingers. Between little nips his gaze rose to meet hers.

"Why do you always wait for me to come to you?" he asked softly.

Her mind was in a clamor of confusion. She could barely think as his lips nibbled at her fingers. She answered quickly, impulsively, "But I came to your room the first morning I was here."

"That was by mistake." His tongue touched her palm, sending a swirl of sparks through her warmth. All the while he watched Minda's eyes, darkly shadowed like a jungle river where the trees dipped low over the water.

"I thought it was a mistake then, but I've wondered since if some wiser part of me had known where I was going even if I wouldn't admit it to myself," she murmured.

Still watching her eyes, Britt said softly, "We've spent so much time fighting our feelings, it may be hard for you to initiate lovemaking."

"That may be true," she agreed.

Britt lowered his eyes as his lips nibbled Minda's wrists and he thought about what she'd said. Between caresses he admitted, "Sometimes I'd like you to come to me, to say you want me as you did that first time in the cottage. Sometimes I need you." He looked up and saw that her eyes suddenly lit with radiance, as when the sun broke through the trees to strike emerald glimmers on a river's surface. He lifted her hands to press kisses into her palm. Though their hands were a fragile barrier between them, as he bent to touch his mouth to Minda's, the abrupt flaring of his passion scorched his intention to linger. He turned his head so his lips were at the corner of her mouth.

Between kisses Britt murmured, "I'd be tempted to say we should make tonight a new beginning, but I don't want to forget, even if I could, everything we've already shared. We once loved each other innocently as children; it was like a light that was always glowing in me. When you left Java, the warmth remained, but the light was gone until we met again. Then it no longer was warmth and light, but a flash of fire that burned and blinded us. We've tempered it now, learned how to warm ourselves at it without getting scorched. We can enjoy it, let the fire burn again brightly, as it always was meant to do for us."

Still holding her hands, he put his arms around her waist; so her body was arched against him as he kissed her. Minda's lips joyfully clung to Britt's; the power of his response rocked him, threatened to unleash the desire he was trying to keep banked.

"If you'd come to me, how could I have refused you?" he breathed as, releasing Minda's hands, he slipped his arms under hers so his fingers curled over her shoulders and held her snugly to him.

The sensation of her breasts crushed against Britt's chest was like a fire rippling through her, and she wanted more of it. Minda's arms slid around his hips and clasped him tightly to her. Britt's mouth moved slowly over Minda's, his tongue tracing its outline then its parting. Her lips were soft, silkily moist, an invitation to love. He felt as if a channel of molten lava lay within him, shimmering with golden fires, seething a little higher with every move she made against him. Still caressing her mouth, he reached back gently to break her hold on him.

A mass of amber sparks shone in his eyes as she gazed up at him and breathed, "I love you. I'll want you always."

She took his hand and began to walk slowly backwards, drawing him toward the door. He followed wordlessly, knowing, as she led him through the courtyard, that she meant to spend the night in his bed. For the first time since Minda had come to Phoenix House, she was leading him into love. He gladly let her.

Britt's sitting room was bright with the lamp he'd used for reading. As Minda paused to blow out the light, he stood silently watching, longing to kiss those pursed lips, to capture that mouth with his own, to claim her kiss even as his body needed to possess hers. Now. Without waiting for love games. But he'd offered Minda the lead, she'd taken it, and he wanted to learn what she would do. Britt took a step closer and merely kissed the nape of her neck, brushed his lips softly against her skin till he felt her lightly shiver. Then he stepped away.

When Minda lifted her head, a smile was hovering over her lips like a butterfly over a flower, as she led him into his bedchamber. The small lamp Suhadi had left after he'd turned down Britt's bed cast wavering streaks across Minda's face as she paused with Britt beside the bed.

Minda began to undress him, but not hesitantly as before. Now she seemed to have the confidence of Delilah seducing Samson and she made every move a sensuous caress. The secret smile was on her lips, the same promise in her eyes while she looked steadily up at him and, with little tugs, pulled his shirt from his waistband. After she undid each button, she placed a soft kiss on the skin she'd uncovered; then her lips nibbled at his earlobe while she slipped the cloth from his shoulders. Minda rose on tiptoe to kiss his neck, Javanese fashion, brushing her lips, the tip of her nose to his skin, breathing delicately on him while she absorbed his scent and unfastened his waistband.

Although Britt's impulse was to reach out and lock Minda in his arms, to devour her with kisses and pull her into bed with him, he stood motionless, letting her do as she pleased. Even as he watched her dressing gown fall in a lacy heap on the floor, as his eyes moved up her legs and along the curves of her body to stare hungrily into hers, he did nothing. He watched Minda get into bed, recline with the silken ease of a cat; but he didn't move until she reached out to him.

Britt reminded himself to let her choose the path their lovemaking would follow and sat on the edge of the bed with his back to Minda, trying to regain some control. But his desire was too strong to resist and he half turned to lean on one hip and gaze down at her. Minda's lips parted, she licked them slowly in deliberate provocation, and Britt could bear it no longer. His mouth touched hers, his first kiss softened by the remaining fragments of his will. Then his mouth covered hers, hardened, moved more insistently while a wildfire of passion overtook him. Britt caressed her almost roughly, but his forcefulness was an answer to Minda's own passion. Her mouth as eagerly returned his kisses; the tightening of her hands at his waist urged him to come to her. Though the caresses that crushed her lips mocked his will, he put his hands firmly against her shoulders to hold her back; so he could withdraw.

Britt stared down at Minda a long moment, as if his eyes were absorbing her into their fiery amber depths, before he said, "I wanted you to choose what we'll do, but I wasn't giving you the chance."

"Why do you think I've teased you so? Don't you know I've learned what excites you?" Minda asked in a low, husky voice she'd never used before. "You were doing what I wanted."

A startled look flickered through his eyes; and as if he were speaking more to himself than to her, he whispered, "And to think, when I saw you coming down the stairs in Philadelphia, I'd decided you were cold, like a beautiful crystal statue."

"My flame was turned down low then. It needed you to bring me back to life," she murmured. "Lie beside me, my love. I'll help you forget whatever you've been worrying about tonight, even if it was the tigress you must face tomorrow." Her fingers running down his side, then enticingly along his hip, emphasized her meaning.

"I'm beginning to wonder if I'm not facing another kind of tigress tonight in my own bed," he breathed.

Minda raised her head to nibble away any other words that might have come from his lips; and instead of obeying his urge to lock her in his arms, to kiss her as fiercely as his instincts demanded, he moved away.

Britt closed his eyes, renewing his determination to lift his mind from his body's responses so he could strengthen his will. He felt Minda turn, move snugly against his side, her leg sliding over his, then her lips moving softly on his eyelids, fluttering along his forehead, kisses in the roots of his hair moving to his temple. The tip of her tongue tasted his skin, then unhurriedly explored his ear until he felt as if his body were pulsing with the need for Minda's touch.

Her mouth sought his, nibbled at his lips, coaxing the hardness from them, her tongue surprising the corners of his mouth with little thrusts of piquant heat, then moving along the parting of his lips to finally capture his mouth in a kiss that made fires spring up in him, like the wind that touched Gunung Mrabu's seething fluid with blue flame. But she withdrew.

Britt opened his eyes and saw that she was kneeling beside him. His heart beat faster. But she merely looked at him for a long moment, as if she were deciding what she would do. He held his breath until she again bent over him. Her lips brushed his throat, nibbled at his shoulder. He turned his face toward Minda mutely asking for her kiss. As her mouth touched his, he closed his eyes in anticipation, but her lips lingered only teasingly over his and eluded the kiss. Then Britt felt her tongue flicking down his body, a line of soft bites along his waist. His eyes leaped open, but he could see only the mass of Minda's hair spread over his chest as she continued to caress and kiss him. The fires growing in him swirled higher until he was quivering with the impulses she was building in him.

When she felt as if her own senses were becoming a sea of shifting orange lights, she raised herself to rest on her elbows and, just brushing her body to his, slid up until she again looked into his face.

Lured to the edge of his endurance, Britt whispered, "I don't think I can bear much more of this."

The amber depths of his eyes had taken on brilliant pinpoints of copper, and looking into them, Minda was shaken by the intensity of the passion she'd stirred in him. She stared at Britt as if transfixed. In that moment, he read the measure of her own arousal and thought her need matched his.

"If this isn't to your liking, you must tell me," he murmured.

Britt's hands at her waist tightened, lifted her, igniting a flurry of sparks that streamed through her blood, making her catch her breath. He moved his hips slowly and she was electrified by the impulse that scorched her with its power.

He said softly, "End it now, my Minda, or I will."

The drumming of her heart blocked out his words. Even the hardening glitter of his eyes was lost on her. The firmer grasp of his hands on her hips didn't penetrate her thoughts, for she had none. She was aware only of the fires that seared her being. His body began to move beneath her. The forces pulsing through her blotted out her awareness that she was matching his rhythm. The exquisite sensations became molten waves coursing along her nerves, carrying her in their cascade toward a chasm of amber lights that sheeted up before her inner vision.

Britt's lashes parted and he saw Minda as if through a tunnel of golden sparks coiling around them. Though he was dimly aware of his previous resolution to let her lead them, he knew that passion had leaped beyond their commanding. Britt sat up rigidly to clasp Minda to his heart. She made a soft noise, like a cry of her ecstasy smothered; and they became wild, mindless creatures with the same raging need shattering their senses into crimson splinters.

They remained that way, locked in each other's embrace, Britt's head at last resting on her shoulder, Minda's face pressed against his chest, until the furious hammering of their pulses slowed and their minds began to function. Though the quiet beating of his heart seemed to confirm Britt's inner peace, Minda recalled the strange mood he'd been in when he'd come to her room. She realized his agitation then hadn't been caused so much by the separation of their bedchambers or her seeming reluctance to initiate lovemaking as by some problem on his mind.

"We've given ourselves to each other so fully neither of us should ever hesitate to confide in the other," she said quietly. "I know something has been on your mind since we left Djakarta. Share it with me."

"I suppose it's the situation in Java," he sighed.

"The assassination attempt made it worse," Minda concluded. She paused to think it over, then, as the answers began forming in her mind, slowly added, "There's more to it than that. You're afraid for me, aren't you? It's why you came to my room that way. You wanted to confirm my existence, to forget for a while that I may be as much threatened as you." When he didn't reply, she said, "Because I love you, I'll be in danger as long as you are, even if I were to go back to Philadelphia and you stayed here."

Britt was silent. He didn't want to talk about Philadelphia. It reminded him of Alden Townes, and he discovered deep in the recesses of his mind a chilling suspicion that Alden would cause them trouble yet. Though he couldn't imagine how Townes would do it, the idea was so strong he felt it like a premonition. Suddenly, he *had* to tell Minda that Townes was in Java, somehow to prepare her. For what? He didn't know.

Britt's hands at her temples asked her to look at him. She raised her head and saw that the autumn haze of his eyes had been darkened by shadows.

"During Matarami's funeral, I saw Alden Townes on the beach."

Minda's eyes widened in shock. *"Alden?"*

Britt drew her head to his shoulder, turned his face into her hair, and said, "Townes has engaged a servant, which makes me think he plans to stay for a while. I'd thought, if he wanted to pursue you, it was odd that he hadn't come directly to Phoenix House after his ship landed. I hoped that meant he wasn't going to bother you and I didn't tell you he was here because I didn't want to worry you unnecessarily. But I can't imagine another reason he'd come all the way to Java. Can you think of any?''

''None except that the Colonial Office must have assigned him to Djakarta,'' Minda said slowly. ''If so, he must have objected to his orders, because he spoke very derisively about Java when we were in Philadelphia. I don't think he'd be happy with an assignment here.'' She raised her head to look questioningly at Britt. ''Why does it worry you so much?''

''I don't know,'' Britt admitted. ''I just feel as if his presence here means trouble.''

''If Alden's position with the government doesn't carry enough influence for him to avoid what I'm sure must be an unwanted assignment, he doesn't have the power to instigate trouble for us,'' she reasoned.

''Perhaps not officially, but maybe in some other way,'' Britt said slowly. He regarded her silently a moment, then frowned. ''It probably means nothing. Don't let my imaginings bother you, Minda. If he comes to Phoenix House and is too much of a nuisance or offends you, I'll make sure he leaves.''

''I don't doubt you would.'' Minda smiled more easily than she felt and again settled her cheek against his shoulder. She, too, couldn't believe that Alden Townes's presence in Djakarta was merely coincidence, and she doubted that an island, even one as large as Java, could hold the three of them without trouble resulting. Not wanting to add to Britt's concern, deliberately using the same low, provocative tone as she had during their lovemaking, she reminded, ''You said, if something isn't to my liking, I should tell you; and too prolonged a discussion of Alden Townes *isn't* pleasing me, especially in our bed.''

Britt turned his face into her hair and asked, ''What would please you, Minda?''

His soft breath in her ear told her he already knew, but he wanted her to say it. Minda turned on her side so she could look into those amber eyes and watch them relight with copper sparks as she told him.

Minda paced restlessly through the garden, ending her walk, as she had the previous day, at the old swing. The little rise in the land at the farthest end of the house grounds faced the direction of the old temple at the foot of Gunung Mrabu. When Arjuna and the other men on the plantation who had volunteered to go on the hunt for the tigress had arrived yesterday at dawn, Minda had come with Britt this far to say good-bye.

She'd sat across the saddle in front of him in as near an embrace as was possible while he was guiding the horse. She'd looked at the curve of his fingers holding the reins, recalling how sensitively they'd caressed her, felt the strength of his arms circling her and remembered the warmth of their embrace all night. Minda had tilted her head to gaze up at Britt, at the clean angle of his chin, the roundness of the mouth that, after hours of kisses, she'd longed to kiss again. But instead, he'd had to go to the ancient temple to face the man-eater. A terrible feeling of grief had swept through her, as if the tigress had already killed him, and she'd stared up at his face, tried to fill herself with the sight of him. She'd leaned against Britt, wanting to absorb his scent and touch while she could. Clear amber eyes shaded by gold lashes had moved to look down at her, then had lifted to gaze into the distance.

When Britt had stopped the horse at the gate, he'd said quietly, "You must get down now, Minda." As if he'd read her thoughts, he'd added, "Don't be so afraid for me. I won't take chances."

Minda had thought about the risk he was taking just to go on the hunt, but she had taken a deep breath, looked up at him, and said only, "Let me kiss you for luck."

Britt had kissed her so long and deeply she'd been breathless before he'd released her. After he'd helped her slip down from the horse, as if she'd been pleading with fate, she'd said softly, "Come back quickly."

Britt had looked at Minda a long, silent moment before leaning over to press his cheek to hers and quietly promise, "We'll return in a couple of days."

The vision of Britt's riding away had been burned into Minda's memory as vividly as the firebrand of his kiss. She'd watched until he'd left the grounds, then had run to the old swing, and stood on its seat to keep him in view until he'd disappeared around a bend in the road. It didn't comfort her to know that Malili and the wives of the other men going with Britt were as anxious as she. Nothing could give her comfort except his safe return.

Though Minda had intended to spend the rest of the day after Britt had left working on the plantation's account books, she hadn't been able to concentrate on the figures and had put them aside. All through that night Minda had lain awake worrying about him; in the morning, she'd felt even less inclined to study bills and receipts.

She'd again wandered into the garden and met workers cutting down a tree. One of the men had planted a twig in the cleft of the stump and told her it was so the tree's spirit had somewhere to live. All she could think of was, if so mighty a tree could be felled, Britt could too, and the charm of the custom was lost on her. She dismissed it as just another superstition like the idea of a *lelembut* inhabiting the tigress and her somehow having the power to dispel the demon. All of it was nonsense, Minda told herself, as foolish as the notion that the crystal she'd found at the volcano was a gift from the fire goddess.

Unlike Arjuna, who had grown skeptical about many of the old Javanese beliefs, Malili swore almost as fervently as Dessa that the crystal was protective. Dessa had so persistently begged Minda to give it to Britt to carry on the hunt that Minda had finally offered him the crystal, and to placate Dessa, he'd put it in his pocket. He, like Minda, didn't believe that a pretty piece of mineral had magical qualities just because it had been found in a volcano, that a butterfly blown by the wind into the crater and pausing on her hand to rest was a gesture from a goddess.

Minda stepped up on the swing seat to peer in the temple's direction, realized what she was doing, and silently scolded herself. It was just as foolish to imagine she could somehow bring Britt home sooner if she kept staring toward a temple miles away and wishing. About to step off the swing and return to the house to fix her thoughts on something more constructive, like the account books, she noticed a horse and a pony coming up the road. The pony's rider was a servant, Javanese, she surmised from his batik pants and the jacket he wore, but who was on the horse? The set of the man's shoulders, the way he carried his head and sat his horse was familiar to Minda. When he took off his hat to fan his face, the sun caught silver lights from gray streaks at his temples, unusual when the rest of his hair was so dark. Suddenly Minda realized with a shock that her visitor was Alden Townes.

She hopped off the swing seat in a quandary about what to do. Why did Alden have to come *now*, when Britt wasn't home to face him with her? Then Minda's confusion changed to annoyance. Why did Alden have to bother her at all? She considered giving Enang orders to tell Alden she wasn't home and not admit him, but remembering how she and Britt had wondered why he was in Java, changed her mind.

Maybe she could learn something about his purpose. She ran back to the house making hasty plans about how she'd receive him.

When Enang led Townes to the study, as taken back as Alden was that Melinda would entertain a visitor in so unlikely a room, he was more surprised to find the former debutante seated behind a large desk surrounded by papers and account books. At Alden's entrance Minda laid down her pen, stood up, and came around the desk. Her smile was gracious but as cool as the one she'd always worn for social gatherings in Philadelphia.

She offered him her hand with the same aloof attitude as she'd have greeted Major Wakefield. "Good afternoon, Alden. After so long a ride from Djakarta, I'm sure you'll find a glass of lemonade refreshing," she said, as casually as if Djakarta was a stone's throw from Pennsylvania. She told Enang to get lemonade from Koki; then, noticing Alden's perplexion that she behaved toward him as if she'd seen him yesterday, she explained, "I'm not surprised you're in Java because Britt saw you at Matarami's funeral. I hope you had a smooth voyage and your stay has been pleasant. Have you been in Djakarta long?"

Alden gazed at her silently a moment before releasing her hand. "You're looking very well, Melinda."

She turned away to reseat herself behind the desk and invited, "Please sit down, Alden." As she resumed sorting stacks of receipts and bills, she said, "I'm sorry to have to entertain you here, but as you can see, I have work to do."

"I'm surprised to find you at such a task," he commented as he seated himself.

Minda couldn't resist flashing him a smug smile as she straightened a pile of receipts. "I told you I intended to learn this business, and I am."

Enang returned with the lemonade. While he gave them their glasses, Alden used the moment to consider this turn of events. He'd never seriously believed Melinda was capable of being a useful business partner for Vandekker. He cautiously remarked, "I suppose working behind a desk is a likelier job for a woman than overseeing the tea fields."

"I've been to the fields too," Minda replied. "I've found myself doing tasks and making decisions I'd once thought were the duties of a man, whether or not I've wanted to, thought I could, or even was afraid to try. I've discovered that I can do things I'd never considered and even enjoy many of them.''

Alden dryly observed, "It does, indeed, appear you're at home here.''

"Phoenix House *is* my home," Minda said pointedly. "I'm running the plantation while Britt's gone to hunt a tigress that's been causing trouble in the district.''

"I know about Vandekker going after the man-eater. My servant's relative told him. In fact, that's why I chose today to visit you. I thought it might be awkward to talk with Vandekker here," Alden admitted. "Out of curiosity, why didn't Vandekker wait for the other plantation owners to go on the hunt with him?''

"He didn't want to delay and give the tigress a chance to escape," Minda replied crisply. Though she'd already considered the possibility of telling Alden she and Britt were lovers to put him off, Minda now changed her mind. She didn't want to endure the discussion likely to result and didn't want him gossiping about her in Djakarta as she was sure he had in Philadelphia. Telling him she and Britt were going to be married, she was sure, would bring the same result.

Minda said tartly, "I can't imagine what you and I might have to say that Britt shouldn't hear, unless you've come to insult me as you did at the Reeds' party.''

"I apologize for that foolishness," Alden quickly replied. "I was angry because you'd broken our engagement.''

Though Minda's momentary silence seemed to be because she was considering the apology, she was really making a mental note to find out which of the plantation workers was passing information to Alden's servant. "I accept your apology, though it's a bit tardy," she said slowly.

"Your mother said things she's sorry for now too," he advised. "She's been frantic worrying about you.''

"I've written to her and described my life at Phoenix House, but you can confirm that Britt has done nothing harmful to me and hasn't shown a hint of wanting to cheat me out of my inheritance," Minda said sarcastically. The old bitterness welled up in her and she asked sharply, "That's why you've come to Java, isn't it? Because Mother's been hounding you? Maybe you hoped I was unhappy and you could persuade me to sell my share of Phoenix House to Britt, that I'd return to Philadelphia and marry you so you and Mother could use the money on yourselves." Minda took a breath and ended icily, "You're an attractive man, Alden. Why don't you find some other heiress to charm into marriage?''

Though Alden had previously felt the edge of Melinda's temper, it had been when she was furious at Jessica and his plot to cheat her. This time Melinda's pique was caused by the remembered offense, but the sting of her words was as sharp. She had found a new spirit Alden discovered he liked, though he knew he wouldn't be able to treat her as he had before. Gathering his composure and his ability to lie convincingly, he asked, "What do I have to do to make you believe me? You misunderstood the bit of conversation you overheard between Jessica and me." He paused to sigh heavily. "I've always loved you for yourself, not your money. I'm not interested in, as you put it, charming another heiress. If I can't get the woman I want, I won't take whatever female comes along next."

Alden seemed so sincerely distressed Minda began to wonder if she really had somehow misjudged him. Then, reminding herself that he was a talented actor, Minda was sure she'd been right in the first place and decided she was likelier to draw him out if she appeared to soften a little. She said, "When you go back to Philadelphia, you can tell Mother I've decided it's best to forget past problems."

"I'll have to assure Jessica that you're well and appear to be happy by mail. It may be a while before I return to Philadephia," he advised.

Minda's heart sank at this news, but she inquired, "Do you plan to stay in Java? That's surprising, seeing as you had such a low opinion of the island before. Have you been here long enough to learn to like it?"

"I only arrived a few days ago," Alden lied smoothly. "I would have visited you right away, but I didn't know what to say and I wasn't certain what Vandekker would do. He'd shown himself to be a violent man on our last encounter."

"You struck Britt with your riding crop," she pointed out.

"A mere tap on his hand was hardly reason for him to drag me off my horse and attack me."

"It was more than a tap," she recalled, "but he did it because you insulted me."

"I was worried about what his intention was toward you."

Minda squelched her impulse to add that Alden had been and probably still was jealous of Britt. Making Alden angry wasn't the way to learn his motives. "As I've already said, the past is best forgotten," she reminded and seemed to dismiss the incident as she took a sip of lemonade, but she was really buying time to think of a way to discreetly ask why Alden was in Djakarta. Finally, Minda said, "Perhaps, to prove that Britt and I hold no grudges, we could have a gathering of some sort to welcome you to Java. If I could know how long you're planning to stay, I'd be better able to make arrangements. We wouldn't want to have a small dinner party if you're going to be in Java long enough for me to arrange something more suitable for a visitor of your position."

Minda's offer astonished Alden. "You and Vandekker would have a reception for me?"

"We could invite Major Wakefield, his officers, and their wives. I'm sure the other planters would be happy to come. You're here on business as well as to look in on me, aren't you? Would your business take long enough to give me time to arrange a reception?" Minda inquired, hoping to learn something of his purpose.

"I am here on government business and I'll probably remain for some months," Alden replied, still trying to recover from the idea of Britt and Minda's having *any* kind of party for him. He wondered if it would be advantageous to accept this offer of a truce. Though he preferred to stay on friendly terms with Melinda so she would turn to him during the stormy times he saw ahead for Java, he didn't want to appear so friendly with Vandekker that he might accidentally be caught up in the destruction of the planter.

Finally, Alden said, "Your offer is generous, but my developing any sort of friendship with your partner, if that were possible, could be awkward in more ways than one. The situation on this island has become very unstable. Rakata and Vandekker are closely related and it would cast doubt on me, professionally, if I associated with him socially."

"Britt has very little to do with Rakata," Minda denied.

"They seemed quite friendly at Matarami's funeral."

"It was the attempt on Wakefield's life that brought them together. Wakefield was questioning them," Minda said.

Alden privately congratulated himself for having persuaded Samarang to have his men assassinate the major because though the attempt had failed, it had cast more suspicion on Rakata. Aloud he said, "The Colonial Office is very suspicious that Rakata is planning a rebellion, and I must tell you, Minda, that it has doubts about Vandekker's part in all this."

"But Britt saved Wakefield's life!" Minda exclaimed.

"He saved *Rakata's* life. Vandekker knew Rakata would be blamed if Wakefield was killed."

Alden's words were like ice water being poured on Minda. She'd hoped no one had thought of that. "It isn't true," was all she could say.

"Melinda, I *asked* to be assigned to Djakarta because I still love you and I'm afraid you're going to be hurt." Seeing she was ready to protest, Alden hurriedly continued, "Whether living on a plantation appeals to you for its novelty, because you want to prove something to yourself or just needed to escape from Jessica's pushing—I can't let you be buried in this jungle. I'm certain that before my assignment here is over, you'll *want* to go home. I hope you'll change your mind about me meanwhile; but if not, at least I'll be here if you need help. I'll be a friend if you don't want me to be more than that to you."

Minda got up from her chair and turned to stare out the window. She knew such an assignment involved a year. Why would Alden volunteer to live in a place he hated for so long unless, in his own way, he did care about her? But if what he'd said was a lie, if he still was after her money or had some other reason for being in Java . . .

Her speculations were interrupted by a tap on the door. She turned to give permission to enter, and Enang stepped into the room.

"Mr. and Mrs. DeGroot are calling, Mem Scott."

Minda frowned and turned to Alden. "I'm sure Mr. DeGroot is a little miffed about Britt having gone on the tigress hunt without inviting him. I think he'll want to find out about it and pretend this is a social call. His having brought his wife along means they'll probably stay awhile."

"I suppose their finding me here with you will start gossip. I'd best leave," Alden said. He put down his lemonade.

"When people have to travel jungle roads to visit each other, they can't send calling cards in advance. This isn't Philadelphia, Alden. Everyone is used to neighbors simply knocking on their doors without warning, so my having a glass of lemonade with an old acquaintance is hardly shocking," Minda explained. "You're welcome to stay if you want to."

"I've met very few people here so far. Perhaps I should begin to make some acquaintances. I think I will stay awhile," Alden said, hoping Melinda might be more favorably impressed with him if he remained long enough to at least smooth DeGroot's feathers about being left out of the hunt.

*   *   *

Later, as Alden rode back to Djakarta, he was glad he'd met the DeGroots. They'd been so impressed to be in the company of an envoy, Mr. DeGroot had restrained his complaints about Vandekker's hunting the tigress without him. The couple's amiable presence had eased the tension between him and Melinda and given them a chance to talk more socially. Melinda had relaxed enough to smile easily and even laugh at a couple of anecdotes before he'd left. She hadn't hospitably invited him to stay overnight, though she knew he and his servant wouldn't reach Djakarta until dawn, but he overlooked this.

Having found Melinda at work on the plantation's accounts and noting during her conversation with DeGroot how knowledgeable she'd become about the tea business, Alden's clinging suspicions that Melinda and Britt were lovers faded. They'd receded even more when he realized that, though the house was full of servants and neighbors could stop in unannounced any time, not one disparaging comment had reached his ears about their relationship. Not even his servant's relative on the plantation had mentioned gossip about the couple. Alden recalled that Melinda's extremely circumspect behavior in Philadelphia had been marred only by that one incident in the meadow at the Reeds' country house—which, he conceded, because of the temper he'd been in, he might have misunderstood. If Melinda really wasn't romantically involved with Vandekker, Alden thought he might win her over yet. This possibility changed his plans slightly, but he had many options on this politically volatile island.

Alden had learned, through what he considered to be a reliable source, that the war in Europe was likely to end soon. He'd been assured that Britain wouldn't return the East Indies to the Netherlands, a surprising move because Holland had been Britain's ally against France. The Hollanders had fought Napoleon and lost; Britain had driven the French troops out of Java and occupied it to protect the islands from French retaliation. If King George wouldn't return the profitable islands to the Netherlands, the Hollanders would probably be driven out. Their plantations could be claimed by ambitious men like Alden, who had the right connections. If Alden could get control of a plantation or two, if Vandekker were eliminated, he was sure he could persuade Melinda to return to London with him. Then they could either sell the plantations or let agents run them and simply collect the profits.

Alden had made careful inquiries about Phoenix House Tea in Europe and had learned it had a lucrative future. He'd also been assured that Vandekker wasn't the sort of man who would be turned out of his plantation without a fight. But because of Vandekker's mixed background and the Colonial Office's suspicions about him, Alden thought he could dispose of Vandekker as a threat even before the war in Europe ended, if he were careful, without Melinda having any idea what he'd done.

With the Hollanders resenting the British occupation and the Javanese wanting *all* foreigners to leave, the country was ready to explode in a civil war, which Alden was certain the British troops would win. He planned to make sure that Britt would be one of the victims of that war.

During the weeks he'd been in Java, Alden had secretly cultivated Samarang's friendship, because he'd learned the Javanese wanted to usurp Rakata's title. Alden had promised Samarang that he would be *raden* when the conflict was finished. As Prince Notokusumo had defected to the British so he could take his brother Hamengky Bwono's throne as *sunan*, Samarang had been happy to have a Britisher on his side; he recognized they were the major power in Java now. Samarang had agreed to lead his followers in attacks that would not only appear to be the beginning of Rakata's rebellion but would finance their plot. Samarang would steal gold from the occasional convoys Wakefield sent to the other military posts on the island, loot some of the smaller plantations, and raid Indonesian villages for the pearls they harvested from the ocean. Alden knew he could trade the loot to smugglers from Singapore.

Though Alden planned to implicate Rakata in these attacks, he also intended to make it appear that Vandekker was in league with his half brother to drive the British out of Java. Alden was certain that, if Britt and Rakata weren't killed during the three-way conflict that was sure to result on the island, Major Wakefield would have them executed afterward.

Chapter Thirteen

Late in the morning, after Britt and the hunting party had left Phoenix House, they entered a savanna and surprised a rhinoceros with a baby. Although rhinos are ordinarily quiet, harmless animals, this mother was alarmed at the crowd of men and horses suddenly intruding on her and charged them. Not wanting to have to shoot the creature, Britt ordered the men to scatter, but the animal was persistent and rushed at them again. After several charges, the men retreated to a dry riverbed, where the water had once deposited gravel in the same swirling patterns of its currents. The men could guide their daintily stepping horses around the worst of the rocks, but the mother rhinoceros ran heedlessly over them. Rhinoceros hide is tough, but its feet are incongruously tender. After a short pursuit the creature slowed, took a couple more steps, bellowed in pain, and stopped. As Britt had hoped, the indignant rhinoceros turned around to gingerly make its way out of the riverbed. It stared at them, snorting empty threats for a few minutes, until it gave up and left with disappointed grunts following in its wake.

The hunting party had to reorganize, then find a route to avoid the rhino's feeding ground. Because of the delay they didn't reach the foot of Gunung Mrabu until late in the afternoon. Britt called the men to a halt before they got too near the temple so he could consider the situation.

"The mountain is giving off more smoke than when we climbed

it," Arjuna said as he gazed at the volcano's crest. "Maybe it will spit fire one day soon."

"I'm more concerned about that tigress now," Britt replied, brushing off the importance of the volcano. "It's getting too near sundown to go into that temple."

"The man-eater will awaken soon if she hasn't already," Arjuna noted apprehensively.

"I don't want to take any longer at this hunt than necessary, but I don't like to send men who are weary from traveling after a tigress who's just had her rest and is probably hungry," Britt said, then reluctantly decided, "I think we'll have to wait until morning and hope she's found a few peacocks or monkeys to satisfy her appetite and make her drowsy."

"Nothing would make me happier than to kill this man-eater today so we could start back home tomorrow, but I, too, think we should wait until the tigress is in a less dangerous mood," Arjuna agreed.

The hunters made camp for the night a little up Gunung Mrabu's slope so the volcano's sulfurous odor would mask their and the horses' scent from the tigress.

Despite Britt's weariness he lay awake listening to the deep rumbles coming from the mountain's core while he gazed at the stars wishing the rhinoceros hadn't delayed them. He knew Minda would worry until he returned. As he'd ridden down the road away from the house, he'd turned to look back and seen her standing on the swing, watching until he'd passed from view. The small, lonely figure she'd made haunted his thoughts for several hours before he finally fell asleep to dream of her in his arms.

After Maoke, the man Arjuna had sent to watch the temple, came back to camp a little after dawn and confirmed that the tigress had returned to its lair, Britt chose several men to guard the horses. The rest of them set out on foot to the temple.

They divided into groups of three, then waited at the sides of every doorway while the torches were lit. They entered the crumbling building at Britt's signal. Each Javanese silently breathed one prayer—the man-eater was in someone else's corridor. Though the man who killed the tigress would be a hero among his people, none of them wanted to face, much less do battle with, a *lelembut*.

Kokoda and Baru, the men accompanying Britt, carried torches and spears; while Britt, needing both hands to keep his rifle ready to fire, had to rely on their light. The pungent odor of the tigress combining with the smell of moldering stones made Baru and Kokoda exchange grim looks, but Britt was listening to the ominous sounds coming from deep inside the mountain. Not only was the volcano smoking more, but it was noisier. He hoped the vibrations, which were causing dust from the stone ceilings to sift down over their heads, didn't loosen any rocks to topple on them. He was again amazed that the tigress hadn't found another den. Were her cubs too small to move or had the volcano's activities accelerated that fast?

The flickering torchlight revealed that the corridor was more treacherous than Britt remembered on his previous visit. He wondered if the mountain's vibrations had speeded the temple's deterioration in only the last few days or if the candle he'd carried then just hadn't given enough light for him to see as much damage as he could now. Brushing aside a shroud of cobwebs, he became suspicious that he wasn't following the same passageway he had before. Had he walked along the wall opposite the webs and somehow not noticed them? Inching his way around a pile of rubble, Britt realized that, because so many of the mildewed stones had fallen to pieces and entire walls had collapsed, there were more openings to other corridors now, which meant more ways for the tigress to slip past them.

A chasm made by a section of the floor's having sunk out of sight abruptly yawned at Britt's feet and he motioned for the men behind him to stop. Baru and Kokoda held up their torches and all three measured the pit with their eyes. It was too wide for a man to leap over, but not too great a jump for the beast. This passageway could provide an escape route for the tigress. Although Britt didn't like to surrender half their light, he took Baru's torch and stooped to prop it in a pile of rocks at the edge of the gaping hole. If it remained upright, the tigress wouldn't spring across the pit, because there wasn't enough room in the corridor on either side of the flames. Britt rose and gestured for them to retrace their steps so he could find the passageway he'd originally taken, the one that had led him to the room where the tigress had made her lair.

Britt discovered that, instead of following the corridor he had on his previous trip, he'd mistakenly stepped through a gap in the wall and led them down a different passageway. Now he recognized the remnants of old carvings in the stone he'd passed before and knew they were approaching the man-eater's lair. He gestured to Baru and Kokoda, but his warning wasn't necessary. They'd sensed Britt's heightened tension and knew from the stronger scent of the tigress that she was nearby. Despite the low grumble of the volcano that would help disguise any sound they might make, the men walked even more cautiously down the last passageway leading to the room where Britt had found the cubs.

The men expected that, despite their stealth, the torchlight would awaken the tigress. They could only hope, after a night of roaming and probably having eaten something, she would be drowsy. The worst they anticipated would be to find her alertly crouching between them and her cubs. Though Britt's rifle allowed him only one shot before reloading, the close range almost assured that would be enough. But if he missed, Baru and Kokoda had spears. Rifle cocked and at his shoulder, Britt entered the room with his friends a step behind. They were surprised to discover only a pair of cubs at the far end of the room.

One of the cubs was sprawled on its side and appeared to be sleeping. The other was struggling to its feet. Its clumsiness told the men that the cubs were barely past the stage of opening their eyes. The cub who had gotten up looked curiously at Britt, blinking in the torchlight.

"The man-eater is gone," Kokoda breathed.

"She must have slipped down another passageway," Baru whispered.

"Maybe she got past us when we went down the wrong corridor," Britt muttered, disgusted at his mistake. About to say some of the other men might trap her, Britt was distracted by a feeling that they were being watched. His scalp prickled when he heard a low, rumbling growl, so close it seemed almost to come from inside himself. The man-eater was behind them.

Britt whirled at the instant the tigress leaped on Kokoda's back. Kokoda screamed only once as he plunged facedown to the floor, but the man-eater sprang away from his body and launched herself at Baru so swiftly the Javanese hadn't the time to raise his spear. Britt dared not fire his rifle and hit his fallen friend, who was desperately grappling with the beast. Britt lowered the gun, and, hoping to club her in the side of the head, to at least deflect those awful fangs from Baru, he swung the rifle stock up. But the tigress swerved away; the stock splintered against the stone wall and the rifle went off. The shot plunged into the ceiling and a burst of rock shards fell on Britt, staggering him. The tigress, frightened by the roar of the gunshot, bounded from the room, her shoulder knocking Britt against the wall.

Britt heard something crunch against his hip and, puzzled by the sound, reached into his jacket pocket. When he grasped a handful of grainy stuff, like coarse sand, he felt as if his skin were being stung by a thousand bees. Britt hastily pulled out his hand and saw that his palm was dotted with blood; particles of Minda's crushed crystal sparkled in the last flickers of Baru's fallen torch. Shaking the splinters from his hand, he glanced at the bodies of his friends and realized they were dead just as the torch went out and the room was plunged into darkness.

Echoes of shouts and running feet somewhere in the temple reached Britt's ears. He knew the other hunters had heard his gunshot and were coming. He realized if he took time to feel around the floor for the spears Baru and Kokoda had dropped, the tigress would get away. Though he was weaponless and couldn't kill the man-eater, he decided to follow her and call back to his friends so they'd know which corridor the beast was in.

Britt raced out the doorway after the tigress shouting, "This way! Arjuna, Maoke, follow me!"

In the gloom ahead he saw the white tips of the tigress's ears veer, then vanish, and he knew she'd swerved into another passageway. A moment later, when he turned the corner and saw the torch he'd propped up to prevent the tigress from leaping over the collapsed floor section, he skidded to a stop. Afraid to jump because of the torch flames, the man-eater had turned to face him. Her eyes glowed like topazes in the flickering light as she began to crouch.

Britt felt as if ice, not blood, were pumping through his veins. He knew the other hunters were too far away to save him. If he turned and ran, the tigress could catch him in a few bounds. Suddenly remembering the splintered crystal in his pocket, he reached in and took out a handful of the stinging grains.

"Beast or *lelembut,* your eyes will feel *this!*" he shouted and threw the crystals into the tigress's face.

The man-eater roared in pain and shook her head. She went down on her shoulders to paw her face, then tried to rub her head on the floor. Britt could see the crimson spotting her muzzle, and despite the people she'd killed, though she'd been ready to maul him, he pitied her.

"Arjuna! Maoke! Over here!" he shouted, wishing someone would come to end the tigress's pain.

But at the sound of Britt's voice, the beast raised her head and turned toward him. Although the man-eater was blind, the low growl in her throat told him she was going to make one more rush at him. Britt took a soundless step backward as the tigress's muscles coiled to spring.

A shot rang out from behind Britt and the man-eater abruptly flopped on her side as limply as a discarded rag. Britt leaned back against the wall, head bowed to his chest, and let out a heavy sigh of relief as Arjuna sprinted toward him.

"Are you all right?" the Javanese anxiously asked.

Britt nodded. "Thanks to you. Baru and Kokoda weren't as lucky."

Arjuna gripped his friend's arm. "I know," he said, then spying the blood on Britt's hand, lifted it. "What happened here?"

Britt finally raised his head. "I guess Minda's crystal saved me after all. At least, it bought me the time to come for you and kill the beast, but it's smashed to dust now."

"It *was* protection, as Malili said," Arjuna commented wonderingly.

"What is this?" Maoke's voice demanded.

Britt stepped away from the wall and turned to see that Maoke had just entered the passageway. Following the line of Maoke's gaze, Britt saw one of the tiger cubs standing in the corridor midway between them. It looked first at Maoke then toward him and Arjuna.

"Now, what will we do with those cubs?" Britt said gruffly.

"The other one is dead." As Maoke started toward the cub, he explained, "It had a twisted leg as its mother did and looked like it had died from something that was wrong inside it." Intending to pick up the live cub, Maoke began to stoop, but the little tiger turned and ran clumsily toward Britt.

He gazed down at the cub, who'd stopped at his feet and was staring up at him. "This one seems to be normal, but it's much too young to have been weaned."

"What will we do with it?" Arjuna asked. "It will starve if we leave it here."

Britt knew the only alternative was to kill it now. Not wanting to look too long at the cub, he stepped over it and walked a little away. At Arjuna's chuckle, he stopped and turned. The wobbly cub had followed him. It sat down and again stared up at him, as if awaiting his verdict.

"I *don't* want you, damn it," Britt said brusquely. The cub rolled over on its back, as if in surrender. Britt gazed down at it a long moment. "But *you'll* need someone. For a while anyway." Finally he bent to pick up the cub and said, "I suppose Minda might like you."

"When she was a child, her mother was very distressed about the kinds of pets she carried home," Arjuna recalled, then added, "You could call it Dalang—to come."

"It docs keep coming after me, doesn't it? If it must have a name, Dalang it will be." Sighing in resignation, Britt turned and started down the passageway with the cub nestling comfortably against his chest. Startled by a ragged, little purr as he walked, Britt glanced down. A pair of tawny eyes looked up at him and he commented softly, "You knew all along I couldn't let you die just because you had an evil mother."

On the morning of the day Britt had hoped to return, Minda stationed herself in the garden to watch for him. After hours of fruitless waiting broken only by occasional trips into the house, at twilight Minda gave up. She lay awake that night reassuring herself over and over that Britt's plans had simply gone awry, there was some good reason for his delay. When Britt didn't come back the next day, Minda told herself that if anything had happened to him, the other hunters would have brought him home. She spent that night in his bedroom weeping into his pillow and got up the next morning pale and wan with shadows beginning to circle her eyes. A couple of days later, despite the growing heat at noon, Minda wouldn't go into the house; and while everyone else was taking their afternoon nap, she sat on the motionless swing, gazing at the road Britt had taken, feeling as if all vitality, even life itself, was slowly draining out of her.

When Minda saw the group of horsemen round the bend in the road, her exhausted mind didn't immediately react. The heat waves made the figures seem to shimmer and she wondered dazedly if they were an illusion. Finally, she got to her feet; but when the riders moved away from the trees and the sun made a golden blaze of the first man's hair, her weariness and nightmares were swept away. She gathered up her skirt and, with a little cry, began to run.

Britt saw Minda racing toward him and urged his horse into a trot. At the entrance to the house grounds, he barely had time to hastily dismount before she flung herself into his arms. The joy of his embrace was like a burst of sunlight in her mind.

Britt quickly explained, "We're late because we brought the tigress's body to Rakata rather than home. I didn't think you'd want to see it."

"I saw enough of that man-eater in our garden to spend every minute you were gone terrified for you," she said against his shoulder.

"You don't have to be afraid anymore," he soothed, then, holding Minda away, saw the marks that sleeplessness had left on her face. He said, "I brought something back I thought might cheer you, but maybe it will only remind you of fear. Perhaps I should have left it to die."

"Die?" she echoed in surprise.

Britt released Minda and walked around to the far side of his horse. She knew he was doing something with his saddlebag, but couldn't see what until he returned, holding the tiger cub a little hesitantly out toward her.

"Oh!" Minda stared at the creature, which was barely the size of a housecat. She reached out and gingerly touched a paw that hung languidly over Britt's arm.

"This one is normal, but her brother wasn't. He was dead when we found him. She'd have starved if we'd left her behind. The only other thing to do was kill her and I couldn't." Britt slowly, almost apologetically added, "If she reminds you too much of her mother, Arjuna said he'd take care of her until she's old enough to fend for herself."

Minda's fingertip tentatively brushed the cub's forehead and found its fur as soft as down. "When will she be old enough to manage on her own?"

"Over a year," he answered cautiously, knowing it was closer to two.

"By that time, if we got along at all," Minda said as she started gathering the cub from his arms, "we might get too attached to her." When the miniature tigress gave Minda's chin a lick, she smiled and asked, "Do you think she'll frighten away some of those little lizards we keep finding in the house?"

Finally sure that Minda wasn't afraid of the cub, Britt relaxed and answered, "As time passes and she grows, I suspect Dalang will scare away a lot more than lizards." He put his arms around Minda's waist and as they started toward the house, explained, "Arjuna suggested the name because she kept following me."

Minda nodded approval of the name and, suddenly recalling her visitor of a few days before, said, "I'm glad you warned me that Alden was in Java. I wasn't quite so shocked when he called on me."

Britt's sideways look was brief, but she saw the annoyance sharpening his glance. He stopped walking, turned to her, and asked, "What did Townes say?"

After Minda had described Alden's visit, Britt remarked, "He has some scheme in mind, I'll wager."

"His taking an assignment that will keep him on an island he hates for at least a year has made me wonder if he really does care about me," she commented.

"Trying to win you back is obviously part of his plan or he wouldn't have been on the doorstep right after I left," Britt said curtly. "But I think an assignment here must also be a good move for his ambition with the Colonial Department. After all, nothing controversial is happening in Philadelphia these days, so he has little chance of doing something noteworthy there to advance his career."

"Whatever Alden intends, I think he's still afraid of you."

Britt's voice had an edge as he resumed walking toward the house. "Townes will have good reason to be afraid if he tries to instigate trouble between us."

Minda privately agreed, but said aloud, "Talking about trouble reminds me that Rakata may have caused some; at least, Major Wakefield seems to be blaming him." At Britt's alarmed expression, Minda explained, "I sent Suhadi to Djakarta on some errands. He said a courier was killed on the way to the military post at Bogor and his pouch was stolen. There also was a raid on a small rubber plantation near the coast. A man named Voorne ran it. The house was burned to the ground. Mr. Voorne, some field workers, and his house servants were killed."

Britt's shock was apparent as he exclaimed, "But I saw Rakata at Talu when I gave him the tigress's body! He can't be in two places at the same time!" Then Britt suddenly realized Rakata didn't have to take part personally in such attacks. The *raden* could order his men to accomplish them. Finally, Britt said, "Rakata never even hinted he knew about this. If he's innocent, it's possible he isn't aware any of it happened."

"If he's guilty, would he tell you?" Minda asked.

Britt had to admit, "Though Rakata and I have become friendlier, there's a lot about him I don't know."

"That's what Major Wakefield would say about you, and Rakata would probably agree with him," Minda observed.

Britt had to concede that was possible, but not wanting to believe Rakata had been involved in the attacks, he said, "Whatever else Rakata may be, I don't think he's a thief, and I'm certain that's why Voorne was killed. Though he lived like a miser, it was rumored he kept a lot of gold hidden in the house. I was inclined to think it was true.''

"What about the courier?'' Minda inquired. "The stolen pouch contained Wakefield's orders to the officer in charge of the post at Bogor. Who would be more interested in knowing about those orders than Rakata? Although very few Javanese can read English, Rakata seems much better educated than the majority of his people. Do you know if he can read English?''

"I don't think so,'' Britt answered. "If Rakata did have his men attack that courier, he's asking for trouble; because it wouldn't take much to turn this island into a battleground.''

Seeing how upset Britt was, Minda quickly said, "If any charges were going to be made, I should think Rakata would already have been arrested.''

"Charges will be made the instant any shred of evidence shows up,'' Britt grimly assured, then fell silent. He reflected that Wakefield knew *he* could read English and the major had always been almost as distrustful of him as of Rakata. But wouldn't his having saved Wakefield from assassination make the major realize he didn't want a rebellion to break out? Britt wasn't sure of that or anything else about the situation, but he didn't mention his doubts to Minda. He was silent until they went into the house.

They were immediately surrounded by the servants, who oohed and ahhed over the cub Britt had brought back and wanted to know about the hunt.

Britt's answers were so abbreviated the servants turned to Arjuna, who had followed Britt and Minda into the house, for details.

Dessa was elated that the pulverized crystal had played a part in saving Britt from the tigress. "I *knew* the fire goddess would protect you from that *lelembut*!'' she triumphantly exclaimed.

"The goddess will rid our island of the soldiers too,'' Enang declared.

Britt's sharp glance stopped him from saying more. "It's best not to speak too loudly about soldiers,'' Britt warned. "Minda told me that someone at Phoenix House is related to Alden Townes's servant and was talking to him about what goes on here. Townes is working with the Colonial Office.''

Arjuna's cheerful mood vanished as he turned to the servants and demanded, "Who has been talking to Townes?''

The servants stared at each other in astonishment.

"Alden didn't say it was a house servant. It could be anyone on the plantation," Minda reminded. "From the offhand way he mentioned it, I suspect the worker didn't say anything important, nor does Alden expect him to."

"Maybe not, but I still want to know who that person is," Britt said.

"I'll find out and bring him to you," Arjuna promised.

Wanting to change the subject and ease the tension, Minda looked at Britt and said, "If that crystal helped save your life, I'm glad I climbed Gunung Mrabu to get it, and if the fire goddess would get rid of the soldiers on Java, I'd crawl over every inch of the crater looking for more, then help you smash them all."

Britt had turned to regard Minda and his eyes softened as she spoke. Then he said, "The crystal wasn't completely destroyed. I found part of it still intact." He reached into his jacket, then dropped a piece of the stone into Minda's hand.

It was about the size of his thumbnail, flat on two sides like a coin, but its outline reminded her of something. She stared at the orange-red lights in the crystal's heart and finally said, "It's even prettier than the whole piece was. It looks a bit like a rose petal, doesn't it?"

"The goddess preserved it for you," Dessa advised solemnly.

Minda glanced at the maid, then looked at Britt and said, "Whether or not it has protective power, it would make an attractive piece of jewelry. Maybe I should have it put into a pendant on my next visit to Djakarta. If it's trimmed and polished, it will be less likely to break."

"It's yours to do with as you please," was all Britt would say. He'd thought that the crystal's being in his pocket when he'd faced the tigress had merely been a fortunate coincidence, but he was beginning to wonder where coincidence ended and fortune or misfortune began.

At Koki's reminder that even little tigresses needed sustenance, Britt explained he and Arjuna had devised a kind of waterskin for Dalang to nurse from and had learned in Rakata's village that the cub accepted goat's milk. Koki promptly sent Enang to borrow a nanny goat from one of the Javanese who lived on the plantation.

Britt went to bathe and Minda distracted herself from worrying about problems by playing with Dalang until Enang came back with the nanny goat.

After the cub had been fed, Britt returned from his bath wearing a robe and rubbing his hair with a towel. He watched Dalang curl up for a nap with the pair of kitchen cats Koki kept and couldn't help smiling as he commented, "They're all friends now, but I wonder what those tabbies will think of Dalang next month."

"Maybe by then they'll be so used to her they'll accept her being larger than they are," Minda said as they left the kitchen to stroll in the courtyard.

"The cats aren't going to have much choice." Britt's smile faded and he paused in his steps. "I'm sorry I was so short with you when you told me about Townes's coming."

"I realize there's a lot on your mind and you know I could never be interested in him." Minda brushed away his apology. "I just wonder why you seem so bitter toward him."

"I'm not bitter; I just have no use for him. Townes didn't come here because he cares one whit about what happens to you. People like him do nothing out of love. They aren't capable of it," Britt said tensely. Without looking at her, he added, "Even if Townes were my rival for your love, I would respect him, providing he deserved it. But he doesn't. He reminds me of the kind of people I prefer to forget exist when I'm at Phoenix House." Britt felt Minda's hands on his arms and finally turned to look at her.

"I was in the garden when I saw Alden coming up the road. My first reaction was resentment, so it seems that you and I feel the same way about being imposed on," Minda said thoughtfully. "I allowed him into the house only because I'd hoped to learn why he'd come to Java. I think one sometimes has to temporarily set aside a personal preference in order to benefit in another way."

"You think I'm being inflexible, that I should be more willing to unbend," he concluded.

"I think you don't like anyone to interfere with your life and you know that being too flexible can be a trap," Minda answered more brightly. Rising to her toes, intending to plant a cheerful kiss on his cheek, she leaned against Britt. The sensation of his taut, lean body, the silky texture of a wisp of his hair brushing her skin, its freshly washed scent made her linger to add softly, "You seem to know how to unbend at the right moments. Didn't you teach me how?"

Although she moved away, her face remained uplifted to his and he saw a kiss waiting on her lips.

The last shadows of annoyance in Britt's eyes faded as he gathered Minda in his arms. Britt's mouth was as warm as sunlight, his kiss as soft as the courtyard's fragrant breeze, and she melted against him. As his lips moved pliantly over hers, his arms tightened.

Between the kisses he was tenderly placing at the corner of her mouth, she whispered, "I want you."

Britt leaned over and, picking Minda up in his arms, started carrying her toward his room. His lips continued to caress hers as he walked and he said quietly, "I suspect I could even live in Townes's kind of world if I had you."

"No matter what Alden or anyone else may do, I shall love you," she promised.

"Then I can endure anything," he breathed.

Chapter Fourteen

The servant who was offering to help Rakata take off the loose, cotton robe he'd worn from the bathhouse finally lowered his hands and prompted, "Isn't my lord going to take his afternoon rest?"

"I have too much on my mind to sleep," the *raden* brusquely answered.

"Can I get anything for you, my lord?" the servant inquired.

Rakata wasn't thinking of personal needs and replied automatically, "A cup of pear wine." Then he turned away.

After the servant had given his *raden* the wine, he hovered solicitously near until Rakata waved him away. The servant went to a corner of the room, where he sat on the floor to watch for a sign of the *raden*'s needing anything else.

Rakata was only dimly aware of the wine he was sipping as he distractedly began to pace his chamber. He was too absorbed in his thoughts about the messages Britt had sent since he'd delivered the tigress's body almost a moon-month ago.

The first letter, which Maoke had brought to Talu, had informed Rakata of the attacks on Wakefield's courier and Voorne's plantation. The second, delivered last week, described more incidents—a raid on another small plantation, a British patrol that had been waylaid in the jungle, and attacks on two Indonesian villages whose people were known to cooperate with the occupying army. Although the messages carefully avoided any hint of accusation, Rakata sensed Britt wasn't convinced he was innocent. Both letters had discreetly reminded him that the violence could cause suffering for everyone in Java and urged Rakata, if he knew the identity of any Javanese taking part in these attacks, to stop them. Britt promised that if he got evidence that Hollanders or British were causing the trouble he'd take it to Wakefield.

Evidence was the problem. Rakata frowned as he thought about Britt's messages and the man he suspected most, Samarang—not because he had any evidence, but because he'd learned long ago to distrust his cousin.

During their childhood, Rakata had innocently puzzled many times about why the challenges boys normally flung at each other in play had always seemed to take a sharper, more threatening turn when Samarang had aimed them at him. After Rakata had accepted the idea that Samarang disliked him, he'd wondered what he'd done to earn his cousin's aversion, but he didn't court Samarang's friendship. Rakata wasn't easily influenced by his peers and had refused to let his cousin goad him into doing things that would have gotten him into trouble with Matarami or were foolishly dangerous. When he had accepted Samarang's challenges, he'd known in advance that he was strong and quick enough to succeed.

By the time they'd reached adolescence, Rakata had finally realized Samarang had always been driven by resentment that he would one day assume Matarami's place. He'd been surprised his cousin seemed to view the title only as an avenue of power and overlooked the often onerous problems that went with it.

Among the Javanese, puberty was the direct entrance to manhood, and because accidents or mistakes would no longer be blamed on childish misjudgment, Samarang dared not used the same methods as before. His rancor had taken other forms of expression. He'd competed against Rakata in all possible ways. One legitimate competition open to Samarang was women. He'd taken an immediate fancy to any girl Rakata noticed, but it was the future *raden*'s sincere love that had won the heart and hand of the beautiful Lady Surana. Whenever Matarami had asked for opinions on official matters, Samarang had taken the side opposing Rakata's view and, during the inevitable debate, had tried to make Rakata appear foolish. But the future *raden* had learned to avoid these new traps of his cousin as well as lay a few of his own, with the result that Matarami and his council had finally become aware of the young nobleman's antipathy.

Rakata suspected, too, that Samarang had exaggerated and spread gossip about a couple of impulsive remarks he'd made and caused Rakata to appear to be a hothead who wanted a rebellion. As angry as Rakata was that foreigners had taken the government of the island from its people, he knew the Javanese couldn't win a war against the superior weapons of the occupying army. Even if desperation eventually drove them to rebel, Rakata would never order his men to face the foreign soldiers on an open field, but would be forced to carry on the battle bushfighter style in the jungles his people knew so well, a tactic Samarang was well acquainted with and could be using now to incriminate the *raden*.

Rakata's becoming Raden of Talu had silenced Samarang, but Rakata knew his cousin's jealousy had become like a demon possessing him. Samarang would gladly take advantage of any opportunity to have Rakata deposed so he could become *raden*. But the title was Rakata's; he meant to keep it.

Rakata saw how the problems forced upon the island by its invaders could be used to so discredit him the council of noblemen would banish him or Wakefield would arrest him, which meant almost certain conviction and execution. If he were *sunan* of all Java, his personal suspicions would have been enough to condemn Samarang, but a *raden*, though powerful, needed evidence to lay before his counselors. Rakata and his agents had found none. If Samarang was guilty of any of these crimes, he had so cleverly covered his tracks that even Rakata sometimes wondered if he was wrong about his cousin's being behind these raids. He realized that others could as easily benefit from them.

Why would Samarang, who spoke only enough English to make himself understood in simple matters and couldn't read one word of it, steal messages from Wakefield's courier? Although loot taken from the raids was a language anyone could understand, searches of Rakata's walled city had produced nothing. It was possible that Samarang and those secretly working with him had found a place somewhere else to cache the stolen goods, but what purpose did it serve on an island where it had to surface eventually if the thieves were to profit from it? All that Rakata could think of was that the thieves must somehow have made a connection with smugglers to get rid of their loot.

Such an arrangement was unlikely for a Javanese because the smugglers from Singapore were so elusive and dealt only with known contacts, usually Chinese compatriots. The Javanese had always been law-abiding people. Their rare serious crimes were the kind more inspired by passion than greed. Any stealing had always been a matter of petty pilfering rather than taking items of enough value to interest smugglers. Even Javanese criminals had never established contact with them and had no access to the ships that, like ghosts on moonless nights, lowered anchor in secluded inlets to silently take on forbidden cargo.

Aside from Samarang's doubtful ability to contact smugglers, Rakata had never thought his cousin was clever enough to plan a series of crimes in such careful detail Rakata couldn't catch him at it. There were only two conclusions that might answer all Rakata's questions. Either a non-Javanese—one who knew enough about Rakata to cast blame on him—was guilty or Samarang was working with such a person.

Rakata considered, as he often had, who among the British, the Hollanders, or those of mixed blood had the brains to plan all this, the ability to move freely enough to establish a connection with Singapore plus an intimate knowledge of the Javanese. Though Rakata wasn't personally acquainted with every soul in west Java, his network of agents were effective eyes and ears. There was no one he could think of who was a more likely suspect than Britt, but he didn't want to believe that Britt's concern for the Indonesians and their island was sham.

As always, when Rakata's mind sorted through these possibilities only to arrive at the same answer, he frowned. At this sign of the *raden*'s displeasure, the servant hastily rose and, noting Rakata's cup was empty, quickly offered to refill it. The *raden* seemed to pay no attention, but when the cup was half full, he lifted a finger in signal that it was enough, then turned away to walk outside.

The first floor of the building jutted out past Rakata's apartments so its roof formed a terrace for the *raden*'s private use. The decorations around the top of the lower floor made a lacy balustrade of stone carvings that Rakata leaned his arms on as he gazed unseeingly over the city.

Britt had told Rakata little about his personal habits, ways of life, or beliefs, but once in a while Britt's reserve had momentarily lowered and Rakata had been able to glean some personal insight into his half brother. Although Rakata had made no decisions that couldn't be altered, he found it very difficult to believe Britt could be a thief and murderer; but he could understand why a man in Britt's position might be tempted.

"You're thinking about your brother with the golden hair?"

Rakata nodded but didn't turn at the sound of the voice he loved more than any other, Surana's. As Rakata anticipated, his wife's perfume came nearer, and he sensed her presence close behind him before he felt the butterfly touch of her fluttering robe as she stepped around to his side, then leaned lightly against him.

"Thoughts of this brother are more important to you than I am," Surana remarked as she slipped her hand inside his garment and caressed his chest.

It was a game they sometimes played. She accused him of not caring as much for her as what he was thinking about so he would say he loved her. It was Surana's way of distracting him from his worries.

"Nothing is more important to me than you are," Rakata answered.

Surana stood on her toes and lightly nuzzled Rakata's neck, a gesture that usually sent fire swirling through his veins, but his hand on her waist didn't move. She whispered against his skin, "You have tired of me and are thinking of taking another woman."

This, too, was part of their game. He replied, "If the *sunan* himself had a wife like you, he'd send his other women away."

"You aren't my husband today, but Raden of Talu only; for you're thinking about the problems of your people," she concluded. "If this Hollander brother is causing the trouble, I'll make him a gift of a venomous serpent to end the problem so your eyes will have time to see me again."

This seemingly fierce offer was as much part of their game as the rest of it. Surana was too gentle to harm anyone, and she wouldn't go near even the most innocuous snake. Rakata's dark eyes, now softened by humor as she'd planned, finally moved to gaze down at her. "I *am* looking at you. How could my eyes ignore so beautiful a woman?"

It was true that Surana's delicately boned face was as flawless as a golden lily, and Rakata was much tempted to caress the ripe petals of her lips as her wide almond-shaped eyes were asking him to do.

"If I did what you're wishing, I'd forget my problems. But that wouldn't be the way to find solutions to them."

Rakata's answer was Surana's permission to ask, "May I lighten my lord's burden by taking some of it on myself?"

He put his cup down on the balustrade, then slid both arms around her, laid his cheek on the glossy black hair at her crown, and sighed.

"Though your hands are too small to hold the staff of my rank, without your counsel I'd be less a *raden*. I only wish you could meet Britt. Your judgment of a man is sometimes better than mine."

"You longed for many years to meet him. Now that you have and discovered you like him, you don't want to think he's the cause of this trouble," Surana surmised.

"As always, your words are like a sword that, in one quick stroke, slices through a coconut's tough husk to reveal its fruit," he commented. "Yes, I like Britt though in many ways I don't know him well."

"Doesn't he belong to this land the same as you? He's your mother's child too."

"Britt's father was one of Java's invaders." Rakata lifted his head and stepped back a little to look at Surana. "Gerard Vandekker and his partner, Charles Scott, were different from many of the foreigners that came, I admit. They never treated the Javanese they employed like slaves, as so many others did. Gerard and Charles toiled beside their workers to three times rebuild their plantation, and Britt, I'm told, goes into the fields and factory with his workers. His skin confirms this, for he's darkened from the sun, not pale like those who sit under awnings counting their money and give little of it to the men and women who earn it for them."

"The tigress skin now gracing the floor of my bedchamber wasn't the gift of an indolent man or a coward," Surana reminded. "Still, you ponder the reasons Britt might betray us. One you're considering is revenge for your mother's banishment and death."

"Britt seemed angry with me the first time I spoke to him in that village where his partner was killed," Rakata remembered, then added, "But Charles was his friend and had just died in his arms."

"Some people would rather appear angry than grieved because they're too proud to weep," Surana suggested. "Then, too, you'd just saved his life. The old feud between Matarami and Gerard had taught Britt to think of you as his enemy, and it's difficult to owe your life to an enemy."

Rakata nodded agreement. He'd seen the surprise that had lit Britt's eyes turn to abashment when he'd recognized who'd saved him. Rakata had also noted the tears of grief for Charles that Britt had tried to hide.

"I know enough about enemies and death to understand. But I wonder if Britt ever realizes Sukadana's banishment took her from me when I was a child and I grieved for her. If Gerard hadn't killed her murderer, I would have done it, even if the man thought he was obeying Matarami's wishes," Rakata confessed. His mind returned to Britt and he recalled, "Britt's anger that day we met seemed directed at the present, not the past, but I sometimes have to wonder if it's all a role he's playing."

"Confused emotions make you as suspicious of him as he probably is of you. It isn't right for brothers, even those with different fathers, to suspect each other," Surana pointed out. "Perhaps the goddess of fire is warning you with Gunung Mrabu's awakening."

Rakata lifted his eyes to gaze at the volcano's distant crest, which was more heavily circled by smoke than he'd seen it in his lifetime. "I've thought of that," he admitted.

About to say more, Rakata was stopped by a quick succession of knocks on his door. He looked at the servant, who was hesitating because he'd learned from past experience that the *raden* didn't always allow interruptions when he was with Lady Surana. At Rakata's nod the servant hurried to the door and admitted one of Rakata's most trusted agents, a man named Anambas, whom he'd sent to Djakarta to pose as Major Wakefield's gardener.

Rakata didn't wait for Anambas to come out on the terrace. He walked swiftly into his suite, with Surana at his heels, to meet the agent halfway. After Anambas had made *dodok,* Rakata reminded him, "You have orders never to leave Djakarta. You're supposed to send Kalao with messages."

"My son is only a boy, not as easily noticed as I when the major is talking about matters we need to hear. My lord, I left Kalao to continue listening if more is said about the news we heard yesterday. I thought it best to come quickly myself to tell you," Anambas explained.

Rakata was surprised the agent had made the trip from Djakarta to Talu in so short a time. Even if he'd used the hidden jungle trails only Javanese knew existed and had traveled at night, he must have killed his horse, which he treasured. The message had to be of the greatest importance. Having pity on Anambas's obvious weariness, Rakata invited him to sit down and directed his servant to give Anambas a cup of wine.

Anambas thanked the *raden,* took a quick swallow of wine, then said, "A soldier from Jogjakarta came to Wakefield's headquarters yesterday to report that a convoy he'd sent carrying gold and pearls had been attacked. Some of the soldiers in the convoy were killed by arrows, spears, and blowpipe darts that mark someone in this city as guilty.''

Rakata's eyes widened in alarm. ''Are you certain the weapons were ours?''

''The soldier who brought the news to Wakefield also had samples of the weapons used,'' Anambas said slowly, as if reluctant to tell the *raden*. ''I got a glimpse of them as he carried them into Wakefield's office. One quick look was enough. The design is Talu's.''

''Guns and arrows with no identifying marks were used for those other attacks—why should weapons with what amounts to my city's signature have been used on this convoy?'' Rakata exclaimed. Anger was a dark flame that sprang up in his eyes before he turned away. He already knew the answer. Someone wanted to make sure he was blamed. It was a source of pride that the dyes used in Talu's insignia colors were made by a special process no other district could duplicate. Now the secret skill was being used to condemn him. Finally Rakata asked, ''How much gold was taken?''

Anambas took a deep breath and said to Rakata's rigid back, ''The gold was in coins that were to be used for the operation of the military post at Jogjakarta for the rest of the year and came to a considerable sum. The pearls, which are of exceptional quality, were to be a special gift to their queen across the ocean.'' Anambas paused and tried to gather his composure, but failed. He said anxiously, ''My lord, the major has decided to come to Talu and personally question you! He's preparing soldiers, and they're bringing cannons to destroy the city walls if you won't admit them!''

''What do you think Wakefield will do if I admit him cordially, like the innocent man I am?'' Rakata's inquiry was bitter.

Anambas answered dejectedly, ''I think he'll arrest you anyway, my lord, for you have only your own people to swear you were here when the convoy was attacked. The major wasn't in a mood to believe the word of *any* Javanese when I saw him.''

Rakata considered this. Anambas's opinion of Major Wakefield's attitudes had always been accurate in the past. The *raden* turned to Anambas and gestured for him to rise. ''I'm afraid, after your travels, I can offer you no rest, not even to show my gratitude. Go to my council chamber and have the guard strike the gong. Don't allow him to stop sounding the call until every nobleman has come.''

Anambas ducked his head in an abbreviated bow and hurried from the room.

Rakata caught up Surana's hands and said solemnly, "Tell your servants to begin packing immediately. We'll have to evacuate Talu before Wakefield and his cannons arrive. I'm not sure if we'll ever be able to return, and I don't know what the soldiers may do in the meanwhile. Take whatever you have that you wish to continue possessing."

"That will be easy to decide, my love; for you're all I can't do without," Surana replied.

Although Rakata was in a hurry to change his clothes, he paused to draw her into his arms and murmur, "Except for the welfare of our people, I would rather hand Samarang my title than lose you."

The noblemen watched Rakata's green-and-gold-clad figure pacing slowly at the front of the council chamber as he explained Anambas's report. Their initial shock became indignation when the *raden* concluded that the city must be evacuated. Samarang had his own reason to be alarmed at this decision, and his expression of horror was genuine. He *wanted* Rakata to stay and be arrested.

When Alden Townes had visited Phoenix House, he'd found a child's locket he'd said Vandekker wore on his watch chain. It had been lying on the floor as if it had broken loose and dropped off. Townes had surreptitiously picked the locket up and had later given it to Samarang with instructions to leave it in some easily noticed place after the convoy had been stripped of its gold and pearl shipment. He'd also given Samarang orders to have his men use firearms during the raid so Vandekker would be blamed for the attack. But Samarang was more interested in Rakata's being arrested; so he'd had his men use the arrows, darts, and spears of Talu's design as well as guns, and had left the locket to implicate both men. Samarang had anticipated that Wakefield would be so enraged he'd march on Talu, but Samarang hadn't known Anambas was Rakata's agent and the *raden* would learn enough in advance of Wakefield's coming to escape.

In the stunned silence of the council of noblemen, Samarang was desperately trying to think of a way to stop, or at least postpone, the evacuation. Only one day might be a long enough delay for Wakefield to catch Rakata.

Lord Sirik, who loved the city with a fervor second only to Rakata's, finally asked in a hoarse tone, "My lord, if we aren't going to fight for Talu, how soon must we abandon it?"

"Major Wakefield will probably have his men ready to leave Djakarta by tomorrow morning. He doesn't know about the jungle trails we would use to shorten the march, and because he'll be slowed by the artillery he's bringing, it should take his soldiers three full days to get here," Rakata estimated. "We will have to leave Talu no later than noon on that day."

The noblemen were aghast. How could the people of an entire city pack their belongings and leave *that* soon?

"Why can't we make plans to defend Talu?" Samarang asked, hoping Lord Sirik's love for the city would make him want to fight rather than abandon it. "You just said we know trails through the jungle that Wakefield doesn't. Why don't we use them to circle around him and his soldiers, then attack from their flanks and rear as well as from the city when he comes? Our soldiers could even lessen Wakefield's ranks by sniping at them from the jungle before they get here."

Rakata had anticipated Samarang's opposing him, if only from habit, but he answered tolerantly, "Your ideas will be good strategies if we someday have no choice except to fight. I'd like to postpone that kind of war and the casualties we'll surely suffer when and if we *have* to fight it."

"They'll see our tracks coming out of the city and follow them into the jungle," Lord Tumai warned.

"We won't be in the jungle for long," Rakata replied. "I plan to follow the rocky slopes beyond Gunung Mrabu. We won't leave a trail there."

"Where are we going?" Lord Kinabalu inquired.

Rakata braced himself for a chorus of protests as he answered firmly, "The village near the old temple of Durga."

"The temple of the goddess of death?" Kinabalu exclaimed.

Cries of protest filled the council chamber. "It was abandoned because it teemed with *lelembuts* and *memedis!*"

Samarang was even more horrified by this plan than the other noblemen, but it wasn't because he was worried about demons and ghosts. The temple had been deserted so long ago its existence had almost been forgotten. Its location was known to very few except priests. Samarang himself had no idea how to find it or the village. *How could he let Townes know where he was?*

"The temple was abandoned when Matarami's grandfather was a boy. The goddess would surely have left it by now or starved from lack of offerings. The *lelembuts* and *memedis* said to have haunted the place had little reason to stay where there are no mortals for them to influence or terrify. We'll have our own priests with us. They can drive away lingering spirits, if any yet remain," Rakata was saying patiently. "No one will believe we'd go there. Even if someone did, its reputation will make them reconsider. In any event, it's so remote I doubt Wakefield has ever heard of it, and if he has, I'm sure he couldn't find it."

"Leaving this beautiful, safe city to live in a wretched, unholy place like that is a blow the people won't take lightly," Samarang commented, then, hoping Sirik would protest again, added glumly, "Wakefield's soldiers will probably desecrate Talu's temples and surely will destroy our city out of frustration after they discover that we've left."

But Sirik already seemed to have resigned himself to the destruction of Talu. He flinched at Samarang's words, and his pained look deepened, though he remained silent.

"We can rebuild a city if necessary, but we can't call back the lives that will be lost if we stay," Rakata said.

"If our temples are destroyed, the gods and goddesses will surely be offended. Maybe they'll send the demons back to Durga to punish us," Kinabalu, who was very devout, warned.

Lord Allang, who had long tried to give the impression with showy offerings that he was more devoted to their religion than Kinabalu, exclaimed, "Gunung Mrabu's stirrings have been a warning to us! The fire goddess has foreseen this and is angry."

"Maybe the goddess is angry at the foreigners; and if they destroy our city and temples, she's planning to punish them, not us," Rakata suggested, more tolerantly than he felt. He was weary of this discussion, and precious time was passing.

"That is possible," Kinabalu conceded.

"Maybe she's going to send an army of fiery demons to protect us," Allang remarked.

"Would you like to wait for them?" Rakata asked. His tone was quiet, but no longer disguised his growing impatience.

"Fleeing Talu will seem to admit our guilt!" Samarang vehemently declared. "We'll be hunted until these foreign soldiers leave Java, *if* their king across the ocean ever decides to call them back. Why should he? We are such docile slaves."

Rakata's answer came in low, measured words that were like drum-beats rolling across the room. "Someone in this city is guilty of at least that attack on the convoy because the design of our arrows, spears, and darts is like no other. Anambas managed to get a glimpse of the weapons used to kill the convoy's escort, and he wouldn't mistake them.''

As Rakata's dark eyes slowly moved over the noblemen's faces trying to glean some hint of guilt, the men cast looks of anger and suspicion at each other.

Finally, in a tone as quiet as before, Rakata said, "I don't like having to shelter the guilty along with the rest of us, but I can't sacrifice everyone in Talu because whoever is causing this trouble clings to us like the little fish who swim close to a shark for protection from other fish.''

Samarang got to his feet and turned to address the noblemen. "It grieves me to have to bring up a possibility no one else has dared mention, but how can we be sure our *raden* hasn't been involved in those attacks?''

Lord Tumai leaped to his feet, livid with anger that Rakata should be accused. Rakata quickly walked over to put his hand on Tumai's shoulder and firmly hold him back. "But, my lord, that puppy . . .'' Tumai began.

"Let him speak," Rakata said. "I would finally like to hear what has been on my cousin's mind for so long.''

Tumai saw the flash of dark fire burning in the depths of his *raden*'s eyes and sank back into his seat.

"I never paid serious attention to the stories that our *raden* is guilty of leading the raids, but they've become so widespread they no longer can be ignored," Samarang said, trying his best to seem sincere. "While Raden Matarami spoke of restraint, didn't Rakata swear that the only way to get the foreigners out of Java was to drive them away or kill them?''

"We've all said that one time or another," Sirik reminded.

"But who among us can read English? Major Wakefield's messages would be meaningless to us, so why would a Javanese attack the courier to steal them?'' Samarang reasoned. "But our *raden* has a brother who can read English, who can move about freely in Djakarta and even sail to Singapore to make arrangements with smugglers to collect his loot. None of this trouble began in earnest until after Vandekker's partner was killed. Maybe it was Charles Scott's disapproval that prevented Vandekker and our *raden* from joining forces and making this plan to enrich themselves.''

Although Samarang's charges seemed plausible and Rakata wished his cousin hadn't laid such a good case against him, he dryly reminded, "Britt and I are already rich, and Britt has another partner."

"A woman! What could she do to stop him?" Samarang demanded.

"From what I've heard, Minda Scott would have the spirit to go to Wakefield if she thought Vandekker was guilty," Sirik commented, then asked, "Didn't it take courage for her to leave her home across the ocean? Didn't she face that tigress with nothing more than a tree branch to save Arjuna's daughter? Why would Minda Scott hesitate to have Vandekker arrested? Should he be convicted, he would be hanged or shot and she would be sole owner of Phoenix House."

"Make no mistake about it, Wakefield would charge anyone he arrests for these attacks with murder, including me," Rakata said quietly. "Do all of you think I'm capable of murder? If so, you must depose me—and deposing a *raden* is a grave matter."

"Think back to when those attacks were made," Samarang urged the noblemen. "Our *raden* was often in the jungle with some of his men at those times. How can we really know he wasn't conducting the raids?"

"I was here in Talu when the convoy was attacked," Rakata said, his temper rising higher.

"Couldn't he have sent his men with instructions?" Samarang questioned.

The noblemen, not knowing what to say, were silent. It could be true, but they didn't want to believe it.

"Do you think I'd be stupid enough to have my men use weapons so easily traced back to us?" Rakata demanded.

"Major Wakefield is certain our *raden* is guilty," Samarang persisted. "He just hasn't had evidence to arrest Rakata until now."

"If I thought I could save Talu, I would walk through the gates and surrender myself to Wakefield, though I'm innocent," Rakata declared. "But Wakefield will want the other men involved in the attacks, and I can't surrender them because I don't know who they are. I think Wakefield is angry enough to fire his cannons on the city to try to force the guilty men to surrender even if I give myself up to him."

Stunned by Rakata's willingness to sacrifice himself to save Talu, Sirik burst out, "I will *never* believe the *raden* is guilty! We've known Rakata all his life. Has he ever done *any* dishonorable thing?"

"Since when have Wakefield's opinions decided *our* council's judgments?" Tumai suddenly demanded.

The rest of the noblemen, except Samarang, swore that Rakata must not sacrifice himself, protested that Wakefield couldn't make decisions for them. To quiet them, Rakata held up his hands.

"The major will soon decide whether this council lives or dies unless we leave Talu," Rakata sternly reminded. "If you aren't willing to depose me or let me give myself to Wakefield, you must obey my commands. It's my decision that beginning a war with the English now will only result in the needless slaughter of our people and we must withdraw." Rakata turned to lock Samarang's eyes in a contemptuous glare. "Unless the council unanimously declares me a traitor to our people, you, Lord Samarang, will be silent." Without another word he left the chamber.

Although Samarang had realized he'd gone much too far, he'd pressed on in the hope that some of the other noblemen would agree and at least add credence to his charges. But Rakata's offer to sacrifice himself, his challenging the noblemen to depose or obey him, had brought the matter to a head. Rakata's offer wasn't an empty gesture, for the noblemen could have deposed him on the spot and decided to hand him to Wakefield. But they'd believed in Rakata's innocence and had remained loyal to him. When Samarang had finally found himself standing alone, he was much afraid of what Rakata would do with him now.

After Samarang left the council chamber, he considered how he might lessen the impact of what he'd said and decided that humble apology was the only way. He went home and rinsed his mouth several times with a strong liquor made from bananas, then resolutely went to the *raden*'s personal suite.

One of Rakata's harried servants admitted Samarang and told him to wait while the *raden* was meeting with Anambas. Then the servant left the apartment on an errand. When Samarang heard Anambas speaking to Rakata in the next room, he crept closer to the partly open door and listened.

Rakata began to read a message aloud, as if he were checking its content. Then he told Anambas to stop at Phoenix House on this trip back to Djakarta and deliver the letter to Britt. Samarang saw in this an opportunity he couldn't deny himself, for the letter was so discreetly worded it could be interpreted more than one way. If the message was put into Wakefield's hands instead of Vandekker's, it could seem to be a piece of evidence against both Rakata and Vandekker, especially if someone swore that the meeting being arranged was only one of many between them.

Samarang could imagine Anambas's hesitation to approach Vandekker now, after all the accusations that had flown about, when the *raden* inquired, "Has Lord Samarang given you suspicions about me?" Anambas sputtered his denial, but Rakata said, "Since Britt and I seem to be getting blamed for the attacks, I want to discuss it with him. This letter tells him to come to me; after we leave Talu, it will be too much of a risk for me to go to him."

"You just surprised me with this mission, my lord, and that your Hollander brother knows where Durga is," Anambas quickly said. "I never doubt your motives and have never questioned, even in the silence of my own heart, that you're innocent."

"I can only *hope* that Britt remembers where Durga is. He hasn't seen it for many years," Rakata said slowly. Then, more briskly, he urged, "Get as much rest tonight as you can, Anambas, for you must leave Talu before dawn. I'll make sure your family is taken care of when we evacuate the city."

"When I think that this night will probably be the last I'll spend at Talu, I feel as if my heart is being torn in two," Anambas commented.

"You and I have spoken of fleeing to Durga before this, but I, too, find my heart unprepared for this moment," Rakata sadly agreed. "I can only hope we'll be able to return after this time of trouble has passed, that Wakefield isn't the kind of man who will destroy the city when he finds it empty."

"He never seemed so, but it's difficult to judge what he'll do now. He's very angry," Anambas replied, then bowed and left the room. He was so absorbed in his worries that he looked neither right nor left as he walked through the room where Samarang had hidden behind a decorative bamboo screen.

Samarang hardly dared breathe until the hall door closed behind Anambas. He crept silently to the door, opened and closed it as if he'd just entered the *raden*'s suite, then more noisily approached the room Anambas had just left. He didn't call to Rakata but entered hesitantly, as a man would who was seeking forgiveness.

Rakata turned in surprise at Samarang's entrance. He hadn't thought his cousin would have the courage to face him after the scene in the council room, but he decided that Samarang had little choice. Samarang immediately lowered himself in *dodok*, an appropriate gesture even for so close a relative who had seriously offended the *raden*, but Rakata was startled that Samarang sank to his knees on the floor and kissed his sandaled foot in the most abject gesture of humility. Such servility from Samarang under any circumstances made Rakata suspicious, and he stepped backwards.

"Why have you come?" he asked coldly.

Remaining where he was, Samarang kept his eyes downcast and replied, "To beg my lord *raden*'s mercy. I hadn't expected the council to be called and had been drinking. I confess I was more than a little intoxicated when I spoke before the council. I'd never have said such things if I'd been thinking clearly."

"I'm sure you wouldn't—unless you thought there was a chance of getting away with it," Rakata answered sharply. He noted the odor of the liquor rising faintly from the kneeling nobleman. "I can smell the banana now, but I didn't in the council chamber."

Samarang kept his eyes on the floor as he answered, "Perhaps my *raden* wasn't close enough or was too distracted by the terrible news Anambas brought."

"Get up and leave my chamber," Rakata commanded.

Samarang slowly rose to his feet. Not sure if he was being grudgingly forgiven or simply dismissed, he kept his head bowed as he promised, "I'll go to each nobleman and tell him I was wrong, that my brain was addled and my tongue loosened by drink."

"You will, indeed, do at least that," Rakata replied.

"Do you forgive my indiscretion?" Samarang asked hopefully.

Rakata's hand gripping Samarang by the hair forced his cousin to meet his eyes. Incredulous at Samarang's effrontery, the *raden* demanded, "Can you call denouncing me before the council a mere *indiscretion*?"

Samarang dared say no more.

Rakata's words became darts impaling his cousin with slowly working poison as he added, "I've been aware of your lifelong desire to usurp my place, but this is where your ambitions end. Though I have no proof of your taking part in those attacks and so can't drag you before the council to charge you with the crimes, your guilt will soon be revealed. From this room you will go directly home. You will not step out of your house until it's time to leave for Durga. I think the raids will come to a sudden stop because you won't be able to get away and lead them. If so, it will be all the proof the council will need of your guilt."

Rakata released his cousin's hair and turned away in disgust before he gave one more command, "Get out of my chamber and take the stink of your dubious intoxication with you."

It wasn't until long after night had enveloped Talu's streets and courtyards with darkness that Bedug, an officer in Talu's army who had ridden at Samarang's side in every raid, dared make his way to Samarang's house, which was being guarded.

Bedug arrived like a shadow that slipped through a side door, an entrance few remembered existed because of its closeness to a high wall and the thick shubbery growing around it. Only after the door had been barred and Bedug had followed Samarang to a room without windows did the nobleman light a lamp.

"You don't have to tell me what happened in the council chamber today. The news has been carried to every corner of the palace," Bedug said disgustedly.

Samarang's reply was quick and embarrassed, "It was a gamble I'd thought was worth taking. Though I lost, my accusing Rakata will be remembered later in a different light when he's arrested for the raids."

"The *raden* must be a fool for having allowed you to walk out of the chamber today," Bedug said sarcastically.

"My cousin can't condemn me with proof he doesn't have," Samarang answered.

"I don't advise that you walk alone in dark places or you'll find his dagger in your back," Bedug warned.

"Our *raden* is too honorable to do that," Samarang denied, "but he has thought of a way to try to force me to condemn myself. He's forbidden me to step out of my house until we leave Talu. He'll keep his eyes on me in Durga, too, because he thinks if there are no raids while I'm confined it will be proof of my guilt."

"But it will!" Bedug declared. "Rakata's command has rendered you helpless unless you can slip away, which seems impossible with all the soldiers posted in the streets. I was hard put to avoid them myself just to come here. How could you possibly get beyond Talu's walls?"

"I won't," Samarang agreed. "Neither will I be able to leave Durga without Rakata's taking me prisoner. But I've thought of a way to get our *raden* and his golden-haired brother arrested and convicted so I'll appear blameless."

"What magic will you use to accomplish that?" Bedug asked pessimistically.

"There is no magic in it. After Rakata's been executed, the council of noblemen will have no choice but to admit I was right all along and pronounce me the new *raden,*" Samarang said confidently. "The trap is already half laid. I left the locket beside the body of the captain who commanded Wakefield's convoy, which is evidence against Vandekker to satisfy Townes. While I was in Rakata's chamber, I left several of the pearls from the raid in that little urn on the table beside the entrance of Rakata's apartment. Rakata won't take the urn or the table it stands on to Durga, as both were wedding gifts from me, which I'm sure he'll no longer want."

"The pearls from the raid are of such quality any of them would be easily recognized, but how can you be sure Wakefield will find them?" Bedug asked.

"One of Lady Surana's lesser maids is my paramour and I've already persuaded her to make sure she's the last servant to leave the suite. She's going to tip over the urn before she closes the door. When Wakefield stands at Rakata's threshold, he'll have to step over the pearls to enter the suite. He won't be able to miss seeing them scattered on the floor, as if they'd been overlooked during Rakata's rush to leave."

"How can you be certain the maid will say nothing later?" Bedug inquired.

"I'll make sure some accident eventually befalls her," Samarang replied. "But I have a task for you, too, Bedug."

"To be met with a better reward than hers, I should think," the officer said suspiciously.

"Your reward will be, as I promised, that I'll appoint you commander of Talu's army after I become *raden.* In the meanwhile you'll have a share of the loot we've taken," Samarang assured. "Whom would I trust if not you?"

"If you ever consider betraying me, you would do well to remember that my being at your side makes you vulnerable to me," Bedug warned.

"There's no need for you to distrust me," Samarang said. "What I'm going to ask you to do now will prove how I rely on you."

"Which is?" Bedug asked warily.

"You'll have to take my place outside Talu's walls," Samarang said. When Bedug's eyes registered his surprise, the nobleman continued, "Anambas is leaving Talu just before dawn. He's carrying a message from Rakata to Vandekker asking to meet him and talk over their problems. You must kill Anambas and deliver the letter to Wakefield. Tell him that I've learned my brother has met Vandekker in secret before. Wakefield will add the message to the locket and have enough evidence against Vandekker and Rakata to arrest them both.''

"Wakefield might want me to continue with him to Talu," Bedug commented.

"If so, when you get here, act surprised that the city's been deserted. Tell Wakefield only that you're sure I'll let you know where Rakata is hiding as soon as I can," Samarang instructed. "Later, after I've learned the directions to Durga, you can give them to Wakefield. I'm sure you'll be able to get a reward from him for the information.''

"You're being very generous to plan how I can be rewarded by Wakefield," Bedug observed.

"There's no reason you shouldn't collect something extra for your trouble," Samarang said. "Afterward, go to Alden Townes and tell him what happened, that you'll gather together the men we've hired in Djakarta while he plans another raid. There *must* be another attack or two while I'm trapped in Durga under Rakata's eyes.''

"Townes won't care about preserving your reputation so you can be *raden,*" Bedug warned.

"The agreement Townes and I made at the beginning of this was that I'd help him get rid of Vandekker and he'd help me dispose of Rakata. I've kept my part of the bargain so far, and Townes still needs me," Samarang replied.

Bedug was quiet for a moment as he turned away to consider the situation. "What about *my* reputation with the council? How can I become military commander if my absence is noticed meanwhile? They may realize I'm the one leading the raids.''

Samarang stepped around Bedug so he could face him. "When you later go back to Durga, you can make up some story about the English army pursuing you and having had to hide. You'll have to kill Kalao as well as Anambas or he'll come racing back to Rakata to report that you've betrayed him.''

"It seems you've thought of everything," Bedug said with genuine admiration. "The only problem left is that you'll be *raden* and I commander of your army on an island where the real power is still in the hands of foreigners.''

"Townes wants the Hollanders to fight the British so he can claim some of their plantations for himself. As Rakata has said, both factions might be so weakened by their losses in such a battle we might be able to drive all of them from Java. Isn't that our people's wish?''

"Of course it is," Bedug agreed. "But what about Townes? Would you allow him to remain?''

"Why should I?" Samarang inquired. "Townes is the worst of their kind and his usefulness to me will have ended.''

Bedug decided that Samarang would be a *raden* to satisfy *him* if everything came about according to this plan. But a question did occur to him. "Why should the Hollanders start resisting the British now? They've been peaceful because they hope that, as soon as the war in their homeland ends, the British army will leave Java.''

"Townes has told me something of that war. It rages all across the land they call Europe, and many armies are fighting. I think it will go on forever," Samarang scoffed, then added slyly, "If the Hollanders don't want to fight, we'll give them some reasons. We can attack them and make it look as if the British are to blame, just as we've made Rakata and Vandekker look guilty.''

Chapter Fifteen

The late afternoon sun falling through the bamboo latticed sides of the pavilion made a fine shower of golden speckles falling over the three women who sat in the shade. Minda, Malili, and Dessa fanned themselves while they watched Britt, who was sitting in the grass just outside the doorway holding down Dalang with one arm while he struggled to trim her claws.

The task had begun in the pavilion, after the tiger cub had accidentally scratched Panji's leg while they were playing, but Dalang had fiercely resisted her pedicure from the moment she'd discovered that Britt hadn't taken her into his lap merely to rub her ears. Though according to his estimate, the baby tigress was less than two months old, she was twice the size of the kitchen tabbies and already seemed to have more than their combined strength. Her repeated attempts to escape had carried her battle with Britt out of the pavilion.

Minda's lips curved in affectionate humor as the cub twisted until she was upside down across Britt's legs and he adjusted his grip to accommodate her new position. Panji, crawling on hands and knees behind him, trying to catch the tip of the cub's swishing tail, didn't make his job easier.

Britt sighed heavily as he renewed his hold on the miniature tigress and said in exasperation, "Dalang doesn't want you to hold her tail,

Panji. All this wiggling around might make me clip her claws too close and hurt her."

Panji quickly withdrew and peered around Britt's elbow as if to confirm that she was contributing to the mischief. "I thought I might help you, Tuan Britt, by getting it out of your way," the little girl said contritely.

"The kitchen cats don't like you to hold their tails, do they?" he muttered. Then, recalling how he'd complained several times about Dalang's tail flipping across his face, he said more gently, "I'm doing this so she won't scratch you, but I don't want to hurt her paws either."

At the change in his tone, the girl moved more boldly around his side to kneel in front of him and agreed that she, too, didn't want Dalang to suffer. "She didn't mean to scratch me. I was running away and she was trying to stop me."

"I know. You were playing tag," Britt replied, then reflected that, as young as the cub was, she'd instinctively tried to grab Panji's legs much in the way an adult tiger would strike at a deer it was pursuing, but Dalang hadn't used her teeth. He said quietly, "Dalang is still a baby and doesn't always notice that her claws are out. When she gets older, she'll know better, but you must learn now, before she gets too big, that you can't handle her the same way as you do those tabbies. Even though Dalang behaves like a big kitten, she isn't a house cat."

"When Dalang grows up, she'll be a tiger. Like her mother. Won't she?" Panji asked softly, hesitantly, as if she didn't want even the cub to hear about her terrible destiny.

Britt recognized the fear in the little girl's wide eyes and knew she was remembering how the tigress had threatened her and Minda in the garden. "Dalang will become a beautiful tigress, Panji, but she won't be like her mother." He patted the cub's cheerfully waving paw with his free hand, adding, "Dalang has healthy legs. She'll be able to run fast enough and jump high enough to catch even a gazelle, so she won't have to eat people." As if Dalang were agreeing, the cub's throat vibrated in so laughable an imitation of an adult growl that Britt smiled.

Panji relaxed, then asked curiously, "How do mother tigers cut their babies' claws?"

Britt's smile widened. "They don't have to, because there aren't any little girls in the jungle for them to scratch while they're playing."

Malili, who had been carefully listening to Britt and her daughter's conversation, leaned closer to Minda and commented, "Since that incident with the man-eater, Panji has become afraid not only of tigers but of all animals and any bush she can't see through or over. I'm glad he's teaching her not to be afraid, but careful, of Dalang."

"Tuan Britt understands the child's mind," Dessa remarked, then slyly added, "He'll be a good father to your children, Mem Scott."

Minda didn't answer. She was flustered that Dessa would casually mention so intimate a matter. Britt, who'd overheard the servant, glanced up briefly before returning his attention to clipping Dalang's claws.

"Tuan Britt, you're as heedless as a rogue who isn't concerned that his children will have no proper name," Dessa scolded. "You should consider marriage to Mem Scott."

"You're behaving like a mother hen, Dessa," he commented.

"*Someone* must look after Mem Scott," the maid retorted. "When do you expect to marry her?"

"On our trip to London," he answered, then warily added, "You say that as if you know something about Minda I don't."

"Oh, no!" Minda exclaimed. "I'm not going to have a child!"

"If it weren't for the uncertainty in Java these days, I wouldn't mind if you were," Britt said more easily. He paused as he tightened his hold on the again restless cub. "We could be married now, if you wish, by one of the missionaries or in a civil ceremony in Djakarta."

"The priests of your mother's people could marry you," Dessa said, a little indignant that he'd overlooked this possibility.

"That's true," Britt agreed. Though he picked up another of Dalang's paws and kept his eyes fastened on his work, his tone was lightened by humor as he asked, "How much of a bride-price do you think I'd have to pay? A pair of cows?"

"No, Tuan Britt. That wouldn't be enough. For a woman like Mem Scott, not less than three buffalo *and* two cows," Dessa answered solemnly.

"Buffalo and cows!" Minda exclaimed.

"Don't be insulted, Minda. That would be an exorbitant bride-price, probably more than Rakata gave his father-in-law—and Surana was a noblewoman," Britt said.

"Lady Surana is, I've heard, also very beautiful," Dessa advised Minda.

"I've met her and I can vouch for that," Britt remarked.

"I wouldn't like to be bought like an object," Minda said.

"The bride-price doesn't really buy a wife. It's a small compensation to the girl's parents for taking away one of their greatest treasures. The Javanese don't consider their daughters to be less precious than their sons. In fact, as loved as a son may be, he has little social standing until he's properly married," Britt explained. "Actually, since everything I have is already half yours because of our partnership, if you were Javanese I probably wouldn't be able to afford you."

"If I were Javanese, *something* would have to be agreed on or I'd be forced to run off with you," Minda retorted.

Britt said more seriously, "It seems to me that's just about what we did—run away from Jessica because no agreement could be made about anything."

Minda realized with a start that she hadn't given a thought to Jessica since Alden had mentioned her. She wondered if she should feel guilty or be glad that she'd gotten over her disillusionment and sorrow about Jessica. She put the thought aside for later consideration and asked, "Why would I be a more valuable bride than even a noblewoman?"

"You have the fire goddess's favor," Malili reminded.

Britt flashed Minda a wicked smile, adding, "And a few qualities *I* favor."

Dessa gave him a reproachful glance and said, "You would bring good fortune to your husband."

Minda looked down at the crystal she'd had Arjuna take to Djakarta to be polished and set in a pendant. She'd worn it on a chain around her neck ever since. The odd tangerine color glowed softly against her skin. "If anyone else had climbed Gunung Mrabu before me and seen the crystal, they could have picked it up just as I did."

"Many others have climbed that mountain, but the goddess blinded their eyes to the stone. Even if someone had seen it, she wouldn't have allowed them to keep it," Malili insisted. "It would have found its way into your hands because it was meant to protect you and those you love."

"That's a charming idea, I admit, but . . ." Minda began.

"It already has saved Tuan Britt's life. It will continue to help you whether you believe it or not." Dessa's firm tone said the matter was closed; she'd hear no more arguments.

Minda looked up at Britt, who shrugged helplessly, as if it would serve no purpose to protest. His movement relaxed his grip on Dalang; the cub, who'd been pretending to have surrendered to the clipping, instantly took action. A squirm, one backward bounce, a whirl of tawny fur, and Dalang was gone.

Panji looked up at Britt in dismay. "Dalang will get lost!" she cried, then scrambled to her feet to dash off in pursuit of the little tigress.

"It's getting too near dusk for either of them to wander around out there," Britt said as he got up, then trotted after them.

The women stepped out of the pavilion to watch first Dalang, then Panji, and finally Britt vanish into the foliage.

"I guess this means that Panji's fear of the forest has been overcome," Malili said. "I only hope she isn't going to be too brave, as she was before."

"I doubt that will happen," Minda assured, then added, "Don't worry, Malili. Britt will bring them back."

"I know," Malili answered, but her tone revealed her nervousness.

The search took longer than Minda had expected. She was getting restless and trying not to show it when Britt finally emerged from the foliage. He was holding Panji by the hand and had Dalang securely tucked under his other arm. His clothes were soiled, his face smudged, and bits of leaves were caught in his hair. From the way he was frowning she assumed the cub had led him a merry chase. Then she saw the pair of soldiers with cocked rifles following Britt. Horrified, Minda caught up her skirts and ran across the lawn to meet them.

"Britt, what happened? Are you hurt?" she exclaimed. His features were taut with tension and he didn't immediately answer. Her eyes darted to the soldiers, whose impassive expressions told her nothing.

Finally Britt said, "I'm all right." Dismissing his appearance, he added, "Wakefield's men seem to have cordoned off the garden."

Minda gasped. "But why?"

"They won't tell me," Britt replied, then, looking beyond her shoulder, observed, "Wakefield must have entered by the main gate. He's coming around the house now."

Angry at the major, but dreading to learn his reason for this intrusion, Minda slowly turned to watch him approach with Sergeant Moore.

"Good day, Miss Scott, Mr. Vandekker," Wakefield began as cordially as if this were any ordinary afternoon, but his next words shocked Minda to speechlessness. "By the authority of his majesty, King George III, I must take you, Mr. Vandekker, under custody for questioning."

Britt paled under his tan, but his eyes quickly kindled with copper sparks. He released Panji's hand and told her to go to Malili before he looked at the major and quietly said, "As a citizen of the Netherlands, I demand an explanation for your soldiers' manhandling of me."

Wakefield looked at his men. "Did Mr. Vandekker resist you?"

Britt cut off the soldiers' reply. "How could I have resisted when I had no idea they were here? I was crawling under a thicket to get this cub and one of your men pulled me out by the ankles, then dragged me to my feet. The only thing they've said so far was to direct me to return to the house. If they hadn't had their guns trained on me every moment, I would have treated them like any intruders because that's how they behaved."

"I apologize for their discourteous behavior. They'll be reprimanded for it," Wakefield said.

"Discourteous behavior!" Minda exclaimed, but Britt's glance warned her to say no more.

He addressed the major more coolly, "Would you be good enough to tell me what all this is about?"

Wakefield looked at him measuringly a moment, as if trying to decide whether Britt was acting a part or really didn't know what had happened. Finally he said, "I sent a convoy to Jogjakarta carrying a considerable sum in gold coins and a collection of pearls that were to be a royal gift." He paused, still gauging Britt's reaction, but could see nothing in the planter's face other than an attitude of waiting for him to continue. Wakefield said, "The convoy was attacked and everyone in it was killed. The gold and pearls were stolen as were the horses and firearms."

"This is the first I've heard of any of this, so there's no information I can give you," Britt said tightly. "If you're accusing me of having something to do with the attack, I've been here day and night since I returned from Matarami's funeral with only one exception. That was when I took nearly thirty men to hunt down the man-eater at Gunung Mrabu's temple. We were gone almost a week."

"Are your witnesses all employees of yours?" Wakefield inquired.

"One of those witnesses is *me*," Minda declared. "I should think, Major, that you might give us some sort of explanation as to why you're arresting Britt."

"I've already said I intend to question Mr. Vandekker, not arrest him," Wakefield reminded.

"Do you always drag people away from their homes at gunpoint merely to question them?" she asked icily.

"Only very good suspects, Miss Scott," Wakefield replied. "Truth is, I'll have to send Mr. Vandekker to Djakarta to await my return. I must press on to Talu and collect another excellent suspect, Raden Rakata."

"So you're back to your favorite old theory that Rakata and I want to start a rebellion," Britt commented in disgust.

"It hasn't been *my* favorite theory, Mr. Vandekker," Wakefield denied. "Whether you believe me or not, I personally regard you with a certain amount of respect and hope you're innocent. It isn't a pleasant task for me to accuse you, but I have evidence in my office that was found among the remains of the convoy. It points to you and the *raden*."

"*What* evidence?" Britt asked derisively.

"A pile of spears, arrows, and blow darts of the design used exclusively by the *raden*'s men as well as a trinket known to belong to you," the major answered crisply. "Come along, Mr. Vandekker. Evidence can't be denied, and because of it, you must be thoroughly investigated."

"I'm not guilty of this and I doubt Rakata is either," Britt said firmly. "Anyone from Talu could have used those weapons because they wanted Rakata to be blamed. If he had led the attack, he would have been too smart to leave what amounts to his signature."

"It isn't my job to analyze the workings of your or Rakata's mind," Wakefield said. "I can only gather evidence and suspects."

"Then tell me about this so-called piece of evidence you have against me," Britt urged. "I have no idea what that trinket is."

"A small gold locket was found beside the body of the captain who commanded the convoy. The locket has long ago become so familiar a sight on your watch chain everyone knows it's yours, including me," Wakefield answered confidently.

"Are you talking about a child's locket with rosebuds and forget-me-nots engraved on the front?" Minda questioned. When Wakefield nodded, she declared, "That's *my* locket! I gave it to Britt as a keepsake before I left Java as a little girl. When he went to Philadelphia to tell me about my father's death and my inheritance, he gave the locket back to me. If you expect to use it as evidence in a trial, you'd be well advised to arrest me, not Britt."

To Wakefield's silence, Britt said quietly, "That happens to be the truth, Major."

"And I'd certainly swear to it in court," Minda promised. She looked at Britt and hastily explained, "The locket has so much sentimental meaning I didn't want to admit I'd lost it. I was hoping, if I just kept looking, I'd find it."

He briefly squeezed her arm with his free hand but asked Wakefield, "Is there other evidence?"

"*You* have no real proof of where you were when the convoy was attacked or, for that matter, when most of the other raids took place," Wakefield advised, warily watching the cub in Britt's arms. She'd been quiet, as if dozing, but now she seemed to be stirring.

Insulted that Wakefield had seemed to dismiss her so easily, Minda coolly inquired, "Doesn't *my* word mean anything to you?"

Wakefield raised his eyes from the cub. "I'm a soldier, not a barrister, Miss Scott, so all I can do is investigate this situation. Someone else must decide its outcome. If charges are pressed and Mr. Vandekker goes to trial, I believe that, once the prosecution has pointed out you're Mr. Vandekker's partner, a judge would realize you'd be hard put to run this plantation without him and probably would have to sell if he's convicted. Seeing as how you've come all the way from Philadelphia and appear to be happy here, a judge could see you'd *want* to believe Mr. Vandekker is innocent and would go to all lengths, perhaps even lie, to save him and Phoenix House."

Wishing she could cry out that losing Britt would break her *heart*, that Phoenix House would mean little without him, Minda dared not. If Wakefield knew she loved Britt, he'd have more reason to believe she'd say anything to save him. Putting on her old mask of composure, though her heart was pounding with fear, she said coldly, "You think I can't run the plantation because I'm a woman."

"Minda is capable of operating Phoenix House," Britt put in. "She's been an enthusiastic student and has become a real partner. The workers, even a couple of the other planters—Mr. DeGroot, for example—can verify that. Ask him," Britt invited. He paused to think a moment, then added, "Most of the other planters have become little more than tenant farmers since your army arrived and they're not very happy about it. The way you and your soldiers invaded this plantation today will be one more reason for the Hollanders to believe your government is going to steal this colony from the Netherlands no matter how Napoleon's war turns out."

"Maybe they'll join the Indonesians and together try to drive you out of Java," Minda suggested.

Despite the gravity of the situation, the hard line of Britt's mouth lightened with humor. "*There's* a twist to the situation I'll wager you and your superiors never thought about, Major."

"Major Wakefield takes orders; he doesn't think for himself," Minda noted sarcastically.

"Miss Scott, remarks like that aren't called for," Wakefield snapped.

"If Mr. Vandekker hadn't intervened, you wouldn't even be alive. The assassins would have killed you at Matarami's funeral. And this is how you thank him!"

Minda's words hit Wakefield like a spear and he flushed with embarrassment. That Britt had saved his life and he was repaying Britt by taking him prisoner weighed heavily on Wakefield's conscience. He gave her the same explanation he'd tried so hard to use in soothing his own qualms. "I'm grateful to Mr. Vandekker for that, but I can't allow my personal feelings to interfere with my job. I've even wondered if, knowing suspicion about them was growing, Mr. Vandekker and Raden Rakata might have planned the incident and its outcome in an effort to distract me from their guilt. What would make them appear more innocent than Mr. Vandekker's foiling my would-be murderers while Rakata stood a dozen yards away on the beach?"

"What a disgusting thing to say!" Minda declared. "Do you actually think Rakata would send several of his men to their deaths just to deceive you? How could Rakata even be sure Britt could succeed in stopping the assassins?"

Wakefield's eyes were again on the restless tiger cub, who was trying to push herself away from Britt. He said quickly, "If the *raden* chose men he knew weren't Mr. Vandekker's match, who had no idea it was a plot and Mr. Vandekker had a concealed pistol ready to fire, Rakata could have been pretty sure the plan would work. It's also possible that was an isolated incident having nothing to do with Vandekker and Rakata's possible plans to overthrow the military government in Java. But the fact remains that Mr. Vandekker has no alibis for the raids and I daresay neither will Rakata."

"He won't if he's been in Talu minding his own business," Minda shot back. "It's obvious you won't accept the word of a Javanese, and those would be the only witnesses Rakata could have at Talu."

Britt's glance warned her not to arouse the major's anger further and he suggested, "Major Wakefield, why don't you search Phoenix

House for the loot taken in those raids? You have our permission to go over every inch of our land if you wish.''

"You could already have shipped it off to Singapore if you're guilty,'' Wakefield replied.

"Not the items that were taken in this most recent attack,'' Britt said. "Phoenix House is some distance from the coast, but I've heard that the waters around the western part of the island have been too rough lately for ships to dock. That's why you sent the pearls to Jogjakarta in the east, isn't it? If legitimate shipping has been disrupted, the smugglers, who must come at night to inlets that are hazardous when the water is calm, can't approach this part of Java either. The gold and your precious collection of pearls are still on the island, I'd say.''

"If you were to spend more energy looking for them, you might recover them before the ocean quiets and they can be spirited away,'' Minda suggested.

Britt let Wakefield absorb this idea a moment, then said quietly, "I don't want a rebellion because I could very well be caught in the middle of it. I think Rakata doesn't want one either, because his people don't have the resources to win and would be decimated.''

"You can't deny that Rakata has sworn to drive all foreigners from Java, and Matarami hoped, if the British and Hollanders could be set at each other's throats, they'd kill themselves for him,'' Wakefield pointed out.

"Rakata was younger when he said that. He's less impulsive now. I think the responsibilities of his new title have also sobered him,'' Britt insisted.

"What if you're all being led into a trap?'' Minda inquired. "Maybe someone is deliberately encouraging your suspicions because he wants you to be distracted from what *he's* doing? Maybe someone is simply interested in stealing all he can.''

Britt saw the possibility of this truth flash behind Wakefield's eyes like a light and he said, "Whatever the reason behind all this, I must think of the plantation. A field of tea is being harvested for the first time, and I think you know, Major, despite your lack of experience growing tea, that the initial harvesting of a plant produces the finest and costliest product. Supervising this particular field is one job Minda can't do for me, because the tea is a particularly delicate variety I'm experimenting with at the request of both Amsterdam and London. The tea must be processed under my supervision, too, because the entire crop could be lost if the smallest mistake is made. By insisting on sending me to Djakarta now, you could cost Miss Scott and me a great deal.''

Britt paused to let Wakefield think about what would happen if the tea was lost and he was proven innocent, then suggested, ''Why don't you leave me here until you return from Talu? I'm not going to run away. Innocent or guilty, you *know* everything that matters to me is at Phoenix House.''

''Your arguments have given me pause for thought,'' Wakefield admitted, then fell silent.

''While you're considering your decision, may I put this cub in the house? She knows it's time for her meal and Koki has it waiting in the kitchen.'' Britt looked down at the little tigress squirming in his arms. ''I really don't relish chasing Dalang again if she escapes me.''

''Yes, yes, go ahead,'' Wakefield said irritably and gestured for one of the soldiers to walk with Britt. After they'd left, he looked appraisingly at the gathering shadows and commented, ''It's getting a bit too late for me and my men to push on. I think we'll have to stay for the night.''

''Do you suppose I'm going to offer you and your officers our hospitality when you've come to accuse Britt?'' Minda asked bitterly.

''Miss Scott, I'm only doing my job as best I can. And I might add, under difficult circumstances,'' Wakefield began.

''We realize that, Major,'' Britt said as he approached, ''but you must understand how we feel too. If you want to remain overnight, you may sleep in the meadow with your soldiers.''

Wakefield frowned. ''I'll have to assign guards to the house.''

''Just make sure they understand they may patrol around the house or post themselves at the doors, but they are not to set foot inside,'' Britt directed.

Still frowning, Wakefield turned to give his men their orders, then made his way back to where his horse and the rest of the soldiers were waiting in the driveway.

After Britt and Minda returned to the house, they went to Britt's study. Its window overlooked the meadow, and they stood holding hands, watching Wakefield and his men in the distance setting up their camp.

Finally Minda said in a low, angry tone, ''I hate to think of them being *anywhere* on our property, but seeing them in the meadow, where you and I played as children, makes me so furious I want to rush out of the house and somehow drive them away.''

"Tomorrow morning they'll be gone except for the guards. If you feel so strongly, why not stay indoors for the next few days?'' Britt suggested. "Then you won't have to see them until Wakefield comes back from Talu and they leave.''

"How can we be sure they'll go? Maybe Wakefield will drag you off to Djakarta anyway,'' Minda worried.

"I think he was in a temper when he came. After he's had a few days to consider what we told him, I'm sure he'll be calmer,'' Britt soothed.

"But what if he isn't?'' Minda tried to blink away the tears that blurred the scene in the meadow. "What he can do to you, to us, is frightening. It's an awful feeling to know that our futures, our very lives, are in the hands of someone else and we can do nothing about it.''

"That's how Rakata and his people have been living these past years. I can finally appreciate how frustrated they've been,'' Britt mused, then, putting his arm around her waist, added, "We'll get through this, Minda, even if we have to leave Java.''

"I don't want to leave Phoenix House. It would be like abandoning a dear friend.'' She brushed away her tears and tilted her head to look up at him. "How could we even get out of the house? Though you aren't under arrest now, only accused, we can't open a door without bumping into a soldier.''

"Despite the guards at our doors, even with all the soldiers camped nearby, we could leave Phoenix House tonight, if we needed to,'' Britt said. Noting Minda's amazement, he explained, "After our families had been burned out the last time, our fathers decided to make certain there was a way to escape in the event of future attacks. They had a tunnel dug that leads beyond the garden. It opens into what looks like an abandoned storage building, but the building never was used. Its sole purpose was to hide the tunnel. The stones from the old kitchen were salvaged so the storage building would appear weathered and neglected.''

Still staring at him in surprise, she breathed, "You'll have to show me where the entrance to the tunnel is in the house!''

"It's under the flags in the courtyard, a place easy to get to from any room and that can't be seen from the outside windows or doors,'' he replied. "No one ever had to use the tunnel and I'd forgotten it existed until now."

"But how could we live, where would we go if we managed to escape?" Minda asked.

"There are many places in Java Wakefield doesn't know about," Britt assured. "I learned how to survive in the jungle a long time ago. We could manage until we made contact with one of the smugglers and arrange to be taken to Singapore. We have money invested in other countries that we could get a new start with. Remember, your father and I traveled to a lot of places to attend tea auctions."

Minda silently digested this news.

Britt knew Minda's surprise at his escape plan was mixed with sorrow at the thought of having to leave Phoenix House, and he said, "You *know* we wouldn't leave except as a last resort."

"It's good to know it would be possible if we had to escape," Minda said slowly, "but I'd rather think of how we might solve our problems so we can stay."

"Samarang is probably causing some of this trouble as Rakata suspects," Britt surmised. "He would have access to the weapons used in the attack on the convoy, and if Rakata was convicted and executed for those crimes, the normal line of succession would give Samarang Rakata's title."

"Why didn't you tell Wakefield about Samarang?" she asked.

"Do you think he'd pay any attention to Rakata's suspicions when he barely listens to what you and I say?" Britt inquired. "Wakefield needs *evidence* to show to his superiors. That's why he's being hard on us. Someone else is demanding it from him." Britt drew Minda a little closer and again raised his eyes to look at the soldiers in the meadow. "It isn't likely that Samarang could make contact with the smugglers when he dares not show his face in Djakarta and risk being recognized from one or another of the raids. He's either found a partner who can or the loot is hidden somewhere."

"How could he have gotten my locket?" Minda puzzled. "I had it when we came back from Djakarta and I must have lost it here."

"I don't like to think that someone at Phoenix House is involved in this," Britt said reluctantly.

"What about that relative of Alden's servant?" she inquired. "Did you ever find out who that was?"

"Merely a harmless gossip who, once he'd learned I was trying to discover who'd passed news to Townes's servant, came to me and begged my pardon. He'd never repeated anything important because he works in the tea factory and can't know much about what's happening in the house. He was terrified of losing his job and vowed never to say a word about us again.'' Britt brushed off the incident, then asked, ''Can you remember when you last saw the locket?''

''It was while you were on the tiger hunt,'' Minda answered promptly. ''I was wearing it the day Alden and the DeGroots visited, but I didn't have it that night when I undressed for bed. I was still wearing the chain, but the locket had dropped off sometime during the day and I'd been too distracted to notice. I could have lost it in the garden or anywhere in the house.''

Britt carefully considered the possibility of the servants and gardeners before he concluded, ''Though it's possible one of our workers is involved in this, it doesn't seem likely. I choose only the most trustworthy of them for jobs in or near the house. I think it's safe to take DeGroot off our list of suspects too. He's too honest to think of a scheme like this, and he certainly isn't a murderer.''

''We know Alden is devious,'' Minda reluctantly said, then shook her head incredulously. ''No, I can't believe it! He'd never attack plantations and military convoys like a highwayman. If he wanted to steal something, he'd do it by lying and cheating, not violence.''

''Townes could have thought of the scheme, but Samarang would have supplied the violence. They were standing near each other at Matarami's funeral, and we can't know how long Townes was in Java before that, maybe enough time to have made contact with Samarang,'' Britt speculated, then was quiet a moment before adding, ''Townes might be after a lot more than what's being stolen in these raids. He could have his own reason to encourage a rebellion.''

''But why? He's a stranger to Java. How could a rebellion benefit him?'' Minda asked in surprise.

''He may have learned through his government connections that the East Indies won't be given back to the Netherlands after the war in Europe ends. If this should happen and both the Hollanders and the Javanese rebel, this island would be plunged into such chaos that, afterward, opportunists could come to claim whole plantations for very low prices. The British government would need men willing to operate the plantations and bring a profit from this colony,'' Britt said slowly, as if he were thinking aloud, then abruptly declared. ''That *must* be the answer!''

''Alden couldn't run a plantation even if he wanted to, which I'm certain he wouldn't. I know he wasn't lying when he said he didn't like Java," Minda denied, then asked, "Are you really sure the British could put down a rebellion?"

"Yes, and so is Rakata or he'd have started the fight when Matarami died," Britt said grimly. "Townes could hire an agent or agents, depending on how many plantations he could afford to buy with the loot he's been collecting from the raids. Maybe he thinks he could get Phoenix House as some sort of revenge on me for stealing you from him."

"Alden doesn't know I love you. I'd thought if I told him, he might cause a scandal," Minda said. "I was very careful to convince him I'm only your business partner and friend. Alden even commented how surprised he was that I'd learned so much about tea." She paused, then sighed, "How ironic it was for me to have worried about a scandal if he's trying to destroy our lives."

"Maybe Townes thinks, after he has a plantation or two of his own, he could woo you back, providing you didn't learn about his scheme," Britt said angrily. "Maybe he thinks, with me out of the way, he could still get control of Phoenix House Tea through you."

Minda shuddered. "This is like a nightmare."

"If it's true, we *have* to find a way to stop him, but I don't know how," Britt admitted. "No one would be inclined to believe an envoy attached to the Colonial Office, a relative newcomer to Java, is guilty of all this, not unless we could produce the most damning kind of evidence. And we have nothing except theories."

Despite the way Alden had tried to cheat her in Philadelphia, Minda found this new scheme hard to accept. It wasn't a matter of simply lying; it involved armies and people being killed. All this to satisfy one man's greed? She whispered, "It's hard to believe. Maybe we're wrong."

"We could be," Britt conceded. "But no one had a better opportunity to take your locket, and I don't know anyone who hates me more than Townes does. Unless we learn something to the contrary, we'd be foolish to ignore the possibility of Townes and Samarang's guilt."

Minda couldn't deny this. Their situation had become too desperate for them to overlook the only theory that supplied answers, however outlandish. She finally said, "We'll have to discover some way to learn the truth."

They fell silent, each so absorbed in their dilemma they didn't notice Dessa enter the room until she spoke. "It's getting late, Mem Scott. Koki is asking when you'll want dinner."

Minda turned from the window to answer wearily, "I don't know. I have a dreadful headache and no appetite."

"I'm not hungry either. Maybe we can have a light supper later," Britt suggested.

Minda looked up at him and, noticing some leaf bits from his pursuit of Dalang still clinging to his hair, reached up to comb them out with her fingers as she said, "Maybe I should have a glass of sherry. It might ease my headache."

Britt glanced down at his soiled clothes. "I'd completely forgotten how dirty I am. I think I'll go for a swim."

"Mem Scott, will you join Tuan Britt?" Dessa inquired.

Britt, who had gone to the doorway, paused to look back. "Why not come with me?"

Minda shook her head. "You go ahead. I feel like being alone for a while."

After Britt and Dessa had left, Minda continued to stand by the window and gaze at the soldiers in the distant meadow. Though she'd been stunned at the theory she and Britt had evolved about Alden, Minda realized, even while she'd tried to deny it, she'd known all along that he hadn't come to Java for the reason he'd told her.

Minda's resentment of the soldiers in the meadow was steadily growing, and so was her anger at the possibility of Alden's ruthlessly scheming to ruin Britt, win Phoenix House, and even win her. Knowing that her anger was reaching such proportions she must distract herself, Minda tried to think of what she could do, then decided that staring out the window at Wakefield's camp wasn't going to help her forget the guards patrolling around the house or the plausibility of Alden's perversity. Frowning, she resolutely turned from the window.

Britt's love was the only thing in her life that had the power to turn her mind from such thoughts, she finally realized; and seeking comfort, she envisioned him swimming in the twilight. The peace of the scene was like an invisible line persistently tugging at her. The high wall enclosing the pool and bathhouse to insure privacy made the area seem like a haven from everything that was causing her pain.

Chapter Sixteen

The sky's daytime face of bright azure had deepened to a rich indigo tint. The sun had paused on the horizon to fold fiery wings that left glowing trails of orange and crimson as guides for the first timidly appearing stars. The bathing pool's surface was a mirror of the heavens broken by wavering gold reflections from the torches Suhadi had lit before Britt dismissed him.

Britt had plunged into the water to swim as fast and hard as if he were in a race. After crossing the pool's length several times at this frantic pace, he'd realized he couldn't outswim his troubles and finally slowed down in the hope that deliberately languid strokes would relax him a little. But angry, fear-filled thoughts of the snare Townes seemed to be drawing around him persisted.

Even if Wakefield accepted the plantation workers as witnesses to his whereabouts on the day the convoy had been attacked, Britt knew the major's superiors wouldn't. He doubted that Minda's testimony would convince anyone of his innocence either. Though as Britt's partner she would profit from his conviction by inheriting Phoenix House Tea, everyone knew she also was his lifelong friend, and Britt was sure any prosecutor he might ever have to stand before would remind the court that his living with Minda, however the house was sectioned, made their becoming lovers possible. In that case, even if Minda could conceal that she loved him—and her volatile emotions made it unlikely—

the puritanical attitudes that men held in public, if not in private, would negate her denial.

Britt dreaded to think of what Wakefield would learn at Talu. If Rakata was innocent, Britt wondered how the *raden* would receive the major's troops at Talu's gates. Although Rakata had good reason to avoid battle, would his pride, trampled on so often during these last years, force him to say or do something impulsive and unwise? A *raden* had to answer to the noblemen of his city. Would they demand that Talu defy Wakefield? Could they, hoping to save themselves, even hand Rakata over as a sacrifice, a gesture that would condemn Britt as well?

Aware that his worrying was making his swimming uncoordinated and he was accomplishing nothing by continuing, he finally made his way to the side of the pool. He stood in the waist-deep water gazing at the shadowy tops of the palm trees rising from the other side of the wall and tried to think of what he could do.

Britt knew he had to stay in Java as long as there was any chance he wouldn't be arrested. Fleeing now would be like an admission of guilt; and no matter how the political situation changed later, he wouldn't be able to return unless he could prove his innocence. But remaining in Java to see the thing through now was a gamble Britt knew he could lose. Despite his encouraging Minda, he was haunted by the fear that now, when he finally saw his dream of love within his grasp, it could be snatched away. He was more afraid than he'd ever been of anything in his life that his and Minda's tomorrows would be stolen from them.

Britt had to admit in the privacy of his own soul that Wakefield might change his mind in the morning and march him off to Djakarta for questioning that could evolve into his arrest and trial. Arguing with himself that he was being foolish, this wasn't possibly his and Minda's last night together, Britt knew only one thing for certain. He couldn't bear to tell Minda about his fear. He couldn't go into the house with this on his mind, because she would see it in his face and question him.

A bird trilled its nesting song and Britt tried once again to convince himself that his speculations were merely dark imaginings; then, as the breeze gently strummed the coconut fronds, he decided he must concentrate on the beauty of his surroundings in an effort to cleanse his mind of worry.

The sweet and spice of a thousand kinds of jungle flowers blended their perfumes into an exotic bouquet Britt closed his eyes to inhale. In his darkness, the clamor of his thoughts gradually subsided to be replaced by the sound of the water gently lapping at his waist. Then he slowly became aware of another's presence. He opened his eyes and turned his head, already knowing who it was.

Minda stood motionless by the door she'd just closed behind her, fingers still resting on the handle, as if she suddenly weren't sure she should stay. Her voice was little more than part of the murmuring air currents as she said, "You were so quiet, looked so deep in thought, I didn't want to interrupt you."

"I wasn't thinking, at least not like human beings do, with words to pinpoint every detail of their problems," he replied. "For a moment I was pretending I was just another animal, letting my senses absorb the twilight without words."

Minda sighed. "Maybe it's because animals don't have a language that they can't worry."

"They're capable of it, but they don't pore over their fears and prolong them by inaction as people do. They solve their problems quickly by running away, if they can, or by fighting." Britt turned to look at Minda more steadily.

She was wearing a sarong, one of the gifts she'd received after she'd defied the man-eater in the garden. The sarong was dark blue and coral like the evening sky. Her hair was brushed loose, its soft waves auburn where they caught the torchlight, deepening to sable in the shadows. She was a sight to distract him, he concluded, but recognized that she, too, was worried.

"Come closer, Minda. I'll teach you how to think like an animal does, without words," Britt suggested. "Once in a while, when you need respite from troubling thoughts, it helps to be able to do this."

"Human problems are more complicated than the things that make animals afraid. I can't just run away from them. I can't bite or claw my enemies as animals do." Minda walked slowly toward Britt. "I'm pretty sure that Alden is causing this. I suspected it the moment I realized he could have taken my locket. I feel like a fool for denying it. Why do people insist someone is innocent of wrongdoing just because they know the person? I wonder if it's conceit—they don't want to admit someone they've associated with is wrong or even wicked."

"It's your own goodness that makes it difficult for you to acknowledge the evil in others," Britt said quietly. He tugged at the hem of her sarong until she sat down at the edge of the pool. Then he reasoned, "There's nothing either of us can do at the moment about our problems. Don't let them steal this night from us by thinking about them. Come into the water with me. Let me show you how to distract yourself from all this trouble."

While Minda hesitated, Britt reached for the edge of her sarong and pulled the tuck loose that held the garment closed. The sarong fell into a twilight puddle around her hips. He grasped her waist and gently swung her down into the water.

"Lean against me," he said and drew her near.

Britt's nakedness was a surprise running pleasantly along Minda's nerves and she glanced up at him.

"Close your eyes and listen to the evening's sounds," he directed. "Smell the flowers in the air. Don't let one word creep into your mind. Don't think at all; just enjoy your senses. Feel the breeze and the water against your skin."

"And you?"

His eyes shifted down to meet hers. "Yes. And feel me."

Britt's hand coaxed her head to rest on his shoulder. Minda did as he'd asked and closed her eyes.

The fragrance haunting the air was an intriguing blend. She briefly wondered which flowers composed it, then realized her busy mind was using words to analyze something that didn't matter. All she needed to do was enjoy the scent. Minda resolved to follow Britt's suggestion and not think about anything. She was surprised it was so difficult to do but, after several efforts, discovered it was possible.

Suddenly Minda could hear the water rippling around her, the airy whir of a bird swooping low over the pool, the soft crackle of the torch flames, the whispering foliage moving in the breeze. Minda opened her eyes but didn't raise them. Instead she watched the sky's reflection in the pool, the last streaks of its colors dimming until the stars made a bold slash of silver glimmering across the dark water. She was aware every moment of the warmth of the body touching hers, of the strength of the arms enfolding her, the fingers lightly patting her hair. She felt so removed from the rest of the world that the soldiers, even Alden and Samarang, no longer existed. Minda forgot she was in Java. The name men had given to one of the world's islands didn't matter.

Minda reclosed her eyes and knew, without Britt's speaking or moving, without the knowing having to take on the shape of words in her mind, that he was thinking of kissing her. It was an awareness, a sultry current transferred from his skin to hers wherever they touched.

Britt's kisses became warm breaths in Minda's hair. When she tilted her face to his, Britt's lips were moist and cool from the water as they moved over hers. His fingers wove through Minda's hair, drew her head back, while his kisses slipped down her throat, found the place on the side of her neck where his mouth knew how to evoke a piquant thrill. Then Britt kissed and caressed Minda's neck until he felt her shivering. He raised his head and his arms drew her more firmly to him.

The tip of Britt's tongue traced the outline of Minda's mouth, slowly, thoughtfully, as if he'd never kissed her before, as if he were exploring her response and letting her discover his touch. The edges of Britt's teeth drew at Minda's lip until he gently captured the bow of her mouth, coaxed it into a softer curve, then released it to catch her lower lip and seduce it into roundness too.

Minda knew that his subtle caresses were as much a search of his own senses as hers, but the realization shaped no words in her mind. It was a message borne by the touch of Britt's lips, the contact of his body, and as he dipped his head to kiss her shoulders, by the texture of his hair, damp from swimming, that brushed her cheek. It was the cool, clean water-scent of Britt's skin, the taste of his kiss lingering in Minda's mouth. Wanting her sight to take part in this, she opened her eyes and saw that his hair, like the tips of his lashes, was catching gold flecks from the torchlight. He raised his eyes; copper streaks were glimmering among their amber shadows.

"This is a way to distract me from our problems," she murmured against his cheek.

Britt turned his head so his words became a caress as they brushed her lips, "Your mentioning those troubles in itself tells me you haven't forgotten them—yet."

He released Minda and moved away to grip the edge of the pool, then, in a smooth, quick movement lifted himself out of the water. He turned to offer his hands and pulled her from the pool. Though Britt's skin was cool from the balmy air, the heat in his depths radiated out through his pores; when he drew Minda to him, the naked length of his lean body lit an ember in her. Minda's arms tightened around him, the warmth of his hips moved sinuously against her, and a flurry of sparks rose from the glow he'd begun in her.

Minda anticipated that Britt would passionately kiss her and the flame he'd ignited would burst into a blaze, but his flattened hands lightly grasped the sides of her face, his fingertips twining in her hair as his lips wandered over her eyelids to her forehead, his tongue leaving dots of moist fire along her hairline. Britt's mouth moved to nibble the skin above Minda's lips, then he quickly shifted, the tip of his tongue licking along the edge of her lip to its corner, the edges of his teeth gently drawing at her skin until Minda felt as if she were suspended by a thread over the volcano's glowing core. She swayed closer, wanting to lure him farther into the desire he was so carefully building in her. But his hands slid down the sides of Minda's neck to her shoulders and he held her away.

Feeling as if her body were pulsing with the need for Britt's caresses, she looked up at him and discovered, though the torchlight cast a warm gleam on the surface of his eyes, there was a darkness in their depths she'd never seen before, one she couldn't fathom.

Britt noticed the surprise that briefly flashed over Minda's face and knew she had sensed the nearness of the shadows moving in his soul. He wouldn't talk about it; he had no intention of putting what he dreaded into words that would give it a clearer shape. Britt scooped Minda up in his arms. Forgetting his robe and her sarong, two piles of discarded cloth beside the pool, he bent his head and, with his kiss, silenced any questions she might ask as he carried her to the door in the wall that surrounded the pool.

Though the walkway leading to the house was covered by a bamboo roof, its sides were open to the breeze and the moon was flooding it with silver. The short distance seemed like a gauntlet he must cross, but the only concession Britt made to the soldiers patrolling the grounds was a quick glance in both directions to make sure no one was in sight before he walked swiftly through the moonlight to the house. Minda's old room was nearest and he carried her there. After he'd put her on the bed, he turned away.

Minda watched Britt return to the door, then pause with his back toward her. She'd been made so uneasy by the strange mood she sensed in him she wasn't sure, despite his arousal, that he would come back to her and, if he did, whether he'd want to talk or would silently continue making love. She heard the door click shut, but the moon vanished behind a cloud and the chamber was abruptly plunged into darkness. There wasn't a sound to tell her if Britt was still at the door, pacing the room, or sitting in a chair as he had on the *Harini*, when he'd wanted her and had tried to fight his feelings. Then luminous silver again flooded the room and revealed that he was standing beside the bed, holding back the orchid netting. The level of his desire reflected from the hard glitter of his eyes, the sharpened look of his features, and the tension of his body. One impatient hand swept the gossamer net closed around them as he sat on the bed.

Again the sense that Britt was withholding something stirred in Minda's instincts. As he turned to put his arms around her, she began to ask, "What is . . ."

But his mouth covered hers, effectively stopping the words as he hungrily caressed her lips, rekindling the heat that, in Minda's worrying, had dwindled. Britt's kisses ignited a fire that momentarily burned away the questions she might have asked. He released Minda for only the moment it took to draw his legs into bed, then swiveled around to grasp her shoulders and, with his own weight, ease her to the pillows. He moved provocatively, but when she tightened her embrace, he lay solidly flat. Reaching back, he gently broke Minda's hold on him and took her hands to place them above her head, then firmly held her wrists to the pillows so she couldn't clasp him to her.

Anticipating that Britt's kiss would again scorch her with passion, she was surprised when he tipped his head to nuzzle her shoulder, pause where it met the base of her neck so his caresses could light a new flame in her. His tongue flicked a warm path to Minda's ear, and its restless search sent ripples of pleasure through her that were climaxed by their sudden oneness.

His breath formed whispers, themselves caresses, in her ear, "Don't ask questions tonight, Minda. Don't even ask them tomorrow. Just live every moment we spend together."

The pliant movement of her hips against his was a mutely eloquent answer Britt's instincts begged him to echo now. The hunger pulsing through him was of such power he wondered if it could be appeased, then finally realized the commands of his body wouldn't be silenced until he was exhausted; depletion was the only way he could banish his fears. But how could he behave that way without Minda's sensing that his dread was so great he knew of no other way to hold it back? Britt's need made him feel as if he were in the heart of a wildly throbbing drum, but he still had enough will to force the impulse to recede and keep his rebellious hips still. He leaned on his forearms to nibble gently at her lips, and Minda, aware of the raging desire Britt was controlling, felt as if she'd be driven mad by the tenderness of his caresses.

Then, abruptly, as if her senses could bear no more, the wildfire racing through Minda withdrew, its heat forming a molten core that radiated a power somehow more manageable, yet no less intense, through her blood. As Britt's mouth slipped over her chin, down her throat, then followed the curve of her breast, the only outward sign of Minda's desire was the growing tension of her face, her head turning slowly from side to side as his lips and tongue led her from one piquant delight to another. All the while, his eyes held blazing copper sparks that denied his seeming calm. A pressure was growing in Minda, a craving so acute she wondered how long she could endure it; her wrists strained against the bonds that were his hands. His hips moved in supple provocation, as if to acknowledge her desire, but he continued to elude her.

"Please, Britt," she urgently whispered.

"Not until you stop demanding," he murmured, his body still moving slowly, temptingly against her, "or this fire will be too easy to put out."

Minda stared at him, realized what he said was true. Fulfillment would come like a streak of lightning that glows for but an instant before it fades.

"Then you must stop," she breathed and wasn't sure she was glad when he withdrew to lie at her side.

Trembling with the passion that surged through her, Minda closed her eyes and wondered why Britt had driven her to such madness if he'd wanted a more languorous love and, because she knew she wanted the same, why she'd responded like a racehorse to a starter's gun. There was a kind of desperation in both of them, she realized, and wondered why. The sensuality of his caresses had seemed too subtle to be those of a man who had anything except love on his mind. Finally, as if his thoughts had suddenly been transmitted along her own nerves, she knew Britt was afraid Wakefield's arrival meant that he was being drawn into a trap he wouldn't escape. He thought he wasn't merely facing questions, but arrest, trial, execution, and he didn't want her to know it.

Although Minda was horrified at the idea, not a flicker of apprehension was revealed in her expression. She couldn't believe Britt would be arrested or convicted. She resolved not to let him dwell on that prospect. It didn't occur to her that she was doing the same as he; each was trying to protect the other from the same fear.

"You've given me enough time to compose myself," Minda said in a tone that gave no hint of what she'd decided. "I think my desire has dimmed."

Startled that she sounded more subdued than he wished, Britt turned his head to stare at her. The copper sparks in his eyes blended into a sultry blur as he commented, "I hope not too dimmed."

Minda's gaze was deliberately innocent as she suggested, "You can relight it."

The prospect of rebuilding her ardor when he was already so highly aroused made him sit up. "You're teasing me," he said, but he wasn't sure.

Minda forced herself to answer lightly, "I'm afraid we'll just have to find out."

Britt kept his eyes steadily on her and leaned closer. As his palms moved slowly along the curve of Minda's waist and his lips softly caressed hers, the autumn haze in his eyes sharpened and took on amber streaks. His hands slid to her hips, held them firmly, and their bodies easily flowed into oneness as his mouth again claimed hers. Though Britt's kiss was like a whip lashing Minda's already racing instincts, she didn't let him know it. At her seemingly pallid response, Britt kissed her even more searchingly. His body moved seductively against Minda's, coaxing her fires to renew themselves quickly. She opened her eyes, hoping to slow her responses by watching him. Britt's face was taut with the desire he held in check as he waited for her passion to rise higher. He didn't know she was fighting to conceal the impulses streaking through her, that she wanted him to become so aroused all thought of the evil threatening him would be obliterated.

Britt's kisses moved over Minda's face while his hips' supple rhythm sent ripples of impulses along her nerves, coming one on another, closer together and growing stronger until she finally could no longer restrain the waves of pleasure that coursed through her. His eyes opened, luminous with desire, to meet hers filled with emerald smoke, and he knew at last that she'd deliberately lured him to this pitch. The joyous tremor flashing through Britt made him catch his breath.

The knowledge that it was her decision driving him to these heights was a triumphant fire racing through Minda's blood, igniting every cell in her being until she moaned and didn't know it.

The sound was a streak of lightning burning away the last thread of Britt's control. His eyes lost their focus and closed. Passion became his master and her seducer, drawing them both into a firewind of forces that erupted to consume them both.

*   *   *

Britt lay, eyes closed, so far beyond the reach of his scorched senses that, for a time, he was conscious of nothing except his soul's searching for the scattered fragments of his being. It found them fused with Minda's spirit and let them remain. Then, gradually, he became aware of her breath's rhythm softening against his neck, the pulse of her temple like his own heartbeat slowing, the balmy night air on his skin cooling its film of moisture.

She finally whispered, "I want to be this way with you all night."

As Britt thought about the prospects of such a night, he opened his eyes to find her hair like a web, burnished by the moonlight, spun over his face. He gently brushed it aside and murmured, "I think dawn would find not us, but ashes, in this bed." He smiled faintly, realizing he wasn't inclined to shrink from that danger.

Minda turned her head to meet his eyes. They were a soft blur of amber, and though the pinpoints of copper light had receded in them, they hadn't dimmed. She said quietly, "I would rather be consumed by your fire than charred by any other."

Britt knew then that Minda would ask no questions about tomorrows being snatched away. She'd already faced that possibility. He decided that Dessa was mistaken about the goddess of fire living in Mrabu's crater; the goddess was at Phoenix House and her arms were wrapped around him. Whether they would have only tonight or all those waiting at tomorrow's door, Minda was the torch that could light their way through the darkness gathering around them. Her love was the flame that would burn away the fear.

When sunrise came, its luminous golden fingers caressed not ashes but the warmly pulsing bodies of lovers, still so enthralled by the enchantment of each other they weren't aware that the meadow's gentle hush was broken by men's voices harshly issuing orders, the receding staccato of horses' hooves, the rattle of distant wheels turning.

For the next week neither Britt nor Minda mentioned what the soldiers might have found at Talu. Love isolated them from Alden's possible plots for their destruction and from the major, who seemed to be his unwitting instrument.

Minda knew, if she stayed home while Britt was in the field or at the factory, the only way she would be able to forget the guards Wakefield had left would be to remain in the house and never look out a window so she wouldn't glimpse them. Instead, she insisted on going with Britt to learn about the experimental tea being harvested. With him at her side she could ignore the presence of the soldiers as if they didn't exist.

Each day at noon they returned to the house, and because they bathed together before lunch, they usually forgot the meal as well as the paperwork waiting for them in Britt's study. A casual kiss, a look, even a simple gesture, could stir them with such power that they would spend the afternoon behind closed doors. Though love, day or night, could ignite their passion to as high a flame as Gunung Mrabu's smoke was billowing, it sometimes evoked a tender intimacy that was like a channel joining their spirits. Then their hearts spoke of dreams neither had told anyone else, fantasies so removed from reality they had no other purpose than to give life a piquant flavor. They made plans for the future they wanted to build together that ignored the schemes of other men.

But the morning came when, in the early gray light before the sun washed the land with gold, one of the gardeners, who had been sweeping the blossoms fallen from the mimosa tree by the gate, raced into the house to warn that the tuan major was coming up the lane with his men.

Britt set down his breakfast cup. His and Minda's hands crept over the tablecloth to meet and clasp like their eyes. Neither spoke, and when Wakefield and his officers entered the dining room, the silence was like drapery the major felt he had to tear aside before Britt and Minda could even see him.

When Wakefield strode to the table and his gaze fell on their clasped hands, he realized finally that love was at the heart of their many-faceted partnership. Their eyes, as if drawn by one line, lifted to meet his, and he had the startling feeling that he was looking into the faces of all the lovers in the world who were being tormented by others jealous of what they'd found together. In that moment, Wakefield wished, however damning the evidence he'd found at Talu was, he could turn away and leave them together. But he had a job to do, orders to follow.

Anger at himself for what he was compelled to say sharpened Wakefield's voice and made his words seem like the measured shots of a firing squad. "Mr. Vandekker, I must arrest you for conspiring with Raden Rakata to overthrow the authority of King George III and for attacking his majesty's convoy."

Although the words he'd dreaded had finally been pronounced, Britt was surprised that he seemed to feel nothing. He turned to look beyond Wakefield and his officers, expecting to see Rakata in shackles in the doorway. Instead, he saw a Javanese dressed in the uniform of one of Rakata's officers. The Indonesian wasn't bound in any way and seemed not to be a prisoner. Britt released Minda's hand and got up from his chair.

Remembering how Britt had leaped on the assassins on the beach, Wakefield involuntarily took a step backward; Sergeant Moore put his hand on his pistol, and the several soldiers standing with Bedug in the doorway cocked their rifles.

Britt's eyes flickered with wry amusement. He knew that if he'd wished, he could have captured Wakefield or Moore to use as his shield before any of the guns could have been raised to fire. He looked at the major's grim expression and, wondering if he'd made the right choice, if he should have traded Phoenix House for escape now, commented, "Apparently you believe you've found additional evidence."

"Several of the pearls stolen from the convoy were in the *raden*'s private quarters," Wakefield replied.

Surprised at the discovery of the pearls, which seemed to confirm Rakata's guilt, Britt assumed Wakefield had conquered the city. Although pain stabbed him at the thought, Britt asked quietly, "Rakata is dead?"

"No, Mr. Vandekker, the *raden* escaped before we reached Talu's walls," Wakefield answered disgustedly. "The entire city was deserted, as you already know."

"How would I know that?" Britt inquired, then, realizing that Wakefield thought he'd sent Rakata a warning, added, "If I were Rakata's accomplice, why didn't I try to escape before you returned? There were several times, when I was in the tea fields, that I would have had a good chance of getting away from your guards."

"Perhaps you thought I didn't have enough evidence and you could brazen it out," Wakefield dryly suggested. "Of course, you didn't expect Bedug to be so weary of the *raden*'s intrigues and deceptions he'd volunteer a piece of evidence that ties you and Rakata together in this plot."

Britt turned to look searchingly at Bedug, then spoke to him in the accents of the lowest caste of the Javanese social order, which was especially insulting to a well-born officer, "If you, who have pledged your life to the *raden*'s protection, can so easily betray that trust, anyone who believes what you say is a fool. Who paid you to do this?''

Bedug's face flushed and he angrily started forward, but the nearest soldier swung his rifle to bar the way.

Wakefield, who didn't understand the dialect Britt had used, asked, ''What did you say to him?''

Britt kept his eyes on Bedug as he answered, ''Major, Bedug knows who's guilty. Let me have a little time alone with him. Then I'll be able to answer any question about this plot that you can think of putting to me.''

The fury in Britt's eyes had reminded Bedug of Rakata, and the menace in his voice suddenly made Bedug afraid of the golden-haired man he'd thought was another soft planter. Bedug took a step backward, protesting, ''The Hollander *is* in league with the *raden*! Major Wakefield, you have the pearls. They are proof!''

''You also thought that locket was evidence against me, but it turned out to be Miss Scott's,'' Britt reminded Wakefield.

Minda, who had leaped up from the chair, cried, ''Major, if this man claimed to have found the pearls in Rakata's house, how do you know he isn't lying to deflect suspicion from himself?''

''Bedug didn't find the pearls. I did,'' Wakefield said coolly. He reached into his tunic to extract a small roll of kidskin. ''*This* is what Bedug found. Here, Mr. Vandekker, read it aloud for Miss Scott. It's in Javanese.''

Britt took the kidskin and, unrolling it, translated, his heart sinking with each word, for the message was so ambiguous, it seemed to implicate him. '' 'Britt, I give unhappy tidings. I am moving my people to a safer place, a place where you and I met several times in the past. Come quickly to talk about our problem. Rakata.' ''

''Where have you secretly met him?'' Wakefield demanded.

Still staring at the letter, Britt said slowly, ''There was nothing secretive about any of the few times Rakata and I have been in contact. I don't know where Rakata has moved his people, but I guess the problem he wants to discuss with me is your belief that we're guilty.''

''They *have* had secret meetings before! I have seen them,'' Bedug insisted.

Britt flashed the Indonesian an angry glare, then met Wakefield's eyes and said evenly, ''That is a lie. Have Bedug give you dates and times so I can confirm where I really was. Or will you believe *him* before you would Miss Scott and everyone else here at Phoenix House?''

''Your workers' jobs depend on keeping your favor, so they'd make poor witnesses,'' Wakefield said, then slowly added, ''Miss Scott is in love with you and likely would lie.''

''You'd believe that brigand before me or Britt or anyone at Phoenix House?'' Minda, in a fury, gestured toward Bedug.

Britt took her hand and said, ''Minda, I'm afraid I've overestimated the major's character. It seems he'll take the word of anyone who points a finger at Rakata and me because his superiors are demanding an answer and he hasn't been able to learn the truth.''

Wakefield said angrily, ''The pearls in Rakata's quarters, this message to you with Rakata's seal on it, the locket which the king's prosecutor will point out was a love token to you from Miss Scott, the weapons Rakata used on the convoy, all add up to an excellent case against you and Rakata. Mr. Vandekker, please come along without resisting. I truly would dislike having to use force on you.''

Britt had been desperately trying to think of what he might do. The snare had closed around him after all. He wished he'd tried to escape before. Now there were too many soldiers and Minda could get hurt in the struggle if he tried to get away. He decided there was no choice. He struggled to compose himself, to erase the fear in his eyes before they met Minda's. ''Arjuna will help with anything you need while I'm gone,'' he said assuringly, then added, ''Don't be too worried, Minda. None of this so-called evidence can convict me, because it's false. I *will* prove that I'm innocent.''

Minda reached into her soul to find the courage she'd been gathering up during the past week and fixed its mask on her face. ''I know we'll get through this,'' she said firmly, then unclasped the chain she wore and pressed it into his hand. ''Since Wakefield has my locket in Djakarta, this time you'll have to take the goddess's crystal to remember me by.''

Britt leaned nearer to brush his lips to her cheek and murmur close to her ear, ''I need nothing to remind me of you. This past week you've burned yourself into my soul. Don't come to the post to visit me, Minda. I don't want you to see me in the stockade.'' Then he straightened and turned. A pair of soldiers moved into place at his side.

Minda's attention was so riveted on Britt she didn't even hear Wakefield's apology for distressing her. She trailed after the soldiers to the front door and stood silently watching as Britt was searched. Then his horse was brought for him; she stared fixedly at him as he mounted. Tears stung her eyes, but she kept them from falling even as Britt gave her one last, lingering look before Wakefield signaled to the soldiers and the column started forward.

Dessa, who had followed Minda through the house, said comfortingly, "You were wise to give Tuan Britt the crystal. The goddess will protect him until he returns."

Minda watched until Britt disappeared down the palm-shaded lane and, feeling that her life was going with him, whispered bitterly, "The goddess would have better protected Britt by keeping those pearls and that message out of Wakefield's hands."

"Maybe she's arranging things so the one who is guilty will reveal himself while Tuan Britt is in Djakarta," Dessa hopefully suggested.

"I suspect I already know who the culprit is, and if I'm right, he doesn't believe in your gods and goddesses or any other," Minda said brokenly, then buried her face in her hands and wept.

Chapter Seventeen

Britt stood in stocking feet, hands raised, watching one soldier inspect his boots while another patted his clothes searching for weapons. His eyes shifted to regard Wakefield, who was looking on. "What do you think I could hide in a shirt, breeches, and riding boots? You already had your men do this at Phoenix House. I told you then that I don't carry a firearm unless I expect to go into the jungle. All I take into the fields is a knife because it's often useful in my work. I don't wear it in my dining room and you arrived before I'd finished breakfast."

"It's to make sure you have nothing you might use to escape, a formality before we lock you up," Wakefield said, looking faintly embarrassed to have to do this. His temper had had a chance to cool long before they'd reached Djakarta, and he wished he could have avoided arresting Vandekker. After the soldiers had finished their search, the major told them to give Britt his boots, then directed, "Come into my office, Mr. Vandekker. I want to talk with you."

"As you wish." Britt bent to retrieve his boots and followed the major. He noticed that no guard accompanied them into the office, and Wakefield closed the door. Curious about the major's purpose, he sat in the chair Wakefield indicated and inquired, "Aren't you worried about a brigand like me attacking you to escape?"

"If you were the kind of man to run, you would have tried the first time we went to Phoenix House."

"That was before you actually arrested me," Britt muttered, and leaned down to start pulling on a boot.

Wakefield spoke as he crossed the room to a cabinet. "The only way out of my office is through that door or this window, where there are guards to stop you." He paused by the cabinet to turn and comment, "I don't think you'll try to escape. You have too much to lose by becoming a hunted man—Phoenix House, your good name, and of course Miss Scott."

Britt frowned as he pushed his foot into the second boot. "If I stay, I'll have my *life* to lose," he said. "I don't intend to be shot or hanged for something I didn't do."

Wakefield regarded him silently a moment, wondering if he'd made a mistake in trusting Britt to be a reasonable man while they were alone. He said slowly, "When I returned to Phoenix House, I was angry that the *raden* had slipped out of my hands. I was more curt with you and Miss Scott than I prefer." Wakefield opened the cabinet door. "Would you like a brandy, Mr. Vandekker?"

Britt glanced up in surprise. "That's very hospitable for a jailer."

"I thought, after all that's happened to you since yesterday morning, you might be a little unnerved," Wakefield said as he poured drinks for both of them.

"I'm not unnerved, Major. I'm damned angry." Britt stood up to push his feet more solidly down into his boot. At his movement, Wakefield turned quickly. Britt replaced himself in the chair, commenting, "It seems you're more nervous than I."

"You just said you might try to escape. I've seen how fast you can move and I don't want my face smashed as you did to the man who tried to assassinate me," Wakefield said warily.

"You're not trying to kill me," Britt noted. "It's only your law doing that, and you don't know how to prevent it."

Wakefield sighed and handed Britt the brandy. "Mr. Vandekker, I'm chagrined to confess what you said about my having to arrest *someone* is true, but you have to admit that every piece of evidence I've collected points at you and the *raden*. Still, if this comes to a trial, a judge would take it as a sign of your good faith if you were to tell me where Rakata is."

"It's only been about a year since I first talked to him at all." Britt recalled the village where Charles had been killed and said cautiously, "That was in the jungle, when Rakata had some men with him and Charles was with me. Then Rakata came to Phoenix House to tell me about Matarami's death on the night of the party for Miss Scott. Of course, we spoke briefly at Matarami's funeral, as you know. I've stopped at Talu a couple of times since, but there was nothing clandestine about those visits or any of the other meetings. He and I have never been alone to plot anything.'' Britt paused to sip his brandy before adding, ''I don't know where Rakata has moved his people, but I wish I could question Bedug about how he got that letter. The story he told you about sneaking into the courier's room while he was asleep is ridiculous. It's far more likely that Bedug murdered the man in the jungle. I assure you, I'd get the truth about that and many other things out of Bedug.''

''I can't allow you to threaten one of my witnesses. You know that,'' Wakefield said. ''Assuming you're telling the truth, Rakata *must* have some reason to think you'd know where to meet him. Think about it, Vandekker. It would help your case.''

Britt did think about it, but not because he intended to betray Rakata. He was glad he was staring down into his brandy glass when the memory of the few childhood meetings in Durga struck him. He waited a moment for the revelation to fade from his eyes before he raised them to tell Wakefield, ''My mother was banished from Talu before I was born. That meant anyone who contacted her would have been put to death if they'd been discovered. Rakata and I were raised as separately as if we'd been living on the opposite sides of the world. By the time our mother had been killed, he had his life, I mine.''

''It's odd and rather sad that brothers should live almost three decades on an island yet not know each other,'' Wakefield reflected. ''Still, Rakata has gone somewhere with his people and seems to think you'd know where that is.''

Hoping to get Wakefield off that line of thought, Britt speculated, ''It's possible Rakata didn't write the letter, that someone else managed to gain access to his chambers to use his seal, someone who wanted to trap us both. I know Rakata is convinced his cousin, Samarang, would like to see him deposed because Samarang is next in line for his title.''

''Samarang is Rakata's cousin, but not yours?''

''Their relationship is through Rakata's father,'' Britt explained. ''I have no relatives now except Rakata.''

Wakefield absorbed this information, then said thoughtfully, ''Samarang has been cooperative with us in the past, but that was before Rakata became *raden*. We've had no contact with him since, and I'd assumed he'd decided to be loyal to his new ruler.'' Wakefield paused a moment before adding, "Even if Samarang is trying to get Rakata's title, he has no reason to drag you into this, does he?''

"If you mean, would I have any claim to the title, no, I do not,'' Britt answered. "Samarang wouldn't care about me one way or another, but I know of someone who'd be delighted to see me hanged—a European. Samarang would need a European partner, who could move more freely in Djakarta than he can, who could make certain contacts for him.''

Wakefield looked at Britt with new interest. "Who is this enemy of yours?''

"Alden Townes.'' Britt was instantly sorry he'd mentioned the name, because he was sure the major wouldn't believe him.

Wakefield said, "I don't like Mr. Townes personally, I must admit, but he hardly seems the sort to gallop into a Javanese village or a plantation to loot it, much less attack a British military convoy. Certainly he wouldn't set up such an elaborate scheme merely because he has some quarrel with you.''

"Despite the impression of old wealth he gives, Townes is in desperate need of money, and if he's cultivated Samarang's friendship, he doesn't have to do the dirty work,'' Britt pointed out.

"Alden Townes needs money?'' Wakefield exclaimed.

"I shouldn't have bothered to say it. I knew you wouldn't believe me.'' Britt sighed and, taking a sip of brandy, thought about his situation a moment before he said, "I might as well explain my theory. If you already think I'm a blackguard, I suppose your concluding I'm foolish is no worse.''

"The only reason you're in this office is because I've had doubts for some time about your guilt. I've never thought you were a fool,'' Wakefield said. "Tell me your theory, Mr. Vandekker. Whether or not I agree or can do anything about it, I don't know, but you've certainly piqued my curiosity.''

Britt finished his brandy, then began to explain what he and Minda had discussed. Though he could see Wakefield was very interested, he was pessimistic about this affecting charges brought against him. Despite that, Britt left nothing out and finished by describing the disappearance of Minda's locket on the day Townes had visited Phoenix House.

"If you're right, it's incredible how far that man would go,''

Wakefield finally said. "And everything does depend on Great Britain's refusing to return the East Indies to the Netherlands. I doubt that would happen."

"Someone privy to the royal court might be convinced otherwise and Townes may have access to that sort of information," Britt reminded. "If Townes is behind all this and the East Indies isn't returned to the Netherlands, he'd be disappointed, but what would he have lost? Nothing, as long as he wasn't found out. Meanwhile, I'm sure he'd have made a tidy profit from his share of the loot."

Wakefield put down his brandy snifter. "It would be very difficult to convict someone in his position, even if you had evidence rather than a theory."

"It would be embarrassing to your government," Britt observed dryly. "Yet Townes and Samarang's working together is the only answer that makes sense to me. But then, I *know* I'm innocent."

Wakefield didn't want to think about the implications. He said firmly, "I still have no proof that Townes is doing what you've suggested, but I do have evidence against you and Rakata—and I have orders to follow."

"Unless I get evidence against Townes and Samarang, which I can't while I'm shut away in your stockade, you'll put me and Rakata on trial," Britt concluded grimly.

"If I can catch Rakata, yes."

"And *if* you can hold me that long."

"Don't try to escape, Mr. Vandekker. I wouldn't like to see you shot in the effort," Wakefield warned. "It would be a waste if you could convince a judge of your innocence."

"If there were any chance of that, I'd willingly stand trial, humiliating as that would be, but as things are, it seems unlikely," Britt reflected. As Wakefield leaned closer to pour a bit more brandy, Britt looked up at him from determined eyes, adding, "If it came to my having to flee Java and I could manage that, I'd still do everything in my power to exonerate myself. Unlike Rakata, I have the resources to carry on the battle for the rest of my life, even if I had to do it from hiding and in another country."

Wakefield took a sip of brandy. "You truly are a blend of two cultures. On one hand you talk about a legal fight and, on the other, about breaking out of the stockade. Perhaps the greatest part of my difficulty in keeping order in this district has simply been that I don't understand the Javanese mind. They're polite and civilized one minute, ferocious the next. They can be loyal to the point of willingly sacrificing their lives, yet can, it seems, just as easily turn their backs on what they profess to love. Look at what Matarami did to your mother. I've seen similar things happen a hundred times. Bedug, pledged to protect Rakata, has betrayed him. Even my own gardener, Anambas, whom I've treated fairly, has gone off to Rakata, deserting his wife and children, his oldest lad only fourteen, though I'd thought Anambas adored his family.''

"Families are divided for many reasons, and in Java, especially these days, a fourteen-year-old sometimes must be an adult. A man like Bedug is a traitor wherever he's born,'' Britt said. "I can't understand why you'd listen to a liar like him. That he's obeying someone else is obvious, seeing as how he's implicated me in all this and we don't even know each other.''

"Bedug has brought evidence, however he obtained it, that I can show to a judge, and you've only given me a theory,'' Wakefield reminded. "If you were to tell me where the *raden* is so I could question him, or if Rakata would present himself to me voluntarily like a reasonable, law-abiding man instead of behaving like a bandit on the run, I'd be able to put more credence in what you claim. Perhaps then I could question Samarang, even Alden Townes. As it is, my hands are tied.''

"Even if I knew where Rakata is and could get a message to him, he'd never come to you. Why should he? Your laws are different from his and he has no reason to trust them. You know you'd have to take him by force. Who would be initiating the violence then?'' Britt asked pointedly, then commented, "He's already shown more restraint than I'd have expected of him.''

"Is that an admittance that you know him better than you've been letting on?'' Wakefield inquired.

"I've merely heard the same stories as you have about what a firebrand he is,'' Britt said disgustedly. "Why can't you or your superiors look at it from Rakata's viewpoint? His country has been invaded by settlers from one country and armies from two others. All but the last remnants of the authority he believes is his by birth have been taken from him. His society's structure has been disrupted down to the last peasant. The invaders have ignored his laws, insulted his philosophy, and disparaged the religion of his fathers. His people are beginning to turn against him, not necessarily because they think you're right, but because they need to survive whatever comes. Now that you're hunting him like a criminal, what would be the next logical step for him to take other than trying to win back his people by reuniting them against their common enemy, which presently is you? I don't for a moment doubt that Samarang hopes a British bullet in Rakata's heart will give him the title of *raden*. A rebellion the Javanese can't win will result in exactly what Townes might want— temporary chaos, which could make it possible for him to get Phoenix House Tea and as many of the other, already established plantations he can scoop up.''

Later, Britt lay on his bunk reviewing his conversation with Wakefield over and over all afternoon. Though he'd been surprised at the major's willingness to hear his story, the results had been what he'd expected. He'd been locked in a cell with only a monotonously pacing guard to mark the passing time. Britt hadn't changed his mind about telling Wakefield Rakata was at Durga. He knew the major would only march his soldiers there as he had to Talu, and seeing the approaching force, having nowhere else to go, Rakata would have to fight. If Rakata survived the battle, he would be dragged back as a prisoner, his very resistance proclaiming his guilt. Then Britt would be condemned on all sides as a turncoat. The only chance he could see of resolving any of this would be to escape, somehow capture Bedug, and take him back to Durga. If Bedug confessed the plot before Rakata's council, the noblemen would have to believe Samarang's guilt. Then Britt and Rakata could together present Samarang and Bedug to Wakefield along with what they could recover of the loot. If Samarang admitted that Townes was implicated . . . But, Britt reminded himself, there was still a chance, however slim, that Townes wasn't guilty. Britt had no real proof, just a theory formed in desperation, which seemed to supply the answers.

Although the fear Minda was suffering in Britt's absence had haunted him from the moment Wakefield had taken him away, he'd been able to keep that worry at arm's length while he tried to think of a solution to his problems. But after nightfall, as if a dam had broken in his mind, Minda became a torrent of thoughts that flooded out all else, and he paced his cell like a caged leopard. The darkness was filled with visions of her pain and the stillness with her weeping. Britt longed to put his arms around her and kiss away her tears; his helplessness was a bitter wind howling through his soul.

Lying down to close his eyes didn't shut out the visions. They only changed into memories of love. Britt could feel Minda's body, like warm velvet pressed against his, her lips moving softly over his face, the silk of her hair spread over his chest. Such thoughts were more than he could bear. He got up again to pace his cell until he was so weary there was nothing left to do except lie down and be tormented by dreams.

Alden Townes sat up in bed with a start and peered into the darkness of his room. Although he could see nothing, he had the eerie feeling that he wasn't alone. The room was like pitch and, without a breeze, stiflingly hot. Had his servant pulled down *every* reed shade before leaving for the night? That must be why he'd awakened so suddenly, Alden decided in relief. He simply was too hot. The rash the Hollanders called "red dog," prickly heat, would return if he didn't open the shades, but if he came out from under the protective netting and the right mosquito bit him, he'd probably have a bout with malaria and have to take that grayish powder called quinine, which seemed as much a staple for the Europeans in Java as rice was for the Indonesians.

"Ah, well," he muttered and swept aside the insect net to grope for his slippers.

"They are here. Take them," a soft, sibilant voice came from the darkness as the slippers were thrust into his hands.

Fear prickled Alden's neck as he realized it wasn't his servant's voice. "Who is that?" he whispered in alarm.

"It is I, Bedug," the voice said and moved to the table to light a lamp.

Alden let out a breath of relief, but he demanded, "What are you doing *here*, of all places? Someone might have seen you—and at this hour?" He almost added "like a murderer or a thief," but changed his mind. Bedug was, in fact, both, and it bothered him not at all.

Despite Bedug's coming to the little house Alden had leased, a very dangerous thing if he were to be seen, Townes was relieved that Bedug could bring Samarang a message about news from Europe he'd received that afternoon. But Alden was angry that Samarang disobeyed his orders in using Talu's weapons on the convoy, that Samarang often did as he pleased, not as Alden had planned.

The lamp cast only enough glow for the men to see each other. Bedug's eyes were like jet beads moving amusedly over Alden's nightshirt as he said, "I came without a sound and closed the shades. No one saw. My lord sent me. Too much news to wait."

Bedug's heavy accent, the way he shredded the king's English, made Townes flinch, but Alden's Javanese, too, left much to be desired. Between their mutual shortcomings, each using what he could of the other's language, it was possible to carry on a conversation.

"I heard about the darts and arrows used on the convoy. Samarang wasn't supposed to use Talu's weapons. He disobeyed me," Alden complained.

Bedug's eyes hardened. "Lord Samarang does not have to obey you. He is not your servant. He also is not pleased. The trinket you gave him to put by the soldier's body is a woman's. My lord said a man should know his enemy's possessions from a woman's trinket."

"It was Britt's. He must have given it to Melinda." Alden was embarrassed at his mistake and he quickly added, "I didn't tell Samarang to put those pearls in Rakata's room either. It seems that Samarang does what he pleases, not what we've planned."

"My lord wanted Rakata to be blamed, but you seemed not interested in that, too much thinking of what *you* want." Bedug leaned closer, and Alden seemed to shrink away, though he'd slid his hand under his pillow where he kept a loaded pistol. His fingers curled around it, reassuring him as Bedug hissed, "Lord Samarang is not your footstool."

"Yes, yes, I know that," Alden hastily agreed.

"Good things have come from what Lord Samarang decided, also some not good, but these can be fixed," Bedug murmured, and seeming ready to move away, instead caught Alden's wrist in a grip that seemed to paralyze his arm to the shoulder. Bedug took the gun from under the pillow and said, "I am not your enemy."

"I keep it there in case of a thief," Alden added quickly.

"Which you think I am and worse," Bedug commented as he laid the pistol out of Alden's reach. "I am a soldier, obedient to my lord." Alden nodded and Bedug went on, "The weapons of Talu and the pearls left in the *raden*'s chamber put guilt on him in the major's mind, as my lord wished. The woman's trinket cast blame not on your enemy, but my lord mended that. He told me to take the *raden*'s letter from his messenger and give it to the major. Your enemy, the Hollander, is now the major's captive. You should be happy for this, grateful to Lord Samarang and me.''

"Yes, I am," Alden had to admit. "Tell Samarang I *am* very pleased about that.''

"One thing to fix now. The *raden* has hidden himself and his people. He suspects Lord Samarang and thinks if there is no raid while he watches my lord, it is proof of guilt he can give to the council. Lord Samarang has ordered a raid or two while he is under the *raden*'s eye to prove he is not guilty. I will lead the attack myself, but you must make the arrangements.''

"I can't be bothered with that now," Alden snapped. "A ship from London docked today. On it was a man I'd paid to rush here with important news about the war. He told me that the fighting is finally over. Though it will take months before Java is actually returned to the Netherlands, our plans must be changed. I *must* talk to Samarang about them.''

The unexpected ending of the war across the sea made Bedug frown. He said, "I cannot go back just now. Must kill someone who saw me with the major and will tell the *raden* I am traitor.''

"Then kill whoever that is tonight and go to Samarang right away. Samarang *must* get away from Rakata for a couple of days," Alden insisted.

"If Lord Samarang leaves Durga, he cannot return. The *raden* would have his head," Bedug said.

"If there are no raids while Samarang is gone, what could Rakata accuse him of?" Alden reasoned. "Samarang could say he had something to do before he went into hiding, unfinished business, maybe a woman. Wasn't he interested in a woman who lived near Bogor?''

Bedug considered this. It was true Samarang had been seeing a lady from Nanti who had welcomed his attention. If Samarang were to pick her up on his way back to Durga and tell Rakata he went to get her, of what could Rakata accuse Samarang—love? The council would frown on Samarang's disobedience, but they wouldn't behead him for wanting a woman. Finally Bedug said, "My lord might do this, if what you want to talk with him about is important enough for him to take the chance.''

"What I have to tell Samarang means *everything* to our success," Alden declared. "We must make new plans now or we might lose everything we've been working for. What Rakata suspects of Samarang won't matter after Rakata has been executed along with his Hollander brother. The council will believe Rakata has been leading the raids and they'll have to make Samarang *raden*. Who else will they have?''

Bedug saw visions of Rakata hanging from the gallows or shot by a firing squad and commented, ''That would be a happy day for my lord.''

''And a good one for you. Didn't Samarang promise that you would command his army?'' Alden reminded. ''We all will be rich too.''

''I will have to kill Kalao before he can tell the *raden* he saw me with the major. That should not be too difficult. Kalao is only fourteen,'' Bedug commented. ''If any of the *raden*'s guards catch me sneaking back into the village, I can tell the *raden* I was delivering a message from Lord Samarang to a lady and was delayed returning because I was pursued by British soldiers and had to hide. I will give him the news of the Hollander's arrest. I hope that will distract him from thinking too much about my absence.''

Alden inwardly shuddered at Bedug's casual mention of killing a fourteen-year-old boy, but he urged Bedug to hurry to the task, then go to Samarang and arrange their meeting in three nights at the cave where the loot was hidden at the foot of Gunung Mrabu.

The place was nearer to Djakarta than Durga, but Bedug didn't argue. It was secluded enough to hide a treasure in loot so no one would discover the meeting. Then, too, Samarang had already mentioned they might have to move their spoils if the volcano became more threatening. Perhaps this could be done at the same time. Bedug left the way he'd come, out of a window at the back of the house, where the jungle was close and shielded him from discovery.

After Alden had put out the lamp and pulled up the shades so the night's breezes could cool the room, he crept back into bed and replaced his pistol under the pillow. Though Bedug was supposed to be an ally, the Indonesian was utterly loyal to Samarang. If Samarang told Bedug to kill him, Alden knew Bedug would come into his room as quietly as he'd done tonight and cut his throat without his having a hint of what was happening, unless he awakened for the couple of seconds it took before he died. Bedug would set about that task as dispassionately as he was now going to murder Kalao. When it came to his work, Bedug was like a machine, without emotions.

Anambas was several days late in coming back from Talu. Although Kalao was uneasy about his father's absence, he told himself the *raden* could have sent him on another task that had delayed his return home.

Then, when Major Wakefield and his soldiers had marched out of the post to go to Talu, there had been nothing Kalao could do. His father had forbidden him to leave Djakarta, had told Kalao he must be the man of the family while Anambas was gone and take care of his mother and brothers. Kalao had assured his family that the *raden* would find answers to the major's questions and Talu's walls were too strong to fall to the soldiers' guns, if it came to that.

When Wakefield had returned, not with the *raden* but with Britt Vandekker as his prisoner, the Javanese community had been as shocked as the British and Hollanders. The news that the *raden* had vanished along with Talu's entire population was a wildfire roaring through the Javanese. Some speculated that Rakata had fled because he was guilty of leading the attacks that were causing so much trouble. Most loyally insisted the *raden* was innocent, that he had taken away the people to keep them safe. Like Anambas, Kalao believed Rakata was innocent.

Having seen Bedug at Talu, Kalao recognized him immediately, despite his not wearing a uniform now. Kalao knew that no officer loyal to the *raden* would have walked unshackled beside Major Wakefield while guns were trained on Rakata's Hollander brother. It was a stunning piece of information that had to reach the *raden*'s ear.

Kalao hastily explained to his mother that he must tell Rakata Bedug was a traitor, and she didn't argue. Sinaga knew Bedug would try to kill her son if he stayed in Djakarta. Kalao assured her that he was certain he knew where the *raden* had taken Talu's people because Rakata had once mentioned the place to Anambas as a possible refuge and Anambas, as a precaution, had told his son its location. But Kalao didn't tell his mother it was Durga. He knew Sinaga would not view Durga as a sanctuary but would wail that it was cursed and haunted. While Kalao took his knife, a blanket, his bow and arrow case, he didn't bother with anything to make a fire. Bedug, who would surely try to track him, would see a fire, and Kalao could live on the fruits and vegetables of the jungle.

He promised he would be careful, assured his mother he would come back with Anambas as soon as possible, then gave her one last embrace before slipping away. Sinaga watched her oldest son for the few minutes it took him to disappear into the jungle, a silent prayer on her lips that Kalao and Anambas would safely return.

*   *   *

As Minda bent to peer under a clump of bright poinsettias, a drop of moisture clinging to the curve above her lip dropped to flavor her tongue with salt. "Dalang, Dalang! *Where are you*?" she pleaded. Seeing no hint of the little tigress's tawny fur or a glimmer of her golden eyes, Minda straightened to blot her forehead with a handkerchief. She turned slowly, running her eyes over the foliage edging the garden, hoping Dalang hadn't run into the forest again.

Minda wondered, as she fanned herself, why the air had suddenly become so oppressive these last few days. This wasn't the hot season, and even at midsummer, Phoenix House's location on the mountain slope always offered them a cooling wind. There'd been no breezes lately, and the morning skies, normally a fresh, clean azure, had taken on a faintly ashen look. Instead of the late afternoon being washed with copper light as clear as Britt's eyes, it had an ocher tint. Was it because Britt was gone that the world had become so drab for her? The grass that, at early dusk, used to appear blue-green had taken on an odd cyanic cast, and the once violet shadows were murky purple. Everything white at this hour usually reflected rose, but her dimity skirt was wearing the same angry-looking red as the clouds that shrouded the sun's descent.

"Is something wrong?" Arjuna, coming across the lawn with long strides, asked as he approached.

"Dalang's name may mean 'to come,' but she won't come to *me*," Minda answered with a sharp edge to her voice. "That cub seems to run off at every chance it gets lately, and she's too small to be in the forest at dusk."

"She's searching for her master," Arjuna surmised.

Minda quickly glanced away; for, at even this mention of Britt, her eyes had filled with tears. Trying to disguise her mood, she grumbled, "Dalang had better learn to come at my call too. I can't spend half my day chasing her. It's too hot."

"Gunung Mrabu is causing this heat. I think it's going to erupt," Arjuna said quietly. "I can find Dalang for you. Go into the pavilion where it's a little cooler and wait."

Minda brushed away her tears only to find her eyes quickly refilling. She looked up at Arjuna, a droplet running down her cheek. "I'm sorry I spoke sharply, Arjuna. I suppose I'm peevish because of the heat."

Arjuna was quiet a moment. He knew Minda was weeping because

Britt was gone, but he didn't know what to say. "You needn't fear the volcano. It never seems to do much except shower sparks. Even if it did more, I think Phoenix House is too far away for it to affect us." When Minda again averted her eyes, he finally touched her shoulder and said quietly, "I miss Britt, too, but he'll be back soon. You'll see."

Minda nodded in silent reply because she couldn't speak. She was using all her strength to hold back the sobs that were welling in her throat, and she was grateful Arjuna didn't linger. As he'd suggested, Minda went to the pavilion, but not to rest or because she hoped it would be cooler there. She only wanted to cry without having someone rush to give her comfort as Dessa had since Britt had been taken away. Minda wondered if she could really help Britt by speaking to the barrister or the major. Longing to visit Britt, Minda reminded herself that he'd asked her not to come. It had been his pride speaking, she knew; but would he truly be angry if she did?

Arjuna crept as quietly through the foliage as if he were himself a tiger, for he doubted Dalang was any more likely to answer his call than Minda's. Although Dalang was a baby, nature had furnished her with a coat that was as hard to see in the tall grass as her mother's; Arjuna looked for the puff of ivory fur on the cub's chest, the white tips of her ears, rather than her body. He wondered if Dalang might be persuaded to wear a collar, something brightly colored, to make her easier to find. Then he stepped out from a thicket and discovered that Dalang hadn't been hiding after all. The cub was pouncing at the trunk of a *sempur* tree as if she wanted to climb it. Had she, at such a young age, actually treed something?

Approaching cautiously so as not to warn her and have to search for her again, Arjuna found that he wasn't quiet enough. Dalang glanced his way, but instead of running off she dashed toward him, then ran back to the tree as if trying to enlist his help. Shaking his head at the cub's audacity, Arjuna followed, but he caught the cub securely in his arms before he looked up.

Stunned to see a boy clinging to the tree trunk, he exclaimed, "Who are you? Come down from there!"

"Are you alone?" Kalao asked cautiously.

Arjuna looked surprised. "Yes, except for this foolish cub. What are you doing in the tree? I don't recognize you as being from this area. Are you lost?"

Kalao wondered if he dared trust this stranger. The man could be one of Bedug's gang searching for him. Yet, he wore no weapons, only a knife of the kind used on the plantations. "Who are *you*?" Kalao ventured.

"Arjuna, overseer of Phoenix House. But you still haven't answered me. What are you afraid of?"

Kalao dropped down from the tree and admitted, "I was stealing fruit. I'm hungry."

"You can eat in the house and welcome. If you're lost, I'll help you find your way. This is a dangerous time to be in the forest," Arjuna said. Then, thinking of the possible reasons a lad his age would be alone in the jungle, he surmised, "You're running away from a plantation where you were treated badly."

Kalao considered telling Arjuna that he was one of the *raden*'s messengers, but recalling how some of the Javanese in Djakarta thought Rakata was guilty of the crimes Wakefield suspected him of, he decided not to give this stranger a hint of his real purpose and remained silent.

"If you're afraid we'll send you back to your master, Phoenix House Tea isn't run that way," Arjuna said. "No one here will force you to do anything."

Kalao sighed with genuine relief. He knew Bedug had been getting closer, and staying here for the night might throw the traitor off his trail. "I am grateful," he finally said. Again glancing warily around at the bushes, he dropped into *dodok* and just as quickly straightened. "My name is Kalao."

"If whoever is after you is as close as you seem to think, we'd better go into the house," Arjuna said, and turned to lead the way. Neither of them guessed that Kalao's pursuer was standing in the bushes watching them with disappointed eyes.

Bedug, taking Arjuna's measure, decided that he would be enough of a match without the boy to contend with as well, and waited until they disappeared through the foliage before stepping from his hiding place. Unlike Kalao, Bedug knew who owned this plantation. He also was aware that the workers went home each night and that Britt's partner, a woman, would be alone in the house with only servants to protect her and the boy. He wondered if he could silence Kalao that night and be on his way back to Durga by sunrise.

* * *

Arjuna led Kalao back to the pavilion where Minda was waiting; and after handing her Dalang, explained what he thought was Kalao's plight. The boy, looking into the troubled eyes of the woman, sank into *dodok* at her feet.

"Go to the kitchen and tell Koki to give you supper," Minda said in Javanese. "Perhaps she can find a place for you to sleep in the servants' quarters. We can talk about a job tomorrow, if you'd like one here."

"You're kind to let me stay the night, *mem*," Kalao said, then lied, "but I'm on my way home. I'd thought I could make my way alone in the world and ran off. I'll return to my parents with new wisdom."

Arjuna was suspicious of the story. Though it was common enough, there was an air of urgency about Kalao that spoke of a secret purpose. Arjuna put Dalang into Kalao's arms and told him to take the cub for Koki to feed as well. He watched until they disappeared into the kitchen building, then, turning to Minda, offered, "I could tell Malili I'm staying at Phoenix House tonight."

"Are you worried about Kalao's being here?" Minda asked in surprise. "He's just a boy!"

"Kalao is lying about something. Trouble is following him. *I know it*," Arjuna said tensely. "If Britt were here . . ."

"Maybe you should stay, but not just because of Kalao. I've decided to go to Djakarta in the morning, and I'd like you to come with me. Maybe we could get an earlier start if you stay at the house," Minda said.

"You're going to visit Britt, despite his telling you not to?"

"I know why he said that, but, Arjuna, I *have* to see if he's all right, if he needs anything or I can help him somehow." Her eyes begged Arjuna to understand.

He sighed. "Britt will be glad to see you, no matter what he said before—as I would be happy to see Malili if I were in his place. I'll send Suhadi to tell Malili I won't be home tonight."

"I'll tell Enang to have one of the guest pavilions prepared for you," Minda offered.

"They're too far from the house. I'll stay in the servants' quarters with Kalao and keep an eye on him," Arjuna said firmly.

"Are you afraid he'd harm me?" Minda asked. Kalao's being a threat seemed unlikely.

"I don't believe that Kalao's just a disappointed runaway going back home. If he started out to make his way in the world, as he claimed, why wouldn't he accept a job here? I don't know of one Javanese who wouldn't be happy to be offered a job on a plantation like Phoenix House,'' Arjuna reasoned. ''I'm sure Kalao is afraid of something, and I want to stay near him. Maybe he'll tell me the truth.''

Minda felt more at peace with herself after she'd made the decision to visit Britt. Arjuna's comment that he would be happy to see Malili even through bars encouraged Minda to think Britt wouldn't mind her coming, and she was too excited from thinking about seeing him to sleep. Finally she got out of bed, relit her lamp, and opened her wardrobe cabinet to choose what she would wear to Djakarta. Smiling at herself for being up in the middle of the night like a schoolgirl planning a costume for tea with a new beau, Minda was looking at hats when the sound of horses being drawn up in front of the house surprised her.

Minda's heart seemed to stop for a moment, then began with a wild rhythm. Was Britt coming back? Had Wakefield released him, and had Britt raced through the night not caring about the hour he'd arrive? But Britt needed only one horse; she'd heard many. Had Wakefield and his men returned? But why? Minda pulled on her dressing gown and was tying its sash with trembling fingers when someone began to pound on the front door. Suddenly there was a cry from the back of the house and she remembered that Kalao was in the servants' quarters. Arjuna had said Kalao was afraid of someone. Perhaps the riders were searching for *him*.

Minda hurried into the corridor, then entered the courtyard. For a moment she didn't know which way to turn. Finally she ran toward the servants' quarters. Just inside the doorway she found Arjuna stooping over a shadowy form sprawled on the floor.

''Kalao!'' she cried, then noticed the lad cringing near the wall and hurried to him. ''Who is that on the floor?''

Arjuna looked up. ''When the horses awakened me, this man was standing over my bed with a knife in his hands. He's from Talu. I've seen him there.''

''But who is he?'' Minda breathed. ''Why would he threaten you?''

''He's one of Rakata's officers, but I don't know his name.'' Arjuna straightened and caught Kalao by the arm to demand in Javanese, ''Why was he after you? Are you, despite your age, a traitor to the *raden*?''

Kalao's fear-glimmering eyes stared out of the shadows at Arjuna, and Minda could see he was too frightened to speak.

Minda turned to Arjuna to ask, "Is that man dead?"

"Just unconscious. I'll find out what Kalao's story is while you see who those riders are. Maybe it's Wakefield searching for this soldier or Kalao. If so, don't say anything to him until I've had a chance to learn what this is about." Arjuna returned his attention to Kalao and demanded, "Why was that officer chasing you? You'd better tell me or I'll hand you both to Wakefield. We have enough trouble now without your bringing us more."

Minda gave the two a worried glance, then, reassuring herself that Arjuna would get to the bottom of the matter, hurried back through the courtyard toward the door to the foyer. If Wakefield had come to drag someone else off to his stockade, she wanted to be sure who should go, and she didn't want Enang blurting anything until she found out.

Before Minda had reached the French doors that opened to the foyer from the courtyard, she saw through the panes not Wakefield, but Rakata, facing Enang, who had dropped into *dodok* before the *raden*. Minda hastily drew back into the shadows to listen.

"I've come to speak to Britt Vandekker, as I've said three times," Rakata said in Javanese. "Will you awaken him or must I get him out of bed myself?"

"But he is not here, my lord. He was taken to Djakarta by Major Wakefield several days ago," Enang answered.

"You're lying," Rakata snarled.

Minda saw several of Rakata's guards step out of the darkness and enter the foyer. Their rifles were held at the ready and the swords at their hips clanked ominously. More guards stood in the shadows beyond the threshold outside. Uncertainty that Townes and Samarang were the cause of her and Britt's troubles suddenly flashed through Minda's mind. Was Rakata guilty after all? Armed men forcing themselves into the house in the middle of the night, the realization that Britt wasn't there to defend her, made Minda's blood run cold. Not knowing whether to run for one of Britt's guns or hide, she hesitated.

Suhadi, stooping in obeisance beside Dessa outside the light Enang's lamp cast, got to his feet crying, "My lord *raden*, it's the truth! Major Wakefield arrested Tuan Britt. He came from Talu with pearls from the convoy he'd found in your chambers and a letter with your seal on it telling Tuan Britt to meet you. The major thinks you and he attacked the convoy together!''

Rakata waved back the men standing over Enang and Suhadi. He was silent a moment, as if considering this story, then said coldly, ''Where is Miss Scott?''

Enang and Suhadi exchanged fearful glances.

Finally, Suhadi cried, ''Do not frighten Mem Scott, my lord *raden*. She has nothing to do with any of this!''

Enang slowly stood up and said in a resigned tone, ''I would not tell you if you said you'd shoot me now, my lord. If I did and harm came to her, Tuan Britt would kill me later.''

''No servant in this house, not a worker in the field will hand Mem Scott to anyone, not even you, my lord *raden*,'' Suhadi confirmed.

''You are indeed loyal. I wish I could be as sure of everyone in my council,'' Rakata commented, then turned to his men and ordered, ''Search the house, find her, and bring her to me.''

At this command Minda turned and ran back into the courtyard toward the clump of camellias where the entrance to the tunnel her father and Britt's had built so long ago was hidden. She was too terrified to think of anything but escape. Before she could reach the camellias, she heard the door to the foyer open and she dashed off the path to hide behind some shrubs. Sandaled feet lightly running across the courtyard's flags made her crouch lower and wonder how she could hope to reach the tunnel's entrance.

Something warm and furry pressed against Minda's side; she started in surprise, only to discover that Dalang had, ironically, finally learned to follow her.

''What's going on here? Stop or I'll shoot!'' came Arjuna's shout. Then his voice changed to an exclamation of surprise. *''Raden Rakata?''*

Minda heard the feet pause and knew that Rakata and the men in the courtyard were facing Arjuna.

''Put down that pistol,'' Rakata said. ''Where is your mistress?''

''Why do you want her?''

Arjuna's tone told Minda he, like Enang and Suhadi, wasn't going to obey the *raden*. Afraid that Arjuna would be killed resisting Rakata and his men, Minda got to her feet and stepped from behind the shrubs. ''What do you want of me?''

At the sound of Minda's voice, Rakata turned. His narrowed eyes moved over the figure clad in a dressing gown who was approaching as coolly as if she were in command of the situation, not he. During the distraction, the pair of men standing nearest Arjuna sprang on him to wrestle for the gun.

Minda's composure dropped away as she rushed forward and cried, "Don't hurt him! *Please!*"

But Rakata stepped in her way while several other men leaped at Arjuna and the struggle ended quickly. Held securely by Rakata's men, Arjuna looked regretfully at her and said simply, "I'm sorry, Minda."

She turned to Rakata, her eyes ablaze with green fire. "You *are* a brigand just as they said—a murderer and a thief! What do you want here? Why are you doing this?"

"I want you, as I said before. You will come with me," Rakata replied.

"My lord *raden!*" Kalao came dashing across the courtyard to throw himself at Rakata's feet. "Bedug is in the servants' quarters! He's a traitor to you. I found him out and he was trying to kill me before I could tell you. Arjuna stopped him."

Arjuna exchanged glances with Minda, and she said coldly, "After what's just happened here, I'm not sure if we should have sheltered Bedug instead of Kalao."

Rakata took a moment to recover from his surprise at his officer's treachery, then said, "However this looks to you, Miss Scott, Bedug is a traitor to us all. Now, come with me."

As Rakata took a step toward Minda, Dalang spat at him, then sprang. The cub's claws tore a slash in the *raden*'s pants leg and he leaped back. "I don't want to harm this little one," he warned. "Please get it out of my way, because I *am* going to take you with me."

Minda bent to pick up Dalang and cuddled her a moment before pushing the cub at Arjuna. The men looked at Rakata, who nodded, so they released Arjuna.

"Don't try to do anything more," Minda told him. "I'll go with Rakata."

The *raden* looked at his men. "Get Bedug," he commanded. Then, taking Minda's arm, he pulled her away from Arjuna. Without a word, Rakata tugged her after him through the courtyard, then into the foyer.

"Mem Scott!" Dessa cried, but Minda waved her back as Rakata hurried her past.

Outside, the *raden* helped Minda up on his horse, then mounted to sit behind her, so his arms strongly enclosed her, making escape impossible.

"When Britt hears about this, he'll find a way to get out of the stockade and come after you," Minda warned.

"I'm counting on that," Rakata said.

She looked up into his face and saw that his dark eyes were glittering with an expression she couldn't read; it frightened her even more. She breathed, "You're setting a trap for him! But why?"

The hard line of the *raden*'s mouth curved in a triumphant smile, but he didn't answer. Instead, he kicked the horse's sides and they galloped off into the night.

Chapter Eighteen

Britt stood with his back to the cell door, forearms on the ledge of the barred window, chin resting on them as he gazed at the darkening sky thinking of the week he'd spent as a prisoner. Although the local barrister had gushed assurances, Britt realized his chances of being exonerated by a military court on an island under martial law weren't encouraging. He'd written to his regular attorney, an officer retired from the British army who now practiced law in Hong Kong, but because of the time it would take for his letter to be delivered, Britt knew he could very well have been tried, found guilty, and executed before the attorney reached Java. His freedom seemed to lie in the hope that Wakefield had seen enough logic in his story about Alden Townes to make him curious and ask questions, but a conversation Britt had overheard last evening made the possibility of the major's looking into Townes's activities dim. Wakefield would soon be immersed in other pressing tasks.

Djakarta's military business was conducted in a single, large room with Wakefield's office adjoining. Because the building was the only suitable one on the post made of stone, prisoners of any importance were kept in a section adjacent to the administration office while others were held in a separate stockade. Britt was the only man presently confined, and because he was a quiet, well-behaved prisoner, the door between the main office and the cells was left open so air could circulate.

Britt had suspected, when Wakefield had remained at work past dinnertime the previous evening, that he was doing more than catching up on reports. Before very long a courier, just off a ship that had been sighted earlier, had arrived with a message that stunned Britt. The war had finally ended in Europe and Great Britain had signed a treaty with the Netherlands promising to return possession of the East Indies. Wakefield had orders to quietly begin preparing his troops to leave and was instructed to keep this news in strict confidence until the new governor-general arrived and the transfer of authority could be made smoothly.

Because Townes was an envoy, Britt was sure he must have learned the war had ended, but if the treaty was to be kept secret for a while, Britt wondered if Townes was aware of its contents. If so and Townes was guilty as Britt speculated, might Townes order another raid or two to fatten his profit or would he quietly convert his share of the loot into unidentifiable gold, then leave Java as soon as the Colonial Office permitted?

No matter which way Britt looked at the situation, unless evidence was found to implicate Townes in the raids, he would go free, and no one in Wakefield's command was likely to search for it now. Britt was going to have to produce the evidence himself. To do that, he had to escape.

He was considering possible ways to persuade the soldier who stood guard at night to enter his cell when he was startled by Arjuna's voice coming from the office. Though Arjuna's English normally carried only a slight accent, he now was speaking like a villager who had to think hard to recall English words, and Britt wouldn't have recognized his friend except for the sound of his voice. Britt realized Arjuna had never spoken a word to the major, so it was possible Wakefield would believe the sham. Finally, as if exasperated at trying to decipher what Arjuna was saying, the major gave permission for the Indonesian to visit Britt.

Wondering why Arjuna was putting on this masquerade, Britt tried not to look surprised when his overseer entered the cell block. Arjuna, who usually dressed in shirts and breeches like Britt, today wore the garments of a Javanese who had dressed in his best to visit the city and was a bit of a peacock. He wore red-patterned, blousy-legged pants held tight at the ankles by tassels, an intricately embroidered tan sash, a dark brown and gold jacket, sleeveless, without closings, that bared his chest and ended short of his waist, as if he wanted to attract feminine interest while he was in Djakarta.

Arjuna approached the cell, then immediately pressed his flattened hands together shoulder level, ducked his head, and began to stoop in *dodok,* which would have been proper to an employer who wasn't a fast friend.

Britt quickly released him from the gesture he knew Arjuna normally despised and, after Arjuna had straightened, warned him with a glance to be careful of what he said. Keeping his eyes on the guard, Britt greeted Arjuna in court Javanese, then asked, "How is Mem Scott running Phoenix House? Tell me what's been happening. Is the experimental tea curing properly?"

Arjuna realized Britt was testing the guard's understanding with the kind of questions any prisoner would be expected to ask and he obligingly answered as if Minda hadn't been kidnapped. Then, certain the guard would react with annoyance if he understood their conversation, Arjuna concernedly asked if Britt had been mistreated in any way, starved or beaten.

Britt noted that not a flicker of interest crossed the soldier's face at this insulting question and said, "He understands only the dialect the traders use among the islands' many peoples. We can speak freely."

"That was what I was hoping when I pretended to speak English so badly," Arjuna admitted, then asked, "Are you well?"

"Well enough for a man who is watching all his chances at legal freedom one by one flying away like little birds," Britt answered, then warned, "Keep the same expression on your face while I tell you what I overheard last night while I was pretending to be asleep."

Although Arjuna was anxious to tell Britt what had happened to Minda, he realized his friend also had important news and listened silently as Britt described the courier's message and Wakefield's orders.

Britt finished disgustedly, "No one is going to bother to investigate further just because I say so. They'll all be busy getting ready to go home. The only way I'm going to be cleared of these charges will be if I find some evidence myself. I *have* to get out of here."

"You have more reason to want your freedom than you even know. Now *your* face must remain unchanged while I tell you about something that happened," Arjuna said solemnly, then, to avoid the guard's recognizing names, referred to Minda as "your lady" and Rakata as "your mother's eldest son" while he described Kalao and Bedug's arrival at Phoenix House, then Rakata's carrying Minda away.

Although Britt willed his expression to remain as stolid as if his face were chiseled from stone, he couldn't prevent his paling under his tan. His heart began to hammer so loudly in fear he wondered how the guard didn't hear it, for the room seemed to vibrate with its thumping as he breathed, "But she has nothing to do with any quarrel Rakata may have with me. Why would he do this?"

Noting that the guard had been alerted by Britt's impulsively mentioning the *raden*'s name, Arjuna exclaimed in barely recognizable English, "Mem Scott said it's the *raden*'s fault you are here! Please don't anger yourself because she said she wishes to shoot him herself!"

Britt realized Arjuna was warning him about the soldier. He looked at the guard, who had taken a step nearer, and said disgustedly, "Miss Scott, my partner, can't understand why Rakata is free while I'm here. She's threatening to send all the plantation workers to search for him—a foolish idea because they'd never find him, and Phoenix House would go untended meanwhile. I don't need more trouble, but she has a temper and is sometimes impetuous."

"I've heard that you have a temper too," the guard commented, appearing satisfied with that explanation.

In a tone that seemed to the soldier as if Britt were giving Arjuna instructions to relay to Minda, he said in Javanese, "Maybe my mother's eldest son thinks that when the major stopped at Phoenix House the first time I told him something to incriminate him and get myself out of this. Maybe he wanted revenge on me and, discovering I was gone, intends to take his trouble out on Mem Scott instead."

"That's possible, but I wouldn't have thought he was the kind of man to do that," Arjuna said slowly.

"Abandoning Talu must have been like cutting off a piece of his own flesh, and I can't help remembering how his grandfather banished our mother and allowed the death sentence to hang over her head for years, knowing all the while there was a chance someone might decide to carry it out," Britt bitterly replied.

"But that was Matarami, not Rakata," Arjuna pointed out.

"Damn them both!" Britt burst out in English, satisfying any qualms lingering in the guard's mind. "The old *raden*'s order killed my mother. I've been fooling myself all along about Rakata's being different. Maybe he is a lawless rebel. All I know for certain now is that he's free and I'm in prison for something I didn't do. Tell Mem

Scott I said not to make matters worse. I don't want to have to worry about Phoenix House going to weed while I'm here.''

Arjuna hastily bobbed his head as if he were any employee getting instructions from his angry *tuan*, though he said in court Javanese, "I had thought to find a way of getting you out of here. It's dusk now and there are shadows to hide us.''

Britt paused to consider this, then said, "We'll have to get the major and the guard in the outer office into the cell block.''

"You still look angry. Perhaps if I said something that made you seem to lose your temper and you reached out in a fury to catch me?'' Arjuna suggested.

As if Arjuna had just said something highly offensive, Britt snapped in Javanese, "I'm sorry, Arjuna, but you'll have to get down in *dodok* again.''

Arjuna stared at Britt, as if he were stunned by his *tuan*'s anger, then hastily dropped into *dodok,* but Britt reached between the bars as if to grip Arjuna's hair and drag him to his feet. Arjuna caught the bars, pretending to be afraid to face his master, and Britt's hands closed around his throat. While they didn't tighten, Arjuna made noises as if he were being strangled; the guard let out a shout and ran to try to stop Britt.

Wakefield and the other guard appeared in the doorway looking alarmed, then started closer. Britt immediately released Arjuna, who struck the nearest soldier. The guard staggered against the bars and Arjuna leaped at the other soldier. Britt's arm around the first guard's neck pinned him against the bars while Britt snatched his pistol.

At the sound of the gun in Britt's hand being cocked, Wakefield froze.

"Get their other weapons, Arjuna,'' Britt said, then looked at Wakefield and directed, "Unlock the cell door, Major.''

"Even if you can get off the post, you can't go home! Where do you think you'll hide on this island?'' Wakefield exclaimed as he obeyed Britt.

"There are any number of places where you wouldn't find me, if hiding was what I intended to do.'' Britt stepped through the doorway, then to its side. He gestured with the gun for Wakefield and the soldiers to replace him in the cell. "Tell the guards to take off their uniforms or I'll shoot you.''

"I don't think you'd do that,'' Wakefield slowly said. Looking at the amber fires swirling in Britt's eyes, he changed his mind and did as he'd been ordered.

"Where is my horse being kept?" Britt demanded.

"In the stable across the parade ground," Wakefield said resignedly. "I don't know what you expect to accomplish by this. You're only incriminating yourself further, the way Rakata did when he ran."

"I expect to accomplish my freedom, as Rakata did," Britt answered sharply. "Rakata has kidnapped Minda and I have to get her."

"*Rakata has abducted Miss Scott?*" Wakefield exclaimed. "But what would he want with *her*?"

"Give me those uniforms," Britt said coldly; and after they'd passed the clothes and helmets to him, he closed and locked the cell door. As he and Arjuna began to change into the uniforms, Britt said, "I don't like to imagine what Rakata is planning, but I do know his having to flee Talu, thanks to you, is what touched all this off. If you hadn't insisted on marching with cannons to Talu, none of this would have happened. I still might have been able to prevent it if I'd been free to talk with Rakata, if you'd have listened to me about Townes and Samarang's being at the bottom of this."

"I *did* listen to you. I'd like to believe you're innocent. I told you that, but . . ." Wakefield began.

"Yes, I know, but you have your orders to follow. It isn't your fault that they don't necessarily involve justice." Britt looked up as he slid his arms into the uniform's coat sleeves and demanded, "What investigating have you done about any of this during the past week while I've been locked up? Who's made any effort at all to learn if what I've said is true?"

"I *did* begin inquiries. One has to go about investigating someone like Townes carefully. One must be discreet," Wakefield answered.

"So discreet I'd be in my grave before you found out the truth, if ever," Britt snapped.

Having no answer to this, Wakefield sighed heavily, then asked, "How do you suppose you'll locate Miss Scott?"

"I think I've figured out where Rakata is. Minda must be there too."

"Don't you realize you can't do this alone? Tell me where you're going! I'll accompany you with my soldiers," Wakefield urged.

"You would find the place as deserted as you found Talu. Even if Rakata didn't run again, what would you do, start the war Townes and Samarang have wanted all this time?" Britt shot back as he put on the soldier's helmet. He picked up the rifle and straightened, saying determinedly, "I'm going to get Minda, and afterward, Major, I'm going to find some way to prove Alden Townes is guilty."

"You're only going to cause more trouble for yourself," the major warned.

"I've never caused myself trouble. You and others like you have done it for me," Britt retorted, then turned away.

Arjuna followed him to the office door, but turned to look at Wakefield and his guards and say in fluent English, "*You'll* be able to leave Java and all its problems behind, but this is Britt's home as much as it is mine. We're going to stay here." Then Arjuna closed the door on their surprised faces and looked at Britt to ask, "Do you really think I'll be able to fool the soldiers outside that I'm one of them?"

"Speak like you did just now and keep that helmet on," Britt answered as he went to Wakefield's desk and pulled out a sheet of paper and a pen.

"What is that for?" Arjuna inquired.

"I'm going to draw a map so you'll know how to get to Durga in case I don't come back and you have to rescue me," Britt replied.

"I won't need a map because I'm coming with you." Arjuna swept the paper off the desk and tossed it on the floor.

Britt asked quietly, "If we're both captured, who will know where to find us?"

"If the *raden* wants revenge and catches us, no one will get to Durga in time to save us anyway," Arjuna grimly replied.

Soldiers crossing the parade grounds in front of the administration building paid no attention to the pair of corporals, one leading a horse, as they strolled toward the post stable. In the deepening twilight no one could see that Arjuna's features were Javanese, and the bundle Britt had made of their clothes only appeared to be laundry.

Arjuna paused at the side of the stable doorway, appearing to examine his horse's hooves, while Britt entered and approached the stable master.

"Major Wakefield told me to get Vandekker's horse," he said.

"You're new on the post, aren't you, Corporal?" the stable master remarked. "I don't remember seeing you before."

"I was just transferred from Jogjakarta," Britt replied briskly, hoping if he appeared intent on business the man wouldn't ask too many questions.

"I suppose you're one of the replacements for the men killed in that convoy," the stable master commented, coming a little closer as if he wanted to get a better look at the new man.

"Yes, nasty business that," Britt replied, and turned away to point toward his saddle and bridle. "Is that Vandekker's tack? I'm supposed to gather that up too."

"Why would the major want that, what with Vandekker's being a prisoner and not likely to go anywhere?" the stable master remarked, again starting toward Britt. "How is it that you can recognize Vandekker's saddle?"

Britt pointed to the saddle skirt and said, "His initials are worked into the leather. See there?"

The stable master muttered, "You must have eyes like an eagle if you could spot that from where you were standing." He approached to peer more closely at the saddle in the wavering lamplight.

Britt struck the back of his head once and he fell like a stone. At the sound Arjuna came inside and hurried to join Britt.

"He was much too curious. A minute longer and he'd have been staring into my face," Britt quickly explained as he pulled his saddle and pad off the rack. He slung his bridle and girth over his shoulder adding, "He's just unconscious."

Arjuna bent to tug the stable master's limp body farther into the shadows, tossed a horse blanket over him, then went outside to get on his mount and wait until Britt came out with his horse.

Although they both wished they could gallop full speed across the parade ground to the post gates, they sedately walked their horses, timing themselves to follow closely a supply wagon. They approached the post entrance while the sentry was examining the wagon driver's pass and stopped. But as soon as the gates swung open, they kicked their horses into a gallop, shot past the wagon, then raced into the gathering darkness beyond, the sentry's bullets whining past their ears. Not until they were well past the houses that clung to the city limits did they slow their pace. Then they turned off the road to avoid the soldiers, who were assigned there day and night to question and search the traffic.

Britt stopped his horse and dismounted to start peeling off the uniform. Arjuna was happy to trade the tight helmet and stiff collar for his own clothes.

"I'm glad you wore regular breeches under those pants you had on in Wakefield's office," Britt remarked. "Those colors would have been impossible for anyone following us to miss seeing even at night."

Arjuna smiled sheepishly as he pulled on the slender riding pants. "They were too voluminous for riding on a fast horse, but I have no other shirt. I'm afraid you'll still have to endure looking at the jacket."

"If you don't mind the mosquito bites, I can put up with looking at you," Britt replied.

"Malili would say I deserve the stings for dressing as if I were going to Djakarta to sell myself," Arjuna commented as he remounted.

Britt silently caught up his reins, grimly reflecting on how Malili would feel if Arjuna should be killed trying to help him. After he'd swung up into his saddle, Britt reached over to grip Arjuna's shoulder and urge, "Go back, my friend. You have Malili and Panji to look after."

"Those sentries at the post gates will have guessed one of the riders who just galloped past was a prisoner and will send someone to free Wakefield and those guards. The major didn't know me before, but he'll recognize my face now. If I go home, soldiers will come soon afterward to arrest me," Arjuna reasoned. "Malili will know, when the soldiers come searching for me, that I've been successful helping you escape and we're on our way to get Minda. Malili understands that I'll have to stay in hiding with you until we can prove Townes is guilty."

"What if you don't return?"

Arjuna was quiet a moment before saying softly, "My death was something I didn't have to mention to her and I don't want to discuss it with you. The god of things-that-go-wrong might hear us and be tempted to make it true."

Britt released Arjuna's shoulder and gathered up his reins. "The god of things-that-go-wrong has been so hard at work on me I should think he wouldn't have time to bother anyone else."

"We'll send him to Samarang and Townes before this is finished," Arjuna promised.

"I'd prefer them to meet the goddess of death on Wakefield's gallows."

"We will be near Durga's temple tonight and you can tell the goddess then," Arjuna reminded.

Despite the casual tone Arjuna used, Britt recognized that his friend wasn't eager to approach the dread goddess's temple, but he said nothing. If his childhood memories of the place were accurate, he and Arjuna would have to hide *inside* the ruined temple until they could plan how to rescue Minda. Britt didn't like to think about the prospect; the part of him that still belonged to his mother's people retreated from the idea. Instead, he concentrated on trying to find their way to Durga, a difficult enough task in the daylight made more arduous by the changes darkness cast on the jungle's face.

Britt was relieved to discover that he still remembered the way to Durga after so many years had passed, then realized that seeing his half brother under such mysterious circumstances had impressed him that deeply. After hours of picking their way through the moonless night lit only by the glow from Gunung Mrabu reflected off the cloud-covered sky, they finally approached the area of the temple. Britt turned his horse to thread through the shadows to the rear of the temple wall, chose one of the vine-curtained places where the wall had disintegrated, and entered.

Inside the temple grounds, Arjuna dismounted and gazed apprehensively at the temple, which was cracked and heavy with age. He said nothing as they led their horses through the grounds, which once had been like a park, but the jungle had since invaded and conquered.

They entered the temple, their footsteps echoing hollowly from the mossy paving stones, the sound vanishing into the darkness of the high ceilings, then stopped apprehensively to scan the crumbling walls, the ancient, sagging doorways shrouded by the webs of long-dead spiders.

Finally Britt said softly, "We'd better try to get a little rest before the light comes."

Arjuna glanced at Britt as if he were startled by the idea of even trying to sleep, then realized Britt was right. "I suppose we're safe enough from any of Rakata's sentries. No one would dare hide in this place except men as desperate as we are," he commented, then turned away to unsaddle his horse.

Although Britt was weary from the long ride, his slumber was troubled by dreams of fruitlessly searching for Minda in a labyrinth of rock corridors. He awoke with a start to find himself lying on a stone floor in surroundings that were a replica of his dream. His eyes remained wide open to watch the dawn finally enter the temple, not with the moist, golden light he so loved at Phoenix House, but with a dull, lurid glow that made the temple's murk discernible. He sat up slowly, and the soft scuffle of his bootheel on the stones made Arjuna sit bolt upright.

The first thing that met Arjuna's eyes was a statue of Durga, mottled with the mold and decay of centuries, peering down at him like a monstrous gargoyle. Shuddering at the figure, he wiped his forehead and whispered, "I know the gods and goddesses are made to look terrifying so they frighten away evil demons, but to awaken with Durga staring at me isn't the way I care to begin a morning."

Because Durga's statue was as unnerving to him as it was to Arjuna, Britt quickly said, "Last night, as we walked through the temple grounds, I heard water running. It's probably a little spring or stream that was once used by the priests. Maybe we can find a place beside it where the horses can graze without being seen if anyone walks past one of the breaks in the outer walls."

"I doubt any of Rakata's people come closer to this place than necessary, much less peer through the holes in those walls, but I'll be happy enough to get out from under this roof," Arjuna said and hastily got to his feet.

Because the village had always been inhabited except for the last few generations, most of its stone buildings, though weatherworn, had survived. Talu's population was larger than Durga's had been, and newly constructed bamboo houses to temporarily shelter the overflow clustered around the stone buildings, making it impossible for Britt and Arjuna to approach closely enough to see what was happening at the village's center. The only way they could think of to do that was to climb one of the huge strangler fig trees, whose maze of trunks and large leaves effectively concealed them.

Assuming that Rakata had moved into the largest of the stone buildings, which had once been the home of Durga's mayor, Britt carefully studied it, but Arjuna nudged his side and pointed toward a bamboo hut that stood in the village square.

"A woman went inside carrying food a little while ago. Two men brought a tub of water and left, as if whoever slept there must be given the necessities for beginning the day," Arjuna said softly.

"A prisoner, for instance," Britt concluded.

Arjuna nodded. "One of Rakata's personal guards just went in."

Britt watched the doorway and was soon rewarded with the sight of Minda dressed in a long, brightly flowered sarong emerging with the soldier. She walked more slowly than her escort and fell a few steps behind, so Britt saw that she was bound by a thick vine that had been split into many strands, each braided into her long hair. It was an effective way to hold her captive, because if she tried to escape, her hair would be torn out by its roots, though the vine was harmless if she remained docile. Her wrists were tied together, making it possible for her to use her hands, but not to get her arms above and behind her head to free her hair. She was led to the center of the open space, where an awning was set up over a mat. There the guard attached his end of the vine to a stake driven into the ground. The vine was long enough to allow Minda to go a few steps away from the awning in any direction, but she was as securely tethered as a dog on a leash.

Angry that Minda seemed to have become a display for Talu's people to gape at, Britt could do nothing except look at her. She seemed so small a figure sitting alone in the grass till the sun grew too hot and she moved under the awning. Although the same woman who had brought her breakfast was making regular visits with a water urn and at midday with bowls of food, despite the passing villagers only casting curious glances at Minda, not jeers or threats as Britt had expected, his anger at her being an exhibit didn't fade.

Arjuna had to remind him to come down from the tree for a drink of water, to find some fruit to eat, and to walk a little so he wouldn't become too cramped from sitting motionlessly through the hours. Britt spent a minimum of time on the ground before quickly reclimbing the tree. He considered walking openly into Durga to negotiate or demand her release, but not knowing why Rakata had kidnapped her, Britt was afraid to chance his own capture. He decided that the only option left was to steal her back, and Arjuna agreed.

They waited until darkness crept over the village and Minda had been led back into the hut, then waited for an hour after the last light had been extinguished. Britt motioned to Arjuna to climb down the tree, but Arjuna cautiously held him back. They waited while another hour dragged by so slowly Britt wondered how he could bear each passing minute. Finally, Arjuna was willing to leave the tree.

At its base the Javanese leaned closer to whisper in Britt's ear, "Don't try to get into that hut through its doorway. Go around the back and cut a slit in the bamboo; it looks only as thick as a sleeping mat. I'll stay a little behind and will keep guard while you get her."

Britt nodded and worked his way through the foliage, skirting the village until he was as close as he could get to Minda's shelter. Then, praying no dog would bark an alarm, he slipped from the shadows of one building to another until he was behind the hut that held Minda.

He could feel her presence reaching out to him through the woven wall. He thought he could hear even her breath and heartbeat. It couldn't be his; he was sure he wasn't breathing, and his heart had stopped. He punched the tip of his knife blade through the bamboo wall and found it, as Arjuna had thought, merely the thickness of a mat. Although the blade had as keen an edge as a razor, it seemed to take an eternity to saw a slit long enough for him to look through.

There were no guards inside, only Minda, still dressed in her sarong, sleeping on her mat, surrounded by a cone of fine netting suspended from the ceiling to keep insects away. He realized that, even while she slept, her hair must be bound with the vines so she couldn't escape. Britt resumed determinedly sawing at the bamboo matting, taking another eternity to cut a long enough slit for him to slide through.

Before Britt even reached Minda, he found the vine that bound her hair and sliced through it. Then he carefully moved the netting aside and covered her mouth with his hand. Her eyes sprang open in fright.

Realizing he was only a shadowy figure in the darkness, he bent close to whisper in her ear, "I've come to take you home." Then he replaced his hand on her mouth with his lips. One kiss, so sweetly poignant he could have wept before he withdrew.

"My hair is tied . . ." she breathed.

"I've already cut you loose," he whispered and took Minda's hand to help her to her feet. He put his arm around her waist's gentle curve and turned her, intending his touch to guide her to the opening he'd made in the wall.

Lamplight suddenly flooded the little room. They quickly turned to see Rakata and one of his guards standing in the doorway. Behind them Arjuna, held by two more guards, looked regretfully at Britt.

Rakata said, "I've been waiting for you."

Chapter Nineteen

From the moment Rakata had carried her off, Minda had felt like a Judas goat, but the hope that Britt would fool Rakata anyway had been a bud in her heart waiting to blossom. Because Britt had managed to get into the village and even into her hut without being discovered, the bud had burst into flower and was just as quickly plucked. She looked up at Britt's eyes. They were hard and bright with anger as they regarded Rakata.

Britt said quietly, "Now that you have me, let Minda and Arjuna leave Durga."

Rakata turned to his guards and directed, "Bring all three of them and watch the Hollander closely on the way."

The soldiers parted to let the *raden* pass, then motioned for their captives to follow. More guards were waiting outside, and they closed around the *raden*'s prisoners.

Britt looked at the long, straight-bladed swords the soldiers wore ready for action at their elbows and said, "Don't try to resist them, Arjuna. We've been trained with the sword, but we're no match for a squad of the *raden*'s personal guards, and Minda might get hurt."

Arjuna didn't answer, but his disgust at having been captured was a storm cloud in his eyes.

Minda stared at Rakata's back through a blur of angry tears as they

walked. "It's my fault. I should have tried to get to the escape tunnel
sooner."

Britt's arm slid around her waist. "*If* I'd left Phoenix House before
Wakefield came back from Talu, *if* you'd never come to Java, *if* our
fathers hadn't fought Matarami for Phoenix House, none of this might
have happened." Minda looked up at him, ready to disagree, but he
said, "There's no point in accusing ourselves for doing things we
didn't know were mistakes at the time. Maybe they weren't mistakes.
Let's wait to see why Rakata wants me here." His arm briefly pressed
her closer as they entered the building the *raden* had adapted for his
new home.

Britt noted their surroundings and contrasted Durga with Talu.
Rakata's city had lavish gardens with ponds and pavilions made for no
other reason than the pleasure of their beauty—tree-lined courts open
for coolness; polished marble floors; carved, gilded pillars; high,
slanted roofs with lacquered crossbeams and elaborately decorated
ceiling rafters. Although Britt recognized furniture, rich tapestries, exquisite statues, and vases from Talu, he also saw the walls of Durga,
made porous by years of disuse that no amount of scrubbing now
would make shine again, peeling paint and gilt crusted with mold,
cracked and mottled floors discolored by years of grime working into
the once glowing stone. The perfume that had lightly scented Talu's
corridors couldn't completely overcome the mustiness of Durga.

Rakata paused while a bronze door was being opened before them.
Though the carving on it had been scoured, bits of green still clung to
the design's deepest grooves. At the center of the chamber they
entered, a huge lacy brass lamp was suspended from the ceiling. It lit
a spacious dais where varicolored sitting pillows were arranged
around a low, richly lacquered table. Pillars along the sides of the
room were shedding their paint, but the *raden*'s personal banners as
well as Talu's—fixed on golden poles between the columns—helped
distract the eye with their richly embroidered colors.

The guards followed Rakata to the dais. Britt saw that the table held
Talu's porcelain platters and bowls filled with food. He looked at
Rakata in surprise.

Rakata told the guards to withdraw and they moved on silent feet to
place themselves more discreetly along the perimeter of the room
between the pillars, as if they'd become part of the *raden*'s decorations,
which were the emblems of his power.

"Choose a place to sit," Rakata invited. "After perching in that tree all day, I suspect you're hungry."

Arjuna stared at the *raden,* wondering if this was a trick. Perhaps the food was poisoned?

Britt commented, "You knew all the time we were there?"

Understanding Arjuna's suspicions, Rakata leaned over the table to take a tidbit from a platter and nibble on it. "I admire your courage to stay in that temple last night. I wouldn't have cared to do it; there are poisonous snakes inside."

"Did the *raden* hope we'd be bitten so you wouldn't have to bother killing us?" Arjuna asked bitterly.

"I thought you could take care of yourselves, seeing as you'd managed to escape Wakefield without a scratch," Rakata observed dryly, then added, "I have no intention of harming any of you. Even Miss Scott must, after thinking it over, realize she was treated well."

"I doubt Minda would enjoy being a prisoner, however gentle her captors," Britt answered coolly.

"It was a ruse to get you to come. I knew you'd find a way to escape from Wakefield when you learned I'd taken the woman you love," Rakata admitted.

Afraid that Rakata would use his love for Minda as a weapon against him, Britt quickly said, "Minda is my partner. I would try to help anyone, man or woman, partner or guest, who was kidnapped from under my roof."

Understanding Britt's caution, Minda declared as if she were insulted that her virtue was in question, "We aren't lovers! What would make you think such a thing?"

Rakata appeared amused by their efforts to deceive him. "Dessa is my eyes and ears in your house."

"*Dessa!* My maid?" Minda was too stunned to say more.

Rakata turned to Britt. "Our meeting in that village where Charles Scott died reawakened my curiosity about you personally, and I decided then to place someone in Phoenix House to learn more about you, especially since you were going to have a new partner." Rakata looked at Minda. "The sparsity of Dessa's reports has revealed her growing affection for you. Forgive her for being loyal to her *raden*. It hasn't been an easy task for her to spy on you. In fact, when I came looking for you, Dessa was as adamant as Suhadi and Enang in refusing to tell me where you were."

"Now that you have us, what do you intend to do?" Britt asked tensely.

"Please sit down," Rakata invited. "Talking was all I ever wanted, Britt, though I confess, when I went to Phoenix House to discover you were gone, I was upset. Everyone mistook my annoyance for anger. I've learned since that you weren't ignoring the message I'd sent inviting you here. You never got it."

Britt's eyes held Rakata's a moment longer, as if he still weren't sure what to think of the situation. Then, as he guided Minda toward a pillow and gestured for her to sit down, he said tensely, "Bedug gave your letter to Wakefield to make it appear you and I were meeting secretly to plan those raids."

"That answered one of my questions," Rakata commented and looked at one of the servants, who had entered the chamber to hover near the dais. At his glance the servant quickly began filling finely chased goblets with golden wine. Rakata picked up one of the goblets and took a sip, putting to rest any lingering doubts Arjuna had about poison. "Let me tell you what has happened since I left Talu. After we've put our stories together, you may find we have something of worth to tell Wakefield."

Britt and Arjuna seated themselves, and Arjuna finally reached for some food.

Watching him, Rakata commented, "You're an excellent friend to have taken so many risks helping Britt."

"Britt and I grew up together, my lord," Arjuna reminded.

"As Miss Scott would have, too, but for being taken away, even as I was, to serve the purposes of others. But of course Miss Scott wasn't Britt's sister and is even less so now," Rakata observed as he lowered himself to sit among the pillows. He looked at Britt. "Bedug didn't say much when we captured him other than deny that he had betrayed me, but after we returned to Durga and I presented him to my council, he swore Kalao was working for Wakefield, that Kalao and Anambas were double spies. Bedug claimed Anambas gave my letter to the major instead of you, then disappeared. He insisted everything Kalao had told me about Bedug's betraying me was a lie. He said he didn't want to kill Kalao, but to take him back to me so I could learn the truth."

"Wakefield told me Bedug gave him the letter, and he had no reason to lie," Britt declared. "Bedug strolled in and out of Wakefield's office as casually as if he were at Talu. Kalao couldn't have missed seeing him.''

"That's as I'd thought," Rakata commented and took another sip of wine. "Anambas was a good friend. I was sure he couldn't have betrayed me, but I had to find out from someone else to satisfy my court. I suppose Bedug killed him.''

"Why don't you question Bedug further? He's your prisoner, isn't he?" Minda inquired.

"Bedug was under guard in his living quarters, but he didn't survive his first night at Durga,'' Rakata said regretfully. "Someone managed to put a sleeping potion in the guard's food. Bedug was found dead the next morning. His murderer must have been someone he thought was a friend, because there was no sign of his resisting. The murderer, instead of comforting him in his trouble, drove a poisoned dart into his neck.''

"You have no clue about the murderer's identity?" Britt asked.

"The kind of poison we use on hunting darts must kill our quarry quickly so it doesn't wander too far into the jungle before it dies. The poison works even faster on a human being,'' Rakata advised. "Bedug must have reached out to grasp at his murderer, but only tore off some of the trim on his sleeve. We found it clenched in Bedug's hand. Although I recognized it from one of Samarang's garments and presented it to my council, Samarang had already vanished. I think he didn't notice the trim missing from his sleeve until after he got home and, not daring to return to Bedug's quarters and search, fled Durga. Another thirty men have vanished since. I assume they're the traitors who were taking part in the raids with Samarang.''

"What you've told me would certainly add weight to what I've already told Wakefield about Samarang and strengthen my case against Townes," Britt said slowly, then added, "Just before I escaped, a courier came with a message that the war in Europe has ended. Wakefield has orders to prepare to leave Java.''

"The British are planning to honor their original promise?" Rakata asked in surprise.

"It's being kept secret to prevent anyone from taking advantage of the change in government and causing trouble,'' Britt said. "Townes might learn about it anyway. If he does, he'll either accelerate his plans so a rebellion begins before the British soldiers leave or he'll get rid of the loot and depart Java a rich man while the blame falls on you and me.''

"Many of my people were beginning to believe I was behind those attacks. Their doubts were making them listen to Samarang. I've sent runners to every village to tell the people about Samarang's plot against me, that *he* was the thief. It will be difficult, if not impossible, for Townes and Samarang to instigate a rebellion now," Rakata assured.

Britt concluded, "I'll have to go back to Djakarta and tell Wakefield so he can have Townes watched." He paused, then added, "I suppose the major isn't exactly pleased about my locking him in his own stockade. I can only hope he'll listen to me."

"If he doesn't, I'll have to find a way to get you out again," Rakata said calmly. "You may leave Durga whenever you wish."

"I think tomorrow morning won't be too soon," Britt advised.

"Take Kalao to tell Wakefield about Bedug's part in the plot," Rakata offered. "You can have the trim from Samarang's sleeve and the dart we took from Bedug's neck if you think they will help."

"*Your* coming to Djakarta with me is what would help most," Britt said.

The *raden* was thoughtfully silent a moment before answering, "I'll go to Djakarta after I've caught Samarang. My cousin and the other traitors will be my gift to Wakefield."

"You'll have to find Samarang and his men first. That might take too long," Britt said.

"Every Javanese in the area will be looking for Samarang after they learn what he's done," Rakata declared. "Samarang won't be able to hide anywhere unless he can reach Townes. If Wakefield is watching Townes in the city and my people are watching everything in the countryside, we'll catch Samarang, Townes, and the men working with them."

"That seems too good to believe, like the end of a nightmare," Minda commented.

"And you've had many of those since you came to Durga," Rakata observed sympathetically. "Maybe you'll sleep more peacefully tonight under my roof instead of that prisoner's hut."

As if his mentioning the night had been a prearranged signal, a guard standing at one of the doors to the side of the room opened it to admit a woman. At her entrance, all present rose from their pillows.

Minda caught her breath at the beauty of the lady, whose black hair flowed like silk to her hips, its lengths gently shifting as she walked toward them. She was so graceful Minda wondered if, under the gold embroidered gown she wore, her feet even touched the floor. The woman unabashedly appraised Minda with clear, dark eyes before she finally said in a lilting voice, "Your beauty is worthy to adorn the great Phoenix House, but judging from what I have heard, it is surpassed by your courage."

Minda replied, "Britt told me of Lady Surana's beauty. Now I would add that the *raden*'s wife is gracious. Thank you for the hospitality of your house."

Surana smiled, revealing pretty white teeth, and took Minda's hand. "You have a charming way with our language, Minda, but our hospitality is several days overdue."

To Britt's questioning look, Rakata explained, "This is the first time Surana and Minda have laid eyes on each other. Not knowing how soon you'd come after me, I brought Minda directly to that hut. I wanted you to see immediately on your arrival that she hadn't been harmed; otherwise I knew we would never have so peaceful a discussion."

"There has been enough talk of violence, murder, and abduction," Surana declared, revealing that she'd somehow managed to hear their conversation from the first. "Let me take Minda to bathe in more comfort than was possible in that meager hut. Minda can rest tonight, even if she won't sleep, more pleasantly than she has since coming to Durga." Surana looked at Minda and said, "I regret this place is a poor substitute for Talu. Perhaps you can overlook its less attractive aspects."

Minda's lips parted to deny Durga's meanness, but Rakata stopped her. "What we brought from Talu is all that makes Durga tolerable. It would take a dim eye not to notice the shabbiness of our surroundings now."

"Maybe you'll be back at Talu sooner than you know," Minda said encouragingly.

"It stands?" Surana asked in surprise.

"Our scouts can see only the outer walls," Rakata explained, looking hopeful. "The city within hasn't been destroyed?"

"Wakefield sealed the entrances and left guards, but harmed nothing I know of," Britt assured, then added slowly, "Perhaps this is just another example of what made our problems possible. Everyone has been so suspicious of each other they've always assumed the worst."

Rakata slowly agreed. "The distrust gives men like Samarang and Townes fertile soil on which to cast their seeds of violence." He didn't mention it, but he was thinking, too, of the reasons he and Britt had grown up not knowing each other.

"Maybe through our solving these present problems, a new understanding can develop between our people," Minda offered.

Surana's fingers brushed Minda's chin in a gesture to get her attention. "Let you and me not be distracted from our purpose with discussions of philosophy. Come with me, Minda. We will get acquainted while you bathe. As it seems now that we needn't be enemies, maybe we will become friends."

Longing to kiss Britt again, just once, to say good night before she left, Minda had no choice except to follow Surana. As they left the room, she remarked, "I think too much has happened to me today. I doubt I'll be able to sleep."

"I don't expect you to sleep, yet I suspect you'll pass the night pleasantly enough," Surana commented.

Britt and Arjuna remained with Rakata for a while sipping pear wine, talking about the situation and their plans.

Despite renewing their resolution to help each other in this mutual time of need, Rakata privately wondered if, later, when new problems arose, he and Britt would be so friendly. He hadn't forgotten that the treaty made between leaders of countries across the ocean he'd never see was merely transferring the government of *his* land to someone else. Another crop of officials would arrive, as alien as the French and British had been. They were the sons of the Hollanders who had originally invaded Java. Would they divide the jungles and mountains neatly among themselves and expect the Javanese to submit to their disinheritance without argument? Or would they be willing to let his people rule themselves? Rakata knew that giving up some of their island so they didn't lose all of it was the most the Javanese could hope for. He wondered what this brother, a product of both cultures, would do if he ever had to choose a side.

Britt, too, realized that though he and Rakata were sitting together now, they might have to oppose each other in the future. The thought saddened him, and he wondered why they must inherit Gerard and Matarami's old fight. It seemed as if everything in their lives had been colored by it. His position was more difficult than Rakata's because, though he was part of both worlds, he couldn't be at peace with either of them. Britt had previously considered the possibility of leaving Java to avoid a punishment he didn't deserve. Now that his exoneration seemed possible, he wondered if, afterward, he should persuade Minda to leave the island to escape a heritage he suspected would always bring him pain as long as he was in Java.

Rakata hospitably sent Britt, Arjuna, and Kalao to his private bathing pool. Arjuna and Kalao talked about their latest adventures as they bathed, but Britt said little. His thoughts lingered on leaving the island forever.

He told himself, that if there were future battles, Minda and any children they might have would be in danger. But he couldn't forget how Gerard and Charles had struggled to create Phoenix House Tea from a tangle of mountainside jungle. He couldn't remember ever having considered doing less. Phoenix House was more than a plantation. It was home, the only place Britt had ever wanted to live. If he and Minda were to put it on sale, he'd feel as if he were fixing a price on his own flesh. By the time a servant led Britt to the room where he would spend the night, thoughts of the past and his possible future problems had depressed him.

Then the servant opened the door to a chamber where Durga's cracked walls were hidden by Talu's exquisitely woven draperies and the fragrance of the *raden*'s palace wafted from the lamp oil to blend with the scent of the blossoms that carpeted the floor. The perfumed folds of the bed's golden netting were swagged back, and the linens were covered with flower petals. The shadows of Britt's melancholy faded in the sunburst of his surprise. Minda was sitting on the edge of the bed, her poised arm paused from combing her hair.

She stood up, her long dark locks falling over her shoulders to be burnished by lamplight as she said, "Surana told me that arranging for us to be together this way tonight is the nearest Rakata will come to apologizing for carrying me away."

Britt wasn't aware of the servant stepping back into the hall and closing the door. His senses were fixed on the cream of Minda's skin, which was only partly veiled by the scarlet of the silk nightdress she was wearing. He said softly, "If I never again obey the *raden,* his wishes tonight are the same as mine."

Minda turned away and crossed the room to put the jewel-encrusted comb on a table. She remained with her back toward Britt, gazing down at the winking lights of the gems as she added, "Surana said, if the plans you made with Rakata this evening aren't successful, you and I will be allowed to stay at Durga until we decide what else we want to do.'' She fell silent a moment, not wanting to, but finally admitting, ''I'm afraid, when we return to Djakarta, Wakefield won't believe us and will jail you again.''

Though his steps were soundless, Minda was aware of Britt's approaching; the sensation of his face brushing her hair aside, of his lips kissing the back of her neck, was poignantly welcome.

''Then I'd have to escape again,'' he murmured against her skin. ''Rakata and I talked about that possibility after you and Surana left us. He promised to help me.''

''But what if he can't?'' Minda asked with a catch to her voice. ''When I think of your being tried, found guilty, and . . .'' She stopped, unable to say that he might be executed. A light shiver ran through her as she whispered, ''When I think of *that,* I wish I'd stayed in Philadelphia.''

Britt's arms around Minda's waist pulled her back against his chest. ''While we were in Philadelphia and I wanted so much for you to decide to return to Java with me, I knew we'd have problems because of the political instability of the island, but I never dreamed they would be this bad.''

''The situation isn't *your* doing,'' Minda denied. ''If I hadn't come back to Java, Alden wouldn't have followed me. You wouldn't have nearly so much trouble.''

''I also wouldn't have *you.*'' Britt turned her in his arms to face him, but she wouldn't meet his eyes. His fingers under her chin tilted her face to his as he said, ''Nobody is going to hang me.'' He kissed Minda tenderly, but her lips clung to his in a way that made him suspicious. His kisses moved over her cheek and her eyelids, then withdrew. He commented softly, ''You're *that* afraid.''

Minda opened her eyes to see the tip of his tongue tasting the tear he'd picked up from her lashes. She finally found the strength to say what she'd been thinking. ''I would rather have stayed in Philadelphia, even married Alden and let him and my mother cheat me out of Phoenix House, than see you hanged.''

Britt drew her more tightly to him and vowed, ''If I really thought you'd do such a thing, as I was being led to the gallows I'd find a way to break loose and kill Townes before they put the rope around my neck.'' His emotions were a firewind whirling through his spirit, and he was silent until he could control them. Finally, he lightened his embrace so he could look down at her and say more quietly, ''I've been thinking, even after this is over and the charges against me have been dropped, perhaps we should leave Java.'' When Minda's lips parted in surprise, he kissed them, lingered long enough to stop what she was ready to say, then rested his cheek against hers and explained, ''There will be more problems in the future. I suspect that the other planters, even those who like me, will never fully trust me because Sukadana was my mother. Rakata and I are friendly now, but someday he might again become suspicious of my motives because my last name is Vandekker. If we stay in Java after we're married, the same distrust will be transferred to you and any children we might have. You'll be safer if we move away.''

''It's the same old feud,'' Minda said disgustedly, her words muffled by his shoulder. She stepped back and looked up at Britt. Her eyes had taken on a deeper green, as if they could hold only a certain amount of anger and the excess was being condensed in them. ''You and I have inherited our fathers' places and Rakata has taken Matarami's in this battle. None of us wants it. Why must our lives be controlled by it, as if we'd been assigned parts in a play we can't change? It's tempting to think of going somewhere else, a place where no one will know us and what to expect from us. But I don't want to leave. Neither do you. I don't think we should stay because our fathers fought for Phoenix House; I think we should stay because we love this plantation.'' Minda's anger seemed to drain out of her and she said wearily, ''I used to wonder why Father didn't go back to Philadelphia to be with my mother and me. Now I think I understand.''

Britt looked down at her silently. He knew Gerard and Charles hadn't come to Java because they'd wanted to get rich. They'd been tired of following the rules everyone else had already laid down for them. They liked the challenge of meeting problems and solving them their own way. He recognized he and Minda were like that too. Neither of them would be happy with the properly scheduled, predictable kind of life they'd have somewhere else. Both of them were too independent, not nearly docile enough.

Britt smiled wryly. ''It was a fool's errand from the beginning for you and me to try to leash our emotions. We both seem always to have been driven by Java's fire spirits, if there are such things.''

Minda raised her hands to his temples, as if to hold his attention while she spoke. ''I think I finally understand what the Javanese mean by 'fire spirits.' It's the energy that makes a person have a passion for living. When Mother took me away, my fire spirits faded, almost went out. I don't think, now that they've been reawakened, they'll be willing to dim." She paused, then said solemnly, "But everything in me would die if you did. Tell me truthfully, do you *really* believe you can clear yourself?"

Britt was silent as he considered his chances. "It's a gamble, but one I think is worth trying. I just don't want to put you in danger now or in the future."

"Anything that threatens you threatens me, no matter where we are," she said.

Realizing that she was again near tears, Britt put his arms around Minda. She laid her head on his shoulder, and he wondered if she was weeping and trying to hide it.

After a moment she looked up at him with sad, but dry eyes. "Please, let's not talk about this anymore," she begged. "I want to forget all these problems, *everything,* tonight except you."

He gazed wordlessly at her a moment while every beat of his heart told him she was right. Love was the flame that would survive even if their plans were reduced to ashes. He picked Minda up and carried her to the bed to put her down among the flower petals.

Britt rested one knee on the bed as he began to untie his robe's sash, but Minda's nearness made him forget the sash and it slithered down his hips to join the flowers on the floor. He leaned closer to kiss her, his robe falling open, and at the caressing of their lips, Minda slipped her hands into his robe, wound her arms around him, wanting to draw him closer. Britt reached back, took her hands away, held them lightly in his, and let his lips wander over her fingers.

"You said you wanted to forget everything. So do I," he murmured between caresses. "But if we make love in a fury, as if this may be our last night together, our problems will become specters standing over us, influencing everything we do. I don't want that. Tonight I want to believe, to make you believe, that we have all the time in the world."

Still holding Minda's hand, Britt got into bed. His face turned into her palm and his tongue was a dot of fire burning moistly into her skin. Her fingers curled slightly, making an even deeper hollow of her hand, as if her flesh must recede a little from the piquancy of the sensations he was giving her. Britt's eyes lifted to Minda's. He knew the meaning of the smoke rising from their green depths and smiled against her palm. Still looking steadily into her eyes, he let his tonguetip move to her wrist to lightly caress her skin and then slide up her arm to kiss the inside of her elbow and kindle another small fire.

As Britt moved closer to kiss Minda, his arm curved around her legs and guided them up to their bed of flowers. He lifted the hem of her nightdress, his hands coaxing it up her leg, over her hips, making a caress of his removing it. He bent to kiss the valley between her breasts, as he slipped the nightdress from her shoulders. Finally he tossed it aside. A fold of silk floated down to settle over her face, a veil of gossamer scarlet she could watch him through.

With a quick movement, Britt's face turned, brushed aside the silk cascading over her shoulder; his mouth settled at her waist by the beginning curve of her hip. The insistent caressing of his lips, the burrowing of his tongue, made Minda tense with delight, and he was acutely aware of the thrilling of her senses.

His tongue seemed like a fire licking its way up Minda's side. It swerved to her breast to make sultry circles, lighting a flame to bloom at its center. The exquisite sensations didn't pause, and her hands reached for his shoulders, held them as if she must steady herself, though she was sitting. Her head tipped back, as if it were the only way she could still breathe, while Britt's hands gently cupped her breasts, making ivory mounds of them he covered with soft kisses. Then his lips were at the base of her throat, nuzzling, caressing Javanese fashion, moving up its side to find her ear.

When Minda was shivering from his caresses, he tilted his head to sweep aside her hair so his kisses could reach under it. Her fingers on his shoulders tightened, the edges of her nails pressing his skin briefly, then barely brushing him as they slid over his shoulders to the tops of his arms, as if she would pull him closer.

His lips, returning to her ear, breathed, "Don't."

Minda's grasp on his arms lightened, and Britt's fingers wove through her hair, took handfuls of her curls, drew them over her shoulders toward him. Raising his eyes to hers, Britt kissed one lock then the other and murmured, "You're all I'll ever ask of life. The rest of it doesn't matter, not even Phoenix House."

With his lips still pursed from the last word he'd uttered, Britt touched his mouth to hers, moving softly, but persistently, deliberately teasing Minda so she wanted more. The edges of Britt's teeth gently pulled at her lower lip, coaxing it to roundness, then lightly brushed the edge of her mouth's bow. His tongue fluttered along her lips' parting; then his mouth captured hers and moved restlessly, compellingly, until Minda felt as if she were a triumphant song being written in light, a wild strain rising higher at his direction.

When he withdrew, she swayed toward him; but Britt's hands at her waist guided Minda to her knees as he was, turned Minda so her back was to him. His kisses were warm spots dappling Minda's shoulders, rivulets of sunlight sliding down her spine. A path of gentle nips marked his ascent, and when Britt's arms slid around her waist, she gladly leaned back against him. She turned her head to seek his mouth and, finding, was possessed by it. Britt's fingers moved caressingly down her body, one arm folding around her hips to hold her more securely to him. Desire streaked through Minda, then faded and rose again, making her feel as if she were a flame dancing in a wind. She caught her breath, only to be seared again by his restlessly seeking lips.

Britt sat back on his heels, his grasp on Minda tightening. A new fire surged through her; she reached back, wanting to embrace him, then contented herself with blindly grasping the sides of his waist. Her instincts wanted to blend with the music he was composing in her senses, but thinking this was part of the prelude, she willed herself to be still.

His lips in her hair whispered, "We have not only tonight, but all the tomorrows in the world to love."

Britt's arms tightened, and a vivid shock of delight engulfed Minda. His persistent rhythm quickened her passion to a fiery compulsion. His body tensed against her back; he caught his breath, but gave them no pause. She felt as if she were running toward Mrabu's crater and couldn't stop. Poised at the edge of its molten core, she moaned softly as she plunged into its fire, her senses erupting in a burst of brilliant lights and swirling colors.

Gradually Minda became aware of Britt's arms around her waist, his chest warmly pressed to her back. His cheek, resting against her hair, turned; and he burrowed his face into the locks that fell over her temple so his kisses found her skin to lightly caress her a moment before he withdrew.

Guiding Minda to lie back among the flower petals, Britt cradled her shoulders in his arms. His hands, holding the back of her head, lifted her face toward his. Britt's lips were as soft as gingerblossom petals as they lingered on Minda's, then outlined her mouth with tender kisses. They followed her hairline to her ear, fluttered across her cheeks and nose, dropped kisses on her eyelids. Between caresses, Britt whispered against Minda's skin in court Javanese so eloquent it was like poetry as he told her she was the dawn lighting his skies, the rains nourishing his earth, and the shimmer of the moonlight through the haze that quieted his evenings. Maybe it had been the fire goddess's will that had brought Minda back to Java and caused her to stay, Britt murmured and promised he would make a little shrine for her at Phoenix House in the garden by the swing.

Then Britt raised his head to gaze silently into the perfumed shadows of the room as he thought about the pledge he'd impulsively made. He finally decided, if he could survive the trials that still lay before them, he would keep his promise. The fire goddess's shrine could be decoratively included in the stones of the wall he intended to have built around the garden to discourage possible future man-eaters.

Minda watched the streaks the lamplight cast across Britt's eyes and guessed what he was thinking. Although part of her reasoned that fire spirits were a symbol of the vitality in mankind and the goddess was a myth, there was something else in Minda, a force she couldn't silence, arguing that there was more to Java's ancient beliefs than mere superstition. She reached up to touch Britt's face, to lay her hand against his cheek. He tilted his head to look down at her, the lamplight making golden glimmers slant across his hair.

"I have to wonder why the volcano's guardian is supposed to be a goddess rather than a god," she mused, then, meeting his gaze, added, "The Javanese said the fire spirits entered me when I was born, but it seems truer of you. I was cold until you gave me love."

Britt ran a fingertip lightly along her shoulder, then down her arm. He took the hand resting at his cheek and held it to his lips, kissed her fingers while he considered his answer. "I didn't create your emotions. You always were passionate, but your feelings were waiting deep inside you, like a sleeping volcano's fires. When you were ready, they came exploding out and captured me as well as you."

Minda was silent a moment, then recalled, "That first kiss we shared in the carriage in Philadelphia made me feel as if I'd been dipped in fire, and I've felt that way with you ever since."

Britt's eyes traveled slowly, appreciatively, along the lines of her body to her toes and returned to her face, wearing a glint of humor. "You look more as if you've been dipped in flower petals now."

She lifted her head and saw it was true. Varicolored bits of flowers clung to her moist skin. Britt turned away to reach into a bowl of blossoms on the table beside the bed, then offered her a crimson bloom.

As she inhaled its fragrance, Minda commented, "Camellias were in my room that first morning I awoke at Phoenix House, but those were pink, not red."

"If passion can be given colors, the way we felt about each other then was pink, like the sky awakening with dawn," he said quietly. "Our feelings have since gotten deeper, and what we are together now has become as rich a crimson as that flower."

Britt leaned closer to blow, with warm little breaths, the clinging petals from her shoulders. His tonguetip brushed aside those dotting the moist satin of her bosom. He kissed away the bits of flowers pressed to Minda's waist, then continued to her hips and thighs, moved slowly down her legs, seducing away each flower petal and replacing it with delight.

When Britt reached Minda's feet, he bent to kiss her toes, brush the tip of his tongue to the bottom of Minda's foot as delicately as if he were using a feather. He moved to the inside of her ankle, then left a trail of soft kisses up her leg. Pausing, he tilted his head to tease the sensitive skin at the back of her knee. His kisses spiraled up her thigh, caressed her lingeringly, insistently, awakening a piquant ache impossible to deny. The tingles running along Minda's nerves became currents of growing pleasure. Britt's hands on the curves of her hips held them still while he evoked exquisite sensations that swirled through her spirit, igniting each cell in her body. She made a soft noise, as if she suppressed a moan. The sound was a cloud of sparks falling over him. He opened his eyes to find that hers shimmered with streaks of emerald lightning. He looked measuringly at her a moment, then, as if he'd already been planning other caresses, sat up.

Britt dropped a line of quick, soft nips across her abdomen and nibbled a path to her waist. The tip of his tongue persistently teased Minda's side until the sharply tantalizing sensation made her gasp and try to flinch away. But he wouldn't let her.

Britt held her firmly until she writhed with the impulses that were like lines of fire sheeting through her. His mouth moved to her lips, then slipped down her throat to crisscross her breasts with kisses. His tongue fluttered over her nipples, his lips teasing her into a torment of delight.

His fingers, curved around Minda's hips, began to move slowly up her sides until his thumbs were tantalizing the beginning swells of her breasts, and he bent closer to kiss her. Britt's lean, hard body resting lightly, warmly, against her turned Minda's blood into a molten fluid that rippled through her veins and scalded her. Anticipating his ardor, she was surprised at the controlled delicacy of his lips brushing hers. Wanting more than such maddeningly elusive kisses, Minda reached hungrily for Britt's mouth while her hips moved in deliberate provocation.

As if he'd been waiting for that moment, his response was immediate. His lips, growing more demanding, moved as possessively as his body over hers. Minda's desire spread through her blood, and Britt, too, felt as if his nerves were set ablaze and his will was dissolving in a frenzy of impulses. His flattened hands slid under Minda's hips, and at the sweet sensation of her against him, he pressed closer, then caught his breath at their blending. He waited a moment, opened his eyes to distract himself with sight from the clamor of his other senses. Thinking he'd finally leashed his passion, he began a sinuous rhythm that coaxed Minda to the beginning of ecstasy, withdrew to let her descend, again and again teasing then evading her. All the while, he watched her steadily, measuring her response and giving her less than he knew she wanted.

Britt's artful delaying filled Minda with so powerful a need she reached out to grasp his shoulders. He leaned closer. Her lips groped for his and, finding them, felt his hips swivel in suddenly blatant invitation. Her fraying nerves became threads of flame, filling her with so great a hunger she felt as if she might explode and, instead, opened her eyes; his were a glimmer of amber lights slowly blurring as they lost their focus.

His mouth crushed Minda's as he twisted his legs around hers, and his desire became a wall of flame rising as though from Mrabu's shuddering core, towering over him, incinerating the last shreds of his control. Britt heard Minda's soft cry as if it came from within his own spirit when their passion crashed over them, shattering their spirits into countless glimmering sparks that lit the infinity of time before them.

Minda lay with her face tucked into the curve of Britt's shoulder until her heart gradually resumed its normal beat and her pulses stopped their hammering.

Britt was aware of her face turning, then of her breath against his hair as she whispered, "You and the fire goddess have sealed our destiny. Our love will burn as brightly as our souls—together always."

"I am here."

The murmur at Alden's ear startled him; he turned quickly to face Garuto, Samarang's bodyguard. Chagrined that the Javanese had been able to creep so close without his becoming aware of it, Alden frowned as he breathed, "Where's Samarang?"

"In the deeper shadows. Follow me," Garuto whispered and turned away.

Alden caught up his horse's reins and obeyed, though he fervently wished that he didn't have to meet his partner at midnight in Djakarta's alleyways. When Samarang stepped out of the darkness ahead, Alden wondered how the pair of Javanese could move silently in the hush of night when they were so heavily armed. Each wore a dagger, a long, straight sword at his elbow, a bow and arrow case slung over one shoulder, and a rifle over the other. Alden guessed that they probably had blowpipes and poisoned darts as well.

The greetings Alden and Samarang exchanged were brief. Not only were they risking discovery by the meeting, but each man had bad news to tell the other.

"Rakata kidnapped the Scott woman and brought her to Durga," Samarang began. "Kalao was with her and betrayed Bedug to Rakata. I killed Bedug to silence him, but I had to flee Durga."

"Melinda's at Durga?" Alden stared at Samarang in amazement. "But if you'd already killed Bedug . . ."

Embarrassed that he'd left evidence to identify him as Bedug's murderer, Samarang hastily said, "Rakata will use any flimsy excuse to point a finger at me."

Alden brushed aside the importance of Samarang's quarrel with the *raden* and said, "At least now it's possible for you to move about as you wish."

Samarang's usually impassive face contorted with anger as he hissed, "I cannot do as I wish unless I can become invisible like a *lelembut*! Every Javanese on this end of the island will know Rakata is hunting me and why as soon as the *raden*'s runners reach them. Everyone will be watching for me and my men."

"How many of you escaped Durga?" Alden inquired, his mind already spinning webs of plans to accommodate this turn of events.

"Twenty-eight," Garuto answered. "They're waiting in the jungle near Djakarta until we decide what to do. It's a great risk for them to be so close."

"The situation has changed for me as well," Alden admitted. "I've learned that the British army will leave Java and the Hollanders will take over the government. Also, someone who works at Phoenix House, a man named Arjuna, helped Vandekker escape from Wakefield; so he's loose now." Despite the darkness, Alden could see the stunned expressions on Samarang's and Garuto's faces. He quickly asked, "Could Vandekker and Arjuna take refuge at Durga?"

"They probably came after we'd left," Samarang said glumly. "Where else could they go?"

"Where, indeed, especially if Melinda's there," Alden commented. "That will only make Wakefield's job of capturing them easier."

"Who will lead Wakefield to Durga? I cannot," Samarang protested. "Neither can any of my men."

"You'll be a hero to your people in a few days if my plans work out," Alden promised.

That idea seemed impossible to Samarang. Afraid to hope Townes was right, he said derisively, "You've made several plans; none have succeeded."

"That's because *your* people made mistakes," Alden retorted.

"If I haven't obeyed every detail of your schemes, it was because they ignored Rakata. You only wanted to get the Hollander out of *your* way," Samarang accused.

"I always understood that *both* Rakata and Vandekker had to be destroyed, but you didn't have the patience to do it my way," Alden said to defend himself. "If you'll do as I say now, you can still become *raden*."

"How can that happen when I must hide from my people?" Samarang asked bitterly.

"We'll make one last raid that not only will add much to our profits, but will give me so much satisfaction I'll take part in the attack myself," Alden said smugly.

Samarang and Garuto exchanged surprised glances.

"No one is at Phoenix House except servants. The place is full of valuables, including a large amount of gold Vandekker would have to have on hand for expenses and the jewelry of two very wealthy women, Sukadana and Melinda," Alden said. "We'll take everything and burn the house, so it will appear Vandekker came back and destroyed it himself."

"Why would he do that? I've heard he loves Phoenix House like Rakata loves Talu," Samarang said.

"Vandekker doesn't merely love Phoenix House—he's *obsessed* with it," Alden explained. "It's common knowledge that Vandekker and his father have fought everything and everyone to keep that plantation. Gerard stayed at the cost of Sukadana's life, and Britt wouldn't leave even for the sake of that girl from Brussels he was going to marry. Gerard went mad there, and Britt has lived almost like a hermit since. He's only left the plantation on business, and the party he had to introduce Melinda to the other planters was the first social event at Phoenix House in years. Everyone knows he would likely have been convicted, and his escaping Wakefield only makes him look guiltier. Now that he's a hunted criminal, everything he and his father worked for has been taken from him.''

"It will appear that Vandekker wanted to destroy Phoenix House Tea if he can't have it for himself," Samarang concluded. "Many field workers as well as the house servants live on the plantation and would resist anyone trying to destroy it. To Wakefield it will seem that, if Vandekker had the men to overcome them, he also had enough men to make the other raids; so he and Rakata will look doubly guilty.''

"Wakefield is fuming over Vandekker's escape. He'll be horrified that Vandekker is so bent on revenge he'd kill his servants. Vandekker will appear to be as insane as his father was and Wakefield will be all the more anxious to recapture him. When you come with me to Djakarta to give Wakefield the directions to Durga, he'll be only too happy to march his men there. If Rakata and Vandekker resist, they'll be killed on the spot; if they don't, you can be sure their trial will result in their conviction and execution.''

"Then it will seem, even to my people, that Rakata and his Hollander brother were guilty from the first," Samarang commented.

"Your opposing him all this time will make you a hero. You'll become *raden* and I'll return to England—not a plantation owner, as I'd hoped, but far richer for this venture," Alden said.

"We must quickly move the valuables we've already taken. That cave we've stored our spoils in is too close to Gunung Mrabu. If the volcano erupts, we might lose it all," Garuto reminded.

"*Everything* must be done quickly," Samarang agreed.

A smile of satisfaction crept over Alden's mouth as he saw that Samarang wasn't going to argue with the plan, and he said, "I'm ready to leave now. Is that soon enough?''

Chapter Twenty

Britt, Minda, and Arjuna left Durga with Kalao acting as their guide. Rakata had explained that Kalao could show them a faster way to Djakarta than Britt knew, one where they wouldn't be likely to be seen by any of the patrols Wakefield had searching for him. The jungle lane Kalao led them along was so narrow they had to ride single file—Britt ahead of Minda, Arjuna guarding the rear. Conversation wasn't possible, and they were left to their own thoughts under trees that dripped scarlet flower petals on the path.

Watching how the sun flickered over Britt's hair and dappled his shoulders, Minda wished she could have ridden double with him so his arms would be around her. Lured by the gentle swaying of his hips with the horse's movements, she relived that morning, when they'd awakened on their bed of flowers.

Minda had opened her eyes to what had at first seemed like a golden cloud of fragrance. Half asleep, she'd reclosed her eyes thinking that the night had been a dream and she was still caught up in it. It wasn't possible Britt had come to rescue her, that instead of Rakata's killing them both, as she'd anticipated, he'd discussed a plan with Britt that might foil the trap Alden and Samarang had made for them. The night in Britt's arms couldn't have been real, she'd thought; it was only a dream too beautiful to let go.

Then a bird had started singing from somewhere nearby and Minda

had suddenly realized no trees were that close to the hut where she'd
been kept prisoner. The bird's song had changed to a trill, as if it was
laughter turned into music, and Minda had opened her eyes to confirm
she wasn't lying on a mat in a hut. It was the sheer veil of the netting
draped over and around the bed that had seemed to fill the air with
gold smoke. The perfume was from the flower petals that covered the
linens. Still unbelieving, Minda had gazed wonderingly at the bird in a
lacy bamboo cage by the window, then had finally turned to see Britt
lying on his side still asleep. She'd sat up to look at his profile,
untroubled in slumber, at the straight line of his nose, the soft curve of
his mouth. Only then had she been convinced that he and Rakata had
finally made peace with each other.

After Britt's golden lashes had parted, he'd turned his head searching for Minda, his hair making sunny whorls among the flower petals;
and when he'd found her, his amber eyes had filled with warmth. Britt
had reached up to touch Minda's cheek, to run his fingertip slowly
along her lip as he'd said softly that he loved her.

There'd been no talk of the possibility that something yet could
happen to dash away their hopes, no discussion about the lonely past
or the dangers of the future. As they'd again made love, there'd been a
light shining from behind the autumn haze of his eyes that was the
triumph of decisions made and doubts left behind. Their kisses and
caresses had held the exhilaration of their new freedom from the past,
the building excitement of the victory ahead.

Now, while they rode through clouds of yellow butterflies shimmering in the sun, Minda knew Britt's thoughts were the same as hers.
They longed for the moment when they could be alone with time as
their servant instead of their master. Only a few days more and the
nightmare would be over; only a few days more seemed too easy to be
true.

In a place where the path began to widen, Kalao rode a little farther
ahead, then stopped his horse, and gestured for Britt to join him.
While they spent a moment talking in murmurs, Minda watched
anxiously, not because she was afraid anything was wrong, but because she hoped Britt would return to pass some message or directions
to her. Then she could look into his face, perhaps even briefly touch
him. Her heart leaped in joy as he stood in his stirrups to pluck a
crimson flower from a twig overhanging the path, then made his way
back to her.

A smile was in Britt's eyes as he leaned closer to tuck the blossom into her bodice. The camellia was a message letting her know he was thinking about last night too. He said, "There's a river ahead; and though Kalao has done a lot of traveling as Rakata's courier, it's mostly been on foot. He isn't a good rider and he's queasy about fording rivers. I told him we'll go in pairs. He and Arjuna will start across first."

Britt turned in the saddle and gestured for Arjuna to go ahead, then nudged his horse closer to Minda's to make room for his friend to pass. Britt's leg brushed Minda's and the same small shock of pleasure that went through her was mirrored in his eyes.

He leaned closer to touch his lips to hers briefly and assure, "The river is shallow and the current isn't dangerous. I'll stay close to you."

Minda looked up at him from under her lashes and replied, "If you say it's safe, I won't be worried about fording; but you can't, for now, be as close as I'd like."

"Nor as I'd prefer," he said softly, then moved his horse forward.

The river came from between the walls of a gorge, where its distant reflection was the sky's blue. Then it widened as it approached the fording place. It took emerald tints from the arching trees, moved lazily past to disappear around a bend. Its smooth surface was broken only by the ripples Kalao and Arjuna's horses made as they waded out from shore. The water barely reached higher than the horses' hocks, Minda noted, and she was glad that the beautifully sewn boots and the softly draped cotton skirt Surana had given her wouldn't get a soaking. She and Britt were a third of the way across when he pointed out a pair of rusta on the riverbank a little upstream. As Minda watched the deer daintily drinking, she remembered her first trip to the tea fields, when she and Britt had been startled by the buck who had been decorating his antlers with flowers and leaves to impress his doe. Minda looked at Britt and saw the memory in his eyes. Britt's easy smile was his wry comment on how different things had been for them then, how fiercely and uselessly they'd resisted the inevitability of their love. The deer abruptly lifted their heads, for a moment stood rigidly still, then whirled to vanish into the foliage.

Britt's smile faded; he hurried their horses to catch up with Arjuna and Kalao, who had stopped when they'd noticed the deer take flight.

"The rusta weren't afraid of us, but of something upriver," Arjuna said. "Do you think it could be soldiers?"

Britt peered warily at the liquid avenue shimmering with sunsparkles down its center. He could hear a sound, so faint it was barely perceptible, and was chilled by the possibility that struck him. "Did it rain in the mountains last night?" he asked.

Kalao paled. "Perhaps. I saw distant lightning. Do you think a flood is coming?"

"I don't know," Britt answered slowly.

Arjuna observed that their horses' ears were all pricked in the same direction and he urged, "Let's get out of the river. Stay close to me, Kalao," he added and started hurrying toward the opposite bank.

Britt didn't notice Arjuna and Kalao's retreat, for his attention was concentrated on the sound, still too faint for him to identify. A rockslide in the gorge? Faraway horses? Aloud he said, "If it's soldiers, we'd make a good target in the middle of the river." When Arjuna didn't reply, Britt glanced to the side and, seeing that the Javanese were nearing shore, guided his horse around Minda's to put himself between her and whatever danger might be upstream. Then he told her to follow the others. Their now obviously nervous animals eagerly plunged forward. Above the sound of the horses' splashing, Britt recognized a growing rumble to confirm what he had feared—a flash flood. He leaned over to slap Minda's mount on the rump and it leaped out ahead.

Already in the shallows, but knowing the flood could carry uprooted trees that might snap a horse's legs, Arjuna snatched the reins from Kalao's hands. "Hold on, Kalao!" he cried and kicked his horse into greater speed.

The rumbling sound burst into a roar. The river at the gorge, which had a moment before seemed so placid and friendly, became a swell dotted with broken branches and debris rushing toward them. Aghast at how swiftly it was coming, Minda was for an instant frozen with shock. Her horse took advantage of her lightened grasp on the reins and, snorting in fear, swerved its hindquarters toward the oncoming torrent. Caught by surprise, Minda was thrown off balance; and she grabbed two handfuls of his mane to steady herself.

"Forget the reins and let him swim! Just stay in the saddle when the current catches you!" Britt shouted above the noise.

Minda glanced sideways at him the instant a tangle of branches, carried by the water, pounded into his horse's flank. The animal screamed in pain, scuttled sideways as the debris jammed against him.

Britt, struggling to keep the animal on its feet, realized it was a lost cause and threw himself from the saddle an instant before the horse went down.

Driven mad by terror and pain, the animal kicked and flailed the water. Minda felt as if her heart had stopped as she tried to see in the churning and splashing if its hooves had struck Britt, but she felt her horse rise under her with the water's swelling, his legs striking out in a mighty effort to stay afloat as the current picked them up and sent them swirling downriver. Muddy spray sheeted over Minda's face and blinded her, poured into her mouth to drown her call to Britt in a spasm of choking. Then Minda's instinct to survive overtook her consciousness. She was compelled to fight for her own life, to stay on the struggling horse and somehow catch breaths between dunkings as they were carried away. She felt her horse's shudders when debris smashed into him and wondered how he could swim despite the blows. His head bobbed back and forth with his lunges, whipping his mane across her face like a lash. All the while Minda withstood the forces battering her with more strength than she'd known she possessed, her tears for Britt joined the muddy water streaming across her face and her sobs were turned into gurgles.

As abruptly as the torrent had struck, it faded. The water that had rushed through the gorge and broken on them with such fury spread into the valley ahead and subsided. Only then did Minda finally become aware of something dragging at her stirrup. Blinking and gasping for breath, she looked down.

"Thank God! Oh, thank God!" she choked when she saw Britt clinging to the stirrup with one hand, his other hand clenched around the girth. At her words, he glanced up at her and she saw that the side of his face was smeared with blood.

"Just a cut," he said between coughs. "Let this animal—get to shore—anyway he wants."

Although the horse's legs kept pumping, his ebbing strength was apparent in his slowing progress. As soon as his hooves touched bottom, Minda slid from the saddle to lighten his burden and waded beside Britt, who put his arm around her waist and trudged doggedly to shore. When they reached the bank, they wordlessly fell to their knees and, too weary even for that, slid down to sprawl on the ground.

Britt turned his head, leaving blood smears on the grass, and reached for Minda's hand as he anxiously asked, "Are you all right? Are you sure?"

She nodded slowly, then again as she struggled for breath to whisper, "You aren't. Your head is bleeding."

"Your horse's foot grazed me while he was swimming. I forgive him. He saved us both," Britt panted, then turned his head to look at the animal.

The horse was on his feet though his legs were spread wide to brace himself while his head hung down, nostrils distended, as his sides heaved.

"I vow that's the strongest . . ." The sound of a distant gunshot stopped Britt's words. He didn't turn again toward Minda, just tightly closed his eyes. Finally his muffled voice came to her. "I'm glad Arjuna survived the flood. I hope Kalao did."

"Was that Arjuna's signal?" she asked breathlessly.

"Arjuna wouldn't risk being heard, not to signal us. He'd just wait for us to come back." Britt fell silent until his breathing slowed, then said quietly, "The branches that hit us impaled my horse. That was why he went down. I'm sure the gunshot was Arjuna putting him out of his misery."

Minda squeezed Britt's hand but said nothing. She knew the horse had been his favorite and he was grieved.

They lay silently recovering their strength, Britt regretting the loss of his horse; until, finally, he sat up and, in a voice still roughened by emotion, said, "We should start back as soon as you think you're ready."

Minda wearily propped herself up on her elbow, then, gazing at the blood trickling down the side of his face, moved closer to study the cut. "We aren't going anywhere until we've done something with that," she said firmly. She slowly got to her feet, then pulled up her hem and started tearing a strip of cotton from her petticoat. "I wish we could rinse off that wound and this cloth. I don't like to think of what might fester from that muddy river water," she said apprehensively.

Conceding she was right, Britt got up and, taking out the knife he had sheathed at his waist, slowly turned to scan the surrounding foliage. When he saw what he wanted, he walked toward one of the vines that, rooted in the soil, climbed high into the trees to reach the sun.

Minda watched curiously as he sawed away a section of the arm-thick vine, which was a common plant in the jungle she'd seen often.

Britt handed her the piece he'd cut loose, advising, "There's water inside. Use it to rinse off that piece of petticoat." Then he turned away to saw off another section of vine. When he tilted his head and held the cut end over his wound, she could see liquid dribbling out, washing away his blood.

"Are you sure that's safe? It isn't poisonous?" she asked warily.

"It's just water the plant stores for its own use. I've drunk it many times," he assured, then, looking down at her, added, "Didn't I tell you, if we had to hide in the jungle, I'd know how to survive?"

Minda nodded and discovered there was just enough water in the section of vine he'd given her to rinse the strip of cotton she'd torn from her petticoat. Then, while Britt sat down so she could reach him, she wrapped the makeshift bandage around his brow. As she was knotting it, the distant crack of another gunshot sounded.

Minda stiffened in surprise, then hesitantly asked, "Do you think Arjuna had to shoot another of the horses?"

Britt waited a long moment, head up, listening; there were no other sounds. Finally he said, "I suppose that's possible, but he might be frightening away an animal. If something is wrong, he may have risked a signal. Let's just hope nothing else has happened."

Minda hurriedly finished knotting the bandage, then stepped back to inspect her work. When Britt glanced up at her, his features had taken on a sharpened, wary alertness, like a hunting animal. He suddenly seemed so different she was startled, as if she were looking into the face of a stranger.

"With that bandage around your head, you somehow remind me of Rakata or, perhaps more properly, of a Javanese bandit, except for your hair and eyes," she commented. "All you need is a pair of those blousy pants they wear and one of those long swords at your hip."

"In Surana's clothes, you look more Javanese than I do," Britt remarked.

Minda looked down ruefully. The green and yellow flowered skirt slapped wetly around her ankles; the abbreviated blouse was still dripping water on her midriff. The buttonless jacket was caked with mud. "I'm afraid Surana wouldn't recognize her clothes now."

"Appearance is the last thing that concerns me at the moment. I know how to use a Javanese sword and I wish I had one." Britt got to his feet in a smooth, easy movement, then put his hands on her shoulders as he explained, "My rifle was on my saddle and I lost my pistol in the river. Judging from the sound of that gunshot, we were carried a couple of miles by the current. We'll have to lead this horse, because he's still too tired to ride, and I don't relish walking so far in the jungle with nothing except this field knife to defend us.''

"I think you'd know what to do if any animal should threaten us," Minda said confidently.

Britt didn't want to frighten Minda more than she'd already been by reminding her of the possibility that Samarang's renegades or Wakefield's soldiers were in the area. He said only, "If we're going to find Arjuna and Kalao before twilight, we'd better start back now.''

The river's overrunning its banks had formed new channels and pools in the jungle that Britt, not knowing what was under their surface, swerved to avoid. Because of skirting these areas, they trudged twice the distance they would have if the river had been in its banks.

When they finally reached the place where Britt said the flood had caught them, Minda wondered how he recognized it, because to her it only looked like another newly made marsh. He turned to follow the soggy edge of the inlet, explaining that Arjuna would have tried to find a dry place to wait. Britt didn't mention that Arjuna would have wanted to stay a little away from the river because of the predators that soon would be approaching the water for a drink as well as hoping to find prey.

The sun was rapidly fading and the jungle floor was hazy with gathering shadows when they saw in a clearing ahead Arjuna sitting in the grass a few feet from Kalao. Noticing that Kalao's arm was in a sling made from Arjuna's shirt and one of Arjuna's pants legs was blood-soaked, Britt hurried his steps so Minda had to almost run to keep up with him. Arjuna and Kalao turned bruised faces to watch their approach. Arjuna's eyes were grim and Kalao looked frightened.

Britt reached Kalao first and asked concernedly, "What's wrong with your arm?''

"It's broken," the boy mumbled.

Surprised that Kalao said no more, Britt looked past him at Arjuna. "And you, my friend? What happened to your leg?''

"Shot," Arjuna said angrily.

Assuming that the second gunshot had been accidental and Arjuna was embarrassed, Britt quietly inquired, "How did that come about?''

Minda, who had hurried to Arjuna's side to bend over the still bleeding wound, exclaimed, "Why didn't you at least wrap this with something?''

"Because we wouldn't let him.''

Minda's heart lurched at the sound of the familiar voice behind them. Although she straightened in surprise, she didn't turn.

Britt whirled to face not only Alden Townes but Samarang and his men coming out of their hiding places with guns leveled at them.

"If you move, I'll have to shoot you, as I did Arjuna," Alden warned.

Britt looked measuringly at the pistol in Alden's hand, then at those Samarang's men held, and decided he'd better not try to resist them.

After one of the Indonesians had taken Britt's field knife, Alden motioned with his pistol. "Sit down next to Arjuna. You, too, Kalao. Get closer to them. Melinda, get back, away from them."

Finally turning to face Alden, Minda breathed, "How did you find us?"

"We were nearby and heard Arjuna's gunshot when he killed the horse." Alden reached over to catch Minda's arm roughly, to pull her to his side.

"Let go of me!" she cried, resisting his grip. "Why separate me from them? You're going to murder us all anyway!"

Samarang gave an order, and several of his men came forward. One of them poked at Kalao with the tip of his rifle barrel to prod the youth to his feet. Another waved his pistol at Britt, then gave him a shove toward where Arjuna was sitting. Although Britt's temper flared, he had no choice. All he could do was hope Townes would approach closer so he might spring on him and wrestle away the gun.

The Javanese who had pushed Britt motioned for him to sit down beside Arjuna, and he angrily obeyed. When he saw several others coming with ropes to tie them, his heart sank, but there was nothing he could do. One of the Indonesians held them at gunpoint while the others tied his and Arjuna's hands behind them, then tied their ankles. They bound Kalao's wrists together in front of him, making sure that if he moved his uninjured arm, he'd wrench the broken one. Then they tied his ankles together, as they'd done with Britt and Arjuna.

Seeing the pain that flashed across Arjuna's face as the men unfeelingly tugged him about, and Kalao's eyes bulging with tears of agony when, uncaring of his broken arm, they rolled him on his side, Britt snapped, "Are you enjoying causing them torment, Townes?"

Alden gave Minda over to one of the Javanese, then stepped closer to Britt. He reached down to tear the bandage from Britt's brow and toss it aside. "It doesn't matter to me one way or another, Vandekker.

But now that you're helpless and trussed up like a roast ready for the spit, I can say all three of you will be taken closer to the riverbank, where the horse's corpse is, and left as a meal for any of the beasts that come prowling here tonight.''

Minda gasped in horror. ''You can't mean that, Alden! You *can't* do such an awful thing!''

Noting with satisfaction that Britt's head had begun to bleed again, Alden said, ''The scent of your blood added to the horse's should attract any number of predators. Whether it's crocodiles, a leopard, or even one of those giant lizards called dragons that find you to its taste, I'm sure there won't be much left of any of you by morning. If Wakefield himself were to come by here tomorrow night, I'll wager he'd never guess you'd been here.''

Minda's horror turned into overwhelming fury. She wrenched herself free of the man holding her and ran to rake Alden's face with her nails. With an oath of surprise and pain, he caught her hands and held them, but she kicked at his legs. He struggled with Minda a moment, then flung her away. Although her scream of despair sounded genuine as she tumbled toward Britt, she was using the blur of her whirling to disguise her real purpose. She snapped the fine golden chain from her neck. Falling over Britt's chest, she threw her arms around him and appeared to be weeping hysterically, but before the nearest of Samarang's men came to pull Minda away, she'd pressed the crystal pendant into Britt's hands.

''Let me stay with him!'' she sobbed. ''Let me die with him!''

''Get her up on that horse,'' Alden snarled over his shoulder as he marched closer to Britt. He glared down at his prisoner and said derisively, ''The wonder of it is that Melinda was ever roused to such passion by the likes of you, a damned half-breed, though she was so icy with me I'd begun to think she was incapable of it.''

Britt's eyes flickered with copper lights as he looked up at Alden to retort, ''Your pride is stung because Minda chose me over you, but you never wanted her. It was always her money you were after.'' Britt gasped as Alden's boot crashed into his ribs.

''If I had the time, Vandekker, I'd take great satisfaction in watching Samarang's men geld you,'' Alden snarled, and again kicked Britt in the side.

The pain momentarily took Britt's breath away so he couldn't have answered if he'd wanted to, but beside him, Arjuna said contemptuously, ''He would still be more a man than you.''

Alden glared down at Arjuna. Infuriated beyond replying, he aimed his pistol straight at Arjuna's face. Sure that Townes was going to fire, Arjuna didn't even breathe as he stared defiantly back for the long moment until the gun was lowered.

"You wanted to goad me into shooting you so a bullet would save you from death by fang and claw. That wouldn't do, not at all. I only wish I could stay to watch the beasts fight over your carcasses," Alden said venomously.

"You hate Vandekker, anyone on his side, as I hate Rakata and his friends," Samarang commented in English, then turned away to order his men to carry their captives closer to the river.

As Samarang's men picked up Kalao, despite his resolve, he cried out in pain, and Minda winced to see blood dripping from Arjuna's leg while they carried him away. Though her vision was blurred by tears for their suffering, when Samarang's men dragged Britt off into the shadows, the tears finally streamed down her cheeks.

After Alden had mounted the horse beside Minda's, she whispered, "What more can you possibly hope to gain from doing this? You already have the loot from your raids and there's nothing you can get from me unless . . ." Shocked by the idea that streaked through her mind, Minda brushed away her tears and looked at him from eyes fired with new fear. "Surely you aren't thinking, you wouldn't . . ."

Alden's eyes were on the dark mound Britt's body made in the shadows. "I'd wager it's what Vandekker is thinking too, that I'll rape you. Let it be his dying thought," Alden replied. Then he looked appraisingly at her to add, "Vandekker was only partly right when he said I'd always been after your money. I was actually fascinated by your aloofness, and I thought, after we were married, it would be interesting to teach you about passion. You have little resemblance now to the lady who was able to freeze me with her glance; and you are, finally, more in my power than you would have been even as my wife."

Minda felt as if her spirit were shriveling, but she stared at him defiantly and said, "Don't you think Wakefield will question my disappearance when he discovers Rakata doesn't have me? Whatever else Major Wakefield thinks of the *raden*, he knows Rakata wouldn't kill me."

"Your death is one thing Wakefield won't blame Rakata for. I'm going to burn Phoenix House to the ground. With Britt's seeming to be a hunted criminal, it will appear he fired the plantation out of revenge that he can't have it. Your body will be found in the ashes," Alden said coolly. "If you can be identified, even if anyone knows you and Vandekker were lovers, it will be supposed that, upon learning he was mad, you refused him, perhaps that, as half owner of the plantation, you tried to save it and resisted him, and he, in a rage, killed you. Wakefield will believe you were merely another victim of Vandekker's insanity. Although they'll never find Vandekker, his seeming guilt will add substance to Rakata's, and the *raden* will eventually be killed or captured. Then Samarang will get the title he's always wanted. I, of course, will leave Java a rich man, accused of nothing by anyone."

Minda shuddered, not only at the macabre plan but at the matter-of-fact way Alden described it. She finally said, "It's you who are mad."

"If you ascribe to the theory that a man must be insane to plan to kill another, you're wrong," Alden said. "I'm quite sane. I'll just go to whatever lengths are necessary to get what I want."

Minda turned to stare at Alden and felt as if she were looking into the face of pure, grinning evil. Unable to think of a word to describe how she abhorred him, she finally turned her horse to follow Samarang.

Alden had no idea how far sounds could carry in the hush of the forest at twilight. Neither did he realize that Britt's ears, sharply trained by the jungle, could hear his low conversation with Minda. Britt was appalled by Townes's plan to rape her then destroy her body and Phoenix House by fire, but he dared not move a muscle until all of Samarang's men had mounted their horses. Even then he only flexed his hands so he could work the crystal from his palm to hold between his fingers. By the time the riders were far enough away that he was sure they wouldn't see him and come back, he rolled over on his stomach and began to rub the crystal against the cords binding his wrists. Though its sharp edge was cutting his fingers and he felt blood trickling into his palm, he kept sawing at the rope.

Arjuna, too, had been watching the riders. After they'd disappeared into the jungle, despite the pain he caused his wounded leg, he squirmed and rolled until he managed to work his way to Britt's side. "I'm like a snake without the use of arms and legs, but my teeth can pull those loops loose if you'll turn away from me."

"How much blood do you suppose you lost getting here?" Britt chided, but he rolled over on his side.

"No doubt I left a trail," Arjuna replied.

Britt frowned as he felt Arjuna's tugs on the loop. "Maybe I should just keep using the crystal to cut myself free. If you bleed too much from moving around, you'll faint and fall out of the saddle on the way back to Durga."

Arjuna paused to retort he wouldn't faint, then continued pulling at the loop until he announced, "That one is loose. Cut the rope beside it and your hands will be free." When Britt started working on that, Arjuna said, "We have only two horses for the three of us."

"I know that," Britt muttered, then added, "Kalao isn't a good enough rider to manage a horse when he has a broken arm, so I think you and he should ride double back to Durga and get Rakata."

"What about you?" Kalao's whisper came from the shadows.

"Alden and Samarang are on their way to pick up their loot. I'm going to follow them," Britt answered.

"What can you do alone and without weapons?" Kalao anxiously asked.

"Probably little more than leave a trail Rakata will be able to follow at a gallop," Britt answered. He winced as one of the crystal's corners stabbed his thumb, but after another moment cut through the rope. He broke its last fraying strands and was free.

Britt turned over and sat up to untie his ankles, then started on the ropes that bound Arjuna's hands. After all three were loose, Britt pulled off his shirt, tossed it to Arjuna, and suggested, "While I'm getting the horses, see if you can use part of this to stop your leg from bleeding." Then he hurried into the jungle, leaving Arjuna tearing off the sleeves.

Wary of the scents of animals prowling closer, the horses hadn't wandered far, and Britt caught them easily. After he'd returned to his friends, he quickly put on his now sleeveless shirt, then helped Kalao and Arjuna into the saddle.

Arjuna was mounted behind Kalao so he could put his arms around the boy and take the reins. "Your legs and my hands will make us a whole rider," he assured Kalao, then looked down at Britt.

"Though the horse Minda is riding looked all right to Townes and Samarang, he's badly bruised and still tired from fighting the flood this afternoon. He's going to slow them all down," Britt said encouragingly.

Arjuna nodded agreement, then promised, "We'll be back with Rakata, at least as far as this place, by morning."

"Have a care you don't try to go too fast in the dark. If your horse stumbles or you faint and fall out of the saddle, neither of you will be able to remount," Britt warned.

"I've been through too much to end this adventure sprawled on the trail bleeding to death," Arjuna said tightly. "Just don't let your temper overrule your judgment when you catch up with them. I know you have one, my friend, and many reasons to be angry, but Samarang has a lot of men with him. They all have weapons and you don't."

Britt nodded and stepped back from the horse.

"The goddess's crystal saved us tonight. Maybe it will protect you," Kalao hopefully suggested.

"Blinding a tigress with volcano dust and cutting ropes is one thing; fighting almost thirty men is another," Arjuna said grimly.

"I won't be careless," Britt promised.

Kalao looked up at the crest of Gunung Mrabu, which glowed with a new crown of fire against the darkening sky. "Even if the crystal can't help Britt, the goddess who made it seems to be getting ready to do something soon."

Arjuna muttered, "I hope the goddess will be silent until we get to Durga. If Gunung Mrabu starts to make noise to frighten this animal, we might not be able to control it." Then he chirped to the horse and started away.

Britt watched apprehensively, hoping his friend would reach Durga safely, not only for their sakes but for his and Minda's. If Rakata and his soldiers didn't come in time to help rescue Minda, Britt knew he'd somehow have to try it alone. Remembering what Kalao had said, he glanced down at the crystal in his hand, then looked up at the volcano and decided that if there were such a thing as a goddess living there, he could certainly use her help. Then he swung up into the saddle and turned his horse in the direction Alden and Samarang had taken Minda.

Chapter Twenty-one

Britt's emotions urged him to gallop full-speed after Minda and her captors, but wisdom held him back. Although the fire at Gunung Mrabu's summit had brightened and sent slivers of its lurid glow like bloody fingers through the trees, the light was deceptive. Britt dared not miss any signs of horses having passed lest he follow a false trail and, while circling back, lose the right one. Eyes previously trained by the years of tracking the man-eating tigress through the jungle picked up his first clue. Under the low-growing palmetto fronds, a shadowy cluster of fungus had been crushed by a hoof. Farther on, a path through a clump of ferns, as if a careless rider had swerved into them, pointed like a guidepost. Britt couldn't know that Minda, pretending to be nodding with weariness, had deliberately nudged her horse into the ferns to leave a mark for him. He assumed that Alden and Samarang were so confident he was helpless and couldn't follow they weren't being particular about hiding a trail.

Alden and Samarang did know that, unless Rakata had some idea of where to look, he wouldn't send his men to comb the jungle for Samarang at night, and that even if Wakefield had any patrols in this area, they'd sleep in their camps until dawn. By then the fungus would have crumbled into indistinguishable dust, the ferns would have sprung back into place, and the other signs that the renegades had left would have vanished. To make good his promise to leave a trail Rakata could follow at a gallop, Britt paused to hastily uproot shrubs, break off palm fronds, and tear out vines to point the direction he'd taken.

A shower of palely glowing blossoms brushed from a branch; the muddy ribbon that Minda had used to bind back her wet hair after the flood now clinging to a twig told Britt he was on the right trail. When he saw a hoofprint too recently made in the moss for the depression to have sprung back, he was able to judge the distance separating him and Minda. Realizing that he was closer than he'd anticipated, Britt took even more care to avoid making the smallest sound that might reveal he was stalking them. He watched his horse's ears swiveling at the normal sounds of the forest, and when they pricked up at something straight ahead, Britt stopped his mount and listened. Faint voices muffled by distance. Because the voices weren't moving away, Britt realized Minda's captors had also paused. He dismounted, tethered his horse, then crept closer to discover his quarry was in a clearing.

The volcano's ruddy glow combined with the smoky moonlight tinted the foliage purple and gave the atmosphere an eerie effect, but the sight of Minda lying in the grass, Townes and Samarang standing over her, made the scene a nightmare. Heedless of the certainty that he'd be killed, Britt was poised to dash into the clearing and leap on his enemies when one of Samarang's men began to speak excitedly.

"I didn't touch the woman! No one did! She just fell off the horse!"

Although Britt's temper lowered only a little and his instincts yet screamed at him to snatch Minda away, he crouched behind the foliage to listen and watch with eyes that were a solid glaze of copper sparks.

Alden stooped beside Minda and, gripping her shoulders, pulled her up to a sitting position. Though her head lolled back, he shook her and demanded, "Stop playing the fox. You aren't fooling me. Open your eyes."

As if Minda were too weary to even lift her head, she moaned, "I can't go any farther. I just *can't*."

Samarang turned to look appraisingly at Minda's horse and after a moment gave an order to his aide. Then he turned to Townes and said, "I think the girl is telling the truth. Her horse also looks too tired to continue. Let us shoot the horse and leave the girl here."

"No!" Townes declared, but not out of compassion for Minda. He quickly added, "Melinda's being found in Phoenix House's ashes will be the final proof that Vandekker's guilty. It will add conviction to

Rakata's guilt as well. You'll be able to return to Talu, not Durga, in triumph, and I'll sail back to my own land without the smallest blot on my reputation or career.''

"Then we must spend the rest of the night here," Samarang replied.

Townes returned his attention to Minda. "I know you're putting on an act to delay us, Melinda, but there's no purpose in it. No one is coming to save you."

"I've been riding all day and we were caught in that flood before you found us. There's a limit to how much flesh and blood can endure. I don't have the strength to stay in the saddle. What can you expect of me, a woman, when my horse is ready to collapse? *Please* let us camp here." Minda's tearful pleading wrenched Britt's heart and he clenched his fists in anger as he listened.

Samarang spoke quickly, impatiently, "I see no reason to ride all night. Gunung Mrabu is causing the earth to tremble too often. If there's a rock slide while we're on the trail in the dark, we will be in great danger."

"I want to get those pearls and the gold, all the valuables we've stored in that cave, before the damned volcano erupts and buries it," Townes snapped.

"Since my grandfather's time, Gunung Mrabu has done no more than send up smoke, sparks, and a little hot mud that went down its other slope facing the sea," Samarang coolly advised, getting annoyed at Townes's attitude.

"There's still a chance it can explode with lava just as some of the other volcanos on the island have done," Townes insisted.

"I am giving orders to my men to rest here until morning," Samarang returned, then, as if dismissing the conversation, spoke sharply to his men.

Alden released Minda's shoulders and stood up. "You've gotten your way, but don't think you've fooled me," he told her. "You can take care of your horse and make your own bed, because no one will help you. If you must persist in this charade, you can sleep where you are." Then he walked away.

Although Britt knew Minda was hoping that their stop in the clearing for the night would give him a chance to catch up, he also realized she was nearly as exhausted as she appeared. She lay in the grass exactly as Townes had left her for so long a time that Britt began to wonder if she really had, as Townes had suggested, fallen asleep. Finally, she dragged herself to her feet. Minda's slow movements as she unbuckled her saddle girth were confirmation of her weariness; when she tugged the saddle from her horse, its weight almost sent her to her knees. Watching Minda, Britt fervently wished he could race into the clearing, gather her into his arms, and carry her away.

Instead, he watched Minda lie down, using the saddle as her pillow, and was disgusted he could do nothing for her. He crouched in the foliage as tensely silent as a leopard watching its prey, his eyes on the pair of men guarding the camp. Neither of them came close enough in their pacing for Britt to drag into the bushes without being noticed. Finally, recalling that his horse was tethered in the jungle and would be helpless if a predator approached, Britt gave up the vigil and made his way back.

He found a little patch of ground between the trees, where he and his horse could rest for the few hours of darkness left, then spent most of the time staring at the ruddy glow Gunung Mrabu spread across the night sky, wishing that, if there were such a thing as a goddess in the volcano she would, as the Javanese at Phoenix House claimed, protect Minda.

It wasn't dawn's light that awakened Britt from the restless sleep he'd finally fallen into, but the anxious whickers of his horse. He opened his eyes to discover a velvet nose almost touching his cheek. Alarm that the horse's noises would reveal their presence vanished when Britt's slowly focusing mind realized there was another sound in the air—or was it running through the earth itself? The deep rumble was more like pulsation than noise.

Britt got to his feet, stroked the horse's neck, and spoke soothingly to it while his eyes scanned the arch of the trees. The sky wasn't merely colored by dawn, but by the brighter and now ominously scintillating glow of the volcano. Britt decided that Townes wouldn't waste time calculating the dangers of an eruption; he'd urge his companions to greater speed so they could get their loot before Mrabu did more than threaten. With that in mind, Britt hurriedly saddled his mount.

Although he approached the clearing cautiously, it was, as he'd expected, empty. Britt turned his horse to walk slowly around its perimeter and soon found what he'd been looking for—marks in the jungle that told him which way Minda's captors had gone. He stood in his stirrups to pull down a tangle of slender vines that were hanging over the path and tied them together so they resembled a giant tassel suspended from the trees, a sign Rakata couldn't miss when he arrived. Britt hoped the *raden* and his soldiers would come soon. With the volcano threatening, Townes could move so swiftly that Britt knew he might be forced to try to rescue Minda without help, a prospect that seemed impossible when he didn't even have a weapon.

As if his horse sensed the mixture of resolution and desperation in its rider, it trumpeted a challenge, tossed its head, and pawed the earth.

"You're right, boy," Britt said softly, patting the horse's neck. "If we have to face them alone, we'd best throw all our spirits into it."

Minda had forced herself to stay awake long after everyone except the guards had fallen asleep. Then, as if she'd feared mosquitoes, to the sentries' amusement she'd finally pulled the blanket over her head, and she'd spent an hour very quietly tearing the hem of her petticoat into narrow strips like a row of fringes. She hoped that one quick tug later would release one of the tatters so she could leave a trail Britt would be able to follow on the rocky slopes she anticipated traveling over after they'd left the jungle.

In the morning, when Alden shook Minda's shoulder, she felt almost as tired as when she'd lain down. It was then that Gunung Mrabu began to rumble. She looked up at the sky, was alarmed at its shifting crimson lights, and new strength poured into her limbs. Assuming Alden and Samarang would be afraid to go nearer the volcano and planned to flee the area, Minda quickly prepared her horse. After she was in the saddle, she was stunned to learn that Alden and Samarang had no intention of even temporarily leaving their loot in its hiding place.

Minda remembered the awe she'd felt when, with Britt and Arjuna, she'd looked into Mrabu's crater at the seething cauldron of liquid, which had crackled with fires each time a breeze touched its surface. Visions of the molten rock exploding not only over her but Britt, who she knew must be following, filled her with terror so great she could hardly endure its shock. Wanting only to find Britt and escape from this place with him, she leaned toward Townes, whose horse was drawn up beside hers, and plucked at his sleeve.

"Alden, don't make me go any closer to that volcano. Let me stay behind."

Minda's quiet but strained tone startled Townes; he turned to look curiously at her. Minda's eyes were wide and glistening, their color deepened by fear. He commented, "No matter what Samarang says about that volcano's not being likely to erupt, you're really terrified of it, aren't you?"

Although Minda was afraid, it had also occurred to her that Britt would have a much more difficult time reaching her if she were with Alden in the caverns. She said in a tone softened by awe, "I stood at Gunung Mrabu's summit at a time when it was more peaceful. Even then it was like looking into hell. Please don't take me any closer to that mountain."

"You must really think I'm stupid if you could even hope I'd give you the smallest chance to escape," Townes said.

"One of your men could guard me. Take my horse with you until you come back down. Even if I could somehow escape your guard, I'd be afraid to go anywhere on foot," she pleaded. "Alden, please, *I'm begging you!*"

"I never thought I'd see the day when that patrician air of yours would disintegrate, but since I found you last night, you've resorted to begging several times. It's very satisfying to see you so helpless," he gloated.

Minda recalled what he'd said in the clearing before they'd left Britt and looked up to see the desire awakening behind Alden's eyes. She glanced away quickly. She wanted to think of something defiant to fling back at him, but suddenly couldn't. It was as if courage had run out of her. It was that too many kinds of terrors had saturated and were slowly smothering her, she realized. Alden's laughter broke into Minda's silence and taunted her, but she was mute. When he reached over, snatched away her reins, then spurred his horse forward, Minda could do nothing except dig her fingers into her horse's mane and hold on. But the light in her spirit hadn't been completely extinguished; for her hand cautiously reached under her bunched-up skirt hem to pluck a loose piece of her shredded petticoat, and drop it.

It wasn't long before the jungle fell away and they entered a narrow canyon. Minda raised her eyes to see that the canyon became shallower as it approached the foot of the volcano, and partway up the slope it blended into Gunung Mrabu's incline. It was like a huge trough, she noted, and thinking of how easily they could all be trapped if a river of lava found the channel, shuddered. Despite her disgust at having to plead with Alden, Minda tried again to convince him to let her and a guard go back down the mountain. He cast her an amused glance before turning his horse into an even narrower stone corridor she hadn't noticed. It, too, led up an incline, then widened into an area that reminded Minda of the bowl of a ladle. There they stopped and dismounted.

Alden's hand on Minda's shoulder roughly turned her toward a steep path that led up the slope to the entrance of the cave where they'd cached their loot. She hesitated, doubtfully eyeing the treacherous incline. Alden gave her a push, and she stumbled and fell to her knees. As Minda started to get up, she began to say angrily, "If you expect me to . . ."

Minda's words were stopped by an explosion that shook the mountain and threw her flat down on the trail. Before she could recover from her surprise, a loud hissing noise filled the air, as if a monstrous snake had reared up in their path. Numb with terror, sure that a wave of lava was ready to roll down on them, Minda raised her head to stare at a geyser of orange-gold sparks shooting out of the volcano's crest to fall like a comet's tail down another slope.

"I told you that Mrabu always sends its fire to the sea!" Samarang triumphantly exclaimed.

Minda struggled to her feet and as if the goddess of fire had suddenly reawakened her spirit, shouted in crisp court Javanese above the volcano's roar, "You have the brain of a tree toad if you truly believe the goddess won't point her finger at us next! Your stupidity is reinforced by your greed, and we'll all die because of it!"

Having until now only heard Minda speak a word or two in his tongue, Samarang was momentarily too surprised to respond.

She'd spoken too rapidly for Alden to follow, and he demanded, "What did you tell him?"

Minda's answer was filled with scorn. "I said he was a fool to think we're safe, and that applies doubly to you."

Samarang, meanwhile, had recovered from his surprise; he moved forward threateningly. Townes quickly stepped between, and Samarang said angrily, "That worthless woman cannot speak so, not to *me,* the next *raden!*"

"I'll make sure she regrets it after we've gotten into the cave," Townes promised, then gave Minda another shove up the path.

The murderous look in the Javanese's eyes made his intention clear, and now Minda didn't resist Alden's pushing. She hastily began to scramble up the incline, sending a shower of pebbles in her wake. Samarang's malevolent stare was a tangible thing following Minda, and she was afraid she'd momentarily feel the sting of a poisoned dart in her back. In her concentration on getting up the path, she forgot to wonder what Townes's threat might mean. Slipping and slithering on the rocks, catching bits of scrub or outcroppings of stone as she climbed, Minda was panting when she finally reached the top.

She straightened to look into the cave. Her sun-blind eyes couldn't penetrate its darkness, but Alden pushed her, blinking and stumbling, inside. Then she saw a man carrying a torch step from around a curve in the passage a dozen paces away.

"Tuan Townes! Lord Samarang!" The man lowered the pistol he carried in his free hand and, hurriedly fitting the torch into a holder in the cave wall, dropped into *dodok* before Samarang.

After the man had risen, Samarang said, "The end of our waiting has come, Mapla. We're taking everything out of the cave."

Minda could see that Mapla was relieved his vigil as guard was over. As he asked questions about the plan to carry out the loot, Minda recognized from the way he spoke that Mapla had been a sailor before joining Alden's gang. After Mapla had turned to follow Samarang and several men farther into the cave, she said, "There's no purpose in my staying here while your brigands haul out your loot. Why not let me at least sit by the entrance, where I won't be underfoot?"

"You and I will wait in Mapla's quarters," Alden replied. He took Minda's wrist and thrust her toward a narrow corridor. Pushing her ahead of him, Alden steered her around a sharp bend in the passageway, and they entered a small chamber naturally formed in the rocks. The light of a torch set in the wall by the doorway revealed a sea chest, a cot with a rumpled blanket, and a charcoal pot where Mapla had cooked his meals.

"It's hard to imagine a seaman living in this dreary hole," Minda commented.

"This is an improvement compared to the quarters he had on the scows he worked," Townes replied. "It wasn't hard to persuade him to leave the wharf. His share of the spoils, though a pittance by our reckoning, is a treasure to him."

Minda shuddered. "He's murdered people in those raids for the promise of a pittance."

Townes confirmed, "And he'll be glad to do it again. People will do what they must to survive, even you." His hand grasped her chin, forcing her to look at him as he recalled, "Just a few minutes ago you begged me not to take you into the cave because you were so afraid of the volcano. What would you do, I must wonder, to avoid being thrown into the crater? Perhaps you wouldn't fight me?''

Fresh terror poured into Minda's eyes and her lips parted in shock. Finally, she regained herself enough to whisper, "Even *you* wouldn't do so hellish a thing."

"Samarang would be delighted to throw you into Gunung Mrabu as a living sacrifice to his goddess," Alden said softly.

Minda tried to pull away, but his grip on her chin and wrist tightened painfully. "You're going to kill me anyway!" she cried. "What difference does it make if I burn in the volcano or in Phoenix House?''

"A lot can happen before we get to Phoenix House," Alden pointed out. "One of Wakefield's patrols might surprise us in the jungle or you might find a way to escape. While we're at Phoenix House, during the fight that I expect the servants will put up, I might even be killed. Doesn't the prospect of seeing what the next few days will offer tempt you at all?''

Minda wondered, If Britt didn't come before they left the cave and Alden dragged her to Phoenix House, could she escape down the tunnel their fathers had dug as protection from Matarami? Silently cursing Alden, aloud she could only say, "I can't tell you in English or Javanese how much I hate you."

"Nevertheless, you do want to buy those extra days," he replied smugly.

His hand released her chin, dug into her hair, and knotted it around his fingers as he bent closer to capture Minda's lips with his. Thoughts of Britt and of the escape tunnel at Phoenix House were all that kept Minda from struggling as Alden's mouth ground hungrily against hers, but he was encouraged by her seeming lack of resistance. Alden released Minda's wrist, and moving his hand over the thin cotton of the blouse Surana had given her, began to explore her breast. His hand in her hair slid down her back to her hips, locking her to him.

Minda was thinking she could endure it no more; she would bite Alden, pound at him with her fists, *anything* to get away from the caresses that disgusted her, when Gunung Mrabu exploded into a new sound, like a deep growl coming from its depths. Alden's grip on Minda loosened as he listened. Then the mountain began to vibrate under their feet, the tremor increasing until the cave shook so violently Alden released her and caught the rock wall to keep his balance. Minda spun around and ran with staggering steps toward the doorway.

With an oath, Alden struggled across the lurching chamber to pursue her.

Samarang and his men had dropped their spoils in the corridor and plastered themselves against the walls just inside the entrance. They watched Minda rush into the corridor leading deeper into the mountain, the tremor dashing her first against one wall then the other, and assumed she was crazed by fear. But Minda's thoughts had never been more ordered as she determinedly followed the passage. Stumbling around a curve, she saw a dark corridor that seemed to double back toward the mountain's outside wall. She snatched a torch from its holder and staggered into the tunnel just as the tremor ended.

Minda was grateful that the soft boots Surana had given her made no sound on the stones as she ran. The passageway turned, but because it hadn't veered completely away from the course she wanted to follow, she continued running. Minda came to a division in the corridor and paused. Calculating her position, she chose the tunnel that seemed to head more in the direction she wanted to go and raced down it. The passageway forked again; she made another decision and resumed her flight. Once more the tunnel curved, and a little farther on she found another bend. Beyond that, still one more branch in the passageway made her stop and consider. Minda was aghast to realize she wasn't certain whether, if she needed to retrace her steps, she could remember all the turns she'd made.

She tried to recall the way she'd come, then noticed that the walls glistened in the torchlight as if they were wet. A tentative finger, then her palm flattened against the rock, discovered the wall was dry. When Minda realized the tunnel had a glassy coating—lava that had cooled and hardened—her heart sank. How long ago had these caves been ducts for the molten rock—a century, eons? Would lava flow through this channel again? Suddenly the full weight of the mountain seemed to bear down on Minda as she finally admitted to herself she was lost.

Britt arrived at the edge of the jungle in time to see Minda and her captors move beyond the meadow into a canyon. He skirted the clearing, then tethered his horse among the trees while he continued on foot.

Instead of entering the canyon, Britt climbed the slope, then used as cover a rock shelf that ran for a distance along another cliff, to run parallel to the canyon's course. He crouched in a boulder's shadow, glanced at the figures ahead preparing to start up the path, then raised his eyes to scan the trail and saw the cave entrance at the moment the geyser of sparks exploded from Mrabu's summit.

Britt waited, hoping Alden and Samarang would be afraid and turn back. When they began to climb the path, Britt could see from Minda's slow progress how much of a struggle it was for her and wondered why Townes hadn't left her with the men guarding the horses. Then he recalled the last bit of conversation he'd heard between Minda and Townes before they'd left him by the river and was chilled that Alden might be forcing Minda into the cave because he planned to rape her. At the thought, Britt's blood seemed to become a fountain of sparks spurting into his brain. He seethed with the compulsion to run up the slope, throw himself on Townes, and kill him with his bare hands. He turned to look down at the jungle. How long would it take Rakata to come? Britt was afraid they wouldn't arrive in time to help Minda. He tensely watched everyone except the guard Samarang had posted enter the cave.

After a moment the sentry lowered his gaze to check something on his rifle, and Britt shot out of the boulder's shadow to run across the slope. When the guard raised his eyes to watch the meadow, he had no idea that Britt was standing in the shadow of a cliff less than fifty feet away. The sentry yawned, and Britt took advantage of that moment to run a bit closer.

It was then that the tremor struck. The guard was almost pitched off the ledge, and he grabbed at the edges of the cave opening to steady himself. Britt, flattened against the face of the cliff, was in no danger of falling, and he watched as he calculated his next move.

After the sentry regained his balance, he acted as Britt had hoped by stepping away from the cave opening to brace his shoulder against the shuddering rock wall. Britt rushed forward, saw the shock on the sentry's face, his mouth opening to call out; but the guard's warning was never voiced. Britt used his fist as if it were a hammer attached to his arm, striking down rather than out at the man's face. The sentry sagged, but before he fell, Britt caught his shoulders and propped him against the wall. Britt took the guard's weapons—the rifle, a bow, arrows, and a sword. Britt stepped away and released the guard. That the man tumbled off the ledge caused Britt no qualms; his mind was too full of fear for Minda.

After the tremor had stopped, a voice in the cave called, "Tunku, are you all right?"

Britt silently waited at the side of the entrance with the rifle stock raised high. When a man leaned out to look for the guard, Britt brought the stock down on his head. Britt quickly stepped into the entrance, fired at a shadowy figure within, and, as swiftly, ducked back.

"Kumar's dead!" someone shouted in Javanese. "Go on! Vandekker has to reload! Get him!"

But Britt had already set the rifle aside, picked up the dead sentry's sword, and drawn it back. A man dashed out of the cave; the long, straight sword made a shimmering arc that ended at the bandit's waist. Britt stepped to the side of the cave entrance, switched his grip on the sword, and raised it high. A second man rushed out, but the sword again flashed in the sun and decapitated him. The force of the blow dashed the blade against the stone floor; it snapped, the broken piece clanging as it bounced away.

Britt flattened himself against the cover of the rock wall and warned, "I still have the other weapons from your dead guard!" When only silence answered, he called, "I'm alone now, but I think I can hold you off until Rakata and his soldiers come. Send Minda out to me and I'll leave with her. You might have the time to escape."

Inside the cave, Alden looked at Samarang in dismay and said, "She got away from me!"

"We don't have enough men to fight Rakata and his soldiers," Samarang muttered.

"We can't *know* Rakata's coming. It might be a bluff," Alden said. "Even if it isn't, Vandekker's only one man and we have thirty."

"He's in a position to kill us one by one. We have three dead and one who will die soon. Vandekker uses that sword as if he'd been taught by the royal master," Samarang snapped.

Alden turned toward the entrance and shouted, "Vandekker, that little wench got away! She's somewhere in the cave and we have to catch her before we can do anything!"

Britt was taken aback by this. He wondered if Townes was trying to buy time so some of Samarang's men could get out of the cave by another opening and somehow attack him by surprise. Deciding he had to take that chance, Britt called, "You'd better find her fast! Rakata shouldn't be long in coming."

Alden again turned to Samarang. "You know these passages better than I. Take some of your men and find her. Maybe we can lure him in after she's here."

"All this because of a woman," Samarang said in disgust, then pointed to the men he wanted and waved for them to follow him deeper into the cave.

Britt strained his ears to hear the murmured conversation inside, but failed. Maybe they didn't believe Rakata was coming. Britt himself couldn't be sure Arjuna and Kalao had reached Durga or, if they had, how long their trip had taken. Even if Minda had escaped Townes, she was in great danger wandering around Mrabu's passages. He listened to the ominous rumbling of the volcano and wondered if it would erupt and bury them all in lava or boiling mud.

Another tremor made the ledge vibrate beneath Britt's boots. It wasn't as violent as the others, but he heard rocks falling in the cave, shouts of warning, and scrambling feet. He was thinking he could use the confusion to reduce the bandit's numbers when a cloud of dust sailed out of the opening. He fit an arrow to his confiscated bow and quickly stepped inside. Although the cave was filled with rock dust, Britt saw that one of Samarang's men had gotten to his feet and had a rifle in his hands. Britt's arrow cut a path through the murk, and the bandit, clawing at the missile in his chest, fell. Britt backed into the deeper shadows at the side of the cave as he fixed another arrow to the bowstring. Someone among the dust clouds moved and Britt quickly lifted the bow. Another arrow sang through the murk; a man crumpled to the floor, moaned, was silent.

"Damn! He's in the cave now!" Townes exclaimed.

Certain they couldn't see him standing in the dark corner if he didn't move, Britt dared not even raise his bow.

"Where is he?"

"Do you see him?"

"He moves like a *memedi*. How can we shoot a ghost?"

Britt placed the voices farther back in the cave. Still wary, he remained motionless.

"Where are you going?" Townes cried. A moment later his foot-steps ran farther into the darkness.

Now assured they were retreating, Britt stepped away from the wall, but found too late it was a trick. At his movement, someone tossed a torch that landed almost on Britt's feet. Surprised and momentarily blinded by the light, Britt dropped his bow as he leaped back. Out of the murk beyond the light, a Javanese came flying feet first. His kick caught Britt glancingly in the side; and though Britt was knocked to the cave floor, he rolled and quickly sprang up. When the Javanese kicked again, Britt caught his foot with one hand, and with his other fist dealt the Indonesian one sharp jab. The man's head snapped back. Britt dropped him, whirled, leaped, and kicked another attacker down.

Britt stepped back into the shadows, but as he prepared himself for another attack, he heard several pairs of footsteps retreating.

Alden's voice shouted, "Where are you going? You cowards! What did we hire you for?"

The footfalls disappeared in the distance.

Britt started in the direction of Alden's voice, but scuffed his boot on a stone. As if the soft noise were a signal, Alden fell silent. Then Britt heard another set of boots, Alden's, running away into the darkness.

Minda wasn't sure if she could find the main passage and she dreaded to reenter it, but it was the only way she knew of to get out of the cave, so she started back. Every branch in the passageway meant an agonizing decision because now they seemed identical. The ominous rumble from the volcano's core gave her visions of rippling orange fires; and like the golden butterfly that had rested on her hand at Mrabu's crater, she felt as if she, too, were being blown by forces she couldn't see.

Minda paused to rest for a moment, but the sound of men talking in lowered voices echoed faintly down the stone corridor. Pulses hammering with fear, she hurried into the nearest passageway. Its ceiling was so low she knew she hadn't come that way before. Minda didn't want to go farther down the unfamiliar tunnel so she waited, afraid to breathe, hoping her pursuers would pass by. A shout reverberated down the passage—someone had seen the glimmer of her torch reflected off the wall. Minda didn't dare snuff out the torch and be lost in the darkness. She turned to run down the low corridor praying that if the men had to stoop to follow, they would be slowed. The tunnel became even lower, and Minda found that she, too, had to duck her head. Finally, feeling like a rabbit in its hole, she had to creep on her hands and knees. The torch's sizzling flames singed her elbow and she dropped it. Before she could pick it up, the flames sputtered out; blackness closed in on her.

The volcano's deep rumble seemed to get louder, or was it that sounds were amplified by darkness and terror? Minda didn't know and dared not think about it too long or she would be paralyzed by fear.

Shivering with terror, she crept around a bend and was relieved to see a spot of light ahead. She hoped the exit opened on a slope she could get down, not over a sheer drop, or she'd be trapped. Minda ignored the scrapes stinging her hands and knees and scurried forward.

A shout behind told Minda that the men had found the extinguished torch. She realized they were very close and desperately tried to crawl faster. When she reached the opening and peered out, she was grateful to see a rubble-strewn slope and, at its base, the meadow she'd previously crossed. Relieved, she crept through the hole, then got to her feet.

Minda hurried down the slope, stumbling and slithering on the loose stones. The calls of her pursuers told her they'd begun to crawl out of the tunnel, and she started to run. Leaping and hopping to keep her balance, Minda somehow stayed on her feet as she raced to the bottom. Her own momentum carried her into the wild flowers and grass at the slope's base, and she still couldn't stop. Exhausted, sobbing for breath, trying to stay on her feet, Minda finally knew she could run no farther. But as she pitched forward, it was into a pair of arms that pulled her behind a projecting crag. Weeping with defeat, she hung limply in her captor's grasp.

"Be silent, little bird, so we can snare those others."

Stunned, Minda raised her eyes to look into Rakata's face. Overjoyed, but too breathless to speak, she could only gasp one word, "Britt?"

"I don't know where he is, maybe in the cave," Rakata answered as he guided her to sit on the grass.

New tears flooded Minda's eyes. To her mind, the cave was the deadliest place Britt could be. She felt as if her lungs were on fire; and, wanting to ask the *raden* more questions, tell him what she'd experienced, all she could do was gasp for breath and watch him raise his sword. When it dropped, Minda heard the hum of a swarm of arrows simultaneously released, the horrified outcries of her pursuers when they saw that they'd run into an ambush, then screams and groans of pain.

Rakata stepped from behind the boulder and Minda knew his soldiers had dropped their bows. Like their *raden*, they were wielding swords as they rushed out to meet the renegades. The ring of metal on metal, the thumps of bodies being thrown to the ground, shrieks of pain and triumphant cries filled the air. But it all was lost on Minda. She'd laid her head back against the rock, eyes squeezed shut in despair. If Alden's men had caught Britt in the cave, if the volcano erupted . . .

Unable to bear the anguish of the visions flashing on her closed lids, Minda finally opened her eyes and wearily got up. She turned and saw that, aside from a few individual scuffles, the battle was over.

Some of the *raden*'s men started to collect weapons. Others were dragging the renegades to their feet and herding them into a straggling group. Rakata was pushing his bruised and disheveled cousin to join his companions.

"I should *not* be with those others. I'm a nobleman," Samarang was protesting through bleeding lips.

"The only reason I don't kill you now is that I have to give you to Wakefield to prove Britt and I are innocent of your crimes," Rakata snapped.

"Why should the English major believe you rather than me?" Samarang declared.

"Because you'll be happy to confess everything by the time I get you to Djakarta," Rakata answered, giving the former lord a shove.

The force of the *raden*'s push sent Samarang flying into the huddle of captives and he crashed to his hands and knees. As he got up, he gave Rakata a look of such malice that Minda was chilled to see it as she approached.

Rakata noticed her expression and threw his cousin a withering glare before he regarded Minda to say, "Samarang has lost his fangs and claws. He needs that ferocious mask to hide his fear behind." Rakata untied the mantle he'd thrown back over his shoulders during the battle, draped it around Minda to cover her torn garments, and quietly said, "Anything you can remember about how many Javanese they've hired in addition to these traitors and where the rest of them might be will help us."

Clutching gratefully at the cape, Minda forced herself to recall the nightmare of the last few hours. Finally she answered, "I think they brought only Samarang's partisans from Durga. They left a few men with the horses in a little canyon beyond that crag." Minda pointed out the direction of the canyon, then ran her eyes over the number of captives, glanced briefly at the dead and wounded, then looked up at Rakata in surprise to exclaim, "There can't be much more than a dozen left in the cave with Alden and Britt!" She paused, lowered her eyes, and added, "*If* Britt's inside."

"We found his horse tethered on the other side of this clearing. I'm sure he's in the cave, and if I've learned anything about him at all, I've no doubt he's decreased the number of our enemies in there with him," Rakata assured. "I know about that canyon, and I'm very familiar with Gunung Mrabu's passageways. I spent over a week there once living alone as part of the preparation for a religious ceremony. I'll take the men I can spare. We'll find Britt if we have to search the tunnels from end to end, one by one."

Minda stared at the grass through a blur of tears and said brokenly, "But the volcano can erupt any moment."

"Gunung Mrabu sent up a cloud of smoke and ashes just before you came out. For several generations it has done little more." Rakata squeezed Minda's arm comfortingly, then turned away to give orders to his men.

Minda watched the *raden*'s soldiers gather, but she didn't hear the commands Rakata was issuing. Her ears were too filled with the deep rumbles again coming from the volcano's heart.

Chapter Twenty-two

Only after Alden had turned several corners and raced past as many branches in the tunnel did he pause to peer back down the dimly lit passageway to learn if Britt had followed. No one was in sight and he heard nothing. Relieved that Britt seemed not to have immediately pursued him, Alden wiped the sweat from his brow with a sleeve, then leaned his back against the cave wall and considered his situation more calmly.

It had been the flight of the Javanese that had made him take to his heels, Alden decided. Fear *was* contagious, especially in a cave at the foot of an active volcano when a man couldn't even see his enemy through the murk until he struck. Though Alden had discovered in the meadow near Philadelphia, when Britt had pulled him from his horse, how suddenly Britt's temper could rise and how quickly he could move, Alden hadn't dreamed he could be so lethal. It seemed as if Britt knew how to use any weapon, and when he had none, his hands and feet were enough.

No matter how he looked at it, Alden didn't want to face Britt alone, not in a fair fight, and it appeared that, until Samarang returned from his search for Melinda, Alden was alone. Silently cursing the Javanese who had deserted him, Alden wondered how Samarang and his men could have completely disappeared. Was the mountain so honeycombed with tunnels it could swallow a score of men and not even send back an echo of their footsteps or voices? Was Melinda leading them *that* merry a chase? Then another thought passed through Alden's mind like the shadow of a night-flying bird. Had Samarang privately decided, despite the assurances he'd voiced, that Gunung Mrabu was showing itself to be more dangerous than expected and fled? Alden knew that Samarang was crafty and unscrupulous; he considered the possibility of Samarang's betraying him as well as the *raden*.

 - Nearly half the loot had already been carried out. It wouldn't be too much of a chore for Samarang and the men he'd taken with him to spirit it away. Alden wondered if, while he'd been holding Britt at the entrance, he'd unknowingly helped Samarang escape. If the volcano exploded while Britt and Melinda were in the caverns, Mrabu itself would silence their claims that Britt was innocent of plotting against the government and Rakata would still seem to have been Britt's partner, especially if some of the gold coins taken from the attack on Wakefield's convoy were to be found among Rakata's possessions. Samarang could lead Wakefield to Durga as a sign of his good will. If Alden died in the eruption, Samarang wouldn't have to divide the spoils with him. Samarang would, after Rakata's arrest, have everything he wanted, and Alden would lie with his enemies under tons of Mrabu's ashes.

Panicked that Samarang might have left with the loot, Alden's courage renewed itself in proportion to his greed. He pulled off his riding boots and, in his stocking feet, padded soundlessly down the passageway toward the chamber where they'd cached the spoils. If Samarang, instead of pursuing Melinda, had taken the rest of the loot, Alden had his answer. But, Alden wondered, if the spoils were still there, could he take the jewels and those fabulous pearls and get out of the cave? He congratulated himself for having brought his dueling pistols along on this venture. He'd have two shots if he saw Britt, and the pistols had been custom-made with a particularly accurate aim.

Britt had been warned by the ruse Alden and his companions had already tried to fool him with and couldn't be certain they'd fled the second time. He wished he hadn't broken the sword. The rifle, having only one shot, was too unwieldy to reload and arrows seemed of little use in a cave. He glanced at the bodies of the Javanese and noted that their companions had stripped them of weapons before they'd fled. Resigned to relying solely on himself, Britt moved farther into the

passage with the caution of a jungle cat testing the air currents for
every wisp of scent and whisper of sound for a trap.

Upon discovering the narrow corridor that led to Mapla's quarters,
Britt paused to try to remember if the sound of the fleeing renegades'
footsteps had continued past this point. He wasn't sure but knew it
would be a good place for them to hide until he passed, then step out
behind and surprise him. Britt drew himself closer to the wall and
entered the passageway, every sinew of his body ready. He crept
soundlessly around the last turn only to discover the small chamber
was empty. Suspicious that there might be another narrow passageway,
where men could conceal themselves in the dimly lit room, Britt's
eyes scanned the shadowy walls.

His gaze fell on a shred of cloth caught on the corner of the sea
chest and he pulled it loose. There was enough left of its flowered
design for him to recognize it as part of the skirt Surana had given to
Minda.

Britt's head jerked up to eye the rumpled blanket on the cot. Had
Alden struggled with Minda in this chamber? Had he succeeded in
raping her? Britt's fury was a white-hot poker thrust into the icy water
of his fear for her, and he threw the shred of skirt aside. He turned
toward the passageway with one thought crowding all others from his
mind—*he must find her*.

Britt came to the first of the cavern's branches and looked warily
down the tunnel. Its shadows were relieved by torches placed at wide
enough intervals so the dark spaces between could hold one of
Samarang's men or, even more easily, one cowering girl.

Forgetting to be cautious about attracting an enemy, he called,
"Minda! It's Britt! Are you there? *Minda!*"

The only sound that answered him was his own voice echoing
through the passageway, disappearing into the shadows beyond. Britt
remembered how bravely Minda had faced the man-eating tigress and
thought it was possible she wasn't running in blind panic now. If not,
she was quick-witted enough to realize that darting into the first tunnel
branching off the main passageway might keep her out of her pursuers'
sight long enough to make other turns and lose them. Britt stepped
into the tunnel.

Rakata didn't lead his men into the cave through the little hole
Minda had fled out of like a rabbit, but headed directly to a larger
entrance higher on the slope that, to her glance, had looked more like

a shadow than an opening. Whatever comfort Minda might have derived from this confirmation that Rakata did, indeed, know the maze of tunnels, was canceled out by her realization that Alden might have previously explored the mountain too. Recalling the day she, Britt, and Arjuna had climbed Gunung Mrabu, Minda didn't remember Britt's saying anything about being familiar with the passageways. If he wasn't and Alden was, Britt would be at a grave disadvantage.

Minda watched until Rakata and his soldiers had disappeared into the cavern, then sat down on a flat rock, like a low platform in the grass, to wait and stare at the mountain, wondering what secrets it held. Gunung Mrabu had finally stopped rumbling, and she was surprised at not having previously noticed the absence of the low vibration running constantly through the earth since early morning. She assumed it had faded during the battle when she was distracted. Although the mountain's growl, which had seemed so menacing before, had ceased, the stillness now was ominous and gave her the eerie feeling that time had stopped its march, that the volcano was waiting. The captured renegades, too, seemed to be aware of the feeling, for their clamor had subsided. Even the wounded had stopped their groaning. With the prisoners now subdued, Rakata's guards became quiet, and Minda, sitting with her back to them all, fear for Britt saturating her thoughts, forgot their presence.

The mountain seemed like a giant blue-gray lizard, its back ferociously humped, looming over the jungle. The streaks, where ancient rivulets of lava had trickled down its slopes, dried, and hardened, seemed like the markings of a reptile's scales; Minda felt in the silence as if the beast was watching her. Out of a habit Minda hadn't known she'd acquired, her hand reached for the crystal pendant and discovered it wasn't in its customary place on her bosom. She recalled that she'd given it to Britt so he could free himself from Samarang's ropes.

She tilted her head to gaze at the scintillating gold fire on Mrabu's summit and wonder if the piece of shimmering mineral ejected from the crater's heart carried the fire goddess's protection, as Dessa insisted. Or was it a curse the fabled being would reclaim soon, along with Britt's life? Minda shuddered. If such things as goddesses, *lelembuts*, or *memedis* didn't exist, she yet felt in the hush as if the place were filled with spirits of *some* kind, but they said nothing to each other or to her. They only waited and watched with her as the azure sky over the volcano took on gray tints and darkened, swiftly becoming almost the color of the slope itself.

Minda got to her feet and slowly turned to scan the surrounding sky apprehensively. A veil of orchid clouds seemed to enclose the volcano, like the netting that surrounded her bed at Phoenix House. A streak of jagged white fire lit the purpling haze at Mrabu's crest, then a brief rumbling sounded, this time not from the earth but from the sky.

One of Rakata's men, who had been watching Minda, called, "You needn't fear this darkness over Gunung Mrabu. When a fire-mountain sends its breath into the clouds, there often is a rain."

Minda thanked him, but she couldn't ignore the awe that was pulsing through her blood as the growing wind began to ripple her hair. She stepped away from the rock to pace uneasily through the knee-high grass and wild flowers toward the center of the meadow, then paused and raised her head to again look at the mountain. Was Gunung Mrabu, after all, inhabited by a goddess? The atmosphere was magical enough to tempt the most unimaginative mind with fantasies, but was this magic's strange beauty evil or merely awe-inspiring?

The layers of veiling that seemed to join Gunung Mrabu's slopes to the purple sky had turned from orchid to topaz, and the volcano's fiery summit was almost obscured by the circle of rain that was gradually encroaching on the meadow. Minda watched as the line of showers moved over the guards and their prisoners, then enclosed her with tiny, soft droplets so dense they seemed like smoke turned golden by the light reflected from the sun, which still was serenely shining in the calm turquoise of the western sky.

Then the earth shuddered, wrenched itself out from under Minda's feet, and she was thrown to the grass. Breathless from the shock, she sat up and propped herself on her hands while the grasses around her danced crazily, not only from the wind, but from the earth's trembling. Oblivious to the cries of the prisoners, who were shackled together and tumbled helplessly about, the soldiers' struggles to remain on their feet, Minda saw through the rain and haze, where Mrabu's summit had blended with the sky, a second, false sunburst, like an orange bangle shimmering among the ragged, silver paths of now flimsy-looking lightning.

Shivering with terror that this time Mrabu might not be merely sending a geyser of sparks into the clouds, but, like a giant heart, was pumping the molten lava that was its life blood into the caverns of its arteries, Minda struggled to get on her feet and found she couldn't. The undulations of the meadow threw her back, as if the goddess commanded her, insignificant creature that she was, to remain. Then Minda saw through the grass and flowers, parting in the wind, that the skin of the earth was splitting. Although the crevices were narrow, to her eyes they looked bottomless, and now, as afraid to try to get up and rejoin Rakata's soldiers as she was to stay, Minda lay on the shuddering ground staring in terror at the light on the mountain.

The tremor stopped as abruptly as it had begun and Minda finally was able to get to her feet. Hugging herself to try to control her own shaking so she could walk, Minda crept as warily through the rain as if demons in the cracked earth were waiting to catch her ankles and drag her down. When she reached the comparative solidity of the platform rock, she sank down to wrap her arms around her bent legs, lay her cheek on her knees, and silently weep for Britt and Rakata in the caverns.

Having previously familiarized himself with the way sounds traveled through the passageways, Alden listened for Britt's calls to Minda, which he could occasionally hear echoing down the tunnels, and was able to maintain a general idea of where Britt was and avoid him. Alden heard nothing to hint of a clash or even a scuffle and became even more convinced that, if Britt could move so openly without opposition, Samarang and his men had deserted the caves. He rounded the last bend in the passageway that led to the chamber where the spoils of the raids had been stored and, fully expecting to find it empty, was stunned to see the room was as Samarang's men had left it when they'd gone to hunt for Minda.

The flickering torchlight cast bright gleams from tangled heaps of sterling candelabras, serving pieces and dinnerware, chests with open lids revealing gold-chased clocks, ivory and silver brushes and toilette articles that had once adorned the dressing tables of the plantations they'd raided. There were baskets and sacks of costly silks and uncut gems from the Javanese towns they'd attacked, strongboxes full of gold coins from the convoy, and the velvet-lined containers of fabulous pearls that had been intended as a royal gift.

Alden was baffled. Had Melinda found a way out of the cavern so Samarang and his men were pursuing her in the jungle? Now that the volcano's noises had finally subsided, had the Javanese fled because of some new fear added to by their superstitions? If Britt hadn't been bluffing that Rakata was coming and the *raden*'s soldiers had entered the cave, Alden thought he would have heard the battle sure to have resulted. He didn't know what to think of the disappearance of the Javanese. In his mind, only one conclusion was certain. The spoils they'd collected had to be moved and there was no reason he could think of that he shouldn't take up the job the renegades seemed to have forgotten. If they returned to find him in the midst of the task and were suspicious of his motives, he would give them a tongue-lashing for leaving the chore to him. That Alden was choosing the most valuable and least bulky of the items to carry out was easily explained by his being only one man, and unused to heavy burdens. As he gathered up the boxes containing the pearls, he decided it was only practical to take the things he could use himself if Samarang and his men for some reason didn't return.

Then the new quake jolted the cave. It tossed Alden into a corner while chests and sacks spilled their contents across the floor and the pile of silver became an avalanche he cowered against the wall to avoid.

In an adjoining tunnel, Britt ran through a shower of sparks while the floor danced crazily under his feet, sending him lurching against one rock face then bouncing into the other side. Finally rounding a corner, where he was protected from the sparks, Britt threw himself to the floor, hoping the tremor would stop before the tunnel collapsed.

A hail of falling pebbles flailed Britt's back like the lashes of a whip and he covered his head with his arms. It seemed as if the volcano would never stop shaking the earth, and visions of being buried under the mountain, of Minda being crushed beneath a collapsed wall horrified him.

After the mountain finally quieted, Britt ignored the pain of the welts and bruises he'd been dealt and drew himself to his feet. Praying that Minda would answer, make *some* sound, even a moan to point him in her direction, he trotted down the passageway calling frantically for her.

Rakata and his men had gained entry to the main passage when the earthquake began and they scattered to brace themselves against the shuddering walls until it was over. Then, half suffocated from the choking clouds of rock dust, they straightened and gazed at the rubble that had fallen, trying to locate their weapons. While they sorted out their equipment, the *raden* relit their torches with one whose flames had managed to survive.

Rakata now realized that the volcano could erupt with all the fury that other volcanoes had shown. He ordered his men to divide into pairs and follow the adjoining passages so they could locate Britt as soon as possible.

The soldiers were eager to obey; they wanted to leave the goddess's home quickly. None of them had the faintest wish to touch her fiery hand, a possibility they were afraid was drawing nearer with every minute.

Rakata saw that his men were on the verge of panic and, gathering up confidence he no longer felt to give them assurance, told them he would continue searching this passageway alone to save time. Watching their blinking torches recede down the tunnels, Rakata took a deep breath and resolutely headed down the shadowy corridor.

"Minda, where are you? Minda!"

Rakata was ready to turn into a passageway he knew had a chamber at its end, when he heard Britt's calls floating from another branch-off. "Britt, it's Rakata! This way!" he shouted in relief.

Alden dragged himself from the corner where he'd been thrown and got to his feet. During the tremor the torch on the wall had been jolted from its holder and the chamber had been plunged into blackness. Alden stood motionless for a moment, trying to orient himself, then started to grope in the dark hoping to find the torch. He was feeling his way around a seemingly endless scatter of rubble when he heard Rakata's call and froze.

The voice had come from just outside the passage that led to the chamber he was in. Horrified that Britt hadn't been bluffing about Rakata's coming, Alden retreated farther back into the darkness; hardly daring to breathe, he could only hope Britt and Rakata wouldn't follow the corridor into the treasure room, that the tremor would have convinced them to abandon the caves.

As Britt joined Rakata, he anxiously began to say, "Minda's somewhere in here . . ."

"No, we found her and she's outside," Rakata said quickly in Javanese, then warned, "Keep your voice low while we speak. There may be more of our enemies still in these caverns."

Britt let out a breath of relief and leaned against the wall. "I'd thought, after that quake, Minda must be . . ." He stopped, unable to say more.

"She's safer than you and I. For that matter, so is Samarang," Rakata said softly. Britt raised his eyes and Rakata added, "We caught him and a number of the other traitors, but we still have to find Townes as well as where they've hidden their spoils."

"Townes may have fled the caverns, but I think he's so greedy he'd stay if there were any chance of his figuring out a way to take the loot," Britt murmured.

Rakata whispered, "Some of my men are searching the passageways, but I don't think they'll find any other chambers large enough to store much in. There is a room, though, at the end of this corridor that would be suitable."

Britt straightened. "Let's have a look inside and be done with it. If Townes has fled, he'll get too much of a head start on us."

Because Britt and Rakata couldn't know if the missing renegades as well as Townes might be in the chamber and didn't want to be attacked by them in the narrow, winding passageway, they crept down the tunnel without making a sound to betray their coming. When they were ready to round the last bend, they knew the torch Rakata was carrying would give away their presence. They flattened themselves to the wall, stepped quickly past the curve, and stood to the side of the dark room's entrance to listen. There wasn't the faintest noise to hint that anyone was hiding in the chamber, but Rakata warily extended the torch into the opening. The light revealed only the shambles the tremor had made of the loot.

Regretting that Townes seemed already to have escaped, Britt commented, "It appears that we've found the cache, if nothing else." Then he stepped into the room.

Alden, crouching behind the tumble of sacks and boxes, pistol cocked and ready to fire, realized that the *raden* would soon call his men to carry out the loot. But, he speculated, if he could kill both of them now, snatch up the pearls, and run, it still might be possible to slip out of the cave. The canyon where the pack horses were waiting, already partly loaded with valuables, was well hidden, and Rakata's men weren't likely to have stumbled across it. Alden thought if he could reach the canyon, he could take the horses to the cove where he'd learned the smugglers from Singapore normally landed, hide his spoils until they were scheduled to return, then hurry on to Djakarta. If Vandekker or Melinda dared come to accuse him later, everyone in the Colonial Office would swear he'd been in his hotel room suffering from the attack of malaria he'd previously feigned. Alden hoped though that, in the confusion and delay caused by the *raden*'s death, the volcanic eruption he thought was imminent would bring the mountain down. Then there would be no one left to accuse him—at least no one that Wakefield would listen to.

Unaware of Alden's presence, Britt picked up the torch that had been jounced out of its holder by the quake and ignited it with Rakata's. He turned away to gather up a jewel box's contents, which had been scattered over the floor. He picked up a bracelet with a ruby as its center ornament and wondered what was more beautiful in the ruby than the crystal Minda had found in the volcano's crater. He fished the crystal, which he wore on a piece of twine, out of his shirt. Holding it beside the ruby, he reflected on how the crystal had saved him from the tigress as well as the beasts by the river, yet the ruby would have a far greater value on any market in Europe or the New World.

Alden thought smugly that the second torch had only made Rakata and Vandekker clearer targets and hoped that Britt's momentary absorption in the jewelry on the floor would delay his reaction. Alden raised one of his pistols and took aim at the *raden*.

As Britt put the bracelet in the jewel box, his eyes caught a flicker of movement behind the pile of rubble. Having no weapon, nothing in his hand except the polished crystal, he threw it to mark Alden's direction as he shouted in Javanese, *"Get down, Rakata!"*

Townes automatically leaped backward from the harmless missile and Rakata dove behind a chest. Alden saw Britt start toward him, swung the pistol in his direction and took aim. Britt continued coming at him, watching not Townes but his hand holding the gun. As the trigger began to squeeze back, Britt ducked low, under the pistol; the ball flew so close he could hear its whine over his head. Then he sprang, swinging his forearm to hit Alden high on the chest, his other fist striking out at Alden's chin to snap his head back. As Townes fell, the gun flew from his hand, and thinking that Alden had no choice except to surrender, Britt restrained his urge to do him further damage.

Watching Alden scrambling among the rubble his loot had become, Britt said disdainfully, "Give it up, Townes."

But when Alden rose to one knee, he was pulling another pistol from his belt.

"Don't be a fool," Britt warned.

Townes hurriedly cocked the gun and raised it toward Britt.

"Drop that damned pistol," Britt muttered and, pivoting, caught the tip of Alden's shoulder with his kick.

As if Townes had been brushed away as easily as a leaf by a broom, he toppled to his side and the force of the blow sent him plunging facedown.

Hand still clenched around the pistol, Alden moved as if he were going to try to roll over, but Britt leaped up to drive his bootheel down on Alden's nape. The sound of the muffled crack announced the end of the battle.

"You saved my life," Rakata said quietly.

Britt turned to face the *raden*. "It's repayment for saving mine when Lieutenant Blackburn was ready to shoot me," he answered brusquely, then stooped to turn over Alden's limp body and pick up the crystal.

"*Just* a debt repaid?" Rakata asked pointedly.

Britt raised his eyes to meet Rakata's. He knew it was more than that. There was a bond of friendship as well as of blood between them neither had yet admitted.

Drawn by the sounds of the brief battle, several of the *raden*'s soldiers hurried into the room with weapons ready.

The foremost of the guards anxiously asked, "My lord *raden*, have you been harmed?"

Rakata turned to the soldiers and replied, "My brother saved me."

Surprised because Rakata had never referred to him so intimately, Britt slowly rose to his feet, but anything he might have said was stopped by Rakata's orders to his soldiers.

"Marudi, get some men to carry out this loot. It's evidence for Wakefield that will clear my name of dishonor. Kepi, take out that corpse. We will present it, too, to the major. Isimi, go back to Durga and tell Lady Surana that I am well and will return to her after I've seen Wakefield."

The soldier lowered himself in deep *dodok* before Rakata, then asked, "My lord *raden*, may I tell Lady Surana that our people will be able to return to Talu?"

Rakata's hand under Isimi's arm urged him to rise. "Yes, Isimi, tell her to begin preparations. Our people will return to Talu soon."

Isimi's face was lit by a dazzling smile as he backed away.

Rakata looked at the several other soldiers still awaiting orders and said, "There are other traitors still in the cavern."

"We found several dead by the main entrance, my lord, but none living," one of the soldiers replied.

Rakata looked at Britt. "The dead are your doing?"

Britt nodded. "There were some others that escaped. They must have fled the cave."

"Then they ran into my men's swords, for soldiers were posted at each of the few entrances a man could squeeze through," Rakata said. To Britt's perplexed look, the *raden* explained, "I know these caverns well. Come, Britt. Let us go out of this darkness into the sun once more."

Neither man spoke as Rakata guided Britt through the winding passageways, but their thoughts were the same—speculation about Java's future—for the shadows of the bloody past clung tightly to the island. They reached the cave entrance on the slope above the meadow where Minda was still sitting on the rock, face pressed against her skirt.

Rakata gazed down at her in thoughtful silence a moment before he turned to Britt and commented, "She's like Java now, huddled in fear and weeping, too caught up by sorrow to have become aware that the tears from heaven have stopped and the mountain wears a different face."

Britt's attention had been so fixed on Minda he hadn't noticed the changed landscape. He raised his eyes to look at it.

The raindrops draining off the higher slope picked up reflections of the sun and dripped down in front of the cave entrance like a curtain of golden crystal beads. Beyond the meadow, the sky's bright arch was filled with pink and lavender clouds. The golden light turned the valley's grasses into a luminous, soft green broken by creamy outcroppings of wild flowers. The shadows at the base of the towering cliffs had lifted, and the rocks, normally dull blue and gray, after the rain wore stripes of purple, rose, and indigo, while the jungle beyond seemed to have been dusted with gilt.

Uncertain as to exactly what Rakata had meant, afraid to hope for too much, Britt turned to him and said, "Now all of Talu's people will be united behind you. I have to wonder if you'll be tempted to persuade the other *radens* to join in a rebellion to drive the foreigners from the island."

"It is a thought that sings through my mind, but like the songs the gamelans play in Java's temples, the melody has many interwoven parts my ears must listen to," Rakata replied slowly, then added, "There is but one certainty in all of it. Sukadana bore us both."

Britt said evenly, "The feud was always between Gerard Vandekker and Raden Matarami. This Vandekker and this *raden* were children swept up in it. But you and I are children no more."

"Matarami and Gerard are dead. I would prefer to let their old quarrel die as well," Rakata replied solemnly.

"So would I," Britt agreed.

The men were silent a long moment, continuing to hold each other's gaze, wordlessly sealing a pact both finally knew would never be broken.

Then, the always before unfathomable depths of Rakata's dark eyes softened and warmed as he glanced past Britt at the figure of the girl waiting in the meadow. The *raden*'s lips held the smallest hint of a smile as he said, "You have chosen this love more wisely than your previous. Unlike the other girl, who fled, she is as much a part of Java as you and I. Even the goddess of fire approves of Lady Minda."

When the *raden* referred to a woman by this Javanese title of respect, it was in itself a declaration of the lady's nobility—an unheard of honor to a woman who wasn't one of his people—and Britt was so surprised he didn't know what to say.

The smile that had hovered over Rakata's lips alighted and he said quietly, "Go to her."

In a gesture Britt had never dreamed he'd offer the *raden*, that of his Javanese brother, Britt pressed his palms together, briefly bowed his head, and turned away. As he started down the slope, he heard Rakata's soft laughter floating down over the valley.

A voice speaking in Javanese said at Minda's shoulder, "He is returning from Gunung Mrabu's bosom."

She wearily lifted her head to look at the soldier. "I'm glad that your *raden* is safe," she murmured.

"The *raden* is safe, but I'm not speaking of him."

Minda stared up at the soldier for a moment until what he'd said penetrated her grief. "Britt?" she whispered, unable to believe what her ears had heard and the soldier's smile confirmed.

The guard's hand clasping hers drew Minda to her feet before he backed away. She stared at the mountain, incredulous at the sight of the figure nimbly making its way down the slope.

Had she, weary with grief, fallen asleep and was this a fantasy of her slumbering mind, a wish never in reality to be granted? The meadow itself seemed enchanted, as in a dream, as if the spirits, whose presence she'd sensed before, had opened a window and light from their magic fire was shining on the mountain and its meadow. The air itself added to her feeling that it was all illusion, for it seemed as if she were looking through golden rose quartz. Minda shrugged off Rakata's cloak, then looked down at her ragged clothes to confirm their reality and saw the raindrops clinging to her hands and wrists, like yellow diamonds, melt into streaks as she lifted them. The potpourri of wild flowers, sharpened by the rain, drifted above the meadow toward a double rainbow shimmering against the turquoise sky, inviting her to make a wish.

As when she'd been a child holding a firefly, Minda tightly closed her eyes to beg of the spirits only one thing: *make this dream be true when she looked at it again*. Then she opened her eyes to see that Britt was still walking toward her. A bubble of happiness seemed to burst in Minda, spreading a joyous tingle along her nerves she was yet afraid to believe. She tilted her head to gaze at Mrabu's crest; the orange fires that had burned so ferociously at its summit had lowered to a redder glow. It was the color of the crystal she'd plucked from the crater.

"If this is a dream," she whispered, "let me die rather than awaken from it."

Then Britt was standing before Minda, the copper flecks, like live sparks glowing in his eyes, still held the heat of the battle he'd won as he said triumphantly, "Townes is dead, and we have all the evidence we need to clear Rakata and me."

Minda felt firm arms enfold her, the warmth of his body as Britt drew her close, and finally she believed his reality. She pressed her face to his shirt to listen to the deep, steady rhythm of his heartbeat, but against her cheek, the hard edge of the pendant she'd given him reminded her of the fire goddess and the bitterness Java yet held. Minda turned her head to gaze at the figure standing by the cave entrance watching them. As if her eyes had touched the *raden,* he turned away.

"And Rakata? What will he do?" she asked.

As in the meadow near Philadelphia, Britt caught the curls over Minda's temples to hold her by these fragile bonds as if she would slip away. He said softly, "That old feud, too, is over."

Britt's eyes softened to amber, took on an autumn haze; and he leaned closer to kiss Minda as a Javanese would caress his love.